THE

RING

AND THE

CROWN

THE

RING

AND THE

CROWN

EXTENDED EDITION

MELISSA DE LA CRUZ

HYPERION

Los Angeles   New York

Copyright © 2014, 2017 by Melissa de la Cruz

All rights reserved. Published by Hyperion, an imprint of Disney Book Group. No part of this book may be reproduced or transmitted in any form or by any means, electronic or mechanical, including photocopying, recording, or by any information storage and retrieval system, without written permission from the publisher. For information address Hyperion, 125 West End Avenue, New York, New York 10023.

First Hardcover Edition, April 2014
First Paperback Edition, May 2015
New Paperback Edition, February 2017

10 9 8 7 6 5 4 3 2 1
FAC-020093-16357
Printed in the United States of America

This book is set in Adobe Caslon Pro/Monotype
Designed by Tanya Ross-Hughes

Library of Congress Control Number for Hardcover: 2014001288
ISBN 978-1-4847-9925-3

Visit www.hyperionteens.com

For Princess Mattie

This book owes an empire-sized debt to my lord husband, Mike of Johnston; my lovely editors, Duchess Emily Meehan & Lady Laura Schreiber; my agent, Viscount Abate; my dear friends Countess Margaret Stohl and Baron Bosch; and the royal and loyal court of Disney • Hyperion. Love and thanks from your humble servant.

Table of Contents

WEDDING BELLES

the
HISTORY OF THE CROWN

In 1429, the English army and its formidable magicians were led to victory by their Merlin, Emrys Myrddyn, defeating Charles VI of France and his dark witch, Jeanne of Arkk. Henry VI was crowned King of England and France.

Since the fifteenth century, the sun has never set on the Franco-British Empire. It is the most powerful in the world, with vast holdings in Asia, Africa, Australia, and particularly North America, its rich territories comprising sixty provinces.

Almost five hundred years later, the one-hundred-and-fifty-year-old Queen Eleanor II is at the end of her reign. Her daughter Marie-Victoria, the Princess Dauphine, must marry and conceive an heir to carry on the line.

A marriage has been arranged between Marie-Victoria and Leopold VII, the Kronprinz of Prussia, the empire's most *dangerous enemy. Truce has been called after the Battle of Lamac, which ended the Franco-Prussian War.*

The engagement will bring peace to the Continent, and will be announced and celebrated at London's annual Bal du Drap d'Or, where eligible ladies are introduced to society and presented at court.

The season opens at the beginning of the twentieth century, during what will be known in history as the height of magic's golden age.

Eleanor's DREAM

here are two of them, bent over their dolls. One is small and sickly; the other is strong and tall. Their backs are turned to me, so that I can only see the delicate bones of their necks underneath their ponytails. The girls. While they play they are singing to each other, a song that the music master has taught them on the harpsichord.

Their singing stops. They have noticed my presence. The girls turn, and I can see their faces now.

One is pale and thin, her eyes a waterless blue, their color fading.

One is merry and bright, her eyes a vibrant hue, their color blinding.

After a moment they turn back to their play, ignoring me.

Except now there is no more singing—only the darkness of the room as the curtains close against the light, and the dream fades.

Two girls.

One beautiful and strong.

One plain and powerless.

Only one shall be queen . . .

And the other shall serve her.

But as I awake from sleep, I still do not know—

Which one of them is my daughter?

And which one is the traitor?

THE

RING

AND THE

CROWN

the
LILY
THRONE

A half unconscious Queen—
But this time—Adequate—Erect,
With Will to choose, or to reject,
And I choose, just a Crown—
—EMILY DICKINSON

Who run the world? Girls!
Who run this motha? Girls!
—BEYONCÉ,
"RUN THE WORLD (GIRLS)"

1

Dark
ENCHANTRESS

The streets of London were so much more crowded than she remembered. It was as if everything in the city had multiplied. The buildings were taller and closer together, rows of red brick houses next to the new tall, skinny, cement ones with slate roofs; and there were so many people jostling on the sidewalk, elbow to elbow, shoulder against shoulder, a great army of pedestrians marching purposefully to who-knows-where. For a moment, she felt claustrophobic and trapped; lost, adrift, and alone in a sea of humanity. Her senses were assaulted from every direction: smokestacks belching into the gray sky, newsboys yelling the headlines, the salty-tangy smell of fried fish from the sidewalk vendors. It had only been four years since she'd left the city, but it felt like four decades, and Aelwyn Myrddyn stood in the middle of it all, clutching tightly the battered leather valise that contained all she had in the world. The bag was heavy with bottles of herbs, tonics, and potions from Avalon.

"All right, miss?" the driver asked, tipping his hat in her direction.

She hesitated for the briefest moment, feeling a pang in her heart. She thought of Viviane waving a solemn good-bye from the shore, her golden hair shining through the mist. For a moment, Aelwyn wondered if she had made the right decision in returning to the city of her childhood. When Aelwyn had turned sixteen, Viviane had told her that it was time to determine her fate. Magic users had two options when they came of age: to join the invisible orders, or to choose exile in Avalon.

"Miss?" the driver asked again.

"Yes, quite all right," she said, thinking of the letter in her pocket from her father. She squared her shoulders and nodded. The driver's orders were to take her to the palace directly, but she had persuaded him to stop a few blocks away. She wanted some time to walk by herself, to see the city up close, before she disappeared behind the black iron gates of St. James Palace. Aelwyn watched as the driver whistled and shook the reins, which were connected to an empty harness hanging in the air. The black horseless carriage rolled away slowly down the street and disappeared all at once with a thunderclap and a cloud of white smoke. Viviane's hansoms were a rare sight in the city, and so a few pedestrians blinked in surprise; but most hardly missed a step, and were more concerned with getting out of the way of the newfangled automobiles that were clogging the narrow roads.

"Need a hand?" asked a nearby gent, his eyes lingering over the curve of her form underneath the cloak. "That bag looks heavy, lass."

She shook her head and pulled the cowl over her mass of auburn curls. The ability to command male attention was its own kind of magic, but one that could backfire on a girl if she wasn't careful. Aelwyn had learned caution during her time away from home, and not to waste her charms on unworthy candidates. The nubby fabric of her wrap was cozy and comforting; the cloth was handspun, and reminded her of the island and the simple pleasures of life there. She had given them up to return to this metropolis.

As a child, she had not been allowed out of the palace very often; but, after the first few moments of terror and disorientation, she had navigated her way easily, using the tall tower spires of the castle as a guide and beacon through the crowded streets. Now, everywhere she looked, there were banners hanging from balconies, and storefronts were flying the red-and-blue flags of the empire. They were remnants of last week's victory celebration for the soldiers and magicians, who were finally home from the long war against the Prussian kingdom—although "victory" was a bit of a misnomer. The smaller nation had wrestled the mighty empire to a bit of a truce, a standoff. But in any event, the war was over—and that was indeed something to celebrate.

She walked along the mall, a broad boulevard lined with flowering trees, pretty shops, and gardens, stopping once in a while to peek into dusty book emporiums and bakeries with Cornish pasties in the windows. This is what she wanted—to live in the moment, to live in London again, to *matter*. She had cherished her experience in Avalon, but couldn't imagine living there for the rest of her life as a person out of time, living in an endless present. Alone and apart from the world, she would have watched the ages going by through her aunt's crystal glass. Avalon, for all its glories and beauty, was not enough. She was her father's daughter, after all.

During her exile she had yearned for the city, like a missing limb. She wanted to experience all it had to offer: live in the great palace, participate in the hectic preparations for the coming season, and dance at the Bal du Drap d'Or, the Ball of the Gold Cloth—an annual gala to commemorate the unification of the two kingdoms and the foundation of the empire. She wanted to see the queen again. Emrys's magic might be the shield of the realm, but Eleanor was its center, its great beating heart.

Aelwyn took a shortcut down an alley that led directly to the royal mews, heading toward the side and back entrances for staff, ministers, and courtiers. The elaborate and heavily guarded front gates and reception halls were reserved for honored guests only. Here she slowed down her pace, nervous about seeing her father again. Four years ago, he had sent her away as if she had been nothing to him; as if she'd been just a girl from the kitchens, and not his only daughter. She knew she had done something wrong by losing control of her powers and starting a fire, and she understood expulsion was the only punishment the court would accept for the threat and harm done. But because Emrys never once wrote her while she was away, never once indicated that she was forgiven, Aelwyn had taken her banishment to heart.

In his letter, Emrys had invited her back to the palace, but she was still apprehensive about their reunion. When she was younger, she had sobbed bitterly at their parting; and while she was almost grown up now, as well as Avalon-trained, thinking about him made her feel like that sad girl once more. She wasn't that much different, really, from the group of street kids—grubby little urchins with dirty faces—that had just emerged from the back of a fry shop into the alley. "Want some?" one of them asked with a grin, holding out mushy peas wrapped in greasy newsprint. She shook her head with a smile, and he shrugged, turning back to his meal and accidentally bumping her shoulder.

"Oh, excuse me!" she said, dropping her bag. But when she leaned over to pick it up, it was no longer there.

It was gone.

She stood there, staring at the ground, and realized she had been had. That bump had been no accident. She looked up to see the little thief running away with it, his food scattered everywhere. "STOP!" she cried, horrified. "STOP, boy!" But he paid no attention to her, darting into the busy streets, weaving quickly through the crowd, and was soon lost in a sea of dark coats, hats, and parasols.

Her precious stones, tonics, and herbs. Viviane's crystal glass: her treasured inheritance from Avalon. Aelwyn pushed up her sleeves, hiked up her skirts, and ran after the little criminal, pushing gentlemen to the side and stepping on ladies' toes. Her face flushed with anger and embarrassment. Had she looked that much like a rube? Like such an easy mark? It shamed her to think she had been robbed the minute she set foot in London. Her aunt had cautioned her, had ordered the driver to see her safely into the palace, and Aelwyn had only her stubbornness to blame.

She saw the boy ahead of her—he was about to turn the corner—and once he did, she knew he would be lost, her valuables gone forever if she did not act. There was no other recourse. She had to do it. The boy had given her no choice.

She stopped running and forced her heartbeat to slow, her breath to steady. She closed her eyes and focused. She had seen him for the briefest moment when he'd offered her a bite. She touched the stone she wore around her neck—obsidian, deep as midnight—and called up his face in her memory.

His grubby little face; the face of a young street beggar, a naughty boy with shifty cold blue eyes; an operative of a local syndicate, working for a Fagin who was sure to be lurking somewhere, taking whatever he stole and stringing him along with a pittance. She concentrated and called up her memory of his eyes, and looked through them into his soul.

Aelwyn would not have been able to do this to just anybody, but the boy was young and poor, untrained and uneducated. Children from good families were taught how to protect one's soul from a mage. But the little thief had not had the privilege of learning how to hide his soul from the world, to disguise its nature; and so she had been able to *see* into his very essence, into the spirit that made him who he was. As she looked into that deep abyss, a calm settled upon her.

The name of his soul came to her mind in a whisper.

Bradai, she called. *To me.*

She opened her eyes. Just as she had commanded, a thin gray column of smoke, shimmering in the afternoon light, came streaking toward her. She reached out and caught it with her fist. It was small and cold and shivering. His soul.

No one noticed the little boy frozen in his tracks in the shadows, his mouth agape, his foot hovering above the side-walk in midstep, a large ladies' valise hanging off his arm. Aelwyn took her time as she walked toward him, holding his soul in the palm of her hand. She looked right into his eyes, which were blank now; dead. He did not know what had happened to him; did not understand what had taken hold of his very essence and frozen him into place.

She plucked her bag from him and slapped him, hard, on the cheek. His soul trembled in her grasp, wriggling—gasping for air, for breath—for release. Aelwyn sighed. He hadn't deserved this. It was wrenching to perform an extraction on so small a child. He was only a little boy, a desperate, hungry street urchin, and his gang leader probably wouldn't have even known what to do with the treasures he carried. Most likely he would have tossed the jars of tonics and herbs into the garbage, broken the crystal glass, and sold the stones for a tenth of what they were worth. She turned away. When she was a few blocks safely past, she released her grasp on him and let his soul back into his body.

St. James Palace, the home of the sovereign, was a monolith: heavy, brown, and solid. It lacked the symmetry of Parliament and the Crown's other great structures, as its twin towers were located off to one side, their octagonal turrets standing like two sentries at the ready. The red-and-blue Franco-British flag flew proudly from the roof and whipped in the air. Above, the sky was gray, as it always was; the clouds stirred and streaked across the horizon, but never parted to reveal the sun. Perhaps the great palace would look less dour if the sun ever shone on it, but it rarely did. The gray of London made the castle look darker, more ominous. Aelwyn felt increasingly small and insignificant as she got closer to it. St. James was the seat of the queen, and had been home to centuries of British and Franco-British rulers. Its architecture spoke of unquestioned power, of a strength that had stood for centuries without interruption—of a power that would never bend, never compromise.

Her father was in his study, she was told by his unsmiling secretary. It was the same dour old woman who had ushered her out of the castle four years before. The chamber was tall and narrow; like the castle itself, the proportions of the room were designed to intimidate anyone who entered. Slender pilasters dressed the walls, their thin golden lines interspersed with panels of rich red cloth. In the early morning light, the cloth reminded her of blood. A brazier of candles made the darkness of the room even more intense, more foreboding. Her father's desk occupied a faint patch of light below the flickering candles. The mighty table could seat a dozen men, and the desk nearly dwarfed the man sitting at its head. A globe decorated one side of the tabletop; it spun slowly, apparently of its own accord, and she guessed it was her father's magic that made it spin. Indeed, it was the power of the Merlin that made all things turn. Behind the desk hung a loosely knit tapestry embroidered with a map of the empire. The map's size, its age, its glorious detail, all said one thing to anyone who braved a visit to the first magician of the realm: *Our empire is vast, our power unquestioned; our rule will stand forever.*

She had not seen him in four years, but Emrys Myrddyn looked exactly the same, with his stern countenance and trim white hair and beard. He was dressed in a beautifully tailored morning suit, his gold cuff links catching the light. "Ah, there you are," he said, looking up from his paperwork with a distracted smile, as if she had just disappeared for a moment and not been sent away for four years.

"Hello, Father," she said politely.

"Have a seat," he said, motioning to the chair in front of his desk. "How was your journey? Are you hungry?"

She shrugged. "I'll get something from Cook later."

Emrys took an apple from behind his desk, peeled it, cored it, and cut it into fourths. She was touched by the gesture. He'd remembered that as a child she had always preferred her fruit this way: peeled, prepared, cleaned of skin and pits and stones, which was the way the princess's fruit was always served. When she was a child in this castle, she had insisted that everything she had be *exactly* like the princess's. She had never settled for less than what Marie received.

She accepted the plate gratefully and took a bite from one piece.

"How is my sister?" Emrys asked.

"Viviane is well. She sends her regards."

Emrys snorted. Aelwyn knew that Viviane believed Emrys had sold out the enchanters of the world by making them servants to the throne. "Your father is nothing but a glorified civil servant," the Lady of the Lake liked to grouse. Viviane had chosen exile over subservience. "I will not bow to some lesser creature," she'd told her niece, and made it clear what she thought of Aelwyn's decision to return to the palace. "What is outside this mist that calls to you so? There we are but chattel, performing monkeys. Let them find someone else to create their fireworks and call for rain."

"Is my sister as stubborn as ever?" Emrys asked in a bemused tone.

Aelwyn smiled. Other than inquiring about Viviane, her father did not mention Aelwyn's long absence or its cause; he did not ask about her health or her happiness. Then again, Emrys had never been particularly affectionate. Her father was the nearly thousand-year-old wizard who had advised Artucus, the first King of England, and all his heirs—including Henry VI, for whom Emrys had brought the kingdoms of England and France together to create the foundation of the empire.

Emrys settled back into his chair and drummed his fingers on his desk. "I had to convince the Order to take you in; you know they aren't very fond of Viviane, and were wary of her influence upon you. I had to assure them of your obedience. Do not fail me."

"My will is to serve," she said, showing him she had already learned the vows of her future station.

He nodded, pleased. "Run into any trouble on your

journey?" he asked, taking a pipe out of his pocket and lighting it.

"No, Father," she said with a shrug, fiddling with the obsidian stone on her chain. She thought of the little thief, and how she'd held his soul in her hands. "None at all."

2

House
AQUITAINE

The prettiest room in the castle was built like a jewel box: all pink, white and gold, with gilt molding, pink damask wallpaper, fat cherub murals painted on the ceiling, and a crystal chandelier above the bed. It was a room fit for a sleeping princess. Except the princess, Marie-Victoria, was only pretending to be asleep. She kept her eyes closed and her breathing even as her ladies-in-waiting gathered around the bed, trying to make as little noise as possible. Marie wondered how long they had been standing there—since dawn? Or for only a few minutes? She never knew; only that they were always there when she woke up. There was an audience for everything she did, even the most mundane of activities, from rising to dining to strolling in the gardens. The practice had been handed down from the French side of their family, and even though the court was in London they kept to the French ways.

She supposed she should get up soon. She could sense that her ladies were getting impatient; she could hear them coughing and murmuring to each other. But she also knew what was awaiting her that day, and so she wanted to stay in her soft warm bed for as long as possible. One of her ladies—Evangeline, most likely, the highest-ranking one—cleared her throat loudly, and Marie decided it was time to put everyone out of their misery.

"Good morning," she said, pulling open the bed curtains and yawning.

"Good morning, Princess," her ladies chorused as they curtsied.

"No breakfast today?" she asked, noticing that no one had set the little table at the edge of the room by the windows.

"No, my lady. You have been asked to join the queen this morning."

Marie sighed. It meant that the rumors were true, then—her mother had plans for her. The formal request to join her at breakfast in front of the whole court meant that Marie would discover what those plans were, along with everyone else, in public—with no opportunity to talk about it in private beforehand. Which could only mean that her mother did not want to take any chances, and that any objections Marie might have to her designs would not be taken into account. She began to cough violently into her handkerchief, staining the white linen with blood and scaring her ladies.

"I am all right," Marie said when the coughing subsided, and the ladies helped her dress. Paulette, the Lady of the Robes, decided on the crimson silk.

"Better for your coloring." She smiled as she helped Marie pull the gown over her head. "There, you see? You carry it well—you can hardly tell you are sick."

"Paulette! Watch your tongue!" Evangeline reprimanded.

"Oh! Forgive me, Your Highness," Paulette said fearfully, with a bow.

"It is all right, Paulie, dear," Marie said gently, taking a long wheezing breath. "It is not a secret." As a child, she had suffered from every childhood ailment, from infection to the pox. She had been slow to speak and slow to walk; for a long time, it was assumed she was slow in every capacity, and arrangements had quietly been made for transfer to an institution in Geneva—until she surprised her governesses by speaking in complete paragraphs at the age of four, and discussing logic with her tutors by age seven. She had worn braces on her legs to straighten the tibias, a helmet on her head to round out her skull, and a contraption on her back to make her sit up straight. For most of her life she had felt more like part of a machine than a girl, harnessed and strapped and attached to a variety of painful apparatuses to improve her looks and posture.

Marie scrutinized herself in the mirror. She was sixteen now, no longer shackled by contraptions or sitting in a wheelchair. But a few years ago she had caught the wasting plague, a rare and debilitating illness of the tubercular variety, which caused blood in the lungs, shortness of breath, and weakness in the constitution. It had turned her pale coloring almost translucent. She had thin brown hair, a high forehead, a narrow nose, and intelligent gray eyes. The dress did give her a little bit more color, even as she despaired of ever looking pretty. It took almost an hour for the ladies to get her properly outfitted—to hook every eye in her corset and tie every bow on her skirt, to plait her hair and arrange it artfully around the nape of her neck.

When they were finally satisfied with her appearance they led her to the queen's bedroom, where two hundred courtiers were already gathered behind the railing that separated the private from the public space of the room. The assembled were the great and the good of the realm: the noble ladies and lords, dukes and earls, ministers and officials, high-ranking enchanters; even the Merlin was there for a change, looking impatient as he scanned his pocket watch. She had heard Aelwyn was supposed to return to the palace that day, and wondered when her friend would come to see her. Emrys nodded a greeting, and Marie shuddered inwardly; she had been uneasy in his presence ever since the day of the fire. He had stormed into the burning room and cast a spell to put out the blaze, his face full of wrath and anger. Emrys was a sorcerer, a wizard, a master of the dark arts. Like many of the queen's subjects who did not understand magic or its workings, Marie was afraid of the man who wielded it.

The queen's bed was a grand four-poster draped with the most luxurious of velvets, embroidered with the white fleur-de-lis of France and the white roses of England. Marie held her breath as a gnarled hand reached and pulled the curtains away. The queen appeared in her nightdress: a small old woman, stooped, hunchbacked, balding at the top. She was neither stately nor regal, but when she appeared all two hundred members of the court bowed low. Marie kept her head bent and tried not to cough. She sneaked a peek as her mother walked behind the dressing panels, where her ladies-in-waiting helped her into her morning robe and breakfast cap.

The court kept their bows in place until the queen spoke.

"Good morning," she said, addressing them at last. Her voice had a majestic timbre, powerful and authoritative. It was a voice that made proclamations, turned commoners into lords, and sentenced enemies to death.

The crowd chorused a hearty "Good morning, Your Majesty!"

"Her Royal Highness, Princess Marie-Victoria Grace Eleanor Aquitaine, Dauphine of Viennois, Princess of Wales," said the herald, announcing Marie's presence.

"Marie, my child, will you join me for breakfast?" Eleanor

said, looking pleased and surprised, as if she had not orchestrated her daughter's appearance herself.

Marie took a seat across from her mother at the gold-and-white table in front of the railing, which was set with an exquisite breakfast. It was a command performance; the entire court hung on their every word and scrutinized their every action. Her hand was shaking a little as she accepted a cup of tea, but it was not from being on stage. No, the fear was always there; underneath the love and obedience, thrumming like a barely heard note, there was a cold panic in her bones whenever she was near this strange creature, this ancient mother of hers. Her eyes watered and her throat itched. Marie chastised herself for her cowardice, but she could not help herself. She had always felt mute and powerless and distant in her mother's presence. She glanced at the queen's wizened face, lined with wrinkles as heavy and deep as the folds in the curtains behind her. Queen Eleanor was over one hundred and fifty years old.

Growing up, Marie had noticed that the other children who lived in the palace had mothers whose faces were creamy and soft to the touch. *Who is this old crone?* she'd wondered when the queen visited the nursery. She could still recall the shock and dismay she'd felt when she understood that her mother was not Jenny Wallace, the pretty, apple-cheeked nurse who held her in her arms, but the imposing old woman in jewels and furs who appraised her with a grimace.

Mother and daughter sat across from each other. The queen was dressed in her plain morning robe, which even in its simplicity spoke of power and ease and position. The brocade and embroidery were so fine as to be almost invisible; the fabric was smooth to the touch, weightless on her frail shoulders.

"I am so glad you have joined me today, my dear, as I have a wonderful surprise for you. The Prussian court will be our honored guests at this year's Bal du Drap d'Or."

"The Prussians?" Marie asked. Just a few weeks ago the empire had been determined to crush the tiny obstinate nation, until the smaller kingdom had revealed its trump card.

"You remember dear Leopold, don't you? The *Kronprinz?* Such a handsome boy," Eleanor said, attacking her breakfast with an uncharacteristic ferocity.

Marie felt the blood slowly drain from her face. She was right to fear this day. Her mother meant to marry her off to Leopold VII of Prussia to secure a lasting peace between the two nations. Marie glanced at the Merlin. Emrys's face was impassive, but she knew he had to be behind this. A truce; a marriage; an alliance that would turn a deadly rival into a close friend once again.

The Prussians had once been allies. The royal families of Europe shared common ancestry, and Marie had grown up knowing Leopold. She even counted his younger brother as one of her closest childhood friends. But the relationship between the nations had slowly deteriorated until it reached full-blown hostility, and the Prussians had gone to war with the empire over the Alsace-Lorraine border for several years, with countless fatalities on both sides. The courage and resistance of the much smaller country was impressive, just like the power at their command—one of the last Pandora's Boxes left in the world, which they had put to awesome use at the Battle of Lamac. The victory they'd won had led to the empire's retreat.

Marie heard that the Merlin had been stupefied and Eleanor incensed at this remarkable and astonishing turn of events. For centuries, the empire had maintained a stranglehold over the world's only source of magic after defeating Jeanne of Arkk and her dark witches five hundred years before. How the Prussians had gotten hold of a weapon of such magnitude was unclear, but they had used it to their advantage, and this proposed marriage would be their reward.

She knew from the way the Merlin ignored her and her mother chastised her that they considered her too weak, mild, and sickly ever to become an effective ruler, and the most they could hope for was to marry her off to one. She supposed that with this peace treaty they were forced to accept Leopold, but she couldn't help but think that they must be relieved as well. Leopold VII was one of the most eligible of the royal sons of Europe: tall, broad-shouldered, classically handsome, with bright blue eyes the color of the Danube and a halo of golden curls upon his brow. More than that, he was supposed to have grown up a real gentleman; he was said to be well-read, smart, diligent, and hard-working—instead of the usual lazy Lothario. From his performance at the battle, it was clear he was a real leader, a hero brave and true, who had the love and respect of his subjects. Not that it mattered when it came to her happiness. She remembered him as a sly little boy, one who had little interest in other people, other than as his admirers. He would not care for her as a person, nor should she expect him to. Romantic love did not factor into royal matrimony; the most one could hope for was civility. He was marrying her for the empire, for the crown she could place upon his head; for the chance to be king.

She had known this day would come, but it was still a shock that it had arrived so soon. She knew she had no choice when it came to her own marriage, and that love was the least of considerations when a princess chose a mate—or, more to the point, when a mate was chosen for her. Even though she had been preparing for it all her life, it was still unexpected when it finally arrived. She thought briefly of a person she *would* choose if she were allowed to, but it was too painful to even think of him. Gill Cameron had left her service for months now, and it didn't appear he would be back anytime soon. Besides, there was no possibility of the queen and the Merlin ever approving that union.

Her mother tapped her spoon against her cup, to show she was still waiting for an answer.

"Yes, I do remember Leo," Marie said finally. "But he is engaged, isn't he?"

There was a titter from the assembled courtiers, which the queen silenced with a frown. "Is he?" Eleanor asked pointedly.

"To Isabelle—you must remember—the pretty little French girl," Marie insisted. House Valois was not welcome at court, but like many, she had heard that sixteen-year-old Lady Isabelle of Orleans was very beautiful indeed, blessed with dark eyes like limpid pools in a small, heart-shaped face. Uncommonly breathtaking and lovely: everything Marie was not. Marie knew she was displeasing her mother by bringing up Leo's engagement, but she couldn't help it. What was the use of power and privilege if one could not be happy in life? She missed Gill and wished with all of her heart that she could see him again. If she could, she would tell him exactly how she felt about him this time. She did not want to think about a future with Leopold.

Eleanor raised an eyebrow. "I am quite certain he is unattached. And if not, he will soon be."

Marie nodded. This was not just her mother's will, but the Merlin's. The peace of the empire depended on her taking the Prussian prince as her bridegroom. The sooner she accepted her fate, the easier her life would be.

"In any event, he is to be our guest. I trust you will help make his stay with us more pleasant."

"Of course, Mother." Marie wondered what her father had been like—if her parents had loved each other as history claimed. The great love story of Queen Eleanor and Prince Francis. Or was that another lie? Marie had seen portraits of her mother as a girl. Eleanor had been so beautiful once, with her crown of red hair and dazzling green eyes. They called her the English rose with French charm. Once in a while, she saw glimpses of that fierce, gorgeous girl in the old lady sitting before her—like today, for instance, as her mother planned her daughter's betrothal, her bright eyes flashing.

"I am sure he will be quite taken by you," Eleanor said, her voice brimming with confidence as she slathered butter on her toast. It was clear that as far as the queen was concerned, the courtship, proposal, and wedding were as good as done. "If all goes well, perhaps you will be wed by the end of the season."

It was late March, and the season ended in June, just a few months from now. A royal wedding was just the thing to distract the populace from the costly failure of the long-fought Prussian campaign. The public loved a royal wedding; there would be tea towels with their faces on them before the year was out. At least Leo had a handsome profile. "You will adore him," Eleanor said in that voice of hers that brooked no argument.

"Yes, of course, Mother," she replied automatically, and was seized by a hacking fit that left her red and breathless.

Eleanor was instantly alarmed. "Have you taken your tonic?" the queen demanded.

When she was able to speak, Marie nodded. She had taken the latest tonic, but there was nothing that could be done; no amount of spell-casting or potion-making could ease her affliction. The wasting plague was a disease even the healers from the sisterhood could not cure. Marie had heard the sisters murmur that it was her mother's advanced age that had caused Marie's many ailments, as Eleanor had been over a century in age when she carried her to term. The pregnancy had been an alchemy of creation, made from the preserved seed of Eleanor's long-mourned and long-dead husband when the queen had decided that, at last, she was ready to bear a child. Even so, the wasting plague was a virulent disease, and one that afflicted perfectly healthy people out of the blue.

"Emrys assured me this one would provide the miracle we have been hoping for. He had the herbs brought from the East; the viceroy himself sent it from the mountains of the Himalayas," the queen said, exchanging a sharp look with her enchanter.

"Yes, Mama," Marie rasped, her chest heaving and her eyes tearing as her mother grew more and more upset.

"You must rest, dearest," her mother said, rising from her seat to kiss Marie's forehead. With papery lips against her skin, Marie tried not to shudder.

Marie nodded, still coughing blood, and stood from her chair. She waded through the rows of bowed courtiers, letting her ladies lead her back to her room so she could lie down.

It was an odd thing, her cough; as soon as she left her mother's presence it abated, and she almost felt fine.

· 3 ·

New York
DOLL

he Astor manor in Washington Square had once
been the grandest house in the city. It was built
in the French-Gothic style with a touch of Beaux-Arts flair,
three-and-a-half stories high, with an imposing limestone
façade. But the corners of its cornice were crumbling. A few
slate tiles were missing from the roof, so that copper flashings
left long streaks of gray-green oxide collecting in the cracks.
In a drawing room on the first floor, the formerly vibrant
Renaissance-style space with a scene from the Trojan War
painted on the ceiling was empty, save for a lone ebony desk,
at which the daughter of the house was currently bent over
her studies.

Ronan Elizabeth Astor grimaced at the book in front of
her. The reproduction was badly faded, splotchy, and gray, so

that it was difficult to make out the face of the boy in the picture. He was either afflicted with a bulbous nose and tragically triple-chinned, or it was an unfortunate angle and even worse lighting. She decided it was likely the former, as a handsome suitor's features would be discernible even in an abysmal photograph. As far as she was concerned, he was a dog just like the rest of them—all these princes and barons, aristocrats and lords, dukes and archdukes, and more counts than she could count. Total bow-wow, she thought with a naughty smirk. A collar would have been more appropriate than that ghastly ascot he wore. Her governess glared at her and rapped on the print with her finger. "Pay attention!"

"One would assume that Viscount Stewart would have been able to afford a better court photographer," she finally said in a bored voice. Ronan was tired of all this. For weeks, her governess had been showing her various portraits of titled, single male aristocrats from Debrett's International— that august and authoritative guide to the landed, titled, and moneyed in the empire—and quizzing her on their names, positions and hobbies. It was a special edition, with lavish full-color spreads of their country estates, not the usual roll-call listing of names and titles. And therefore, it was much more helpful for a striving American outsider. All morning, Ronan had dutifully parroted back the correct responses until she knew their names, titles, and interests better than her own.

This was to be her first London Season: a special privilege, as not many from across the sea were invited to court every year. Ronan had merited an invitation through a patron—an old friend of the family, one Lady Constance Grosvernor, who was a favorite of the queen. There were plenty of silly American girls who would jump at the chance to marry one of these fools, but Ronan was not one of them. At sixteen she had a restless, impatient quality that set her apart. It was the best and worst thing about her, depending on whom you asked.

"I believe the correct answer is Peregrine Randolph, Lord Stewart, as that is the *proper* 'courtesy title' of the eldest son of the Marquess of Hillshire," Vera Bradford admonished. Her nanny was very particular about such details, and Ronan's mother had chosen her precisely because Vera had served at several great houses abroad, and knew the names and habits of the important characters intimately. Too intimately, the rumors had it—but then, there were always rumors of lordlings and their pretty young governesses. If one believed all the rumors, then one believed that Vera's son would have been the rightful heir of Salisbury, if not for the absence of a silly little thing like a marriage ceremony. Noble and royal bastards: the world was full of them, babies like strays with Devonshire noses and Aquitaine eyes.

Ronan wrinkled her own nose at the sight of the pudgy, squash-nosed boy in the picture. Peregrine Randolph, Lord Stewart was a handsome name wasted upon someone who was decidedly not. It was grossly unfair to think that *she* would be the one who would count herself lucky if he took a liking to her, and not the other way around. But as the heiress to a bankrupt house, with little access to the power of magic, such was her lot in life.

"Lord Stewart," she said in a flat voice. "Hobbies: archery, still life, and discussing Plato." More importantly, the Hillshire riches included a vast collection of rare and valuable amulets forged by the brotherhood of Merlin. They were said to bring the bearer good life, good fortune, and good luck—though obviously not good looks. She smiled, and supposed that was where *she* came into the picture.

The next photograph filled the whole page, which boded well for the wealth of the family of the aristocrat in question. This one was slightly cross-eyed and buck-toothed, but what did it matter if his family had a powerful enchanter at their disposal? Especially one who could make lands fertile and farms profitable. "Marcus Deveraux," she said. "Or, as you prefer to call him, Charles Arthur Marcus Deveraux, Viscount Lisle. Hobbies include falconry, piano, and romantic poetry." So pretentious. She bet he only knew that one line from Byron, the one everyone knew, about walking in beauty.

She flicked her eyes at the next titled lord in question, a grainy photograph of a dark-haired boy with a prominent nose and chin. "Archie Fairfax," she said. At a sharp glance from Vera, she relented and recited his real name. "The Honorable Archibald Fairfax. He prefers champagne, music halls, and noise." Finally, an honest answer, she thought.

Ronan sighed. They were all the same, these inbred,

weak-chinned boys. They had too much money and time but too little to do, even as they professed a proclivity toward an athletic endeavor, supposedly cultivated an interest in some form of art, or followed the teachings of a great philosopher. Truth be told, it was common knowledge that boys from privileged backgrounds mostly favored cards, girls, and drink. Their only advantage came from their families' magical holdings.

Unlike her own father, who wasted his time on such wrong-headed pursuits as "technology" and "progress" and who would have been dubbed "Empty Pockets Astor" in the papers if anyone knew the truth of their situation. Thankfully, her mother was good at keeping up appearances. No one in New York knew how badly off they were.

Perhaps she was just bitter. The Astors held one of the oldest and most important positions in the Americas; they were deeply loyal to House Aquitaine, and had been well-rewarded for it. If only her father had managed to hang on to more of his inheritance, instead of squandering it all away on frivolities—investing in such notions as railroads and steam engines that would never be built, nor run correctly. He continually assured his family they would soon receive generous dividends. But not soon enough for their comfort, she thought, knowing the vast sum that was mortgaged against the estate. That was the problem with Americans, they placed too much faith in *science*, when anyone could see that such pedestrian inventions as shoulder rifles or mechanized cannons would never beat England and its powerful Merlin. The American rebels had learned as much during the failed Insurrection of 1776, when the Redcoats and Her Majesty's magicians had laid waste to the attempted sedition with their superior spell-casting.

Luckily, her ancestor had been on the right side of the rebellion, and had retained the governorship of New York and all the privileges that came with it. Their country home in Hastings was practically a castle. Of course, nothing could compete with the sprawling and magnificent stone piles that the Europeans called home, but even the queen had spoken fondly of her time at Hudson Park. Maintenance, however, was another matter; keeping up the estates and the staff had all but drained the family finances. Many of their beautiful things had quietly been sold to pay their monthly bills.

Relief was on the way however, in the form of passage on the *Saturnia*, which was to take her across the Atlantic. Once there, she would be presented to the queen. It was her family's dearest hope that Ronan secure a desirable mate and land an engagement before the season ended and all the eligible aristocrats repaired back to their country homes. As it was, her trousseau was not worth its mention in the *Herald*. The enthusiastic descriptions of the fabulous gowns she would be taking to London masked the shabby reality: scraping together the very last of their resources had only resulted in a trunk full of knockoffs of the latest Parisian styles. She had a few of her mother's glamorous gowns, of course, but they were twenty years out of date. Her jewels, or lack of them, were an unspeakable tragedy. No longer did she have her great-grandmother's famed Astor tiara, but only an expert reproduction—it was a fake, paste and glass, and created in utmost secrecy. The real one had been sold long ago to an Arabian princess, who was probably wearing it somewhere in the desert. A shame.

Ronan was sailing across the sea so she could sell herself to the highest bidder, and she *must* make a match—a rich one that would allow her to pay off their debts and secure her future. And if the family came with a retinue of magicians at their beck and call, then all the better. It was tiresome living without a little glimmer every now and then. All of her friends had the latest fripperies from the empire: powders that turned your hair gold, creams that took away blemishes on the skin. She was at least fortunate in that she did not need a magician to appear beautiful.

"There's my favorite girl," her father said, entering the room. He was a large man with a bristly beard and a gruff but gentle demeanor, the type who was called upon to play Father Christmas every holiday. "What's this?" he asked, looking askance at the book on the desk, which was open to a lavish illustration of a ducal coat of arms. He made a face, realizing what was going on.

"Oh, Daddy, it's nothing," Ronan said, closing the leather-bound book with a thump and handing it to Vera, who politely excused herself from the room.

"Your mother puts strange ideas in your head, but an Astor

of New York doesn't need anyone's help—remember that. You have your good name. You don't need to scrape at the feet of those empire snobs."

Ronan held her tongue. To be honest, she did not have it in her heart to resent him. Her father was the one who had played backgammon with her and drawn her pictures as a child. He was the one who had attended her tea parties in the nursery, and read her picture books at night while her mother threw herself into the social whirl of the city. "Did you hear the Haltons have a new fortune-teller?" she asked eagerly. "She predicts a rise in the stock market."

"Bah, that dark magic has no place in the future," Henry said. "Fortune-tellers are nothing but frauds, my girl." She knew her father did not want to admit it, but if she did not succeed in marrying well, they would have to move out west—a last resort—to her mother's people, the "barbarians."

She kissed her father on the cheek and left to dress for dinner, heading up the stairs. Ronan had always been fond of the grand staircase, with its oiled and shiny balustrade, treads that neither creaked nor wobbled, and rails solid as stone. When she was a child, she had turned it into a coliseum full of dolls, placing row after row of silk-garbed figurines on each of the steps. The stairs held her audience, while Ronan performed a dance at the base. Ronan remembered nervously descending these steps on Christmas mornings, her nightdress gleaming against the dark of the wood as she tiptoed toward the dazzling tree festooned with tinsel and presents. She'd miss these old boards when she went off to England. Not that they'd had much of a Christmas last year, anyway . . . and the ancient but beautiful brass chandelier that used to hang in the center of the room was gone now—sold, like all the rest of the most valuable décor.

Rounding the corner, past the now-empty corridors with the scraped-away wallpaper and more missing paintings, she stopped for a moment to stare at the pendant lights, whose candle mounts had been recently retrofitted for Edison bulbs. It looked as if strands of lightning were trapped within their tiny globes. Was this not magic? Wasn't this power just as grand and unknowable as the Merlin's? Her father believed so. Sometimes, looking at those incandescent lights, Ronan thought he might just have a point.

"Is that you, Ronan?" her mother's voice called. She turned toward the sound, knowing it was more of an order than a question.

Ronan entered her mother's bedroom, the only room in the house that still had all of its original furniture. It was the best room as well, with a view of the park and gardens. Outside, the first street lamps had popped to life as the sun hung low near the horizon. Inside, a single Edison bulb lit her mother's room with a strong, consistent glow. The white paneled walls amplified the light, making her mother's chamber not only the largest bedroom, but the brightest one as well. Her father had insisted the house be paneled in walnut, but her mother had disagreed. Against her husband's will she'd had her room paneled in silk sateen, a finish as bright as newly fallen snow.

The bed was done in the English style, tall and canopied, dressed up like a queen's with bunting stuck between four tall poles. The plush white rug beneath her mother's bed abutted a second one that stretched underneath an armoire, a dressing screen, and a powder table. Each of these pieces was framed by a pair of gilded chairs, their backs pressed against the wall. Vera told her that the backs of chairs in great houses like theirs remained unpainted, because no one ever moved the chairs or used them. Ronan had never checked to see if it was true, if the chairs were indeed nailed to the walls, but it made sense. Everything in the room was meant to be admired. Every piece—from the exquisite French clock on the mantel, to the row of perfume decanters on the vanity, to her own mother.

At thirty-five years of age, Elizabeth Astor was still extraordinarily lovely, if a little haunted-looking. Her hollow cheeks and red eyes were the result of many sleepless nights. She came from the provinces—she was from nowhere, her parents nobody. Her only treasure was her arresting beauty, which had won over her husband, the third son of the then-richest man in New York. The youngest boy was traditionally not meant to inherit, or expected to come to much; but when the elder and middle sons of Jackson Pierce Astor were both lost during the War Between the Americans thirty years before, the youngest had inherited the governorship, and little Sue-Beth Morley (the *horror* of that name—so common—it held the stink of dusty towns and tumbleweed)—suddenly found herself the reigning doyenne of New York. Upon her arrival in the city, her mother had had the good sense to adopt the name Elizabeth, and went by the name "Bits."

"Show me your court bow," Bits Astor demanded now. "When your father and I were presented at court to meet the queen, they all said I had the most beautiful one."

Ronan rolled her eyes. Her mother was forever waxing nostalgic about the glories of *her* season. Knowing the ingrained snobbishness of the Franco-Brits, Ronan was sure that was not all they said about the social-climbing young American.

"Yes, Mother," she said, and dutifully displayed what Vera had taught her. The deepest curtsy, almost to the floor. Her head was bowed demurely, lashes against her cheeks, eyes downcast. Not once must she turn her back on the monarch. It was said that Queen Eleanor had her Merlin destroy those who dared to disrespect her, and Ronan did not want to suffer such a fate. She respected the power of magic; it was why she found her dear father so misguided.

"I sense a hint of rebellion in the curve of your cheek, my dear; and we must show utmost deference to the Crown. Again."

Ronan nodded and curtsied again, deeper this time—so low that she felt the backs of her thighs burn with the effort.

When her mother was satisfied with her performance, she crossed the room to stand next to her daughter. She turned Ronan's face toward the Venetian gold gilt mirror, one of the last antiques left. Bits's hands were as delicate as a child's, but her grip on Ronan's chin was like steel. She turned it to the right, then the left, examining her daughter's profile, and finally brought it straight back to face the mirror.

"My lovely girl." Bits smiled.

Ronan looked at what her mother saw. Her otherworldly, celebrated beauty: the porcelain skin, luminescent and pearly; the high sweep of her forehead; a thin, sculpted nose; sharp cheekbones; her pink pout, a proper rosebud, ripe for the plucking. Her long golden tresses, finer than silk, fell on her shoulders loose and wanton; she had been impatient with her governess that morning, and had pulled away when Vera had tried to braid her hair and put it up properly.

"You look exactly like me at your age; thank goodness for that. A consummate New York blonde, as they like to say," her mother said with satisfaction. "*This* is your fate. *These* are your riches. This face will win you a prince; take my word for it. You are an Astor of New York. You should do no worse, as you have much more than I started with."

Ronan flushed. She looked at her face and her mother's closely in the mirror. They were like twin images, except for the very faint lines around her mother's eyes, the faded color in her thinner cheeks.

She knew all of this already, of course. She would choose one of those awful boys from the photographs and make him fall in love with her. And then she would find a way to make this estate matter again. The port town was booming, and

New York City was being compared to the great capitals. If the Astors managed to get some enchanters at their service, they might be able to shape their fortunes and their future.

Her mother's face, and her father's name—her parents thought that was all there was to her, and maybe they were right. She would be married at the end of the London Season—and she determined right then and there that she would make not just a good match, but the *best* match; perhaps even catch the eye of the *Kronprinz* of Prussia himself. She had studied his portrait in the book with the greatest care, and had found much to admire in his noble profile. It was said that the Prussians had used a Pandora's Box during the final battle, which had brought the queen's army to its knees and ended the war. With a weapon of such magnitude, one could rule the world.

Ronan was nothing if not ambitious.

the
SPARE PRINCE

OLF! WOLF! WOLF! WOLF!" The roar of his name made him euphoric as the crowd surged forward, lifting him into the air. He raised a bloody hand to the ceiling. His vision was clouded by sweat and blood, his mouth full of red, his eyes bleeding red, so that everything was red—from the faces of the spectators to the shadows in the dark room. It wasn't even a room, but a space in the bowels of an empty abandoned building by the harbor, once reserved for the coal stocks that powered the boiler. The ground beneath his feet was made of hard dirt, and soot covered every surface. The room was so dark that the gas lamps made the shadows deeper, the hollows blacker. This is a tomb, Wolf thought, a crypt.

The crowd, made up mostly of day laborers and off-duty

soldiers, hard men with stony faces, pressed against him, cheering his name.

Victory. He had bested the fiercest fighter in the city— a soldier in the queen's army, built like a fortress, who'd crumbled like a burnt and broken tower. "WOLF! WOLF! WOLF! WOLF!" They called him the Beast of Berlin, the Animal of the Black Forest, *Lobo Loco* in Spain, *Le Loup Fou* in Montreal; and tonight in New York City, he was the Mad Dog of the East. While he was no hero of Lamac, no soldier, no knight, he was still a winner.

"Wolf!" One cold, disapproving voice stood out in the crowd, cutting through the noise. "WOLFGANG FRIED-RICH JOACHIM VON HOHENZOLLEM!"

"Bollocks," Wolf cursed. The fun was over. He waded above the crowd, touching feet and palms to hands and shoulders and backs as he rode the tide toward the door, his winnings in his pockets. His breeches were torn at the knees, his shirt shredded. He tumbled to the ground at the feet of his closest friend, his advisor, his minder, his mentor; the one who had taught him how to fight, how to stop a man's heart with his hands. An old man, who crouched down low and lifted him up by his ear.

"Ow, ow, ow!" Wolf said, batting Oswald's hand away. "Leave me alone, Oz. I've taken enough of a beating tonight." He winced; he had taken a few good hits from the Brooklyn giant. His back and shoulders throbbed, and he couldn't open his right eye. He would have swooned and fallen, but he had too much pride. Thankfully, Oswald put his arm around him to steady him as they left.

"Your father would have my head if he found out about this, and your brother will be far from pleased," the old man scolded.

"Hang my brother," Wolf said, spitting out a tooth. A back one, thank Merlin, he thought, fishing in his mouth with his fingers, grateful that it wasn't one of the front teeth so it wouldn't show when he smiled. Messed-up chops didn't go far with the ladies. He took a long, loud sip from his flask, felt the liquor burn his throat, and smoothed his dark hair away from his head, knowing it looked better that way. "You won't tell Father; I know you, Oz. You're all bark and no bite, unlike me," he said with a golden smile that gave charm a new name.

Oswald didn't answer as he helped the young prince into his dark jacket. They boarded a waiting carriage that would take them back to their hotel. Once they were in the privacy of the plush, velvet-lined box, he spoke freely. "I suppose not, but the rumors will catch up with him one day. When His Majesty finds out the 'Beast of Berlin' is actually his younger son, you'd better hope we're all very far from the capital." He grimaced as he handed his ward a clean handkerchief. "You're bleeding."

"Just a trickle," Wolf said, taking it and pressing it against his eye. "Nothing permanent, don't worry. All damage is temporary."

"You're lucky. We have a month to get to London, so your

bruises should be healed by then, and your face back to its rightful shape. You're sure about the eye? We can have Von Strasser look at it tonight."

Wolf waved the suggestion away. "Let the doctor sleep. It'll open in the morning. This is nothing compared to what they did to me in Boston. They had a real gladiator there—you should have seen the arms on the man. Tree trunks! No, tree trunks are smaller. So, we're off to the enemy's lair, are we?"

"Hardly an enemy, more like your new family," Oswald sniffed.

"Right. Leo's to marry the princess now, isn't he? That was one of the terms of the peace treaty."

"After all the papers have been arranged, yes."

"Poor Isabelle. She can't be happy about it. She's been looking forward to her wedding since February."

"Her happiness is irrelevant."

"Of course. Although Marie can't be thrilled either. She's never liked Leo very much," Wolf said. Smart little Marie, with her wan face and kind smile. He hadn't seen her in years, since relations between their kingdoms had gone south. He missed her warm and easy friendship. Marie had always been such a sensible girl, the only one apart from him who understood what it meant to be royalty, and the uselessness that came with privilege. The Prussian kingdom was run by its ministers, the empire by the Merlin. Whoever said "uneasy lies the head that wears the crown" knew of what he spoke. It was a pity that her hand and happiness were the price the empire would have to pay for peace with Prussia. She and Leo would be miserable together; a more ill-advised match could not be proposed between two more different people. But it wasn't as if his father had married their mother for love, either. For that, his lord father had his mistresses. This was how it was for the heirs and heiresses of this world: trapped by their families, by their titles. Duty. Family. Royalty. Side dish.

The King of Prussia had forbidden his younger son to fight in the war, arguing that the country needed him safe in case anything happened to Leo. But Wolf became a fighter anyway. There were underground sparring clubs in every city. The staff usually knew where they were located, fond as they were of wagers. The first time he had done it, he'd been fourteen, and ruthless even then—trained by Duncan Oswald, his father's master-at-arms. He'd been itching to show off what he'd learned. In the ring there were no rules, no restrictions. During a fight, it didn't matter if he was a prince or a peasant; he was the same as any other man. In his eighteen years, he had never felt better than when he discovered he could fight, and fight well.

"So, what does that have to do with me? Why do I have to go?" He already knew the answer, but he felt petulant, small, and complaining—the opposite of being a man. But then, what kind of title was "prince" anyway? It was an embarrassing one. It spoke of lace collars and tufted pillows, like the one his sore behind was comfortably seated on now.

"To represent your house and honor. Not that you have any," Oswald said with a raised eyebrow.

"I need to fight, Oz. You know that. Especially since they wouldn't take me to Lamac."

"You know why your father sent you away. If your brother had lost, then you would be king."

"Ha, the odds of that happening are about as good as Leo beating me in the ring." Wolf grinned. *The heir and the spare.* Wolf was the one in the shadows, the one who would inherit little . . . some land out in Bavaria, maybe. There, he would be nothing but a titled and glorified sheep farmer when it came down to it, unless something happened to his brother, the future king, who had the duty and honor to lead the Prussian troops into battle.

"Your brother is a good soldier," Oswald admonished.

"Only thanks to that demon's tool," Wolf said. "Practically cheating."

Pandora's Box. Supposedly it was the last one on earth, able to conjure horror unlike anything seen in this world. "I don't need magic to win my fights," he said bitterly. Leo had been something of an apprentice to his father's oldest and most trusted advisor, Lord Hartwig, who had been intent on finding a way to combat the empire's monopoly on magic. Wolf had to hand it to him; he had certainly succeeded wildly on that front. Growing up, Leo had taken to Hartwig in the same way that Wolf had taken to Oz. Both of them were searching for a father figure, as King Frederick, busy monarch that he was, never had time for either of his sons.

"No doubt your father will find some use for you."

"Ah well, could be worse. Could be goats rather than sheep." Wolf winked. He leaned back into his chair, wondering exactly what he would do with his life. He hadn't a clue. Nothing was expected of him, other than to remain alive in the event of his brother's death.

"We are sailing on the *Saturnia* in the morning. And good timing, too—a quick escape, shall we say—for there is another one now," Oswald informed him.

"Not again?" Wolf groaned.

"Yes. That makes three young ladies of gentle birth accusing you of fathering their babies since we arrived in the Americas. The latest one is a baron's daughter visiting from Sussex."

"She has done this publicly?"

"No. They are—taking care of it," Oswald said delicately. "Unless . . ."

"Unless I marry her. Is that it?"

"Yes."

"She's lying. They all are."

"Oh?"

"I didn't touch her. I didn't touch any of them." Wolf smiled at the memory. "It was merely an innocent game of strip billiards. Surely you know the game?" he teased. The memory of a certain night several months ago flitted into his mind. The eight-ball sinking in the corner pocket. *Click. Swish. Thud.* "*Strip.*" The girls, standing at the back wall, giggling, with only their long hair to cover themselves; not that they hadn't wanted to show him everything they had . . . they were more than eager . . . but he had not touched any of them, and that was the truth. But there was no harm in looking, was there? "Really, Oz, do you think I'm that stupid?"

Oswald looked cross. "You are accusing these fine young ladies of harlotry."

"Whoever they're sleeping with, it wasn't me."

"So you deny it all? Every one?"

"Oz, don't you know me by now?" Wolf said, feigning hurt. "Let them make their accusations all they want; they are without merit. I'm as pure as a maid," he added, his face set. Unlike his vaunted older brother, he had no taste for womanizing, no desire to father a litter of bastards. He vowed that once he was married he would never take a mistress, not after seeing his mother cry in her room over his father's indiscretions. When she was alive, she had cried all the time. He would never add to another person's misery in that way, and his future lady wife—whoever she was—would not suffer the fate of his mother.

It was his darkest secret: Wolf, the Beast of Berlin, was more Labrador than fox when it came to the ladies. "*This* is my only vice," he said, holding up the bloody handkerchief.

·5·

a
COUNTESS SCORNED

*I*sabelle had never been across the Atlantic, but had heard that the richest Americans, whose fortunes rivaled even the queen's, lived in grand, palatial homes. There was no need for fireplaces, as they were built with central heating and wired with electricity. And so, when she thought of that faraway land, she thought of being warm. With their astonishing technical inventions, the Americans had learned to live comfortably without magic. Critics of the Merlin accused the magician of keeping scientific progress at bay. In the empire, if one had no magic, one had almost nothing. It was always cold in this house, ever since her family's witches had been burned at the stake. Not that Isabelle had any more faith in the power of magic; far from being able to save her family, magic had been its destruction. Magic had rendered her a charity case, one to be pitied or cast aside. And now magic was taking her dearest love away from her, along with her dreams for the future. She cursed the Pandora's Box that had won the Prussians the war.

The reality of her situation made the walls feel colder, the ceilings taller, the drafts more intolerable. Her home was more cave than castle. The parlor they were sitting in stank of oil lamps, and the walls had acquired the gray sootiness of a decade's worth of ash and candle flame. The great fireplace in the middle of the room had a hearth taller than her head. The thing was immense, medieval, originally designed for roasting whole hogs—perhaps two at a time. It was all so primitive.

Through the high windows she glimpsed the family vineyards, long rows of knotted vines stretching over rolling hills. The castle was overrun with vintners, field hands, and armies of grape sorters and bottlers. There were hundreds of wine barrels in the cellar, and more in the servants' chambers below the house. Now that she thought about it, she'd seen wine barrels in just about every cool place they could be stacked. The whole castle was one big, rotting barrel, stinking of vinegar and fermentation. It smelled like defeat.

The horrid letter from the solicitor's had arrived that morning.

"This is the Merlin's doing, isn't it?" Isabelle said bitterly, feeling sick to her stomach. She felt like throwing up, she was so upset. "It has his foul hands all over it."

"It is Eleanor's proclamation," her cousin said evenly, reading the paper once again.

Isabelle laughed. "She is merely a puppet at that man's command."

Hugh Borel frowned at his cousin's loose tongue. He was called the Red Duke of Burgundy, not for the color of his hair (which was a nondescript brown) but for the rich, ruby tannins in the wine from their vineyards. Or so Isabelle guessed. She herself had many names for him. "Lech" was one. He was ten years her elder, a squirrelly, myopic man with thinning hair he combed over his forehead, and shifty, bulging eyes. "Even so, you will do as she has asked. You will release Leopold from his promise."

"You *would* like me to sign my future away, wouldn't you?" she said, with an upturned chin that she couldn't keep from trembling.

"Like I've said before, I only want you to be happy, Isabelle. But if you do not do what you are asked, you will face the wrath of all England and France and the power of her magician. I cannot protect you from that," he said with false concern.

You have never protected me from anything, Isabelle thought, balling her fists against the folds of her dress. Her elder cousin had a way of staring at her for too long, and he was always "accidentally" running into her room just as the maids were helping her undress. He gave her the shivers, and she had been counting the days until she would be free of him and this damp, stinky castle. She had a feeling he would change for the worse once her engagement was dissolved. Her betrothal to Leo meant her freedom from Hugh, among other things.

"Leo *loves* me," she whispered.

"His feelings aside, he will marry Marie-Victoria to bring glory to Prussia," Hugh said, almost smugly.

It hurt Isabelle to know he was right. Nothing mattered more to Leo than his country. He loved her, but he loved duty more, and the crown of the Franco-British empire was too tempting to refuse.

The defeat in Orleans had been five hundred years ago, and yet it felt to Isabelle as if she was reliving it at every moment— that she was *still* a victim of that long-ago failure. *She* was the rightful dauphine, not that sickly pretender who was to marry Leopold once she signed the papers allowing it. Her father, rest his soul, would have been Charles VIII of France; but House Valois had lost the throne to the British king, Henry VI, when the Merlin broke the spell cast by their sorceress and won the battle. Jeanne of Arkk had been burned by the English madmen, and her wyrd women disbanded and killed.

Isabelle's family had been banished to their ancestral holdings, and tacitly forbidden to appear at court. Even so, her father had a few loyal allies left, and at birth Isabelle had been betrothed to Prince Leopold of Prussia. It was an alliance uniting them against a common enemy. But who needed

Isabelle of Orleans if Marie-Victoria was being presented as a bride?

"I heard the princess is deformed—a freak—that no one ever sees her, that she is nothing but her mother's pawn," Isabelle said bitterly.

"She is sickly," Hugh said. "And her mother's daughter. But she is said to be gentle and soft-hearted."

Isabelle snorted. Leopold's victory at Lamac was no victory after all, if this was the sacrifice it entailed.

"You will sign the papers when we arrive in London for the season. We must be grateful, as Eleanor was kind enough to extend an invitation for the royal ball to us all, for the first time," said Hugh. "Look at this as your chance to secure a good match."

As if Hugh cared about matching her up with anyone, or about her future away from his influence. When he had arrived in Burgundy to become her guardian, he had made it clear that as highborn as she was, she was completely at the mercy of his kindness. He kept accounts of every piece of bread she ate, every dress or gown that was made for her, against a ledger that he would collect on when her inheritance was settled: when she turned eighteen, or married. Hugh knew she despised him, that she couldn't wait to get as far away from him as possible.

"Why do I need to find a husband?" she said. "Remember? Until yesterday I was to marry Leopold."

"But that is no longer the case," Hugh said smoothly. "Be grateful the queen did no worse."

"Bastard," she muttered.

"Excuse me?" He cocked an eyebrow.

"I am grateful for the invitation," she said, gritting her teeth and lowering her eyes to the floor.

"Good," he said, standing up and walking behind her seat. He put a heavy, sweaty hand on her shoulder.

Grateful.

She had to be grateful for everything the royal family— those British *usurpers*—had given her. Grateful that her family had been allowed to keep their countryside estates after the Battle of Orleans. Grateful that they had been granted their lives and retained their titles, which assured that the Valois line would forever be prostrate to the throne. Forever grateful for scraps; forever in debt; forever losers.

Grateful.

Now both of Hugh's hands were on her bare shoulders, and they were massaging her skin. He had never groped her so publicly before, and Isabelle couldn't help but think it was due to her looming status as a woman without protection. If she wasn't betrothed to Leopold, she was nobody; there would be no prince or royal family to answer to. No one would care what happened to her.

"Leave her alone," said the third person in the room, probably the only person in the world who did care what happened to her; he had remained silent until now. Isabelle glanced nervously at her other cousin, Louis-Philippe Beziers, who had grown up in the castle with her. His parents had been felled by the same wasting plague that had taken hers. Louis had finely chiseled features, dark hair and eyes, and would grow up to be strikingly handsome one day, but right now possessed a gangly, boyish awkwardness. Quiet and reflective, he was the only bright spot to her dark days. They clung to each other against a common enemy, but Louis had never dared speak up to Hugh until now.

"What did you say to me, Jug Ears?" Hugh asked, turning to Louis with a dangerous look on his face. Their entire childhood, Hugh had been dismissive of Louis—continually mocking his interests, calling him names, and making it clear that he was nothing more than a burden. When they were younger, Louis had hardly ever spoken a word.

"I said, leave her alone," Louis said, rising from his chair and standing a foot taller than his cousin.

But Hugh continued to massage Isabelle's creamy shoulders, and she shook her head at Louis to tell him to back down. She didn't want him to get hurt, and even if Louis was bigger than Hugh now, their wretched cousin was still their guardian, with the power to make life difficult for them.

"It's all right," Isabelle said weakly. "Louis—it's all right."

"See? It's all right," Hugh said with a smarmy smile. He gave her one last squeeze and left the room.

"What am I going to do?" she despaired.

"Don't worry, Leo will never give you up," Louis said. "He would be a fool to do so."

"If only that were true." She sighed, looking out the window apprehensively, as if the answer to her dilemma could be found in the serene, rolling hills. "But perhaps you are right," she said, thinking that it might be a good idea to see Leo face-to-face. Perhaps if he saw her, he would change his mind about this so-called peace treaty. Leo loved her. He would never willingly release her from their promise to each other. Once he laid eyes on her, he would change his mind. She would steam into London under the cover of the season, ostensibly to sign the papers destroying her future, but she would make certain to speak to him alone before that was necessary. That was all she needed—time alone with him.

When she could be alone with Leo, as they had been just a month ago, there would be no king or country to contend with, only the two of them; and when they were alone, she would make him remember why he fell in love with her in the first place.

Of course, she would have to be careful. If the Merlin or the queen knew what she was plotting, it would be treason; she had no desire to lose her head, she was quite fond of it. But if she were somehow able to make Leo think it was his own idea—his own love for her that was spurring him to honor their agreement—then the engagement with Marie-Victoria would be forgotten. She would be married to Leo as planned, safe from her lecherous relative. Besides, she had always been curious about the legendary Bal du Drap d'Or. Perhaps it was time to see it for herself.

"Hugh is right," she told Louis-Philippe, fanning herself with the queen's letter. "I am grateful for this invitation."

VANITIES

*I*f Aelwyn had any fears about the quality of her welcome, they evaporated the moment Marie walked into the room and caught sight of her. "Winnie!" her friend cried, crossing the length of the room in quick strides and enveloping her in a warm embrace. "Where have you been? Why has it taken you so long to come see me?"

Aelwyn had no answer to that. It had been a week since she had returned to the palace, and she had been meaning to call on her old friend, but had been overtaken by a sudden shyness. Her last memory of the princess was of her ash-and-tear-streaked face as her bedroom burned. Aelwyn had only meant to make a few sparklers for her and Marie to play with truly, but instead had set the entire east wing ablaze. It had been an epic disaster, a scandal. Her father had paid for it politically, as the queen had insisted that she could not rest unless Emrys sent his daughter away, which he had done without question.

In truth, Aelwyn was also ashamed of what she had done—put the princess in mortal danger—and she had doubted that Marie would even want to see her. What if her friend shared her mother's paranoia? When they had first been separated, they had written letters to each other: long, detailed missives about the injustice that had befallen them, along with their daily tribulations. Marie wrote about the tedium of court life, and Aelwyn regaled her with stories of the strange and fascinating creatures she encountered on the island. But as the years went by, the letters dwindled, until it was only through the crystal glass that Aelwyn was able to keep up with Marie, to sneak a peek into her life. In the past year, though, she'd barely ever bothered, although she had been worried when she heard the princess's health had deteriorated.

Her best friend was a stranger, and even the palace was unfamiliar. Was this really where she had spent her childhood—where she had played hide-and-seek in the secret passageways, stolen pies from the kitchen, and giggled over dolls? This was a stranger's castle, unfamiliar in every way—the ceilings felt lower, hallways narrower. Murals that had for centuries graced soaring barrel vaults were newly restored, but they were repainted in garish colors, hues too bright for the palace's drab interior. Doors replaced blind archways, halls supplanted galleries, leaving St. James neither old nor new, but somewhere in between. Back then, her compatriot had been a gangly, awkward girl in a helmet and a back brace; Marie was now the princess of the land. Aelwyn had always known Marie was special, but it had not stopped her from thinking they were equals when they were younger.

Although to be honest, she did not find her much changed. Marie-Victoria was taller and thinner, maybe, pale as usual, the sickness showing in her sallow color and sunken eyes, but she was as warm and welcoming as ever. "I am so glad you are back. Look," she said, placing a gold foil truffle in the palm of Aelwyn's hand. "Hazelnut, your favorite." In an instant, it was as if they were both twelve years old again, conspiring to nab extra cream puffs from the dessert buffets.

Aelwyn beamed at Marie. "Father said I was to see to your glimmer before the reception," she said. "Send your ladies away. I shall take care of you, Princess."

"Don't call me that! You're being so silly," Marie said, shooing her ladies out the door. "And you don't have to wait on me."

"Yes, I do. No arguments, now," Aelwyn said, leading Marie to the mirrored vanity and picking up a comb.

"Can you believe I'm to marry Leo? That little squirt you used to chase down the hallways? That is, if his people find me acceptable this morning," said Marie.

"Which they will, I guarantee it," Aelwyn said cheerfully, even as she noticed her friend's face fall in the mirror. She ran the comb gently through Marie's fine brown hair, untangling snarls and whispering a few words to give it some luster. She eased into the familiarity of the act, remembering the hours they had spent learning to braid each other's hair when they were younger. This was just like before, except, in a nagging corner of her mind, Aelwyn knew it wasn't. Even if Marie hadn't changed, everything else had, including Aelwyn Myrddyn herself. She was no longer the orphan girl of the kitchens, with a dirty face and tangled hair, but a full-grown sorceress in control of her magic. She was an enchanter trained in the ways of Avalon, able to command wind, water, air, and stone—and what was she doing?

Combing hair.

"Make her look pretty. She will be queen one day, and no one wants to be reminded their queen is ill," her father had ordered before dismissing her that morning. She received the message loud and clear: *You are a servant to the throne. While you might command the power of magic, the royal family has command over you. Your power is theirs.*

In Avalon, Viviane had explained the reasoning behind her brother's decision to bow down to the sovereign. "He did it for our protection. Emrys believes that unless we submit ourselves to their rule, they would hunt and kill us for the rest of our lives. There are too many of them and too few of us. Before the Order was established and the rules set in place, mages like us were tortured and killed. Magic is unpredictable, but try explaining that to a pining lover or the mother of a sick child."

"And what do you believe?" Aelwyn had asked.

Viviane had smiled ruefully. "I believe, my child, that servants or not, they will find a way to use—or kill—us anyway. My brother thinks he can manipulate time and history to remain among the mortals, but he will be proven wrong. Magic has no place in their world, as the glass has shown us time and time again." Aelwyn had seen the other time lines her aunt was speaking about. She had peeked into the crystal and had seen visions of strange, foreign worlds. In one, the very earth had frozen over in ice, its mages destroyed—literally rotting from their own magic.

Aelwyn ruminated on her aunt's words as she continued to comb the princess's hair, so dry and brittle, unlike her own lustrous locks. The difference between them was striking: Marie was frail and delicate, while Aelwyn was tall and voluptuous, her hair a rich, dark red that complemented her cat-like green eyes. She wore the garb of the Order she would soon join—an apprentice spellcaster's midnight blue tunic and long skirt. The uniform was meant to be deliberately drab, but even in such dull clothing her figure was stunning.

Since she had arrived at court the other week, the sight of her had caused pages to run into doors, and lords and knights to stammer and stare. Even the footman who'd carried her bags to her room the first day had hinted that if she ever desired company, he would be happy to provide it. She had turned them all down with a sweet but firm hand. If she *was* to take a lover—a privilege sorceresses were granted freely, as those of the invisible orders were bonded to the throne and forbidden to wed—she would choose a great man indeed, a man worthy and able to bear the weight of her love. Unlike her last choice. But now was not the time to think of that mistake.

"Mama told you to make me beautiful for the Prussian ambassador, didn't she? Perhaps if you fail, they will turn me down," Marie said suddenly.

"Shush, now," Aelwyn said, disliking Marie's defeatism in the face of such privilege. "You are to marry a handsome prince, and live happily ever after like a real fairy tale. You will dazzle them."

"I am not fishing for compliments. They will call me beautiful enough when they see me, I am sure. The Prussians want to end this war and seal this alliance as badly as my mother and your father do. I used to think I was the only one who thought Mama looked old, since everyone around me always talked about how young and beautiful she was, until I realized they were all lying—they were so afraid of her. For the longest time I thought I was out of my mind as well as my health, because no one ever told me the truth."

Aelwyn stared at her. "You see the queen as she really is?"

"What do you mean?"

"The courtiers talk about the queen being young and beautiful because to them she *is* young and beautiful. It is a glamour spell of some sort, but even I cannot see through it," Aelwyn said.

"Do you mean you do not see her as an old crone, as I do?"

"No, not at all."

"How strange," Marie said.

"Perhaps it is your gift." Aelwyn smiled. "That you can see things others don't." She placed a few pins in the princess's hair to hold it away from her face, thinking it would look more striking that way.

Marie nodded. "I am sorry we lost touch—Mother said I was not to bother you anymore. That you were to make your own decision about your future, without me hounding you. But I am so glad you chose to return to us, instead of staying in Avalon! Was it hard to leave Viviane? And you never told me—is Lanselin as handsome as they say?"

"I too am glad to be back, and my cousin is very handsome indeed," Aelwyn said lightly. They were cousins in name only, as Lans was the child Viviane had raised as her own, but he was not of her blood. He had taken to reminding her of that when they were together. "I heard your Leo has grown up to be very handsome as well."

"I suppose. Handsome is as handsome does." Marie shrugged.

"Why are you so against the idea of Leo? You never liked him, even when we were little," Aelwyn said, as she waved an amethyst stone over Marie's hair to create vermilion highlights. "Oh, I remember now—you always preferred the younger one. What was his name again?"

"Wolf," Marie said softly. "I didn't 'prefer' him. We were

friends. Or we used to be, before the Merlin declared war on his family. It was awful during the war; I was always worried he would be killed, although my mother assured me she would only take the royal family hostage, then put them to death if it came down to it. Apparently there's no need to start a precedent of spilling royal blood. Never mind that they were our friends and distant family, and we shouldn't murder them."

"That stands to reason," Aelwyn nodded. "Now, Leo can't be too different from his brother, can he?"

"Yes, he is," Marie said, annoyed. "Wolf is sweet and smart and kind, but everyone thinks he's a troublemaker, while everyone thinks Leo is perfect." She made a face in the mirror.

"Did it ever occur to you that maybe Leopold *is* perfect?" Aelwyn smiled, remembering the handsome young man who used to visit.

"Maybe *you* should marry him, then." Marie sighed. "I don't know, there's just something about him. He's always so proper and polite and, well, perfect." Perhaps she did hold it against him a little, because she'd had such a rough start in life.

Aelwyn considered that. "You're not just saying that because there's someone else, are you?" she asked.

This time Marie wouldn't meet her gaze. Aelwyn realized they weren't twelve years old anymore, passing notes to the young princes who came to court and laughing when one of them tried to kiss them during dancing lessons. Marie was sixteen now, a girl with desires and secrets of her own.

"Marie, who is he?" Aelwyn asked. It had been years, but in the space of a few minutes they had eased back into their familiar intimacy. "You can tell me."

"There's no one," Marie said flatly.

Aelwyn was relieved, until Marie spoke again all in a rush. "It doesn't matter. He's gone now. He was a soldier—a member of the Queen's Guard, actually. But he was sent to the northern front. I don't know when he'll be back, or even if he'll ever return. He just . . . disappeared . . . one day. They said he only went on leave, but I wrote to him, and I never got a letter back," she said, covering her face with her hands.

"Oh, Marie." Aelwyn finished with the highlights and put the stone back in her bag. "This isn't good."

"Like I said, it doesn't matter now. I don't know where he is. I don't even know if he's all right. I wish someone would tell me what's happened to him, but no one will."

Marie had always been so obedient, so agreeable, and Aelwyn felt a pang to see her so low. She loved Marie like a sister, even if she had always been just a tiny bit jealous and resentful of her position. The court fawned over her, and Marie always got the best of everything—the largest piece of cake, the best cut of meat at the table, the prettiest dresses, the most toys, the largest stack of gifts, the white pony at the stables—while Aelwyn always had to make do with hand-me-downs and scraps, never quite knowing her place, never quite having a real home. She was the bastard daughter of the

Merlin, and magicians were not allowed to have children. Her whole existence was a mistake, even if her father never said so. It was only now that she truly understood that Marie was as trapped in her life as she was; that she had little choice or freedom to shape her own destiny. That, like her, she was a prisoner of her fate. "You have to forget about him. You know that, right?"

In answer, Marie kept her face covered with her hands.

"You haven't seen Leo in years. I know you've never liked him much, but you need to give him a chance."

"I suppose you are right," Marie sighed. "You know, they call him the Hero of Lamac, because it was he who unleashed the Pandora's Box that won the battle."

Aelwyn held the comb in midair and shuddered. Viviane was uninterested in the mortal realm, but even in Avalon they had heard the gruesome news. The stones made by the witch Pandora could conjure the horrors of Gilgamesh, Tartarus, and Doomsday all at once. They were stones that held the power of the Dark, of the Terrible. They had the ability to unleash a million hungry mouths with blades for teeth—monstrous creatures, rotten and soulless. She pitied the soldiers that had been on the battlefield that day. No wonder the empire had agreed to a truce, to a wedding. Anything to erase the memory of that dreadful battle, and—it remained unsaid, but it was clear—anything to make sure it never happened again. "However did the Prussians get their hands on one?" she asked.

"No one knows." Marie shrugged.

"Because only a mage tutored in the dark arts could unleash the power of Pandora's curse," Aelywyn said. "And the most powerful enchanters of the world are in service to the queen, and work for the empire."

"Well, maybe he was lucky," Marie said. "That's what everyone says about Leo, you know—that he's blessed. The seers say there was a shower of shooting stars on the day he was born."

Aelwyn shrugged. "Don't they say that about every royal prince? Don't they say that about you?" She smiled as she sprinkled another dusting of powder on Marie's hair to make it shine, and rubbed a rosy pigment into her cheeks.

Marie peered at herself in the mirror. A naughty smile crept on her face. "Remember how we used to play twins?" she asked.

Aelwyn remembered but she shook her head, knowing what Marie would ask next. "No, it's not right."

"Please? It's so fun—please do it! Winnie! Please!"

Aelwyn pursed her mouth in disapproval but as Marie continued to insist, a reckless rebellion overcame her better sensibilities. Marie always could goad her into mischief. It had been the princess's idea, after all, to make the sparklers that had started the fire in her bedroom. "You must never tell anyone," Aelwyn warned.

"I never have. I promise," said Marie.

Taking a quick look around to make certain they were alone, Aelwyn blew a puff of smoke from her hand. It sent a shower of silver sparks dancing around them. "Did it work?" she asked, when it cleared.

Marie laughed in delight. "Look for yourself!"

Aelwyn stared at the beautiful princess in the mirror. Marie's face was vibrant, her cheeks pink, her eyes shining, her brown hair thick and glorious, everything about her blooming in the prime of health—with no sign of illness or the wasting plague. Then Marie put her own cheek next to hers. There were two of them in the mirror now. Two princesses, who looked exactly alike—except that one was just slightly more radiant than the other.

The illusion glamour. One of the most powerful spells known to Avalon, it had the power to make people see only what you wanted them to see. It had the ability to fool the world and blind it from the truth. Viviane had taught her to use her power sparingly, to keep it hidden from those who would use it against her. "Not even your father can know you can do this," her aunt had warned. "He is wary of the glamour mask. It would cause him to be wary of you."

But Aelwyn couldn't resist. And anyway, Marie already knew she could do it.

Her friend brought her back to the moment. "Winnie, there's something I've been meaning to say to you since you returned. When you left, I never got the chance to tell you how sorry I was about what happened, the day of the fire," Marie whispered. "It was all my fault."

"We were children," Aelwyn said stiffly.

"It's no excuse. They sent you away. I know how hard it must have been," Marie said. "I'm sorry, Winnie."

Aelwyn unclenched her fists; she hadn't noticed how tightly she was holding them until now. "I forgive you," she said, blinking back tears.

Marie nodded and wiped the corners of her eyes as well. "Look," she said hoarsely, pointing back to the mirror. "You're me," she said wistfully.

"If only," Aelwyn joked, then snapped her fingers and just like that, she was herself again.

·7·

Cottage
IN THE SKY

The Prussian ambassador was satisfied. He had been very complimentary of her looks, which Marie attributed to Aelwyn's handiwork rather than anything real. "Inspected and found satisfactory," she had joked to her ladies after the gruesome affair that had included a private visit with the Prussian royal physician. She had tried to protest, but her mother had silenced her with a stony frown as the nurses led her away.

During the examination Marie been made to stand this way and that, while the creepy doctor had peered down her throat, inside her ears, and in her unmentionables. Marie had sneaked a peek over her shoulder and caught the doctor scribbling "virgin, fertile," in her chart after the exam. Truly? How could they be so certain she was chaste? And who was to say she was fertile? Just another way to assuage any concerns over the upcoming alliance, she thought. Even so, she was nonetheless relieved to have passed the test. There had been many queens who had been unable to produce heirs to the throne, and had lost their lives and crowns in the process. Marie did not think she would be susceptible to such a fate, but she wasn't certain she was so keen to bear a child so soon, either. She was still a child herself; what would she do with one?

Now that the princess had been deemed acceptable by his advisors, Leo was on his way to the palace to meet his bride. There was still the matter of dissolving his prior engagement, but the ambassador assured them that Isabelle and her guardian would be in town shortly to sign the papers releasing him from his obligation. The prince himself would be in London in the next week or so, and the court was buzzing with excitement and pride, as well as relief that the long war with Prussia was finally over. Yet the more her ladies congratulated her and made a fuss, the more depressed Marie became. She could hardly force a smile during wardrobe fittings, and was absent-minded and distracted at every royal occasion.

As the days went by, preparations for the upcoming season began in earnest, with the traditional opening of Parliament by the queen and the city filling up as noble families from all over the empire arrived for the festivities. Marie was starting to be a bit of an embarrassment to the whole court. The princess, instead of acting like a girl on the cusp of a great romance— awaiting the appearance of her soon-to-be-beloved—was sulking around the palace, holed up in her room, eating sweets and not speaking to anyone.

One afternoon not long after the ambassador's visit, Marie remained in her room once more, rather than taking tea with a few court favorites. Her ladies did their best to encourage her, but she would not be persuaded to change her mind. "I need to be left alone, I feel ill," she insisted, thankful that she always had the wasting plague to fall back on when she didn't want to do something.

The ladies bowed and exited the room, but a few minutes later there was a knock on the door again. "I told you, I want to be left alone," she snapped, then immediately felt guilty for taking that tone with the servants.

"Sorry, Princess, I'll come back later," the voice called.

Gill?!

At the sound of his voice, Marie hustled out of her bed and opened the door in a breathless rush. "I didn't know it was you!" she cried, throwing her arms around the soldier who stood in her doorway.

Gill Cameron laughed, but looked around nervously to see if anyone had seen the princess's enthusiastic display of affection. Luckily, the hallway was empty for once, and Marie was without her usual entourage of ladies. "I just got back from leave. Thought I'd tell you I'm back on duty."

"I'm so glad! I didn't think I would ever see you again!" she said, pulling him into the room, even as her cheeks turned bright pink at her outburst.

"Truly?" he asked, a confused look on his face.

"I wrote you—to your family in Ayrshire—and when you didn't reply, I thought . . . it's so good to see you," she said.

Gill smiled and ruffled her hair. He was a strapping lad of eighteen, with a blunt nose, honey-colored hair, and a strong jaw. His features were more rough than fine, unlike the pretty-boy aristocrats who professed their admiration for her at court, but Marie's heart beat painfully in her chest at the sight of his shy smile.

"So what you're saying is, you can't live without me—is that right?" He grinned, taking the seat recently vacated by her attendant.

"Not at all," she said. "Were you gone? I didn't notice," she said airily.

"I didn't think about you at all either, not even once," he said, stretching his arms across the back of the couch.

"Liar," she said, sitting next to him so that she was curled up against his side. It was his cue to put his arm around her, which he did, and he squeezed her shoulder warmly. "You've heard, I'm sure?" she asked.

"That you are getting a husband? Yes! A fine one too. Leopold the Seventh! The Hero of Lamac!" Gill said affably. "Good on you, Marie."

"Please don't congratulate me," she said stubbornly. "I don't care about him, or the empire. Hang it all, they don't care about me except as a broodmare," she said darkly.

"I'll pretend I didn't hear that. Stop acting so foul, people are starting to talk. Even the stablehands have heard there's something the matter. Luckily, the scuttlebutt is that your ladies are just worried you've taken ill again. Have you?"

"Maybe." She felt a pain in her heart from his genial reaction to the news of her upcoming nuptials. What had she expected? A flare of jealousy? A declaration of affection? For him to whisk her away somewhere? No such luck. He was a practical fellow and knew his place. Gill was a friend, and that's all he would be to her, for his sake and hers. Anything more would have meant treason, or worse. It was wrong to yearn for the impossible, but Marie found she could not stop hoping. She took a deep breath and put a hand over his, her small fingers interlacing with his broad ones. "Shall I read to you?" she asked.

Gill nodded. "Please."

Marie flushed with pleasure and took out a book that had been their latest fancy. "Now, where were we before you left? Oh yes, here we are," she said, finding the page. She settled against the crook of his arm and began to read, her quiet, even voice filling the room.

Gill hadn't been schooled in his letters as well as she, and he delighted in the stories. She delighted in reading them to him, even if her tastes were not as gruesome as his. She often teased him that he only liked books with murder and bloodshed in their plots.

If she could write her own story, it would be a much simpler one than the life she led now. She was a small, plain girl, and yearned for a small, plain life. *If only I wasn't a princess—then I could go away with Gill. We would live in a cottage by the sea and be happy forever.* It was her not-so-secret desire, one she had held in her heart for many months now. One that she knew had absolutely no possibility of ever coming to fruition. It was a cottage in the air. A dream.

Gill pulled his hand away and stood up to face the window, stretching his legs. He yawned with his arms up to the ceiling, lifting the edge of his jacket and shirt, so that she couldn't help but notice the ugly scar on his lower back. It was a gift from the bullet that was meant for her during a failed coup d'état last year, when "progressive"-minded populist rebels styling themselves the League of Iron Knights had somehow been able to destroy the wards around the gates. They'd stormed the castle in an attempt to assassinate the royal family.

The Iron Knights believed magic was a tyrant's tool, and agitated to end the monarchy's control of its source; they believed magic should be for all, not just the rich and titled. Her mother's retribution had been swift and brutal, the traitors hanged or burned in the square. The Merlin's men were still out in the country, flushing out the remaining members. It was a reminder that the empire had as many enemies as allies; there were antagonists and opportunists in the shadows within and without, eager to see the fall of their house.

"Does it hurt?" she asked.

"What, this?" He lifted his shirt higher, revealing his hard stomach as he twisted his head down to look at his scar, and Marie felt her cheeks flush. "Nah, it looks worse than it is."

Marie still recalled the utter terror of that day: the rebels storming her room, and Gill with his pistol, shielding her with his own body. He would have died for her, and almost had. She put the book away. "I don't want to marry Leopold," she said quietly.

"But you don't even know him," Gill said gently, tucking his shirt back into his trousers and buttoning his jacket. "You could learn to love him." He returned to his seat next to her and smoothed her hair away from her forehead, as one would a child.

She shook her head. Tears sprang to her eyes, but she blinked them away. She was being ridiculous, she knew. There was nothing to be done; she was born into her position. She could not change who she was, and she could not change who Gill was, either. She would marry Leopold at the end of the season as her mother decreed, and that would be the end of it.

"I should go—they'll wonder why I'm not at my post," Gill said, getting up and holstering his sword and gun.

"Wait—" Marie said, feeling bereft already, even though he was still in the room. "Gill, promise me—"

"Yes?"

"Promise me, whatever happens, that we'll always be friends."

Gill looked down at her, and his eyes were soft and sad. "I'll always be your friend, Princess," he said. "No matter what happens. I'll be right outside the door, as I always am." Then he closed it quietly behind him.

the PRINCESS AND THE PAUPER

s the carriage approached the port, Ronan felt very smart indeed, traveling abroad for the first time—and without her parents! Even though she did have her chaperone Vera with her, who was nervous about making it on time. Ronan thought it was so silly—they had ample time to spare. They had set off from Washington Square right after breakfast, and the ship was not set to sail until noon. They would have hours to unpack and settle into the grand staterooms for the month-long voyage, and Ronan was looking forward to the thrilling adventure of it all. She had spent summers in Newport, but she had never been outside of the Americas. She tilted her hat over one eye, thinking it looked more fashionable that way. Her mother had allowed her a few new things for the journey, including a hat Ronan had helped design: a massive confection of lace and silk with a curved ostrich plume.

Vera leaned over to rub her cheek. "Street dirt," she explained. "I told you to leave the windows closed."

But Ronan had been too excited to keep her face behind the dark curtains. She wanted to soak everything in, to breathe the sea air, to revel in her newfound freedom. They arrived at the port, which was busier and smellier than she had expected, and she held a tidy handkerchief to her nose and a parasol over her head as they made their way to the ticket office. It was almost April, the first hint of spring was in the air, and Ronan felt as if she were bursting at her velvet seams—she couldn't contain her excitement. After months of penury, this trip was a godsend. She was on her way to make her fortune and her name—to make a life for herself in the world. She could forget, for a moment, the seriousness of her mission, and the parents who had invested everything they had in her success.

But the moment was short-lived; Vera returned from the ticket office looking more anxious than ever. Apparently there was a problem with their rooms. Her father had booked them first-class staterooms, but her governess told her that the ship's officer insisted they were listed for two second-class fares instead.

Ronan was aghast. "We cannot possibly travel in such cramped accommodations. Our luggage alone will take up the entire room. Let me talk to him. Perhaps it is just a mix-up and easily remedied." Her heart pounded in her chest, even as her spirits sank, because a part of her knew there was no mistake. Her father had most likely booked the more expensive passage a year earlier, but as financial troubles accumulated, quietly exchanged the tickets without telling her mother. Ronan thought she might still be able to talk her way into her proper berth; she had seen her mother do the same at restaurants and shops when their credit was called into question. She pushed her way to the front and, in the haughtiest voice she could muster, asked the ship's officer to check again.

The man consulted the list once more with a weary air. The port was busy, with travelers bidding friends and family farewell, great ladies and their servants disembarking from shiny carriages, and tradesmen waving their paper tickets and disappearing into steerage. "Sorry, miss," the officer sighed. "Right here. Astor. Second class."

"See, I told you," Vera chided. Her governess looked almost smug, and Ronan felt an instant of hatred for the older lady, who depended on her family for her well-being. After all, her father had continued to pay Vera's salary, regardless of their financial insolvency.

An impatient crowd had gathered behind them as they held up the line. Even if the air was cool, the sun was hot, and she could feel the sweat forming a thin layer between her skin and her clothing. She had felt every inch a grand lady that morning in her fine coat and new hat, along with her mother's most elegant parasol, but her confidence was shrinking, along with her chances of first-class accommodations. Even Vera had abandoned her, returning to stand by the impatient porter and their embarrassingly large collection of steamer trunks.

Ronan wanted to curse, scream, and cry at the humiliation, but she could not allow herself to make a scene. Second-class cabins! She would die of seasickness! She would rather stay at home. What if someone saw . . . ? But what did it matter where she stayed on the stupid boat, as long as she arrived in London in time for the party? She would sleep on her trunks, if necessary.

"Miss?" the officer asked again, irritated now.

She was about to snatch the tickets from the officer's hand when she caught sight of Whitney Van Owen and her mother walking sedately along the docks toward the gang-plank. The Van Owens were one of the wealthiest families in the Americas, but their *riche* was so *nouveau* that their social ascent was still a bit of a shock to established hostesses like Ronan's mother. It was well known that Colonel Van Owen's father was nothing more than an indentured servant. Their money was tainted, not quite perfectly respectable, in that it was not inherited but earned—hand over fist, blood over dollars, until it had accumulated and multiplied to ridiculous proportions.

"Why, it's Ronan!" Whitney trilled. "Off to London for the season as well, of course!"

"Of course," Ronan smiled, pressing her hot cheek next to Whitney's fair one.

Whitney looked every inch an heiress, cutting a striking figure in a lavish, fur-trimmed coat with ornately jeweled buttons that caught and spun the light into a thousand rainbows. Her elaborate hat was three times larger than Ronan's, with a full crown of ostrich feathers and a dazzling lace overlay. Ronan felt drab as a sparrow next to her, and swallowed a pang of jealousy at the shimmering moonstones nestled in the brooch on her friend's throat.

"Mage-made," Whitney said, showing them off with a wave of her hand. "Pretty, aren't they? You should see my dress for the royal ball! It practically glows in the dark!"

"Gorgeous," Ronan agreed, feeling even more deprived than before.

"Well—see you inside. Shall we meet for breakfast? I heard the chef is amazing. Ta!"

Ronan hadn't the heart to tell her she would be dining in the common area, and not the lavish dining room. The ship was the size of an island; perhaps when they arrived in London, she could say she'd caught the flu and couldn't leave her room during the entire journey.

"Miss? You want these tickets or not?" the officer asked, rapping on the glass to catch her attention.

"Yes—I mean—no—I mean . . ." Ronan shook her head, rattled, trying to figure out her options. She could go back home and yell at her parents, or get herself to England as planned. There was no time to waste; the sooner she arrived in London and accepted a proposal, the sooner she could pay off the debts against the house and estate. Vera had hinted more than once that her own impoverished status was due to a family fortune brought low—that she, too, had been raised in splendor, only to find herself in ashes.

No. No. No. She would find a match, and a title, and the magic to go with it. She had to, she had to, she had to. . . . She wrung her gloves in her hands until they were soiled. Another expense she could not afford. She wiped her palms on her skirts and tried to compose herself.

"Is something the matter?" asked a young man behind her, who must have heard every word. He regarded her with an amused smile, as if he found her situation to be very entertaining.

She turned to him and did not smile back, as he looked a bit . . . battered. He had a black eye and a bruised cheek, dark messy hair, a strong chin; he could be handsome, although it was hard to tell underneath the battle wounds.

"Miss?" the ticket officer asked again.

Vera bustled over. "The porter wants his tip. What shall I tell him?"

"Just please—please—give me a moment," she pleaded with everyone. "Let me think." Whitney and her mother were on the gangplank. If she took the second-class tickets now, they would know how far she had sunk. Perhaps they would spread the word in London; everyone would know the truth about the Astor situation, and Ronan would not be invited to the best parties, which would dash all her hopes even before she had set sail. But she could not stall any longer. It was second class or stay in New York. "Fine, give them to me." She took the tickets, stuck them in her purse, and walked toward the dock.

"All right, miss?" She looked up to see that the roguish young man with the swollen eye had followed her. "You look as if you need some help," he said.

What business was it of his? "I'm quite all right, thank you," she said coldly. She did not speak to strange young men who loitered around docks. He looked almost terrifying with those bruises on his face. She looked around for Vera. What use was a chaperone if they did not *chaperone*?

"You don't have to run away," he said. "I don't bite. Unless I want to."

Her blush deepened. He truly was a sight to look at, but even with the broken nose and face, there was something compelling about him—his dark hair, piercing blue eyes, that dangerously crooked smile.

"I'm afraid no one can help me."

"No one?" he asked. He had an accent she could not place. He raised an eyebrow quizzically.

"No," she said firmly. "I'm sorry, I don't mean to be rude."

"Then don't be," he said reasonably.

She laughed, she couldn't help it. He looked funny, all beat-up like that. What did it matter who she spoke to now? She saw Whitney giving her an odd look, and Ronan waved her handkerchief gaily, as if she spoke to uncouth young men at the docks all the time. "What happened to your face?" she asked.

"It fell on a fist." He shrugged.

"That happens a lot?"

"Enough."

"You say that as if you enjoy it," she said tartly.

"Perceptive *and* beautiful," he said. "I like that." His blue eyes sparkled and there was merriment there, and possibility. What cheek to speak to her so frankly! She was hot all over, but for a different reason now. Ronan had never met a boy quite like him before. All her suitors had been of the starchy variety, and after the parade of uglies she'd had to memorize, his handsome (if bruised) face was very appealing. He was not good-looking so much as striking: the sort of man you could lean on, could count on, who could do hard work and not be afraid of it. She thought of the aristocrats with their wobbly chins and soft hands, and wondered what it would feel like to be pressed against his body.

"What else do you like?" she asked, feeling incredibly daring all of a sudden. It was not the kind of question a lady of gentle birth would ask.

His eyes lit up at her challenge and he moved closer to her. Startled, she dropped her parasol. He picked it up and handed it back just as Vera finally appeared, bustling toward them like a ship with a full head of steam. She gave the boy a sharp look. "Do excuse us." She took Ronan's arm and led her away, as the young man returned to his party by the ticket window. "My dear, you know it isn't proper to talk to strange young men," she reprimanded with a scandalized air.

"What does it matter? Where we're staying, I'm sure there will be a lot more of them," Ronan said crossly. "Let's go." She motioned to the porter, and together they walked up to the entrance of the ship.

The ship's conductor glanced at her tickets and told the porter, "The first-class parlor suite."

She blinked. "Excuse me?"

But the conductor had already moved on to the next group and when he handed her back her tickets, she noticed they were indeed for first-class berths. She stared at them in disbelief. How had that happened? She was certain she had been holding second-class tickets—why was she being led to the first-class suite? Ronan was about to correct the mistake, but decided it was best not to look a gift horse in the mouth. Better to accept it as her due all along, and pretend as if nothing had been the matter.

As they made their way up the gangplank, Ronan saw the young man with whom she had been conversing. He was walking onto a lower deck with an older gentleman.

"Second class," Vera hissed. Making it sound like not just a statement about his ticket, but a verdict on his character.

"Vera, a moment ago *we* were second class," she said, still wondering about her sudden change of fortune. Could it be at all possible that the handsome young stranger had something to do with her new tickets somehow? Was he a thief? Or a lord in disguise? She shook the thoughts from her head—he was obviously neither. Just a handsome, but nosy, pest. Ronan chastised herself for having an overactive imagination. Perhaps the mistake was that she had not been given her correct tickets in the first place, because anyone could see she *clearly* belonged in first class.

On the lower deck, Oswald was admonishing his ward. If he could have hit him with the newspaper he was holding, like a master reprimanding a puppy, he would have. "Wolfgang, what have you done with our tickets? Why are we booked in a lower-class cabin? I can't help but think this must be your doing," he rumbled, his tone dark. "You do realize the beds are stacked on top of each other—they are called 'bunks'— and we have to share a privy with a dozen men? And that there is only one bathtub for the whole lot?"

The prince's smile was glorious. He liked the spirited American girl, and had decided to save her from embarrassment on a whim. "I met a damsel in distress, Oz. She needed the rooms more than we did. Come on, you always said I should be open to new experiences."

·9·

the
ONCE AND FUTURE QUEEN

*L*eopold of Prussia was a fine royal specimen. He looked kingly already as he entered the formal state room in his dress uniform of grays and reds, an array of gold medals pinned to his chest, so tall and proud; a lone scratch on his cheek was his only souvenir from the battle he had won so handily. He looked at ease and exuded confidence—a natural aristocrat, with his brilliant golden hair and generous smile. There was a gasp from the gathered ladies of court—one could practically hear them swooning—and the men were just as embarrassing, subtly edging each other out of the way to be closer to him.

"My princess, it is lovely to see you again." His voice was like honey, full of sweetness and affection, and his smile was kindness personified. Even his hand was warm and comforting as it held hers. Only his lips were dry as they brushed the back of her hand, and Marie was relieved because it meant he was not as perfect as he looked. Maybe Aelwyn was right—she should give him a chance. She shouldn't hold his perfection against him. Some people were as bright as the sun; if the majority of her own days were gray, it was not his fault.

"My prince," she said demurely as she took back her hand. "Welcome back to London." They were standing in front of the full audience of the entire court, from the lowliest page to the haughtiest ladies-in-waiting, innumerable cabinet ministers, the ageless Merlin, and the ancient queen. This was the formal reception of the future king of the empire, and certain rituals must be observed. The grand hall had been given a dazzling shine, from the marble colonnades to the granite floor to the array of crystal chandeliers that marched down the length of the room.

They bowed to each other and, with a signal from Eleanor, Marie took his arm so that she might introduce him to their loyal and noble subjects. Their courtship would be a choreographed performance, from initial meeting to the royal wedding. She saw Eleanor beaming at the two of them, and the queen smiled at Leo in approval before taking his father's arm herself and introducing the Prussian monarch to her lords and ladies.

When they had greeted every member of the court as well as the Prussian delegation, Marie led Leo to the end of the gallery to show him the famous view of the gardens. "Do you remember? You used to run in those mazes," she said, pointing to the topiary.

"I remember a certain little girl chasing me." He smiled.

"Oh, that wasn't me you remember. I had crutches then."

Leo's forehead wrinkled. It was obvious he didn't remember her at all, which was just as well. "My mother tells me you were very brave at the battle," she said. "That you held the Box yourself and loosed it upon the field. You could have been killed! Our Merlin says the Pandora is the world's deadliest and most dangerous weapon, one that only the most talented sorcerer can wield."

"Is that so?" the prince asked politely. "I don't mean to contradict your Merlin, but it just happened that I was closest to it, and any of my men would have done the same."

He was being a little too modest, as a lesser man would have surely been killed by the horrors from the Pandora's Box. She smiled at him serenely. "I know that cannot be true. Not every soldier keeps his head in battle; most are just trying to stay alive. And very few can stand up to such powerful magic."

"You have an interest in the field of war? That is uncommon in a princess," said Leo, walking around the room with his long, loping stride.

"Do you think it strange?" she asked, struggling to keep up with her much shorter legs.

"No. Not at all. I find it charming."

"I don't mean it to be charming. I am simply interested, that is all," she said, a little unsteadied by the edge in his voice.

"I mean—I am just being myself. I am not trying to pretend to be what I am not." She halted their walk and looked him in the eye.

He raised his eyebrow. "I see."

They resumed their stroll in painful, awkward silence. Marie wondered at her outburst. She had only meant that she was not flirting with him, that she was sincerely interested in the art of magical warfare. Her realm and reign were protected by a great and powerful magic, so it seemed only reasonable to try and understand its workings. She glanced at his handsome profile, remembering the arrogant young boy who had paid her no attention in years past. If he remembered their childhood antagonism, he made no sign of it. He was playing the part of besotted lover; his eyes were pure adoration. Across the room she saw Gill, his back to the wall, his eyes blank, his posture straight: a true soldier of the Queen's Guard. Then he caught her eye and winked. She hid a smile behind her fan that, unfortunately for her, Leo did not fail to notice.

"Is that your guard?" he asked.

"Gill? Yes," she responded innocently. "He's a great friend of mine; he saved my life once."

"Then I owe him my gratitude," he said warmly. "For keeping my princess safe."

"How is your brother?" she asked. Her feet ached from walking the length of the ballroom in her new satin slippers, but she knew she must keep up her end of the conversation for courtesy's sake.

"He is well, thank you," he said. "Father sent him to the Americas, and he is on his way back now. I shall tell him you asked about him."

"Please do," she said. "I look forward to seeing him again. Does he still box for fun?"

"Unfortunately, yes. Wolf should really be kept on a short leash. There are rumors that he fights for money. He could get himself in a lot of mischief," Leo said with a forced smile, his jaw clenched tightly. His cheekbones looked so sharp they could hurt someone.

Marie remained silent, unwilling to bash her old friend. "Your English has improved."

"Mon français, c'est encore mieux," he said. *My French is even better.* *"Et vous, mademoiselle,* which language do you prefer?"

"Mama prefers that I speak French in private, but English at court. There is a saying we have in the empire: practical matters *en anglais,* and dreams *en français.*"

"A very wise saying," Leo smiled. His demeanor relaxed. "I will love you, my English rose, and you will fill my French dreams."

Marie burst out laughing, and Leo looked troubled. "Did I say something incorrect?" he asked.

"No it's just—you don't have to be so   " Marie could not stop laughing. She noticed a few courtiers looking alarmed at the sight of the princess caught in a fit of hysterical laughter. Marie knew she looked terrible when she laughed; her face went bright red, her nose especially, and more than once she had overheard her mother tell her ladies that she wished Marie would not laugh quite so loudly and so vigorously. It wasn't ladylike. It wasn't queenly. Marie took a deep, shuddering breath to control herself. "I am sorry, Leo," she said. "But let us not make this what it isn't. You must marry me for my kingdom, and I must marry you for my mother. That is the way of our life, and I am sorry to have embarrassed you."

Leo's smile faded a little, and for a moment Marie worried that she had truly hurt his feelings. "My apologies that you find my emotions . . . amusing," he said. "I hope that one day you will believe in the sincerity of my affections. Excuse me, my lady, I find I am quite worn from the travel after all."

"Yes, please—don't stay on my account. See to your apartments. We have chosen the south wing; it has the best view of Big Ben and Parliament. Your servants have already been housed downstairs. I do hope you enjoy your stay with us."

"I imagine I will. Good day, Princess." He gave her a curt nod.

She curtsied and watched him leave the room abruptly, followed by his entourage, who hurried to keep up with his long strides.

Aelwyn, who had been standing with the members of the sisterhood, walked up to her. "What happened? What was that about? Why did he leave?"

Marie rolled her eyes. Leo was only playing a role, nothing more. He had never shown much interest in her when they were young, and he was only pretending to now for the sake of the treaty. Her sense of despair deepened at the thought of spending the rest of her life with such a man. Even friendship seemed out of reach. They would slowly grow to hate one another, she could tell—if they didn't already.

"What did you say to him?" her friend asked, concerned.

"Only the truth," Marie sighed. "And he didn't like hearing it."

・ *10* ・

the
INVISIBLE GIRL

*H*elwyn did not think Marie had made a good decision in ruffling the future king's feathers by making sport of his soft words. She could guess at their conversation from the looks on their faces. He was only trying to do his duty, and should not have been mocked for it. Marie should take care. The young Prussian did not look as if he would take kindly to an impudent queen. A wife's job was to placate her husband and learn to hold her tongue. It was the beginning of the twentieth century, but a girl could still lose her head—*literally*—for saying the wrong thing. The keys to the empire came through Marie-Victoria's hand, but according to the points of the treaty, Leopold would be an equal sovereign once they were married. Unlike Marie's father, Prince Francis, who had been born into the Danish and Greek royal families and whose title had been Prince Consort, Leo would be king, and kings had been getting rid of their pesky wives for ages.

Queen Eleanor dismissed her court, ostensibly to give King Frederick a tour of the grounds, but also in order to distract them from Leo's hasty exit. The court began to file out of the room according to rank, and the mages standing in the back of the room were dismissed last. The brotherhood of Merlin, solemn-faced men in dark suits, exited ahead of the lady magicians in white habits from the sisterhood of Morgaine.

"Thank goodness that's done," said Sister Mallory, a moon-faced enchantress whose specialty was speaking to animals. "He's handsome and says all the right things, but if you ask me, the princess is better off alone. I don't trust the Prussians. Where could they have found that horrid weapon and learned the ability to use it?"

Sister White, who could conjure weather patterns, nodded. "Yes, if it hadn't been for that, our boys would have won that battle, but there you go."

"Can't imagine the Merlin would bow down so quickly," said Sister Mallory.

"Perhaps he was as tired of war as we were," another sister opined.

"Weapons of dark magic were supposed to have been destroyed after the Treaty of Orleans," Sister White grumbled.

"So it was smart of the Prussians to use one, then, as it gave them the advantage," Aelwyn said.

"Advantage? Cheating is more like it!" Sister White argued.

"Sometimes the only way to win is to cheat," Aelwyn said stubbornly.

The sisters turned to see what the Sister Superior would do, but Sister Mallory only sighed. "You are young still, Sister Myrddyn, but one day you will learn that a false victory is a hollow one."

Aelwyn nodded, thankful that her own loose tongue had not gotten her in trouble. The sisters disappeared down the hallway, and she dawdled behind, uneager to return to the charter house so soon. After her years in Avalon, life as a member of the invisible orders was boring. The sisters lived in a small convent in a remote wing of the palace, next to the home of the brotherhood. Every morning began the same way, with a quiet knock on the door at the first light of dawn. Bonded sister and acolyte alike rose to perform the daily tasks. They were not allowed to waste their magic to sweep the corridors, dust the stairs, or make the preparations for breakfast. Magic was a special gift; it had to be rationed for only the most important tasks, like warfare and security. Aelwyn's morning chore was to wipe down the windows with a rag. Once the glass was sparkling, she was allowed to return to her drab little cell to change into her blue tunic and wash her face in the tiny washbasin.

At breakfast, the sisters would gather at long wooden tables, eating porridge and talking in low voices. She usually joined a group of new acolytes at a table near the window. They knew she was the Merlin's daughter and were kind to her, but they avoided asking her about Avalon, or her time with Viviane. Aelwyn understood what her father had warned her about from the beginning: the sisterhood did not trust her. She would have to prove herself to them to gain acceptance into the Order. After the meal, the group convened to the chapel for silent spell-casting. While the Merlin's men spent their time on strategizing military campaigns and border expansion, the sisterhood was responsible for the health and safety of the empire. The wasting plague was one of their more bitter failures, as none of their healers could concoct a real cure. Shields, wards, and anti-destruction spells were strengthened, renewed, and refurbished on a rotating basis, especially after the failed insurrection only a few months ago that had threatened the queen and her daughter.

Sitting quietly, surrounded by dutiful mages who had given themselves over to magic and servitude, Aelwyn's thoughts flitted back to Avalon. She could chant the shield spell in her sleep. She was so incredibly disinterested in the humdrum nature of the Order's magic. It was strictly by the book, whereas in Avalon magic was wild and mercurial, but extremely powerful. Well—there was no use thinking of Avalon now, was there?

Perhaps Viviane was right.

Perhaps she had made a mistake in choosing to join the invisible orders.

But if she did not take her vows and exchange her blue robes for the white habits, she would be a rogue enchantress, a woman without protection, practically a harlot, and even magic could not protect her from the people's wrath if something went wrong. There were hedge witches and random warlocks in every town and village, scrounging a living from the edges, their magic separated from the true source of power, weak and ineffective.

Viviane had made it clear when Aelwyn left that Avalon would always be open to her—but if she returned, she would have to stay for good this time. Why had she chosen London over the island? Because when she was younger, she had worshipped the white-clad sisters, so beautiful and mysterious? Aelwyn had looked forward to the day she would "don the white and serve the light." Magic was a gift, a calling, a home; especially since her father had asked her to return to the palace in the letter he had sent on the eve of her sixteenth birthday. That letter had sent her running back to the city. She had hidden the letter from her aunt, as Viviane would not have understood. She'd only have accused her of sentiment.

Aelwyn was so deep in her own thoughts that she did not notice the prince in the shadows of the corridor speaking to one of the younger, prettier ladies of the court. The girl was practically throwing herself at him, fluttering her lashes and shoving her cleavage in his face. He seemed to be reeling her in, little by little. She tipped forward, as if to receive a kiss, but he merely brushed her off with a lazy smile.

The girl handed him a slip of paper—no doubt with the location of her apartments in the castle—and sashayed away, promising something delicious and naughty with every sway of her step. But when her back was turned, Leo tossed the piece of paper to the ground. When he looked up, his eyes met Aelwyn's.

She felt a hot spark between them, an electric energy that sent a tingle to the very center of her. He hadn't much changed from the handsome, confident young boy he used to be, the one she had secretly mooned over in her diary. Even then, he had the ability to make you feel as if you were the only person in the room, the only person who mattered. "She'll be sorely disappointed you won't be looking for her tonight," Aelwyn said, motioning to the torn piece of paper.

"I'm glad you think so," he said, a small smile dawning on his face as he appraised her boldly, his stare raking her up and down. She felt as if she were standing naked in his presence.

But Aelwyn returned his stare with one of her own. Her green eyes held his gaze. "You should be more careful. This court is lousy with gossip, if you haven't noticed."

"All courts are. That is the nature of court. Let them talk; words are nothing but air," he said dismissively.

"What are you doing out here, anyway? Are you lost, my lord? The tour of the grounds is that way."

He smirked, still drinking in every inch of her with his soulful gaze. "'Lost' is not quite the word I would choose, my lady."

"I am no lady," she said with an arch smile.

"For my sake, I hope not," he replied. "You look familiar." He studied her face so intently that she blushed. "We have met before, have we not?"

"I grew up in the castle," she allowed.

"*You* were the little girl who used to chase me all over this place," he said. "As I recall, you caught me quite a few times."

"Did I now? You must have been a slow runner."

"Perhaps I wanted to be caught—that was the game, after all, wasn't it? Catch and kiss?" he said.

"Was it?" she asked coolly.

"Ah, the games children play," he said, his smile broadening.

"Except we are no longer children, my lord," she said, shaking her head.

"No," he agreed. "Indeed, we are not. You are a sorceress now. I remember; you are the Merlin's daughter. Aelwyn." Her name on his tongue gave her another secret thrill. He remembered her. Did he remember any more from their past? *Catch and kiss.* They had chased each other down these same hallways. It all came back to her suddenly. Fourteen-year-old Leopold, young and breathless, with his lips on hers. They had kissed right in this hallway. From the smile on his face, it looked as if he did remember.

"And you are soon to be our king."

"Not just yet," he said with a wave of his hand, as if to sweep it away.

"Yes, I suppose you are right. You are not yet crowned, and I am still an acolyte."

He put a hand on his cheek. "A sorcerer's apprentice; a wyrd woman," he teased, as if finding it all so incredibly amusing. "My brother told me there are secret passageways all over St. James, leading from the roof to the dungeons. Funny that I never knew of them during the time I was here, and I have always been curious about the history of this castle. Would you care to discover them with me?"

Would she care to? She could see it now: taking him around, showing him the hidden passageways she knew so well. She and Marie had discovered them as children and the princess must have shared them with Wolf while Aelwyn was entertaining his older brother. Aelwyn imagined she and Leo reconnecting again, reminiscing about their shared childhood, laughing at his witticisms; perhaps even making plans to meet again; perhaps even renewing that little game they had liked to play, catch and kiss.

Leopold of Prussia. So young and handsome, a boy who had everything and everyone he'd ever wanted delivered to him on a plate. When had he ever waited for anything? Even the empire had succumbed to his charms. The queen did not want to risk losing another battle, was tired of losing soldiers and public support, and so had offered up her daughter as a bride—the richest gift yet.

If she went with him now, Aelwyn knew that before long, she would be just another conquest; another notch on the royal bedpost. One more name written on a scrap of paper, crumpled and discarded. Not to mention, he was supposed to be the intended bridegroom of her best friend—although Marie had made it abundantly clear she had absolutely no interest in marrying him, and possibly even despised him.

"Well?" he asked. "Shall we, then?"

Before she could answer, there was the sound of another girl calling his name. "Leo, darling?" There was a distinct French lilt to the voice, and Aelwyn remembered that the French girl, the *faux-phine*, the would-be princess, was supposed to arrive today. Leo's engagement to Marie-Victoria could not be announced until his former alliance was dissolved.

"Someone's calling you," Aelwyn murmured. "The south wing is that way, my lord, and the hidden passageways are easy to access. Perhaps Princess Marie can show you sometime. She knows them as well as I."

"Ah." Leo nodded. The electric charge between them faded.

"Good-bye, my lord. I'm sorry I cannot help you." The rules of the land said the mages were to remain invisible; that their power was reflected through their sovereign's rule.

The bonded sisters served in silence.

But at that moment, as Leo walked away from her, Aelwyn wanted nothing more than to live out loud.

the
ONE THAT GOT AWAY

*L*eo! I was calling for you—I was waiting for you in the east parlor. They said you were to meet me there." Isabelle pouted. She knew she looked pretty when she pouted, and so she pouted often. That he had ignored her call was just the latest annoyance in a long string of annoyances that afternoon. It had taken longer than she had anticipated to travel to London; it was a journey hampered by broken carriage wheels, dubious fare and boarding at a slew of roadside inns, and the knowledge that once she arrived at her destination she would have to relinquish her dreams of love and hope.

She was settled for the season in an apartment at a grand house in Mayfair, and while it was one of the most fashionable addresses, she had found the staff wanting. Isabelle had spent the morning haranguing her maid about her hair—she was certain the girl was conspiring against her by turning her fringe into a row of stiff ringlets more appropriate for a poodle. Isabelle had yanked the curling iron from the hapless servant's hand and taken care of it herself, cursing her family's lack of beauty mages. She wanted to look as dazzling as possible for their meeting.

But Leo seemed distracted when she saw him. He didn't seem to notice her Cupid's bow of a mouth, painted exquisitely so that it was as red as a ripe berry, or the beauty mark she had filled in on her left cheek. Her hair was an architectural creation, a riot of soft dark curls, and her maid had been useful at last—cinching her corset as tightly as possible, giving her that elusive fifteen-inch waist. She couldn't breathe and was terribly uncomfortable, but no matter. She had chosen to wear her dress in the French style, with the exaggerated low neckline and powdered bosom thought too daring for the British sensibilities. Isabelle was set on looking as exotic, foreign, and French as she could—to remind these peasants and usurpers that *she* was the rightful Queen of France. The Lily Throne belonged to her, Isabelle of Valois, Isabelle of Orleans—she still carried the titles bestowed on the French royal family— the French heir to the throne, not this ugly, ancient crone or her horse-faced daughter.

She cleared her throat, and Leo turned to her as if noticing her for the first time. "Ah! Lady Orleans," he said. "How are you?" His tone was vague, though, and he looked as if his mind were still stationed elsewhere.

"Terrible," she said with a dramatic whisper. "But you should know that!" With his usual awful timing, her cousin rounded the corner. Hugh looked irritated, and she knew he was impatient to get on with the program. Isabelle had purposefully wandered away from him when they had arrived at the palace earlier, so that she could meet Leo and convince him no empire was worth the loss of her love forever. After he failed to show up, she had decided to look for him.

"My lord." Hugh nodded his greeting to Leo.

"Burgundy." Leo nodded as they shook hands vigorously.

"I will give Isabelle her moment, as you cannot fail to observe she has dressed for it," he said, with his usual leer. "Isabelle, they are waiting for us in the second drawing room. I think you know the way."

They were silent after Hugh left. Isabelle reached out with her hand and touched his cheek where the wound was still healing. "Does it hurt?" she asked sorrowfully.

He shook his head no.

"I wish you *were* hurt. If you had not won the battle, then we would not be here today," she whispered.

Her words shook him out of his daze and his eyes focused on her, as if seeing her for the first time. "Today? What is today? Oh, that's right—my dear Isabelle, of course—you are here to sign the papers."

"Oh, Leo," she cried. "I can't let you go!"

"My little French nightingale, this is not good-bye. Far from it. You will be with me always," he said. "After today, we will never be separated from each other again."

"Truly?" she asked with a rapturous look on her face. It was exactly what she wanted to hear.

"Do you doubt me?" he asked.

"Of course not, my darling. I will not sign the papers this afternoon. I will not release you," she said, feeling brave and determined.

"No, my dear," he said, the smile fading from his face. "You *must* sign them. Sign whatever Eleanor demands. Our future depends on it."

"Our future?" she asked, her eyes bright.

"Yes, our future," he said. "You must sign the papers so that the treaty is not called into question."

"But—!" she tried to protest.

"Meet me tonight," he whispered, his breath on her skin making her shiver in delight. "I am in the south wing, the third room to the right under the portrait of Henry the Second. Take care that you are not seen; use the stairway from the servants' quarters. My man will let you in with the usual code."

"Tonight?"

"Yes, it must be tonight. But first, you must sign the papers, so that we will never be separated."

They were going to elope tonight! That's what he was

telling her. He was asking her to pretend that she was here to make peace, as he was. But in reality, he was planning to take her away—from St. James, from Orleans, from Hugh and his disgusting attentions on her. Leo was her savior, the only boy she could trust; the only one who loved her.

"Never," she said. "We can never be separated."

"Ma belle. Ma chérie, you will always be at my side," he said. It was what he had called her in February, when they had first fallen in love—when they'd first met. He began to kiss her, and wrapped his arms around her body, holding her so tightly that she was pressed against him. The heat of his body on hers was wonderfully familiar.

"My dearest love," she breathed, and she moaned as he pressed his lips against her cheek, finding her lips, her neck, her collarbone.

Leo's kisses turned harder, more passionate—he was biting her—and she gasped, for it hurt. She had wanted him to respond, but not like this . . . in public where anyone could see. . . .

"Leo! Stop! Not here!" she said, as his hands groped her body in a fever. "Please!"

He was panting. "Tonight, then. Promise me you will meet me tonight."

"Tonight," she whispered. "Yes."

"For our future," he said, with one last kiss. Then he released her and disappeared down the hall.

Isabelle clutched a hand to her neck, where he had left a

red love mark. She looked frantically for something to hide it with, and decided upon her handkerchief, unfolding it from her pocket. She was terrified and elated. Leo was the same as ever, devoted and passionate. She would sign the annulment. She would do as she was told. For him. For them.

Our future, he'd promised.

They were leaving tonight; they were going to be together forever. He'd promised. She wrapped the hankie around her neck, feeling jaunty, triumphant. She had not lost anything. The princess could think she was marrying the prince, but Isabelle was secure in the knowledge that she had won his heart.

·12·

the
LAST WALTZ

old your head up—yes, that's good, very nice, Princess—a little higher—one step, two step, and slide to the right with me."

Marie slid as her dance instructor had taught her, but her foot caught in his shoe and she fumbled. "I'm sorry, I just . . . I can't."

The flamboyantly named Pierre La Fontaine was a man of infinite patience and outrageous wardrobe, but by late that afternoon the brightly colored feathers on his amazing velvet jacket were beginning to droop. "Your Highness, it is simply a matter of finding the rhythm and counting in your head."

"I'm so tired. Can we try again tomorrow?" she asked. They were standing in the middle of the ballroom, with the full orchestra playing the Lovers' Waltz, the dance that would open the royal ball. The party would be held at the Crystal Palace, but the main ballroom served as an adequate rehearsal space. Members of the court were standing at a respectful distance, watching the proceedings as they always did, and probably making fun of her graceless dancing under their breath.

Aelwyn walked up to the two of them. She had been borrowed from the sisterhood that day, as she was the sorceress in charge of the princess's wardrobe and social preparations for the season. Marie shot her a glance, begging her to help. "Can I have a word with the princess?" Aelwyn asked.

The dance instructor nodded and blotted his forehead with a handkerchief. "Yes, yes, go ahead," he said. "Perhaps there is a spell that might help Princess Marie to remember the steps."

Marie and Aelwyn went to the corner of the room to confer. "You're not very nice to him, and you should be," Aelwyn said. "He's only trying to help. You're not even trying."

"I'm tired," Marie said stubbornly. "I need to *rest*."

"You look fine to me," Aelwyn said firmly. "Maybe we should we send the court away?"

"Is that possible?"

"You're the princess; you can do whatever you want."

Marie watched as Aelwyn walked over to the ranking lady-in-waiting and exchanged a few words with her. After a moment, the courtiers left the room, a few of them looking a bit miffed. She had forgotten how strong and forthright her friend could be. When they were little, Aelwyn had often been the one who told Marie what to demand on birthdays and holidays. She knew instinctively how to stretch the limits of Marie's privilege, and when to push back.

"Shall I send away the orchestra, too?" Aelwyn offered. "Maybe everyone but the violinist, for a melody."

"It's like magic," Marie said when the large cavernous room was empty—save for the two of them, the dance instructor, the violinist, and Gill, of course.

"Are we ready to try again?" Pierre asked with a weary air.

"Perhaps the princess should dance with a different partner," Aelwyn suggested. "Her guard can take your place, Master Fontaine. What is your name, soldier?"

"Oh Gill, you don't have to," Marie said, horrified and a bit excited as Gill stepped forward obediently.

"Aelwyn is right. It might help you, because then I can see what you are doing and correct what you are doing wrong," Pierre said. "Over here, please, Corporal; yes, just like that," he said as Gill placed one hand on Marie's waist and took her right hand with the other.

Marie placed her hand on Gill's shoulder and hoped he didn't notice that her hands were sweaty. She felt self-conscious standing with him this way. She was physically affectionate with Gill, always in a purely platonic spirit. But this was the Lovers' Waltz they had to master, and it was disconcerting and thrilling to be practicing it with Gill. Since the reality of the situation meant she would be dancing this with Leopold in a few weeks, it seemed almost cruel to dance it with the boy she wished could take his place.

"All right, Marie?" he asked.

"Let's just get this over with," she said testily.

The violinist played, and Gill moved woodenly through the dance. He didn't hold her any closer or tighter than necessary, and he had a hard look on his face as if he were in pain.

"Hold her closer," Pierre instructed. "You act as if she is a puppet; she is your partner! Dip her lower—*closer*—this is the Lovers' Waltz!"

Marie blushed. "You don't have to do this," she told him.

Gill frowned grimly. "I do as told."

The violinist played the waltz, a romantic, elegant melody, the sound of the first blush of young love. It was traditionally the first dance of the Bal du Drap d'Or, and the most beautiful debutante performed it with her chosen partner as an homage to the enduring power of love. As a child, Marie had loved watching the chosen young couple perform the special dance. She had loved everything about the royal ball, from the heady music to the extravagant magic used on the ladies' dresses. She remembered a dress made from sunshine itself; it glowed golden rays when the dancer twirled. Now it was her turn to shine, her turn to swoon and fall in love in front of the whole court. But she was not in love with the prince. He was rehearsing on his own time, as tradition dictated they would not perform the dance together until the fateful night.

She wished Aelwyn had not suggested Gill dance with

her, he looked so mortified and annoyed. He did not take the least bit of pleasure in holding her this way. She was embarrassed for herself and for her infatuation, for her greedy desire for any excuse to be close to him. She could tell he only wanted it to be over. Mercifully the lesson finally ended, and Marie was free to return to her room. She pushed Aelwyn inside and shut the door in Gill's face.

"Why did you do that?" she whispered fiercely. "Why did you get Gill to dance with me? I was so embarrassed!"

"You need to learn how to dance for the waltz. I thought it would help. Master La Fontaine is so short. . . . I thought if you had a partner who was tall like Leopold, it would be easier," said Aelwyn. "Wait, why are you so upset? The boy you were talking about before—the one who disappeared—it's not—" She pointed to the door. "It is, isn't it?"

"Yes, that's him. Gill."

"But you told me he had been sent away—that you didn't know if you would see him again."

"He came back." Marie said. Except it wasn't the same, not like before. He had returned, but he hardly spent any time with her anymore. After that first day when they'd read together, he never did again. He visited her less and less on his downtime, and if she had thought there was any indication of deeper feeling on his part, it appeared she was wrong, especially after his strained performance at the dance rehearsal.

Aelwyn walked to the sideboard and found a bottle of mulberry wine. "Can I open this?"

Marie nodded and brought out two goblets so Aelwyn could pour them drinks. "Winnie, you can't tell anybody about how I feel about Gill." She knocked back the wine with one gulp.

"No—of course not," Aelwyn said, taking a long drink from her glass.

Marie held out her glass for another and Aelwyn obliged her. She sat down on the couch where she and Gill had spent many afternoons talking and reading books and felt melancholy. There was no stopping the season; every day brought her closer to the formal engagement, and after the engagement, the royal wedding. Already the dressmakers and seamstresses were fitting her for a wedding trousseau. She had argued that she was not engaged yet, but no one would listen. Everything had to be ready if she was to be married by the beginning of June.

"Aelwyn—have you ever been in love?" she asked.

Aelwyn finished her glass and poured another. "Yes," she said quietly.

"With Lanselin, was it? In Avalon?"

"Yes." Aelwyn sighed. "I will tell you one day, but not today. We might need more wine for that story."

"Was it—did he—was your heart broken?"

Aelwyn looked away. "Yes," she said again.

"I'm sorry."

"Marie, I know it is not my place to tell you, but you can't think that anything can happen with this soldier of yours."

"I know. But don't worry, he doesn't feel the same about me. We're just friends, and we'll always be just friends."

"You're certain he doesn't feel the same way about you?"

"I'm sure," Marie said, thinking of Gill's stern demeanor that afternoon. How stiffly he'd held her. This time, she couldn't keep the sadness out of her voice.

· *13* ·

the
GILDED CAGE

he plush, twelve-room parlor suite that Ronan and Vera called home for the month-long voyage boasted the most luxurious accommodations on the boat by far. Even Whitney Van Owen could not hide her surprise at finding Ronan ensconced in such beautiful quarters when she came to visit the first week. "Great digs!" Whitney had exclaimed upon taking a seat by the window nook. "Yours has a library?" she asked, impressed. *As well as a dining room, a dressing room, several sitting rooms and a marble bath,* Ronan wanted to add, but did not. Best to act as if this was all her proper due, and not some strange twist of good fortune that had finally come her way.

"Mama is incensed," Whitney confided, her pinkie pointing straight up as she sipped her tea. "So far we've only been invited to a luncheon with the queen, and not the actual royal ball. The Duchess of Wiltshire promised that she would get us in, but so far hasn't been successful in actually landing us an invitation. Isn't it tragic? To go all this way, only to have lunch!"

Ronan laughed. She found herself warming up to the girl. Whitney had never been so frank with her before, and she realized with a pang that the reason why her friend was being so voluble now was because she thought she and Ronan were equals, due to the opulence of her current surroundings. If she knew the truth of the Astor finances, she would not have been so forthcoming with her own family's failures.

"But you are going, I'm sure?" Whitney asked. "Lucky duck!"

With pride, Ronan recounted how her invitation to the Bal du Drap d'Or had arrived by regular post, but once she touched it, it had opened in a spectacular manner—the envelope bursting in a shimmer of light and stars, gold letters spinning in the air to spell out her name.

"Do you think it's true what everyone's saying, that the queen will announce the princess's engagement at the ball?" Whitney asked.

"Princess Marie-Victoria is getting married?"

Whitney nodded. "Mother heard from a friend in London right before we left. She is to marry that Prussian prince as part of the peace treaty—you know, the good-looking one— and they are already preparing the city for a wedding."

"Leopold? She's going to marry Leopold?" Ronan raised

an eyebrow. She'd set her heart on winning his, but of course he was already spoken for. She should have known better than to hope a common American like her had a chance at a crowned royal. But a girl could dream, couldn't she?

"Yes, that's what Mother said," Whitney sighed. "That princess is another lucky duck!" She set down her cup and gathered her skirts. "You know, Leopold's brother is supposed to be on this ship, but I haven't seen him around anywhere. Anyway, I should go. Mother will wonder where I am, and we're supposed to dine with some friend of the duchess tonight—the campaign for a spot on the guest list continues!" She smirked. "I told Mama to offer her more money!"

"Whitney!"

"Oh please, don't you know that's how it works? Don't be so naïve!"

Ronan bid Whitney good day, and told Vera she would take a stroll around the deck to take in some sea air. Her governess waved her off with a smile. Ronan had noticed she had been decidedly more agreeable since they'd settled into their sumptuous rooms. Luxury had a way of doing that to a person, and far be it from her to begrudge the old girl the pleasure of being catered to, hand and foot, by the state-room's butler. Even their assigned table in the banquet hall was located in the "Gold Coast" area of the room nearest the windows, so they could look out over the serene waves of the Atlantic while they dined on oysters and champagne.

The promenade was nicely shaded, and passengers lounged on the jaunty blue-and-white deck chairs, sipping their mint juleps and Pimm's cups. There were several croquet and *pétanque* games in progress. Ronan said hello to a few familiar faces: dowager ladies in pearls and lace gloves, older gentlemen in ascots and top hats. Many of them were from the finest families of New York, Virginia, and Newport, along with several Europeans heading home as well.

She found a cozy spot to perch and twirled her parasol, thinking she made a nice picture in her pretty pastels against the blue sky and sea. Even so, she was still surprised when someone said exactly the same thing. "What a nice picture you make!" It was the boy from the docks, the one with the bruise on his cheek and the black eye, although both wounds were healing nicely. His face was starting to come into focus underneath all the swelling.

She murmured her thanks and turned away.

"Hey, no need to be so shy. I thought we were friends!"

"Friends?" she said, aghast. "Wherever did you get that idea?"

He grinned and didn't answer. "Having a good trip?"

She nodded curtly and attempted to turn away again, but he wasn't having it. "I'm a little seasick myself, but that can't be helped," he said.

"You could try watching the horizon. Supposedly it centers your equilibrium," she said.

"Is that so?" he asked, staring at the sea. "Hmm. You might just be right about that."

"You're not supposed to be up here, you know," she said. "This is for first-class passengers only. The porter comes around in a bit, and he'll know you don't belong here."

"Oh? That's very nice of you to be worried about my well-being." He smiled. "What will they do? Throw me off the ship? I'd like to see them try."

"You like to live dangerously, do you?" she said.

"Ah, so you do remember me!" he crowed. "See, I told you we were friends." He nudged her elbow. Against her will, she found herself smiling back at him.

"That's more like it," he said. Footsteps rounded the corner: the ship's porter, offering drinks. His smile faded. "Well, I suppose that's my cue," he said. "Like Heathcliff, I've got to run away."

"Wait!" she called.

"Yes, Cathy?" he asked with a grin.

She bit her lip. "Will I see you again?"

"Would you like to?" He winked. "I'm just teasing. Same time, same place, tomorrow?"

She hesitated, unsure why she had asked. Something had propelled her: a desire to not let him get away, not to say good-bye just yet. She couldn't help but say, "No—I mean, yes, but not here."

The next day, Ronan insisted that Vera take the afternoon off to visit with a friend she had made, who was a governess for another family. "Go and catch up over a long and luxurious six-course tea," she urged. "I am quite content to remain here and relax quietly."

"If you're sure, dear," Vera said doubtfully. "Are you sure you don't mind?"

"I'm sure. And take as long as you want. Please."

Once her governess was dispatched, Ronan heaved a sigh of relief.

Promptly at three o'clock, there was a knock on the door. She opened the door and sure enough, the boy who'd styled himself Heathcliff was there with a smile on his face. "Is this your room? All this?" he said, taking a look around.

Ronan nodded, feeling somewhat embarrassed at the luxury. She had been intent on finding a private place for them where he wouldn't be run off by the porters on the upper deck, but it seemed fraudulent to pass it all off as hers. "I mean, it's all my room, but it's not really mine. It's a long story."

He walked over to the library books, pulling out titles, murmuring to himself. "Have you read this?" he asked. "This?"

She shook her head, not paying too much attention to the books. She began to think it might have been the wrong idea to invite him over. Now that he was here, she wasn't sure what to do with him. But he saved the afternoon, as somehow she knew he would. "I say," he said, spying the game room. "Do you play billiards?"

From that day on, every afternoon Vera went to have tea with her friend. Ronan met Heath, as she came to think of him, in her room to play billiards and drink champagne. He was very opinionated on what kind of champagne to order, and gave her a list of the best vintages to ask for from the room's stewards.

"The '87 *Canard-Duchene*! A very good year," he said as he popped the cork and the bottle frothed with bubbles.

She laughed as he poured them two tall stems.

"*Prost!*" he said heartily.

"Cheers," she smiled, taking a big sip. "How do you know so much about champagne?"

He shrugged. "A hobby of mine."

She put down her glass and picked up her cue, and sent the white ball spinning in a complicated move that sank two colored balls in different pockets.

"Good shot," he said, raising his glass in salute.

"My dad taught me to play." She smiled.

"Thanks, Dad. So," he said, "shall we play a game?"

"Aren't we playing one now?" she asked.

"Oh, but this one is much more fun." He waggled his eyebrows and set up his pool cue. He looked like a sleek, handsome panther as he leaned over and elegantly dispatched the remaining balls on the table.

"What kind of game?" she asked.

He told her the rules with a grin and she shook her head. "No, I'm not taking off my clothes for you. Not one glove," she said. "Don't even think about it!"

"It was worth a shot." He smiled. "You can't blame me for trying," he said as he racked up the balls.

Ronan looked over her shoulder at the door. Vera was in the middle of tea right now, on the second course, gorging herself on scones and cream. Ronan, on the other hand, was alone with a strange, wicked boy in her rooms, and he had just proposed they play a game where they take their clothes off. It was the farthest thing from being a lady, and she would never in a million years acquiesce to something so vulgar. . . . But somehow, the way he proposed it, and the naughty smile on his face, made her think twice about saying no. It was just a little fun. . . . She felt a wild impulse to enjoy life, to be a little free-spirited—to be that crazy girl who had no inhibitions, no worries, before she went to London to be a lady and find a husband. She wanted a chance to be young and reckless, and "sow her wild oats," as they say.

"Fine," she said, picking up the pool cue and carefully wiping the ends with chalk. "I have to warn you, though, I'm wearing a lot of layers." She smiled as she sent the balls flying in every direction with the opening break.

· 14 ·

His FAIR LADY

*I*sabelle pulled the sheets up to her chest and turned away from Leo so she could reach for the candle and light her cigarette. She thought her dark hair would make a pretty picture against the satin pillow. She was always very conscious of the best angles and the best light for her features; conscious of her effect on men; on him. Sometimes it was as if she were looking down on her scene, directing it, rather than living it. It gave her a pleasant sensation to have control over the atmosphere, as there were so few things she had control over these days.

"Hand me one, will you?" he asked.

"Sure." She lit it with the gold engraved lighter he kept by his bedside that she had given him as a Valentine's Day present. It was embossed with their initials, L and I; a secret souvenir of their love. She watched as he inhaled deeply and exhaled a ring of smoke in the air. She was glad for the oil lamps in this part of the castle, as the dim candlelight made his hair like burnished gold, his skin a warm caramel color. His cheeks were still rosy from their exertions between the sheets. He was as avid a lover as ever, his ardor for her unquenchable as before.

"So, shall we get ready to leave?" she asked, flicking her ashes into the marble ashtray.

Leo raised an eyebrow. "Leave?"

"I've brought my bag. I'm ready when you are," she said. She had signed the papers that morning, breaking their engagement and his obligation to her, guaranteeing peace between their families. House Valois would not seek recompense or restitution from the Prussian kingdom. He had asked her to sign it to protect their future, and now Isabelle wanted to know what the future held.

She was still smarting from her treatment in the royal court earlier. The assembled audience had all been so sympathetic, so pitying, as they watched her sign the papers. She couldn't stand it. *Leave your pity for someone else,* she wanted to scream at all the smug noblewomen and their ugly daughters who had gathered to watch and celebrate her humiliation. She wanted to laugh and say there was nothing to pity; Leo was hers. They could make her sign all the papers in the world releasing him from his engagement; it would not make the least bit of difference in the temperature of his passion for her. They would be together, as he promised—always.

Only the queen had smiled, gently. And drat it all, even that horrid ghastly princess, that Marie-Victoria, had been truly kind.

"I am so sorry you have to do this," Marie had whispered as she handed Isabelle the feathered quill. "Believe me when I tell you, I do not want to take him away from you."

Isabelle had stiffened. The princess was not half as ugly as they said. She was plain, sure, but had a handsome elegance to her bearing. "I do not want, nor need, your sympathy," she'd whispered fiercely.

"You have it regardless," Marie had said. "I am truly sorry, Isabelle." Then she'd stepped away from the desk to let her have her privacy.

Next to her, Hugh had coughed into his hands and glared at her. Isabelle had pulled herself to her tallest height and nodded. "I am ready." She flipped through the pages: a negotiated treaty between Orleans and Prussia. Her father's hard work to ensure her legacy and safety by marrying her off to the Crown Prince had all been in vain. Her father had been dead for years, she was under Hugh's care now, and Leo had asked her to do this for him. She signed her name with a flourish.

I, Isabelle of Orleans, release Leopold of Prussia from his obligation without penalty of war or threat of battle. . . . Blah blah blah.

She had fled from the humiliation of that moment and packed victoriously, only taking as much as she could carry. She had sneaked out alone in the night, had told no one, not even Louis, what she was doing or where she was going. She'd hailed a hansom cab to take her to the palace, and given the butler the secret code to bring her up through the servants' quarters. If she was afraid, she was also certain that tomorrow she would be his wife. Of course, when she'd arrived in his room, Leo had pounced on her the moment she walked in the door. That was only to be expected, of course, because he loved her so much. They had a little time, she thought; it was only midnight. They could enjoy each other's company before running away.

She nestled herself against him, luxuriating in his slow caressing of her hair as they puffed on their cigarettes. "It was awful, you know, having everyone stare at me as if I were to be pitied—I hated it so! Shall we go now? Do you have the carriage waiting to take us to the vicar?"

"A carriage waiting? A vicar?" Leo repeated, his voice amused. He stopped touching her hair and regarded her thoughtfully through the smoke. She didn't like the way he was looking at her, as if she had suffered a brain injury; as if she were speaking nonsense.

"We are eloping, aren't we? I assumed that was what you'd planned? For our future?" she asked, feeling cold all of a sudden.

He picked up the lighter and flicked it open and closed,

playing with the fire, and continued to look at her in that maddeningly casual way. "*Ma chérie*, you assumed that we would elope tonight?"

"You said I had to sign the papers for our future. That it was very important to you."

He nodded. "Yes, for our future. It is very important to me that I be free to marry Marie-Victoria. Eleanor was quite insistent that the royal wedding should go off without a hint of scandal, of tarnish. She and her Merlin would never have welcomed me into the palace otherwise, certainly not with open arms. I don't know what I would have done then—continue the war, most likely. And then where would we be?" he mused. "Do you know—we were about to surrender when the Pandora gave us our victory? We were so close to defeat—so close! We had hardly a pawn to play, even in the peace negotiations, as I was already affianced—and marriage was off the table. But I told them you would sign it, that you only wanted to make me happy, and you didn't fail me. You were brilliant, weren't you, my sweet French nightingale," he said as he nuzzled her cheek.

"I still don't understand—how is this important to our future?"

"Isn't it obvious? With all the riches of the empire at my disposal, I will take care of you forever. Don't you worry—my sweet Isabelle will have everything she wants for the rest of her life."

It was as if she could not understand English. His words were like hailstones. She could not make them out because her head was buzzing too loudly, sending warning signals. She could not quite believe what she was hearing. "Wait a minute, what do you mean . . . ? Do you mean you are actually going to marry her? You are going to marry Marie-Victoria?"

"Of course."

Isabelle felt her cheeks burning hot, and suddenly realized she was very, very naked. She had never felt more vulnerable in her life. She was in bed with a boy who was not her fiancé anymore. "But what about us?" she squeaked. She sounded just like a stupid little mouse. She wanted to slap herself. What had she done? What had she done?

Eleanor was quite insistent that the royal wedding should go off without a hint of scandal, of tarnish. And they would never have welcomed me into the palace otherwise, certainly not with open arms. I don't know what I would have done—continue the war, most likely, and then where would we be? But I told them you would sign it, that you only wanted to make me happy, and you didn't fail me. . . . I will take care of you for the rest of your life.

She put her hand on his chin and turned it, so he had to look at her directly. "What do you mean, you will take care of me?"

"You will want for nothing, I assure you." He gently took her hand away from his face and kissed her on the forehead. His lips, which had been so soft just a moment ago, were now dry and papery. She was suddenly revolted by his touch.

"But Leo—this—this cannot go on—you cannot mean . . ." she sputtered.

"I will marry Marie-Victoria and become king of the empire. But do not worry your pretty little head. I promise you that nothing has to change between us. You will continue to meet me in my room when I call for you, and I will make sure you are by my side at every occasion. We will always be together like I promised." He put his head on her bare shoulder and kissed her neck. His lips traced a path to her breasts. She felt him pull the sheet away from her body to make his intentions clear.

"But you will be married!" she said, protesting against his kisses.

"Little nightingale, why should my marriage change anything between us?"

You will be by my side at every occasion, never far from me. . . . You will come when I call for you. Then she realized what he was saying, what he was proposing, and finally she saw the shape of the future he had intended for them, even as he kissed her skin and put his hands all over her body.

She wrenched away from his grasp. Her voice was low and hoarse. "You mean to make me your mistress?"

His head on her bare stomach, Leo murmured, "Aren't you already? I have always taken care of you, have I not? Like a proper gentleman? Have you wanted for anything? I have seen to it that you have one of the best houses in the square, that your wardrobe is the latest from Paris. I have even sent you my magician to make your jewels sparkle."

She was Isabelle of Valois, Lady Orleans; she was the

rightful Queen of France. She told him she would never debase herself in such a manner, but he only looked amused. Her words sounded hollow, even to her.

"My dear Lady Isabelle, nothing changes. My love for you remains as strong as ever," he said, taking her hand and showing her. "On the night of the royal ball, you will meet me here, in my bed. You will wait for me. On the night of my wedding, I will come to you, and prove that I am as good as my promise. You must not be seen—but then, you are good at that, aren't you? You have always been good at keeping secrets."

She felt her cheeks turn scarlet. It was true. She had seduced him from the beginning. She had thrown herself at him, flirted with him madly when he had come to Orleans that winter. But it was he who had insisted. It was he who had forced her into taking the next step. . . . And it was too late, now, to take it all back.

When Lord Hartwig and Leo had arrived in Burgundy that winter to meet with Hugh, the Prussians were still at war with the empire and things were not going well for them. Louis-Philippe guessed they were calling on their old allegiance, to ask for aid and soldiers.

The moment he entered the castle, Leo fixed Isabelle with a look. "So, you are to be my bride," the handsome young prince said as an opener, showing he was well acquainted with the agreement between their families. Isabelle would be lying if she did not admit her heart raced from the moment she saw him. This tall and handsome boy, who had come right up to her and claimed her. She would have swooned if she could have. He was her future—the one who would take her away from the sadness of her past, as well as her disgusting cousin.

Later that afternoon Leo whispered in her ear over tea, "My rooms are in the east tower. Meet me tonight. My man will let you in."

She had done it. She met him in his room that evening. At first, they were just talking and holding hands; he was whispering in her ear, and he poured her something to drink. The next thing she knew, he was all over her, untying the stays in her corset. She pushed him away, weakly, asked him to stop. But it was like her arms were made of lead; like she couldn't say no at all.

"We are to be married," he said. "We are doing nothing wrong." And he kissed her hard on the mouth, and his tongue was down her throat. "You are mine," he said. "Pretend it is our wedding night."

And because they were to be married anyway, and because she could not think straight, and because he was so handsome, and because she was so thrilled to know he was so enamored of her, that he wanted her so much . . . and because she just couldn't say no, not once, not ever, could not form the word, no matter how many times she was screaming it in her head . . . he took what he wanted.

Afterward he kissed her on the forehead, as if to apologize.

But the next day he had asked her to meet him again, and the next day, and the next. All that month before he left for Lamac, she met him in his room in the dark of night, and she fancied that she was in love: in love with the boy who was just as in love with her, and who was to be her husband. . . .

But he was *not* to be her husband. . . .

Not anymore . . .

Not since she had signed her life away that morning . . .

Leo leaned over and kissed her again, and now he was on top of her, kissing her again, and she wriggled underneath him, and found she was crying. She was crying without making a sound, the tears streaming down her face as he kissed her, just like the first time, when she had been unable to ask him to stop.

"Come now," he crooned, as he kissed her tears away. He hitched his breath and then he was inside her again, and he held her hands down on either side of her head with his. "Don't be this way. Isn't this what you wanted? I promised you we would be together always. Love is all we need . . . it does not matter if we are married or not, and it never has. Not with us."

No, this is not what I wanted, she thought, turning her face away while he ravished her body.

This was not what she'd wanted at all.

· 15 ·

No Stranger
TO HEARTBREAK

Prince Leopold did not seek her out after their chance meeting in the hallway the day of his arrival. Aelwyn was surprised to find that she felt the sting of rejection. It was she, after all, who had sent him away; and yet, there it was anyway, prickling at her skin. She had expected him to chase her, she realized; had been looking forward to clandestine notes pressed underneath a serving tray, or the knock of his valet at her door, asking her if she would be so kind as to see to some matter—which would lead to meeting him in some secret room. She had even wandered the halls of the palace and the gardens in the hopes of bumping into him again. She had made herself very available. Yet she saw neither hide nor hair of him for days.

It appeared the prince was kept busy by his royal duties: meeting ministers and noble families, familiarizing himself with their ways, and supposedly wooing the princess. The rumor mill had it that the prince was quite infatuated with the young dauphine, and she with him. It was all hogwash, of course, Marie couldn't stand the boy, and Leo was an actor on a stage. They spent as little time together as possible. Perhaps he had found some other entertainment or distraction, which is why he did not seek Aelwyn out. It couldn't be that difficult to keep himself occupied. There were many beautiful girls at court.

The morning spell-casting over, Aelwyn walked with her sisters to a quiet meal of hard bread and cheese. The sisters were eager to talk, and many of the young acolytes wanted to know more details of her life in Avalon. They all wanted to know about Lanselin. His beauty and legend were famous even now, even after a thousand years. Aelwyn told them he was as handsome and charming as the legends said, but she did not tell the entire truth.

She had arrived at Avalon as a child. During her four years there he was always the same age, permanently arrested at seventeen, with his angelic face and curls, and those bright eyes that had taken Genevieve from Artucus. Lanselin would never grow old; he would never grow up. He was trapped in time, old and young, but neither wise nor innocent.

A boy who would never grow up.

They had been friends at first. He was like a brother to her, and taught her how to use the power of the stones to amplify her own abilities.

Things changed as she changed. She noticed how his eyes lingered over her body. "Don't be shy," he'd said to her when she'd tried to cover herself up after bathing, after he'd chanced upon her unawares in the stream. He had taken the cloth away from her, and she had been frightened at first. But then she'd realized that, for the first time, she had something he wanted; she was no longer a child to be dismissed, but a woman.

So she let him look at her.

He didn't touch her that day, but it was only a matter of time.

It happened one afternoon a few weeks before she returned to London. It was a game they played: she'd run all over the island, and he would chase her. Aelwyn remembered the feel of the wind on her back, how fast and strong she felt, the ecstatic high of the chase—how breathless they had been. *Catch and kiss.* A game she liked to play with boys. Lanselin had fallen and tackled her, his lean body on hers, his mouth crushing hers. It wasn't a game anymore. She had whispered in his ear and bit it, sucking on the flesh.

His hand had slipped under her skirts again, and she let him go further than before, and then there was no stopping it, not this time. No laughter, no giggling. He had not asked permission, and he had not needed any, for she had wanted it—had wanted him, had succumbed. Succumbed was too weak a word; she had drowned in his attention, relished it, hungered for it; had been lit up by his infatuation with her; had craved it with every fiber of her being.

"Do you like me," she had whispered, right in the middle of it, while he was thrusting into her, her back arched, her lip bitten, his hands in her hair. "Do you like me?" she had asked, like a child, like a fool. . . .

He had not answered.

Instead he'd cried out, and crashed against her until she thought she might break. . . .

It had lasted for nearly a month—his infatuation. They slept entwined in each other's arms, awoke in the same bed. One morning Viviane walked into the room unexpectedly and saw them together, and walked out without a word. She never mentioned it, and Aelwyn had felt a twinge of shame. Not that she'd done anything wrong, as Avalon did not subscribe to the rules of society and propriety. Viviane knew all that happened under her watch; she was neither mother nor friend, and she had done nothing to encourage or discourage it. But somehow, Aelwyn felt she had shown weakness in submitting to Lanselin—to that ageless, mercurial boy.

Because just as quickly as it began, it ended.

The chase was over.

She had thought that loving him would bind him to her

forever. But he had only turned away. He had lost interest. He was bored again.

He had gotten what he'd wanted after years of pining, but when he finally got what he wanted, she was nothing to him. . . . She would never hold a candle to his lost love, his Jenny. She was gone now, dead a thousand years, and still he mourned her. Lanselin had come to Avalon to repent for the damage he'd done by loving her, and so he was cursed to live on the island alone, forever preying on the young girls who chose Viviane over Emrys. Lanselin would not go with her to London, he told her when she asked him. He belonged to Avalon. He did not ask her to stay, either.

Lanselin had taken what he wanted—her girlhood, her innocence, her love—and shrugged it off. It meant nothing to him. She meant nothing to him. It was a hard lesson to learn.

Like Lanselin, Leopold had looked like the kind of boy who would enjoy a chase—and so she'd meant to give him one. But perhaps Leo was too lazy after all. He was a prince; he was not used to effort. She had piqued his interest, but any more exertion was too costly to him. What was she doing, anyway, thinking about him? It was disloyal to Marie, her friend—his future wife—no matter that Marie did not love him. She would marry him, as was her duty. But Aelwyn couldn't keep him from her thoughts. *You always found him charming; maybe you should marry him,* Marie had said jokingly, even though they both knew that would be impossible.

Lanselin du Lac, Leopold of Prussia. The golden boys everyone wanted, including Aelwyn. When she was a child, she'd always wanted what was the princess's. Even at sixteen years old, it was a hard habit to break.

· 16 ·

a FOOL'S GAME

The first kiss was not their last, and by the end of the trip Ronan was looking forward to the afternoon billiard games with growing impatience. It was all a lark, a tryst, a distraction, she told herself. She didn't even know his real name, and he did not know hers. They were Heath and Cathy, passing the time together on a long seafaring journey. It was their last week on board the *Saturnia*; they would arrive in London soon. It was a pity they would never see each other again after they reached the city. They were not so different, when it came down to it. It was such a shame they had been born into different stations. There were several titled lords on board, but somehow Ronan managed to avoid spending any time with them. If Vera had known that she was spending every afternoon half-dressed with a strange boy, she would have sent Ronan back to New York on a lifeboat.

Right now she was lying with him on top of the billiards table, the game forgotten. She was dressed only in her slip, and he was only in his trousers, his chest bare. Her lips were puffy from kissing. While she would have let him have his way with her, he was respectful of taking it too far; they never did more than kiss. She could kiss him for hours, she thought. She traced a map of scars on his hard stomach with a light finger. She didn't know very much about him, other than what he had told her: he was a fighter, a boxer, returning home to the ring. His mother was dead, and he was estranged from his father and brother. He wasn't cut out for the family business, he explained.

"Don't have it in me to join the firm," he sighed.

"What does your family do?"

"Oh, them? They keep sheep," he smiled.

"I see. And you are not the herding type."

"Not the least bit. I'm not one to follow the herd, if that's what you mean."

She laughed prettily, her long blond hair falling over her shoulder like a silk curtain. "Yes, somehow I can't picture it."

"So what about you? You never told me why you were traveling to the capital," he said. He ran a finger along the edge of the strap of her slip, playing with it. She held her breath, wondering if he would tug it away, but he seemed content to just caress her skin softly with his finger.

Ronan squared her shoulders. "I am going to London to sell myself," she said, her tone hard and brittle. Earlier she had told him about her disastrous family finances, and had finally confessed that she had lucked into the first-class stateroom by accident.

"Such dark words for such a bright girl. I was not aware you were for purchase. . . ." he said, his tone light. "If I had known this earlier, perhaps I would have placed a bid. May I?"

"Oh please, you can't afford me. But it's the same thing, is it not? Because of my circumstances I must marry for money, and not for love. I might as well be one of those painted ladies in Amsterdam, with a red light over my head."

"Then don't do it," he said softly. "You're better than that."

"If only that were true," she said with a bitter laugh, sitting up to wrap a shawl tightly around her shoulders. "No, you will find I will be quite good at it. I will pretend to fall in love with one of these titled dopes, and that will be the end of me. But perhaps all is not lost, after all; there will be all that lovely money, and all the magic it can buy."

He shrugged. "Magic is overrated. I didn't take you for a cynic."

"Just a realist."

"So that is the plan, then? To enter into a fraudulent, loveless union in order to save face and status, and earn a token from the Merlin?" His tone was sharp and disappointed. He sat up as well and put his shirt back on.

"Don't judge me. Without our name, without our

home . . ." She shook her head. "I told you that you wouldn't understand. Your family . . ."

"Herds sheep. Yes. But you are wrong there—I understand perfectly," he said, fastening his cuff links.

Ronan, watching him dress, noticed that his cuff links were gold—although gold-plated, most likely.

"My mother had to do the same thing. She had to marry my father. She had no choice in the matter," he said.

"You're so lucky. You can do whatever you want. You can keep fighting . . . your future is your own. Mine is behind a golden cage."

"Then break the chains," he said, daring her. "Why not do something wild—and consider a different outcome. . . ." He put a hand on top of hers. "Perhaps one that you did not expect."

She looked at his hand. There were faint lines on his knuckles. More scars from his fights, she thought. He was offering her something—she was certain of that—but what could he offer her? He was no one, from nowhere—a nobody. Her mother hadn't pulled herself out of the frontier so her daughter could sink back into obscurity. If she set her lot with his, she would lose the game before the season had even started, by giving her heart to this nameless boy. Ronan knew she should take her hand away from his, but she did not. She clung to him, as if he were a life raft. He was offering something—something—what was he offering her? They stood there for a long moment, holding hands on the billiard table.

The question he posed hovered in the air between them. She was filled with doubt: what was he talking about, really? Was he even serious?

The books she had read as a child were filled with stories of heroes and heroines who risked everything for love and adventure. They left their families and their ordinary lives behind for travails on the road, the oceans, the unknown. She had loved those stories when she was younger. She'd thought of herself as an explorer, an adventurer—a girl with a free and wild heart—which was why she had played the game with him, why she met him every afternoon. To see how far she would dare. How far she would let it go.

But if he was asking what she thought he was asking, she knew she had taken this illicit affair too far. "So, what do you say? Come with me when we get into port. I know a judge in London, a friend of a friend who can see to everything. Or we can pop down to the General Register Office. Whichever you'd like—it's all the same to me," he said.

A judge? A quick trip to the Register Office? Was he mad? Out of his mind? Did he truly think she would consider getting married without the blessing of the sisterhood? Without a sign from the Merlin? She was *Ronan Astor.* Her wedding would be the talk of New York! The queen would be invited (she probably would not attend, but she would be invited nonetheless!), and her bridesmaids would number the wealthy, the beautiful, and the titled! She could not see herself plighting her troth in her traveling clothes, taking a fighter for a husband, standing in front of some sleepy-eyed judge whom they had roused in the middle of the night.

Oh, but he was so handsome and kind. He smiled at her, and she felt as if she would give him anything he wanted. Was it so wrong, what he was offering? They were in love, were they not? She had disrobed in front of him—he knew almost every part of her by now, from all these secret afternoons filled with laughter, champagne, and intimate conversations, not to mention the passionate kisses they'd shared. She had been more honest with him than she had been with anyone in her life. He knew her and he liked her. She had lost her heart to him from the beginning, when he had spoken to her at the port in New York.

Perhaps she would regret it for the rest of her life—in fact, she had a feeling she would certainly regret it for the rest of her life. As a fat matron with a rich husband, she would look back on this proposal from this strange and wonderful boy, and wish with all of her might that she had answered differently—that she had said yes to him. But as it was, she was too much her mother's daughter to throw away her future so recklessly. She couldn't do it. In any event, he could not truly be asking what he was asking, surely? He was just teasing her, trying to make her feel better. For that matter, she didn't even know his real name . . . nor did he know hers. . . .

"So, what do you say?" he asked again, and his grin was wide and confident. It was too bad she didn't know he had a ring in his pocket, and that if she'd said yes, she would have been wearing the famous blue diamond of Brandenburg on her finger when they arrived in London.

"You're such a sweet boy. I'm sorry, but the answer is no," she said, and quickly changed the subject. "My father says our civilization has become stilted, that magic has corrupted reason, logic, and freedom . . . if magic did not exist, we would be living in a different world," she said as she pulled away from him.

The light in his eyes faded as he turned away from her. "Perhaps, but perhaps some things would still be the same. There would still be the London Season. There would still be the Debrett's rankings."

"I think you might be right on that," she allowed. Later she would wonder how a boy from steerage had known about the social calendar, or the name of the social bible. Or, for that matter, how a boy like him would know to order the best types of champagne. Perhaps he read tabloids. Perhaps it was another hobby of his.

"So, that's your answer, then," he said lightly, but his face was pained, hurt. Ronan wanted nothing more than to take that hurt away, but she steeled her heart against him.

"Yes," she said. "Maybe we'll see each other in London," she offered, even though she knew it was insincere.

"Maybe if we're lucky," he said with a sad smile. "So this is good-bye, then, is it?"

"Good-bye, Heath," she whispered, watching as he gathered his things, put his socks and shoes and coat back on.

"Good-bye, Cathy," he said. When he walked out of the room, he didn't look back.

She didn't see him for the rest of the journey. She found that she was more devastated than she'd expected. One lonely afternoon she contemplated looking for him in every corner of the boat, but Vera came back from tea early for once, and the chance passed. Perhaps it was just as well. If she'd spoken to him any longer, if she had let him kiss her again, if they had shared another steamy afternoon, she had a feeling he would have succeeded in talking her into eloping somehow. Ronan had been so close to saying yes that afternoon, to risking the unknown . . . perhaps it was for the best that she'd never see him again. She had done the right thing. She was certain.

the
LONDON SEASON

Everyone's here and frightfully gay;
Nobody cares what people say.
—NOEL COWARD,
"I WENT TO A MARVELLOUS PARTY"

· 17 ·

Friends
OF THE BLANKET

hen the *Saturnia* docked in the Port of London, Wolf felt a heaviness in his step at having returned to Europe. He had enjoyed the Americas; had liked the broad open spaces of the Midwest plains, the awkward and aggressive confidence of the cities, the fact that no one cared who his father was, that no one recognized him. But back in the empire, he was back to being the prince again—back to being his father's son and his brother's wayward problem.

Unlike Leo, he was ushered into the palace with hardly any pomp or fuss when he arrived. Oswald and his loyal valet were his only entourage, and aside from a few giggling ladies of court, no one else seemed to pay him much attention. Perhaps they were all too busy, as the "small season" had already started with the opening of Parliament, and the hectic festivities would build from Easter until the official opening of the season at the royal ball. Wolf tried not to feel too offended that there were no high-ranking representatives from the queen's circle to greet him. While he hadn't expected Her Majesty or the Merlin to make an appearance, a minister or two would have been nice. The suite of apartments he had been given was adequate, but after traveling for months and then spending the sea voyage in second class, he was itching to just go home to the family *schloss* in Brandenburg. The homefront was indeed plagued with the aforementioned sheep, but did boast a very comfortable bed.

That morning dawned bright and early, and at first Wolf was disoriented, unsure of where he was. It was strange to be back on land; he had gotten used to the gentle rolling of the waves on the ship. He blinked open one eye to see a shining apparition at the door.

"So, the prodigal son has returned," the apparition said, stepping into the room and out of the sunlight, so that Wolf could see his brother clearly. Leo walked in with a broad grin and clapped his hands loudly. "Wake up! Wake up!"

"Hello to you too," Wolf grumbled, forcing himself awake and upright. "You're awful cheerful this morning."

"Am I?"

"Isabelle here?" Wolf said pointedly.

"I wouldn't know," Leo said, but his eyes were smirking. "Is she?"

Wolf shook his head. His brother was a pig. Poor Isabelle. She should have known better than to give her heart to Leo. His brother took after their father, with an eye for every pretty girl in his path. And yet, for all of Leo's indiscretions, there was hardly a whiff of scandal about him. He was the golden boy: nothing tarnished his sheen. If anything, it made him more lovable. Wolf didn't know how his brother got away with everything, but he always did.

"How were the provinces?" Leo asked.

"Provincial," Wolf grumbled, even though he had enjoyed his time there. He looked at Leo, dressed in a proper British cricket suit. "Settled in, have you?"

"Fancy a game?"

"Not today, thanks."

"Right, then. Well, see you later. Dress for dinner, will you? And get the doctor to give you something better for that eye. You look like a burglar."

Wolf nodded.

He didn't want to admit it, but he hadn't felt like doing much of anything since the American girl had rejected him. Of course it had been a foolish offer—what was he thinking, going around proposing with his mother's diamond ring? What made her so different from all the other girls he had romanced and left behind? From all the other girls he had played strip billiards with, for that matter? But there was something about her honesty, her brave determination, that had touched his heart. She was trying so hard to be the grand lady, but she was a kindred spirit, wild and uninhibited. He had been drawn to her fire, and to the impulsiveness of marrying her without knowing her real name—the daringness of it. It was a story they could tell their children, something out of a fairy tale. How their mother had not known who he was when she accepted him, and the frog turned out to be a prince. But the princess had been unwilling to kiss the frog, the prince remained warty and unloved, and now there was no adventure to be had. Perhaps the world was right about him after all—without his title, he wasn't much use to anybody.

Wolf thought that maybe he should have been honest with her. Not about his name—he was too careful for that after the latest paternity accusation—not that she would do something like that, but it was safer to remain anonymous. No, he wished he had spilled the dark secrets of his own heart and admitted that, like her, he was not free to live life on his terms—not at all—but instead was as much a prisoner to duty and family as she was. Which was why she should have accepted his proposal, because together they could have forged a new life that was unconstrained by tradition, a new and uncharted adventure. He would have married her then and there if she had said yes. He had never met a girl who didn't know who he was, who his family was, and who only liked him for himself. And she *had* liked him, had liked him fine, *but not enough* . . . not enough to risk it. Alas.

If only she had said yes. . . .

He wondered what he would do when they saw each other again—she had mentioned she had been invited to the royal ball. Perhaps if they met again, he would tell her his real name. . . .

There was not much time to feel sorry for himself, however. Once he arrived in London, there were social and royal obligations to meet. During his first week in town he was a fixture at the opera, the ballet, dinners, dances, and suppers that lasted until the wee hours of the morning. People whispered when he walked past; he could not enter a dining club or a theater without causing guests and patrons to titter, or worse, being obliged to greet and pay homage to the various dignitaries who knew his father and brother.

That evening he tagged along with Leo to a dinner given by one of London's best hostesses, one Lady Constance Grosvernor. It was the standard fancy affair, with the usual mix of the beautiful and the titled, and Lady Constance had remarked to him that she had a friend who had also sailed on the *Saturnia* to London. She had thought of inviting her, but had decided against it at the last minute, as it would have caused their dinner to have an odd number at the table—and everyone knew that was unlucky. Wolf found the prattle as mind-numbing as usual. He was glad when Leo entered the room, and the lady and the rest of the party left him to swarm over his brother.

Wolf was even gladder when Leo decided it was time to

leave the dinner and head to the nearest private club. The night ended at a rather famous bordello, and the next morning at the breakfast table Wolf cursed himself for taking the carousing too far. He looked and felt like death, but of course Leo looked like he always did: perfectly robust, healthy and whole. Meanwhile, Wolf felt as if his head would crack open, it was pounding so hard. He finished off his coffee—so much weaker than they took it back home.

"A note for you, sir," the butler said, placing an envelope with the royal seal on his plate.

Wolf smiled as he recognized his friend Marie's handwriting. He had been feeling a bit lonely and useless at the palace, and it was nice to be remembered by a friend. Dear old Marie, as constant and thoughtful as ever.

My dearest Pup,

Marie had written,

You must think I am so rude to have ignored you for so long. Please forgive me by meeting me for a picnic this afternoon at our usual spot.
Your loving friend, Marie.

"Another game of cricket today," Leo said as he attacked his plate of roasted tomatoes, bacon rashers, creamy spinach quiche and a buttery croissant. A traditional Franco-English breakfast.

"Can't, I've got plans," Wolf said, whistling as he scribbled an enthusiastic acceptance on her note.

Be there with bells on!
Love, your own Wolf.

Leo chewed on his croissant. Bits of pastry clung to his lips. "Plans? With whom? Don't tell me—is it the lovely 'Lady' Marianne from last night? You did seem awful cozy with a few of her dancing girls, eh?"

If "cozy" meant he'd passed out on the floor while they tried to revive him, then sure, Wolf thought. Even he was getting tired of his undeserved reputation.

It's from your future wife, he wanted to tell his brother, but he didn't. He had a feeling Leo had not been, nor would ever be, invited to the roof. "Make the usual excuses for me, would you?" Wolf asked.

Leo grunted and turned back to his paper. "Suit yourself. But don't make plans for the weekend—we're off to Chatham for a hunting party."

"Isn't it a bit early in the season for grouse?"

"Maybe, but I asked him to open it up and he said yes." Leo smiled.

"Of course." Wolf nodded. It wasn't that he was jealous of Leopold—that would be like being jealous of the sun. One did not wonder why the sun shone in the sky; one just accepted it as a fact of life. In truth, Wolf idolized his big brother, as everyone did.

"Hey," Leo called. He tossed Wolf a black object.

"What is it?" he asked, catching the small velvet pouch, although he could already tell what was inside. It brought a smile to his face.

"Your lucky dice. Thought you'd want them."

He did want them. He couldn't risk an underground sparring club for fear of being caught out. It was too close to court, and could potentially harm his brother's chances of marrying the princess. Surely the queen would not look kindly on a bruiser as a sort-of-son-in-law. He had been missing home and wishing he had remembered to pack his lucky dice with him so he could maybe find a game or two, hit the tables, try his luck. He thanked his brother. That was the thing. Leo might be a pig to the ladies, but he was a mate.

With a little help from one of the pages, Wolf remembered how to get to the roof through the secret passageways, hidden doors, and hallways he and Marie had discovered as children. It had been their little secret when the four of them used to play together, although Leo never really joined in the games. And what was the name of the other girl, Marie's friend? The red-haired magician's girl. He couldn't remember. She'd been more interested in Leo than in hanging out with Wolf and Marie. When Wolf was young—six, eight at the most—he'd found the hidden doors. He'd noticed something odd about one of the walls in the east wing. One of the wood panels looked slightly askew, and when he touched the surface, it moved. It was not a wall at all, but a door that had been left ajar.

Now, Wolf approached one such paneled wall, pressed against its edge, and felt the wood bend slightly inward as a spring compressed. The panel nudged aside a little. He wrapped his fingers around the edge and tugged it open. He smiled as he slipped inside the passage and pulled the door closed behind him.

It was dark inside the tunnel, but Wolf found the bronze rail that ran through the entire maze, making it navigable. Marie always said to keep turning right if he got lost. He followed the path and wound quickly around corners and up stairs. The passage had been built behind the backs of closets and bedrooms. It ran above dropped ceilings, and alongside stairs. He suspected the passages had a variety of uses; pinpricks in the walls made it possible to eavesdrop on the occupants of many of the palace rooms. Cool air rushed across his face as he passed one of the tiny apertures. A narrow winding stair led him up one floor, then another. The air grew hotter as he ascended. There was no ventilation in the passages. Mildew and rot filled his nose.

The air cleared when he reached the top of the stairs, which were dimly lit with blue light where an open hatch awaited. Ah, so Marie had used the old way too, he thought. He stepped through the roof hatch and into the sunlight to find the princess at their usual spot, as promised.

He and Marie were called "friends of the blanket," for they had known each other since birth. The story went that as babies, their nurses had placed them in the same crib. He supposed they would all soon be family now, once the marriage was settled; but back then, years ago, when he was just a young pugnacious boy and she was a sickly little girl, they had been friends.

Marie was sitting on a checked cloth with a picnic laid out with a few of his favorite things. His spirits lifted to discover she remembered the old days as well—the picnic was set with their favorites. Peach pie, a pitcher of cold lemonade, bacon butties, French cheese, a bar of chocolate. She was alone except for a member of the Queen's Guard, a rough young man who gave Wolf a stern look as he approached, as if the soldier would have no trouble pitching him off the roof if he tried anything. Wolf wanted to tell him to relax, he was a friend, not an enemy. The war was over, wasn't it?

"Dog droppings!" Marie said, looking pleased when she saw him.

"Helmet head!" he said, pulling her hat down over her eyes and making her giggle. He was the only one who could call her that, because she knew he meant it fondly. When she'd worn a helmet, he had drawn lions and bears on it, the symbols of their houses. "Here," he said, offering her a bouquet of red and pink wildflowers that he had ordered from the shop that morning. They were her favorite kind, and she lamented that the palace gardener would not cultivate them, dismissing them as common and weed-like.

He flopped on the blanket and helped himself to a sandwich. He was glad to see her looking better. The last time they had seen each other was four years ago, right before the empire had declared war on his father's kingdom. She had been just a girl then, but now she was practically a married lady, and he was still . . . well, he was still a brawler. Maybe not much had changed after all. Marie was thin and pale as usual, but she had a flush in her cheeks, and her eyes were bright. She was wearing a pretty white linen dress, and her hair was dark and loose under her white hat. She looked enchanting, like a girl from a painting, and he told her so.

"You're too kind," she said. "And you of all people don't have to blow kisses to me, you know. I've heard what you've been up to." She shook her head and adopted a stern tone. "Too many nights at private clubs! How much debt have you racked up this time? How many hearts have you broken?"

"It's good to see you too, I missed your scolding," he laughed. From the roof they could see all of London, all the new development and construction, the city expanding in all directions. They did not speak of the war, or their long separation. Instead they talked about books and music, like they always did, and their plans after the season was over. Marie thought she would be going to Versailles as usual for the fall, but she did not know. So many things were changing so fast, and she was uncertain if Leo would uphold the usual traditions once they were wed. She thought they might set up house in a wing at Kensington, where her mother had lived as a girl.

"So you really mean to marry my big brother at the end of the season?" he asked lightly, taking a big bite of peach pie.

"I don't have a choice, do I?"

"No," he sighed, "I suppose not. None of us do. I'm sure Father will tell me who I'm supposed to marry soon enough." He stretched his legs lazily and let out a little burp. Marie was like family—not quite a sister, but a distant cousin. They shared a great-grandmother or two somewhere up the line.

"Well, you *are* a second son, so perhaps it doesn't matter so much who you marry," she teased.

"Thanks for reminding me," he growled, pitching crumbs toward the pigeons that had gathered at a discreet distance from their picnic.

"Why so gloomy? Have you met someone and had your heart stolen, for once?" she asked. When he did not answer, she laughed. "Ah! So there is a girl!"

He shrugged, even as his thoughts wandered to the girl on the boat. How did Marie know he was thinking of that girl? Marie had always been too smart for her own good. "I suppose I have met someone," he allowed.

"What happened?" she asked, pulling her knees up to her chin under her skirts and regarding him thoughtfully.

"I asked her to marry me." He grinned.

"Wolfie!" she gasped and rapped his knee with her fan. "What would Oswald say!"

"He would whip me like when I was a kid, I suppose."

"Well, I'm sure you didn't mean it," she said with a laugh, but when she saw his face her tone changed. "Darling! What happened?"

He hung his head. His proposal had been sincere, but he shrugged as if it were nothing, as if he asked girls to marry him every day.

"She said no," he sighed.

"That silly girl," Marie said angrily. "Why on earth did she refuse you?"

"Oh, I can imagine there are many reasons." He frowned. The rejection had stung more than he'd expected. If only she had said yes—and she had been so close to it, he could tell. At that moment, he'd felt as if he were standing at a cross-roads, that his destiny could change on a whim—on her word. He would have run away with her if she had accepted him. And what he wanted more than anything in the world was someone to run away with, he realized at that moment—to be someone else, rather than second-in-line to the throne. It was not to be, and his face darkened gloomily.

Marie returned a hand to his knee and shook it back and forth, as if to shake him out of his terrible mood. "You'll find another girl. There's always another girl."

He put a hand on top of hers and grinned. "Maybe I

already have found one," he teased. He liked teasing Marie; she got so mad at him. It was fun.

She tossed a croissant at him. "Now you're the one being silly."

They ate the rest of their meal in companionable silence, until Marie spoke again. This time, her tone was not teasing, but serious. "Isabelle dissolved her hold on Leo the other day. She didn't look very happy when she signed the papers. Wolfie, tell me the truth. Are Leo and Isabelle truly in love, as everyone says? She is so very pretty."

"If you like vipers," he said. "She has nothing on you, my dear. Do not worry."

She sighed. "I always thought Leo would marry a great girl."

"He is," Wolf said, turning to her in surprise. "Don't be so hard on yourself! My brother is a very lucky man, he always has been." He meant it. Marie would be a good wife to Leo: kind, devoted, helpful, smart. Leo was a great man—generous with his subjects, a forward-thinking statesman, a formidable opponent on the battlefield, a hero to his men—but he had none of the qualities in a person that made life bearable, even—dare he think it?—happy. "You are an absolutely remarkable girl," Wolf said, looking into her fair gray eyes with deep sincerity.

"Why, thank you, kind sir," she said, looking pleased.

"Like I said, I am just being honest," he said. "Yes, absolutely remarkable—you must be the only girl in the empire who isn't in love with my brother. Why is that, do you think?"

"I'm immune to his charm?" she laughed.

"Mmm," Wolf said thoughtfully. She'd drawn the short stick in the bargain, truly. She was a princess, however; she understood the way the world worked. Love was not a priority for the likes of them—it was a luxury they could not afford. Perhaps she would find a way to make peace with the marriage.

"Oh well. At least now we'll see each other more often," she said, brightening.

"Count on it. Every Christmas and Easter at least." He raised a champagne glass and clinked it against hers. "You'll never get rid of me at your table."

"Princess? It's time to take your tonic," her soldier said, looking intently at Marie.

Wolf raised an eyebrow. There was something just a bit proprietary and familiar in that man's tone . . . but he supposed someone who was with Marie day and night would naturally feel that way about her.

Marie nodded. "Yes, thank you, Corporal."

"You're welcome, Your Highness."

"Protective chap, isn't he?" Wolf asked, as the soldier went back to his respectful distance. "He doesn't look like a city boy—where's he from?"

"His family's from the north—Ayrshire, I think," Marie said, blushing unexpectedly.

Wolf squinted at the soldier and saw a meaningful glance

pass between him and his friend. Ah. So Marie was in love as well. Wolf mused on how he felt about that. He felt a little uncomfortable, sure, and more than a little pained for her. He hoped it was mere infatuation, for her sake. He could not imagine Leo would stand for being made a cuckold. His brother would expect his wife to remain faithful, even if he was not. If Marie knew what was good for her, she would put this young soldier aside soon enough. Or not. The wags did say that Wolf closely resembled a dashing Bavarian knight who had served his mother. Not that it had ever mattered. Not that his father, stodgy King Frederick, had ever shown any indication of listening to vicious rumors.

Wolf was the second son. He would never inherit the throne. In a way, it would never matter who his father was.

Not with Leo around.

· 18 ·

Changing
OF THE GUARD

*I*n the weeks since Marie had first been introduced to Leo, since that first abrupt conversation, things had not progressed nor developed for the better. Now that the season was truly upon them, with the royal ball imminent, the two of them had to spend a lot more time together to move the courtship along. The prince was just as charming and sparkling as ever, and although it seemed every girl at court had lost her heart to him, Marie felt as indifferent as before. Was there something wrong with her? Why did she not find him handsome? Or even humorous? While everyone at court praised his good looks and rapier-sharp wit, she continued to find him false and dull.

Even Aelwyn thought she was being too harsh on him. The sorceress had taken to joining Marie at meals. Their old friendship was renewed over many glasses of mulberry wine, and the sense that they wanted to cling to each other as everything changed around them. Aelwyn would soon bond to the sisterhood, and Marie to Leopold. Aelwyn urged her to try and accept her fate, as she had. It was a running joke between them that Leopold was going to marry the wrong girl. If only it was Aelwyn who was the princess . . . if only . . .

Try as she might, Marie could not soften her feelings toward him—could not find a semblance even to her dear friend, Wolf. When she looked at Leo, she saw darkness and despair, a miserable gray future in which she was shackled to him for the rest of her life.

That evening she was suffering through another long and ponderous state dinner in which the health of both nations was toasted, along with the health of the monarchs and the young royals. She sat with Leo on one side and a rather entertaining young man on the other. He was one of the princes from Spain, as London was now full to bursting with the glamorous, young, and titled who had come to the city for the season.

When dinner was over and the servants had cleared the table, it was time for the ladies to depart for the drawing room, leaving the gentlemen at the table to their cigars and brandy. Leo came to her chair to bow and kiss her hand. "Don't," she said.

"Excuse me, my lady?" Leo said, surprised. He looked

uncertain as to whether or not to take her hand, now that she was holding it up in a "stop" signal.

Don't touch me. Don't tell me how beautiful my eyes are, how soft my hair is, how you love to hear my voice. Don't. Don't pretend you are falling in love with me. I know you are lying, and every word you say hurts even more. Let us just be friends, if we can start there. Can't we? Can't we at least be friends? Get to know each other a little? Before the wedding, and the bedding, when I will have to take you as my lord and husband?

But all she said was "Don't." Her eyes dropped, and her hand fell to her lap as well.

"You are tired, my dear," he said, and patted the back of her chair instead of any part of her. At least he had divined that much.

"Good night," she murmured.

He bowed and waited as she stood, following the ladies into the drawing room. Once inside, she took a cordial and downed it in one gulp. Aelwyn raised her eyebrows, but she did not say anything to her friend. Marie played one hand of bridge, listening to the idle chat and speculation about the upcoming royal ball. "I heard the sisterhood is working on a charm spell—that it will be like winter inside the palace!" one said.

"Oooh, I hope it doesn't get too cold!" another gushed.

"I do! Mama said I could wear the white mink!"

Marie smiled at them benevolently. She, too, loved the

London Season. As a child, she had been enamored of the glamour and magnificence of the legendary Bal du Drap d'Or. During her debut year, she had not taken a particular affinity to any of the young men who had come courting, and had been thankful her mother had not pushed her to marry any of them. But the time had come now, and the whole city was buzzing with her prospective engagement. The ladies were all gossiping, talking about her as if she weren't there.

When she felt she had stayed long enough to be polite, she excused herself from their company. She went through the elaborate bowing and curtsying ritual with the queen, and was about to take her leave for the evening when her mother stopped her.

"Marie," Eleanor said, and her face was hesitant.

"Yes, Mother?" Then she noticed her mother was close to tears; her eyes were shining.

"I just want you to know that I am very proud of you, my girl," Eleanor said, her voice trembling. "I know you think I am hard on you, but it is only because I need to prepare you for your future—for the day when you will reign with your husband over our people."

Marie started. Her mother had never spoken to her like this before. She felt a wave of tenderness for her. If only Eleanor showed her true face to her more often . . . if only she allowed her daughter into her intimate conversations, into her plans with the Merlin. But it was almost too late.

She bowed and said good night, and the queen dismissed

her. Finally, she was alone in the corridor with Gill, who was to walk her back to her rooms.

"Thank God that's done," she said, stomping down the hallway. She shook her hair out of its tight braids as if she were shaking Leo out of her life. "If he tells me again how my eyes look like starlight, I swear I am going to have him hexed," she muttered.

"He could be sincere, you know," Gill said, giving her a sidelong glance. "You're far too hard on the chap. Don't give him an inch. You're much nicer to his brother."

"Wolf is my friend. Leo's a fraud, and you know it," she said. "I'm not a fool, Gill. I know love when I see it."

There was a strange silence. She noticed he did not say anything, but instead blushed to the roots of his fair hair. She felt her heart ache painfully at that moment. But no. Gill had always treated her as a friend, nothing more . . . had never given her any hope that he returned her feelings. He couldn't even hold her properly when they had practiced the Lovers' Waltz the other day.

They arrived at her apartments. He held the door open for her.

"Don't you want to come in, for a change?" she asked. "And have tea, and read stories, as usual? I miss you, you know. You told me we would always be friends. . . ." She tried not to sound whiny, and failed.

His open face crumpled. "I would like nothing more, Princess. Especially since . . ." He shook his head.

She was alarmed by the morose tone in his voice. "Especially since what?"

"After the ball, when you are formally engaged to the prince . . . I have been told I will no longer be needed at your service."

"No longer needed? Why?" she asked.

"You will be the responsibility of the Prussian court, and their soldiers will be in charge of your protection."

"What on earth? Are they insane? You're part of the Queen's Guard! Does Mama know?"

"Yes. I gather she and the Merlin don't like it too much, but the Prussians will be offended if they are rebuffed in this matter. They are quite insistent upon it."

"But this is still my home—and the Queen's Guard is our tradition—they cannot do this!"

"My captain tells me that it is a sign of faith. Of peace between the two nations."

"Gill—"

"Don't fear. I don't think the queen would agree to it unless she and the Merlin knew your safety was secure."

"So after next week, I shall never see you again?"

"Surely not?" He smiled. "I will visit the palace sometimes, and you can wave to me from the royal carriage."

How could he be so casual about their coming separation? Why were they taking him away from her? Then she realized. It was because *they knew how she felt about him*. They had noticed that she had been gloomy for weeks. Hardly acting like a girl in love, she was the only girl in the kingdom who did not find Prince Leopold the most fetching prince of all time.

Leopold had said something very pointed the day of his arrival. *You seem very attached to your guard.* The Prussians were worried about scandal, the same scandal that had haunted their very own queen—a royal queen and her loyal guard, fanning the subsequent rumors about a bastard son. They had determined the secret recesses of her heart, even if she herself had never told the boy who held it what she felt for him.

It was Gill's turn to bow. "Good night, Marie. See you around, eh?"

But Marie would not let him go so easily. She had to say something she had kept from him for so long. She had to be brave: she had to speak her mind and her heart. "Gill, listen, they know how I feel about you," she said. "And so they want to take you away."

"What do you mean?"

"You know how I feel about you—don't you?" she asked quietly, so quietly that she was afraid he could hear how loud her heart was pounding in her chest.

Gill looked around nervously, even if there was no one in the corridor. "What are you saying?" He looked so pale and troubled that she thought she would lose the nerve to tell him how she truly felt. But she had no time. They were taking him away soon. If she did not speak now, she might never have the chance to tell him . . . and she had to tell him, it was killing her. She had to tell him—before it was too late.

She looked into his eyes and took his hands—they were so large and rough compared to her small ones. "I can't imagine life without you."

Gill looked askance. She felt her heart drop into her stomach. "Don't talk like that, Marie. It's not safe," he said. "Whatever you feel about me—it's just friendship, nothing more."

She blinked her eyes. "I knew you would say that. I know you didn't feel the same way . . . you can't even dance with me without cringing, but I had to say it, I wanted you to know before . . . *before*. It's all right. I'm sorry, I'm sorry," she said, trying not to sob. She wiped her eyes angrily. Of course he did not feel the same way about her. Who could love her? She was so plain and dull and sickly, and he was so wonderful, and there were many girls—so many prettier, more deserving girls—that he could want. That he did want, she was sure.

"Wait!" he said, holding her hands tightly. "Why are you crying?"

"It's nothing—"

"You cannot think—you cannot mean—is it because you think I don't feel the same way? Is that it?"

She nodded, unable to look at him. Her heart was so open and vulnerable at that moment, and she wanted to take it back so badly, wanted to wrap it up and put it back in the locked trunk where it belonged. She should have never said anything to him; it was stupid of her to think, to hope, that he would feel for her what she felt for him. "You are right—we are only friends . . . of course . . . of course you don't feel the same. . . ."

Still holding her hands in his, he pressed his head against hers, forced her to look him in the eye. "Stop telling me what I feel. Stop it. You have no idea what I feel. All I do is feel. *I feel so much for you*, it's destroying me. It's why I had to leave, I had to go away and I couldn't answer your letters," he said fiercely. He was angry now, his eyes wild, and she was a little frightened of him. But all the same, she felt a sudden, sharp happiness rise in her heart. "You have everything wrong. I don't think of you as a friend," he said.

"You don't?"

"No—Marie—I don't think of you as a friend at all—" And his face was so intense, almost red, and he was staring at her so intently, and his face was so close to hers, and she closed her eyes, and then—and then he kissed her. And he kissed her again, and it was sweeter than she could have hoped, could have dreamed—and he was kissing her, and it was like her dreams were coming true all in one moment. And she kissed him back and forgot to worry, forgot who or where she was, and it only mattered that he had his lips on hers.

"Gill," she breathed, and he began to kiss her neck and press her against his body.

"Marie, my Marie," he said, his voice strangled, wretched. "How could you believe that I didn't feel the same for you, when all I do is think of you? It's why I had to get away—because being with you, but not being able to be with you . . . I couldn't take it anymore."

"Oh, Gill . . ." she breathed, and her voice was a woman's voice, full of promise and seduction.

"But it doesn't matter what we feel for each other. We can't do this. I'm a soldier, your servant . . . and you are the princess."

"But I don't want to be." She held tightly to him. Her hands were around his neck and his back, his entwined in her hair, the two of them so close to each other she could feel his heart beating in time with hers.

"Don't say that. You don't mean it. You can't. You're making this harder than it has to be," he said, and his voice was full of raw despair. "It was wrong of me to kiss you."

"Listen to me," she said.

He shook his head. "No. I won't let you do this. I won't let you throw your future away."

"Then you will let me marry him, then? And live a life where I will never know love?" she said bitterly.

He crumbled at that. "Marie," he said. "Hush." His hand was on her lips, and princess or no, he kissed her again, and she felt alight with love, and she knew that there was no turning back now.

He kissed and kissed her, and he pushed the door open so that they tumbled into the room, alone, and he kicked the door closed, and they fell on the floor, and still they kissed as if they could not stop. She smiled, feeling warm and beautiful and protected in his strong arms. "You were right and I was wrong."

"I never knew you felt the same," he said as he leaned over her, his face full of love.

She arched an eyebrow, feeling coquettish all of a sudden. "Truly?"

He blushed and kissed her softly again. "I hoped. I hoped with all of my heart. But I did not want to take advantage of my position."

"What position?"

"I saved your life; I am with you every day, you are my dearest friend. Maybe you only think you love me because you are grateful to me," he admitted.

"Who says I love you?" she teased.

He turned scarlet. She put him out of his misery, pulling him down to her by the soldier's chain he wore around his neck.

"Maybe we should have done this earlier," he murmured.

"Mmm." She nodded. "If we had, we would have had so much more time." She liked the heaviness of his body on hers, but also the way he didn't rest all of his weight on her—as if she were delicate, and made of porcelain, a china doll he was afraid of crushing or hurting. He was so strong and yet so gentle. "I don't want to let go."

"Neither do I," he murmured.

"Then let's not. Let's not let go." She kissed him again.

He stared at her.

"You are everything I want," she told him. "The only thing."

"I have never wanted anything else," he said.

"Then we shall have what we want," Marie said decisively, propping herself up on her elbows, her forehead scrunched in concentration. She was thinking of options, obstacles, a way out, a way forward. "We don't have much time."

"No, we don't," he agreed in a mournful tone. "We don't have a lot of time together. . . ."

She shook her head. "No, that's not what I meant."

"Time for what, then?"

Her eyes were blazing. An onlooker would have been surprised to see the princess in such a state, sprawled on the floor: her hair a mess, her eyes bright, cheeks flushed. She looked like Eleanor in one of her many portraits, the painting where her mother looked like a warrior on the eve of battle, ready for blood. "Time to change the future."

· 19 ·

CONSOLATIONS

laridge's figured highly in Ronan's imagination of London high society, and it did not disappoint. While pollution had turned the once-red bricks of London's best buildings gray, Claridge's façade sparkled in the sun. There was no wind on the street and the air was still, but the flags above the entry billowed slowly, their folds animated and graceful. Ivy graced a cast-iron awning, milk-white flowers dotting the foliage. Their white petals winked open and shut as she approached. Magic, Ronan thought. How wonderful, and how utterly luxurious it was to use such a power to make things look nice.

The hotel had been highly recommended by Lady Grosvernor, and Ronan thought she recognized a few titled and noble patrons in the hushed room. However, knowing what had happened to their grand staterooms on the ship, she was fully prepared to be booked into the maids' rooms when they checked in. Sure enough, the rooms were as small as could be, with a view of the wall next door.

Still, it was wonderful to finally be in London. Ronan spent an invigorating week taking in the sights and visiting museums. She had left her card with Lady Grosvernor, but the grand doyenne had still not returned her call. Ronan tried not to be put out, but without her patron, she had no entrance to any of the fancy parties and dinners that were swirling around her. She hoped the lady would call on her soon.

The next afternoon, Ronan was sitting in the lobby when she noticed Sigrid Van Owen stomping down the staircase, haranguing the army of footmen who strove to keep up with her while carrying all of her luggage. Whitney was hurrying after her mother, looking abashed and apologetic. She saw Ronan and gave her a hapless shrug.

Ronan walked over to her friend. "What happened?" she asked. "Are you leaving?" She watched as the great Mrs. Van Owen swept out of the lobby and into a hansom cab.

Whitney crinkled her nose. "We can't stay. We just got a letter from the duchess. Apparently she lied about everything, just to get more money from Papa. There was no invitation for the queen's luncheon at all, and the ball is completely out of the question, since it's a special year with the princess announcing her engagement. Mother is furious and mortified—says she won't stay the season if we can't go to anything except a few little teas and dances at minor houses. We're to leave for Italy immediately. She says she'll take an Italian count if she can't get me an empire peerage."

"Oh Whitney, I'm so sorry!"

Whitney laughed. "Me too—all my nice things, wasted!"

"Can't you wear them in Italy?"

"Not a one. We're going to be doing a Grand Tour, so all I'll be wearing are practical clothes and walking shoes."

"Pity," Ronan sighed.

Her friend agreed. "It's such a waste of a wardrobe. And I was *so* looking forward to it, especially—well, you know!" She looked at Ronan. "Speaking of, what are you wearing to the ball? It must be fabulous!"

"Oh, me—" Ronan said. "You saw what I wore to dinner the last night on the ship? That one." It was a serviceable dress, a nice plum color trimmed with lace—not made in the latest style, of course, and no glimmer on it at all to enhance its beauty. But it was the nicest thing she had; the Paris knockoffs were stiff to the touch, and didn't fit well. She tried to put a positive spin on things. "Mother wore it when she was presented at court, so it's a family tradition. It's a sentimental choice."

Whitney looked disappointed. "Oh, of course. I understand. But still, it's a bit out of date, isn't it?"

Ronan turned red and tried to protest—but Whitney suddenly brightened. "Listen, take my wardrobe for the season! I don't need it!"

"Excuse me? I couldn't possibly—!"

But Whitney wasn't finished. "And you might as well use our rooms too. I'm sure your rooms are nice, but Mother booked the royal suite—best room in the house—and it's paid for already. Can't let the whole thing go to waste. It's booked for the whole season. Mother won't care. She's ready to buy the whole stinking town, but our money's not worth anything here, apparently. Hopefully we'll have better luck on the Continent."

"You're giving me your dress?"

"Not just the dress, everything! Didn't you hear me? The whole caboodle! I'll have the bellman bring it up to the rooms. It's all wrong for Italy, I'll have to get a whole new set," Whitney said, perking up at the thought of new purchases. "I mean, wear your mom's clothes if you want, of course, but just in case you change your mind, someone should wear this wardrobe."

But Ronan shook her head. "Whitney—you're being much too kind. There is no need. I can wear my old dress, and I brought my own clothes."

"No I'm not, I'm not being kind, just angry they're such snobs. Thinking we Americans aren't good enough. But you'll show them, won't you, Ronan? Show them we're just as good as any of them. Make a splash, will you?" she said, as the footman came scurrying back to tell her that her mother was waiting impatiently. "Oi!" she called to the scandalized hotel clerk. "This is my friend Ronan Astor—she's to stay at our rooms. And bring my trunks back up, while you're at it!"

"Whitney! Stop! I can't possibly accept all this."

"Yes you can! You can treat next time we're in Paris—ooh, it'll be your turn!" she said merrily. "It will give us an excuse to get together again—you're so much fun! We'll stay at the Ritz! Okay?"

"I . . ." Ronan felt faint, not knowing how to tell Whitney she could not possibly return the favor.

"It's done!" Whitney said. "Paris in the spring is lovely!"

Ronan stopped fighting. Why was she arguing in the first place? Pride? But what was pride, compared to a fabulous wardrobe and the best room in the hotel? "Well, all right, as long as you insist."

"I insist." Whitney kissed her on both cheeks in a breathless rush. "Knock 'em dead. I'll send postcards from Florence. Hopefully the Tintorettos are worth it."

The royal suite was aptly named, sprawling over the entire top floor. Its walls were covered with sumptuous velvet, while delicate silk curtains kept out the worst of the afternoon sun. Whitney's trunks were stacked neatly in rows, ready to be opened; ready for the staff to do their work. Ronan's heels made a sharp click as she entered the room. The floor was mahogany, shipped from West Africa, dark amber swirls with lighter areas in the heartwood. She kicked off her shoes and removed her hat while Vera gushed at the expanse of luxury. The smell of rosemary and lilac pervaded the air; clusters of flowers were arranged on every table. Through the archway was the bedroom, where the enormous bed was set with three mattresses, so high that it required a small stair for access. She wondered what would happen if she woke up during the night, or if she needed to exit the bed quickly. Would she fall?

There was a roaring fireplace across from the bed, and a pair of armoires flanked the hearth. In the room's center, below a candle-lit pendant, arranged upon a brightly woven rug (most likely Tibetan) was a table chess set. On either side of it was a silk upholstered chair. She sat on one of the chairs and picked up a chess piece at random. Turning it over in her hand, she saw it was the queen. She smiled.

However did she land so many wonderful things? First the luxurious suite on the ship, and now the best room in the best hotel in London. Ronan had been prepared to scrape by on nothing for the season, but so far it was as if everything had been handed to her on a royal platter. She was made for this life. Providence was shining down on her, and she was glad she had turned down "Heath." She could not live any other way but in the best way possible.

When Lady Grosvernor arrived that afternoon to call on her, finally, she insisted Ronan call her "Aunt Constance" and nodded approvingly at the pretty lilac gown she was wearing. "I just ordered the same dress in peach for my Melisande," she told her over buttered scones.

Whitney's wardrobe was even better than Ronan could have dreamed. It was full of the prettiest day dresses and glamorous evening gowns, made of gossamer silks and satins softer than butterfly wings; suede gloves lined with fur; and a full riding outfit, with gleaming black boots and a new leather saddle from Hermès. There were hats for Ascot and Covent Garden, as well as nightdresses and robes, a full tray of jewels, and several standing wardrobes that opened to reveal shoe closets. There was one trunk that was bigger than all the others, simply marked DO NOT OPEN UNTIL ROYAL BALL and Vera said it was probably because it had some deep magic in it. The two of them were beside themselves in anticipation to see what it looked like, and had to restrain themselves from opening it immediately. Ronan had sent her own shabby trousseau down to storage, but she did not share that with her guest.

Ronan was glad to find that this "old friend of the family" (whom she had actually never met) was a woman her mother's age, with a warm and friendly demeanor. She was not at all like the frosty English ladies who had raised their eyebrows at her on the ship. Lady Constance had a charming way about her, with her bright dark eyes and neat dark hair. "You are such a great beauty, like your mother," she said.

"Thank you," Ronan said simply.

"Your mother and father and I had such a wonderful time during our first season," Lady Constance sighed, as if remembering. "Oh, to be young again."

Ronan took a sip of her tea. "I've heard," she murmured, thinking of her mother's old stories.

"And do you find the rooms to your liking?" Lady Constance asked, after the usual polite chitchat about the weather in New York, the health of Ronan's parents, and the weather in London.

Ronan allowed that the rooms were fine—in fact, the finest in the house. She wasn't sure how much Lady Constance knew about their finances, but she supposed it was better for everyone to think the Astors were on top of the world. The royal suite on the top floor was practically a little mansionette on top of the building, with a full garden terrace and dizzying views of the city. She and Vera had done a little jig after the butler and footmen had left.

"The season doesn't really start until the ball, but there are a few entertainments that you might find amusing. I'm sorry you missed my dinner the other week; we had the prince as our guest," said Lady Constance.

"Leopold?" she asked eagerly. "You hosted the prince?"

"And his brother—what's his name? I can't remember! The prince is so terribly charming! It's a pity you missed it!"

Was I invited? Ronan wanted to ask, but didn't.

"Anyway this week, Lady Warwick—a friend of mine—is having a little dinner, and is looking for fun young people to invite. Would that be something you might be interested in?"

"I'd love that, but I have to check the diary," Ronan allowed, trying to appear nonchalant.

"Wonderful! I will see what I can do, as she's a bit choosy about her guests. I myself have to attend a hunting party this weekend—such a chore. But I will *try* to entreat her to invite you."

For the first time since she arrived in town, with her beautiful dresses and beautiful room at hand, Ronan was able to banish thoughts of the boy on the boat and what he had asked her. It was difficult, but in the face of such bounty it was easier to forget how much she had liked him, and how much she had regretted letting the moment slip away from them. She could not give all this up, could she? Already she was forgetting that "this" was not actually hers to give up, but a gift from the gods themselves. She could not imagine life with someone of lower station, a commoner (forgetting that she herself was without a title)—no matter how handsome or charming the boy had been. This was what she was used to, what she had set off to London for. Once she met a rich little lordling, her life and her family's would be set.

"What is it?" she asked the next morning, when Vera came marching into the room looking like a general who had just vanquished the enemy.

"Your first invitation! Dinner with Lady Warwick in honor of her son, the Viscount Lisle!"

Ronan smiled. She had, as they say, arrived.

· 20 ·

a
FRIEND IN NEED

hen Marie-Victoria and her loyal guard knocked on her door the night before the royal ball, Aelwyn had been dreaming of Avalon. She was back on that magical island, and Viviane was teaching her the ways of magic and the language of the stones. Stones were the foundation of their magic; the mages of Avalon derived their strength and ability from the legendary stones of Avalon. There were stones that granted power, like the one Artucus's sword was buried in, and there were Pandora's cursed stones, which harnessed the power of evil. Avalon mages learned the language of the stones, from onyx, citron, and opal to musgravite, garnet, jade, and more. There were as many stones as there were spells.

In her dream, Aelwyn was holding a ruby in her hand,

using it to direct the fire on the hearth, making it dance and turning it off. But she was not listening to her aunt, not listening to the song from the stone, because she was distracted—too distracted. So the fire burned as it had when she still lived in the palace. An annoyed Viviane stopped the fire before it could rage out of control. Because it was Lanselin's song Aelwyn was singing when she should have been tending the fire—his face she was thinking of, his name on her lips, when they woke her.

"Winnie—Winnie, wake up, I need you."

Aelwyn opened her eyes. For a moment, she was frightened that it was the night of the fire again—Marie twelve years old, her gray eyes so large and wide in her face.

"What is it? What's wrong? Why are you here?" Aelwyn asked, frantically pushing off the blankets. "Is it a fire? A coup? Have rebels found a way to destroy the wards again?"

"No, nothing of that sort," Marie said anxiously, and it was then that Aelwyn noticed that she was holding Gill's hand in hers.

She blinked her eyes and looked from one drawn face to the other. "What is this, Marie?"

"Winnie, you must help us. Please."

When she found out what they wanted her to do, what they were begging her to do, it was as if they had read her mind. They had known, somehow, that she'd wanted this from the beginning—that what they were proposing was exactly what she'd wanted to happen when she arrived at St. James. That Aelwyn Myrddyn had returned from Avalon for the purpose of becoming the princess.

She bade them shut the door, put a kettle to the fire, and poured them each a cup of tea. Quickly she put a spell on the room so no one would hear, but even so, their voices were low, whispered, urgent. What her friend was asking her to do was treason, a betrayal of everything the empire stood for—everything her father had worked hard to secure. Aelwyn worried that maybe even the walls could hear them; that her father would know, somehow, that she was party to this faithlessness.

Marie sat on the edge of the cot, holding her teacup in both hands. She was still wearing the golden gown she had worn for the state dinner, but her hair was wild, and her dress had a rumpled look. Her lips were red and crushed—*kissed raw*, Aelwyn thought. Her friend had been kissing the soldier. They had come to her room after being with each other, she could tell. "I don't want it; I've never wanted it. I just want to be able to go away, to live a small life. To *be* with him," Marie said, looking at Aelwyn pleadingly.

Aelwyn asked if the soldier—Gill—could leave them alone for a while. He nodded and left the room. She looked her friend in the eye. "Do you know what you are asking of me? If I do this for you, we will be traitors to the crown—to the sacred trust between the royal family and the invisible order. My father, the Merlin, would never forgive us, and your mother! The queen—if she knew what you were planning . . . Marie, this is deep magic, a perversion of the way of things, and if we are found out . . ." Aelwyn shuddered.

Marie put her teacup down on the side table. "We will *not* be found out. And if we are, I will go to the gallows for you, for it was my idea all along, and they will believe me. But we will not be caught, my darling Aelwyn. You are the most powerful sorceress since Viviane. You can make this happen. I know you can, and you know you can."

"Marie—I can't—my vows . . ."

"You are but an acolyte. You have not yet said the words that will bind you to the Crown."

She had her there, but still Aelwyn shook her head. It was wrong; it was cowardly of them. They had roles to play, duties to perform, and one's personal desires did not factor into their lives, into this equation. She could not do what her friend was asking. She knew it would be wrong of her—wrong from the beginning—wrong.

"Please. I beg you. Help me be free," Marie said, her voice breaking now. "I cannot marry Leopold. I cannot—he will make me miserable for the rest of my life. . . ."

"But if I do this, what will happen to you—where would you go?"

"I will marry Gill and we will go far away from the empire—to the farthest reaches of the American frontier, maybe, or even farther away. Somewhere we can never be found—where my mother cannot go, where your father cannot find us."

Did Marie know what she was giving up? She would trade a life bound by duty and decorated with privilege for a life as a frontier wife—a simpler life, certainly, but one that was difficult, poor, and hard. Aelwyn had seen the lives of such women in her aunt's crystal glass: their tired faces, their callused hands, the backbreaking work they did every day in the fields and in the home. Marie had never had to work hard in her life. She'd had a difficult upbringing, yes, one marked by illness and indifference, but she did not know the feeling of poverty, of hardship, of hunger pangs gnawing on your dreams; of falling on a coarse and lumpy mattress after a hard day's work. Did this soldier know what he was asking of her? How could he love Marie if he would take her away from the palace, everything she knew and everyone who loved her? How could one man's love equal the love of an empire, a family, a mother, a people? Aelwyn shook her head. She would not consign her friend to such a fate.

"No. I cannot do it," she said. "Go back to your room. Tell him good-bye. You will hate me tonight, but one day you will forgive me. This is not the life that was meant for you, Marie." Aelwyn took Marie's hands in hers, trying to make her understand. This delicate friend of hers, this princess who had been educated in five languages, who quoted literature and spoke of art, who made music and beautiful embroidery—who, more importantly, had compassion for her subjects—would make a wonderful queen. The empire could not afford to lose her, nor could she lose such a friend.

But Marie was adamant. "Just—just try it. Please Aelwyn, use your power for *one* night, tomorrow night only, for the Bal du Drap d'Or. If we are not caught, if they accept you as me, then maybe . . . maybe we can do it forever. But give me one night. Please? I beg of you—one night," Marie implored, and she knelt before Aelwyn with tears in her gray eyes.

And Aelwyn found she could not refuse her friend one night.

· 21 ·

Eligible
BACHELORS

The Warwick dinner turned out to be a relatively small affair, with only twenty at the table. Ronan tried to hide her disappointment at finding only a handful of gentlemen at the party, and consoled herself with the fact that at least she was seated next to two of the most handsome ones there. Lord Stewart, on her right, insisted she call him Perry. To her surprise he was not fat, puffy-nosed, or squat at all. He was tall, slim, elegant, and handsome, and closely resembled a long cigarette on a slim black holder.

"You don't look at all like your picture!" she exclaimed, as the footmen served the first course, a clear consommé dotted with tiny, perfectly square croutons.

"Oh—that hideous thing in Debrett's?" he said with a wicked grin. "That's because we entered the ugliest photographs of strangers we could find! Howlers! D'you know, ladies use it to pick and choose husbands for their girls? Good prank, no?" he asked, picking up his spoon and taking a sip of the savory liquid.

Ronan blushed, as he had hit it right on the nose, but she kept her consternation hidden. "Yes, too funny."

"*We're* not getting married off, are we, Archie?" he said, smiling at the equally handsome lad on *his* right, who had been introduced to Ronan earlier as his beau, the Honorable Archibald Fairfax.

Ronan admired them with an almost jealous longing. They were both so beautiful, it just made sense that they were in love with each other. They were like a pair of twins—two tall, thin, devastatingly handsome twins. The majority of the laws in the empire concerned the governance of magic, and, as in America, there were very few rules concerning personal liberty. Sir Oscar Wilde was a favorite at court, and lived openly with his partner.

"Sorry we're all there is," Perry said. "I assume you were hoping to meet some lords or baronets, but they're all at the hunting party in Chatham before the big ball-o. The prince went down there, so then everyone else wanted to go. Our hostess is a bit miffed at the turnout."

Ah. So that was why she'd been invited to this dinner. She recalled her last-minute invitation, and Lady Constance begging off because she had to attend "this chore of a hunting party." But in truth, it appeared Ronan had been fobbed off onto the lesser event, and tonight's invitation was not so much a social triumph as a social failure. Then there was the dinner Lady Constance had thrown in honor of the prince, to which she had failed to invite Ronan. She wondered how close this friend of the family really was. Ronan understood the hierarchy of parties; her mother had kept lists of guests divided into desirability, back when they'd had the wherewithal to entertain. Still, it pricked a bit to realize one had been dumped into the C-list.

Archie looked up from his glass. "Well, here's one who didn't go out with the dogs. Hullo, Marcus, come and meet this lovely lady from the Americas!"

Marcus Deveraux, Viscount Lisle, was the eldest son of her host, and the guest of honor. While he was nowhere near as pretty as Perry or Archie, he was titled, male, and apparently available. "Hate hunting, can't stand it," he said, wiping his sticky fingers on his jacket before taking her hand.

"Or he wasn't invited," Archie murmured into his champagne glass.

"Can't ride a horse, that one," Perry whispered in her ear. "Keeps falling off. Can't shoot either, unless he means to aim at his foot."

Ronan tried not to laugh. "Nice to meet you, Marcus," she said with what she thought was a flirtatious smile.

He nodded brusquely and stalked off. Ronan tried not to feel too insulted.

"Ignore him, he's got awful manners," Archie said. "It's

why no one's accepted him yet, even though he's gone and proposed to half the girls in London already."

It was a shame the boys had to go off after dinner; she had quite enjoyed their company. Ronan followed the ladies into the drawing room and sat down on one of the flowered couches. A girl around her age took a seat next to her. She was wearing an obviously expensive but somewhat ugly dress, hampered by an abundance of lace and embroidery. Ronan had chosen Whitney's dove-gray silk for the evening, and she wished she had not wasted it on so trivial a party. The real action, it seemed, was at the hunting party down in the country. There was nothing worse than feeling as if life was being lived better somewhere else. Ronan attempted to focus on the positives instead of the letdowns of the evening, but her first foray into the London Season felt a lot more like tinsel than gold.

"Perry's a laugh, isn't he?" asked the girl next to her, whose name she now remembered was Lady Fernanda Something-or-Other.

She nodded eagerly. "He and Archie are hilarious."

"Life of every party. Thank God they have no patience for hunting, or this shindig would be a total bust."

"Oh, it's a very nice party."

"You don't have to lie, it's my mother's," Fernanda said. "I told her no one would come if the prince went down to

Chatham, but she wouldn't listen. Said she had to do something, as Marcus is to make a match this season or she's going to take away his stipend. She's tired of worrying that the estate will go to my third cousin and we'll be turned out on the streets."

"Is there any danger of it?" Ronan asked. She was fuzzy on the rules of titles and inheritance, but had a vague understanding that only the eldest son could inherit everything. The rules were a bit more lax in the Americas, since there were no titles to fight over.

"Always," Fernanda said. "Speaking of weddings, congratulate me—I just found out I'm to be a bridesmaid for the princess."

Ronan was impressed. "You are friends with Marie-Victoria?"

"Never even met the girl! But Daddy's a friend of the Merlin's, so I'm on the list. There are twelve spots—I hear not all of them are taken yet. Perhaps you'll get a nod," she said sagely.

"Me?"

"The Merlin wants all the empire represented. He'll need an American on the carpet, holding up the gown. It'll look good. Diversified," she said. "Maybe calm down those rebels overseas. Bring the Americans closer to the fold."

Ronan nodded; that seemed like a sound proposition. She imagined herself walking on the carpet, holding up a corner of the princess's long train, a demure smile on her lips.

"Where are you staying?" Fernanda asked, taking a handful of nuts from a silver bowl on the table and chewing noisily.

"Claridge's, in the royal suite."

Fernanda nodded approvingly and gave Ronan a long look up and down, taking in her jeweled fan and the spray of yellow diamonds in her hair, along with the aforementioned gray silk. "Is that Worth?" she asked, meaning Ronan's dress. "Mama wouldn't let me have it when we were in Paris. Said it's frightfully expensive. But no expense is too much for you Americans, is it?"

Ronan smiled mysteriously and did not deny it.

"Remind me of your name, darling," her new friend said. "I didn't catch it earlier. You're a friend of Aunt Connie's, aren't you?"

"Ronan Astor," Ronan said proudly. "From New York."

Fernanda clinked her glass against hers. "Well, Ronan, welcome to London. Here's to a fabulous season."

Flying AWAY

After he revealed his plan for their future, Leo continued to call on Isabelle at every possible moment, stealing kisses and demanding other advantages. She had allowed it until last night, when she told him in no uncertain terms that it was over. She would not come to him anymore when he called for her. She was not a dog to be whistled for when its master wanted it.

How low she had sunk, she thought the next evening, remembering his smirk. Leo seemed to believe that nothing would change between them—that Isabelle was merely having a little temper tantrum, and it would soon pass. Her father and mother must have been turning in their graves. Her father Charles always spoke about the glories of their house and their vaunted bloodline, but it was all so long ago. Charles was no

King of France—had never even been a prince of France, but merely a vintner, a farmer, one who was too proud for his own good. He would have spit on the Bal du Drap d'Or. The annual ball commemorated the victory of the English over the French. It was said that the first celebration had gone on for days on a field of cloth-of-gold. There had been jousting tournaments, a carnival, a castle made of gold, banquets and feasts that went on for two weeks; even a legendary drakon and its rydder had performed aerobatics in the sky.

It was the night before the ball, and Isabelle was accompanying Louis-Philippe to one of the minor operas to take her mind off her pain. Her young cousin looked so handsome in his fine new clothes. She was glad that Hugh had sprung for a decent wardrobe for Louis for the season.

Isabelle recalled now that Hugh was called the "Red Duke" as a derisive nickname because it was only through a fluke of the law that he came into the lands and title, as he was a distant relative through a minor line who had lucked into the claim. He was the Red Duke, as in a red herring, a fraud.

If it were not according to Salic law, the title and lands would have rightly belonged to Louis-Philippe, who had grown up in the castle as a child, since his mother was a Valois. Isabelle and Louis had hated him so much—this interloper who came to the castle as their guardian.

So far, Hugh had kept his distance, and had spoken about setting up a match for her, but Isabelle decided she would go as far away as possible after the season. She would be of age by the end of June; she would take the small dowry her parents had been allowed to leave her, and she would make a life of her own. Perhaps she would be a governess, or a teacher. She would willingly choose a hard and humble life, as long as it was an honest one that took her far away from Hugh. It was better than being the prince's mistress.

"Are you ready?" Louis asked, and helped her into her cloak.

She would miss Louis, she thought as she smiled and nodded at him. He would probably want her to stay, but he of all people would understand that she could not. It was too dangerous for her with Hugh around. She would never go back to Orleans, no matter what happened during the London Season.

The opera was not the escape she had thought it would be. It was about a doomed love affair, and in the end the woman killed herself. Wonderful.

"Did you like it?" Louis asked as they left their seats.

"Not particularly," she said. "But the music was nice."

Over at the front, there was a crowd around the prince, who was leaving the royal box. Leopold was in fine form, as usual—wherever he went there was a crowd of admirers hanging on to his every word. He did not look her way, and Isabelle was glad. He was nothing to her, nobody; she wanted nothing to do with him. Her skin crawled at the thought of him. She wanted to dunk herself in a hot bath, and scrub every inch of her skin, everywhere he had touched her.

"Come on," she said to Louis. "Let's go, before we are caught in the rush."

She would stay for the ball and the rest of the season—for as long as Leo had rented the house for her—but afterward, she was going to leave this all behind.

· 23 ·

Time TO SHINE

O n the morning of the royal ball, Ronan woke up earlier than usual. She could not wait to see her dress, and ran to Whitney's trunk, her fingers shaking in anticipation. But Vera was already kneeling by it, her hand on the latch. Ronan felt the urge to shove her aside, but squelched it. "Well, let's see it, then," she said.

"Oh! Ronan, you're here. I was just so excited!" Vera said, as she opened the lid.

Ronan looked over her shoulder as Vera unwrapped the layers of tissue to reveal the most beautiful dress she had ever seen. It was a sheer white silk encrusted with moonstones, silvery gems woven into the very fabric of the dress. "Look, this is for your hair," Vera said, breathless, holding up a slim tiara made of the same stone. "And matching earrings, too!"

"Let's hope it fits," Ronan said, trying to act nonchalant. She left Vera to admire the dress and went to have her toast and tea, dressed for the morning in Whitney's smart riding outfit. After the party at Lady Warwick's, Ronan met Lady Constance at the park for a ride every morning.

Ronan liked the rigor of the season; her mentor was amusing and knowledgeable, and the morning went pleasantly. While she could not help but feel a bit annoyed that Lady Constance had sent her to a lesser party during the hunting weekend, she did not mention it. After all, she had met some truly lovely gentlemen at the Warwick dinner. At the end of the evening, Archie and Perry had declared themselves her guides for the rest of the London Season.

After an invigorating ride through the park, they repaired to a full breakfast back at the hotel. Afterward, they made a few social calls on "prominent ladies that you *must* know in order to secure invitations to the better dances this season." The great ladies were polite enough to Ronan, but she had a feeling that they were assessing her chances against their own daughters', and finding their daughters wanting. More than a few exclaimed at her beauty, and how she was sure to secure a proposal even before the ball had ended. "The pretty ones always do," Lady Whitmore had said with a wrinkle of her nose. Ronan smiled and said nothing, but hoped that they were right. She had not traveled all this way to return to New York without a ring and a title.

As the carriage ushered Ronan back to the hotel, Lady

Constance explained that the presentation at court used to happen early in the afternoon, but now it had been folded into the ball in the evening. A twelve-course dinner would be served first, followed by the formal presentation of guests to the queen, after which the Princess Dauphine would dance the Lovers' Waltz with Prince Leopold to formally announce and celebrate their engagement. A light supper would be presented at midnight, and afterward the dancing would go on until sunrise. Ronan could hardly wait.

At long last, it was time to dress for the ball. Vera brought out the dress, carrying it as if it were a valuable and precious gem, as if she were cradling her firstborn.

Ronan was a little concerned; she was a bit more statuesque than Whitney, who was built a little smaller. But there was no need to worry. The moment she touched the fabric, the dress and the jewels arranged themselves on her as if they were made for her alone. The dress glowed with silvery moonlight, and with her fair coloring and platinum hair, she possessed a striking similarity to the long-lost woodland sylphs who were said to have left this earth.

"You look . . ." Vera had no words.

Ronan felt chills all over her body as she stared at the dress in the mirror. She had never seen herself look more beautiful. It was as if all her dreams were coming true in one moment. Surely, with this dress, she would be able to melt the heart of any lord of her choosing. Vera handed her the ostrich-feathered fan, helped her draw on the lace gloves, and knelt to slip her feet into the sparkling kidskin slippers. Not long after, the butler announced that the Lords Stewart and Fairfax had arrived to escort her to the party.

When she appeared in the lobby, Perry gave her a long wolf-whistle.

"Need a lift, gorgeous? Told you we were your fairy god-fathers," he said. "My, my, the princess is going to face some stiff competition with you in *that*."

"I only have one question," Archie said, after kissing Ronan on both cheeks.

"Yes?"

"Do you think it would look better on me?"

"Shut up, queen. Let's go see the queen," Perry said.

The royal ball was held in the Crystal Palace, a cathedral of glass and steel—a steel skeleton with glass panels. It had originally been built in 1845 for the Annual Exhibition of Scientific Inventions, but that yearly ritual had ceased years ago, by order of the Merlin. Now it was only maintained for the express purpose of hosting this annual event, after the ballroom at St. James had been deemed too small to fit all the courtiers and guests.

A huge, cheering crowd of commoners lined the circular streets leading up to the palace, waiting to catch a glimpse of sparkle and glamour. The open-air carriage ferried the happy trio to the entrance, where gaily-dressed guests—aristocrats, royals, and prominent friends of the empire—disembarked from a line of coaches and hansoms. Ronan was awed by the size, the grandeur. The great hall loomed over the park, over the trees. Its barrel vault stretched a dozen stories into the sky, and the long axis of the ballroom ran nearly a half mile in length.

Through the entry, beneath the great barrel vault, liveried servants stood in long lines, waiting to take coats, hats, and canes, or offering sparkling drinks and platters heaped high with delicacies. Velvet drapes and richly tufted rugs decorated the interior. Oil lamps hung at intervals were akin to stars flickering in the sky. Music echoed from every direction. The long axis stretched from the left to the right, ending with the podium where the queen sat with her court.

Ronan tried to breathe deeply, having found the oxygen was thin at such great heights. She was glad to have the two boys with her, who made fun of everything and cut it all down to size, although she could tell that they too were impressed and awed by the spectacle inside.

Fountains bubbled not with water, but pink clouds. Dancers resembling sculptures, their faces chalk-white, pranced like living marble creatures. The Crystal Palace was too large for a single band of musicians to fill the hall, and so a dozen or more bands were assigned to the task, playing the same tune in a glorious symphony. The room was alive with half-heard conversations, trumpets and strings.

Everyone was so beautiful. Ronan admired a few girls who

were laughing and talking in a huge circle; they were each more beautiful than the last, and they had a ring of admirers around them. "Ah, the Montrose girls, the ducal daughters," Archie said. "Pretty, aren't they?"

"Loud," Perry dismissed.

They walked toward the dinner setting on one side of the hall.

"A lot more magic this year," Perry said, switching the place cards at the table so they could sit together. He did it so deftly, Ronan was certain he had done this many times before. She would have been too afraid to meddle with a seating arrangement, but it was clear Perry had no problem with it.

"Princess is getting married," Archie reminded him.

"No more war." Perry nodded.

"Come on, let's find the champagne," Archie decided.

Ronan followed their lead, still feeling dizzy, although she couldn't help but notice the many admiring glances thrown her way. Their table was one of the farthest from the queen's table at dinner, but it did not matter. She would have her two minutes with the queen when she was presented. Anything more and she would probably have fainted from happiness.

The queen was seated on a throne on the podium. She was flanked by her Merlin and a slew of attendants: white-robed sisters from the Order, and courtiers in their finest plumage.

Ronan had only seen photographs of the queen, and was struck by how they did not do Her Majesty justice. The queen had an otherworldly beauty; her skin was the color of pure alabaster, her red hair fiery and thick. Her gown, a vibrant emerald color, was deep and rich. The crown on her head was enormous, and studded with the largest emeralds and sapphires (green for France, blue for England) Ronan had ever seen. The Merlin was frightening: a somber man in black, with a face like a mask.

"Ronan Elizabeth Astor, of New York," the herald announced.

Ronan stepped in front of the throne and curtsied to the floor, just as she had practiced, her head almost brushing Her Majesty's feet.

"Rise, child," the queen nodded. "What a pretty dress. Moonstones have always been my favorite."

"Thank you, Your Majesty." Ronan held up the edges of her gown tightly. Slowly, as she had practiced, she walked backward, never taking her eyes off the queen.

"Bravo," Perry said when it was done and she was back in their circle. She was trembling from the roots of her fair hair to her fingertips.

"Americans tend to overdo it, don't you think?" a voice said. "Look at that one, she looks like a bank exploded and rained diamonds."

Ronan stopped and turned around to see a beautiful

French girl regarding her with a sullen frown. The girl's dress was understated and elegant, a simple dress of the palest pink; no waist or corset was discernible, as it was cut in the daring new loose style, and she wore her dark hair in a low chignon. She was exquisite and perfect and tiny, and Ronan felt like a lumbering American giant next to her.

"Now, now, Isabelle. Jealousy doesn't flatter you," the boy beside the French girl said. He was dark-haired and strikingly handsome, his hair falling into his bright blue eyes. There was something familiar about him, but Ronan could not place him until he winked—and then—

"You!" Ronan gasped. It was him—Heath—the fighter from the boat—looking even more devastatingly, knee-tremblingly, breath-caught-in-throat-handsome than he did when she had last seen him. A handsome *devil*. What was he doing at the royal ball? He looked dashing in a red coat with a golden sash and epaulets, a ceremonial saber on his hip. Why, he looked every inch a . . . but she couldn't form the word. She blushed to think of their intimate moments together—the way they had lain across that billiards table . . . "Heath!"

The boy smiled. "Cathy."

Isabelle—the French girl who had made the nasty comment about her dress—curled her lip. "You two know each other?"

The boy raised his glass to Ronan. "You could say that." His bright blue eyes danced with mirth.

"We've met," she said faintly.

"Why am I not surprised," Isabelle said, her voice dripping acid. "Wolf has probably 'met' every girl from here to New York." She unleashed her fan with a snap and walked off without saying good-bye. What a rude little wench, Ronan thought. What had she called him—the boy from the boat? Wolf? Was that his name? What kind of a name was that? Wolf? *My family herds sheep,* he had told her. . . .

She stared at him, alarmed. "What are you doing here?"

He shrugged his shoulders and took a sip of his champagne. "My brother's getting married. I have to be here."

"Your brother . . . ?"

He cocked his head to the front of the room, where the herald was about to introduce the royal couple. He couldn't mean . . . ? Who was his brother?

When she turned back to him, to this Wolf, he was gone.

Ronan felt her heart beating painfully. She thought she might have to sit down. With relief she again found Perry and Archie, who had wandered off in search of more drinks. They were in a corner, guzzling champagne and cutting people down to size while cutting a dashing figure in their tails and top hats. Archie was nuzzling Perry's shoulder. "There she is, the most beautiful girl in the room." Perry smiled. "Enjoying yourself, darling?"

"Do you know everyone here?" she asked.

"Pretty much," Perry said. "We do, don't we, Arch?"

Ronan raised her fan so that no one could see her ask,

"Who's he, then?" Her eyes followed the dashing, dark-haired boy in the red coat and gold sash across the room.

"Oh, him?" Archie said. "Congratulations, you have great taste, darling."

"He's yummy," Perry agreed. "I'd let him conquer me any time."

"But who is he?" she hissed. She almost wanted to cry. He was just the guy on the boat. Some fighter. He was nobody. He was an impostor! He didn't belong here. All those hours studying Debrett's! And she had been unable to see past the obvious—that he had never been "kicked out" of the promenade deck; that he was only pretending to be second-class. His hobbies: good wine and champagne. Those shiny gold cuff links. She felt faint as she realized, her grand rooms— the mixed-up tickets—he must have put them in her handbag. Which meant he knew her plight, and it was he who had come to her rescue. Which meant those first-class rooms were his, and that he was rich, then. *Very* rich . . . but who was he? "Please tell me, I beg of you," she said, to her new friends. "Tell me who he is."

Archie stared at her. "You really don't know?"

Ronan shook her head so vigorously that the moonstones in her ears were in danger of falling out.

"That's the prince, you silly girl," Perry said, putting her out of her misery—or more correctly, adding to it.

"Prince? You don't mean . . . Leo? That's Leopold?" she said. Her mind had turned to pudding. He was a prince! And he had asked her—oh dear God—someone should ship her back to New York. She wasn't worthy of the season.

"No, of course that's not Leo. Don't you Americans pay *any* attention at all? That's his younger brother, Wolf." Archie rolled his shoulders as if she were the silliest person he had ever met.

Ronan had to support herself on the wall. He wasn't Leo, but he was a prince all the same! A real prince! She'd had a chance with him . . . he had asked her to marry him, and she had turned him down. Perry handed her another glass of champagne. "Be careful with that one," he said. "He's a hard one to pin down. Don't let him break your heart."

"Yes, he's got quite the reputation with the ladies," added Archie.

"Mmm-hmm," Perry said.

"Does he, now." She pressed her lips together, thinking of those endless hours playing strip billiards. Of course he did. What handsome prince did not, except for Leopold? They were all rakes and playboys. Was he just playing with her, then, proposing to her like that? Or did he do that to all the girls? Suddenly, Ronan wanted nothing more than to slap him for taking advantage of her.

Wolf walked away quickly before he could change his mind. It was *her*, of course. He had seen her the moment Archie and Perry walked in with her. He had been struck by how beautiful she was, how she'd approached the queen with chin held high, even as her shoulders were trembling. It had made him feel protective and gentle toward her all over again, just when he had written her off.

His feelings were in turmoil. He hadn't counted on seeing her so soon after they'd parted—it had only been a week or two. But, of course she was here. What had she said to him? *I am selling myself to the highest bidder.* The Bal du Drap d'Or was the largest and most expensive auction block in town. He was disgusted by the whole enterprise, and disappointed with himself for being attracted to her anyway. He felt angry, but didn't know why; he felt like throwing a punch, and once again wished he were back in the ring, where things were simple. A fight—he needed a fight, needed to feel the rush of adrenaline as his fist made contact with flesh. Maybe he would look for a fight later, even if he had promised Oswald he wouldn't. He had to—there were so many places to have it—all those secret dungeons in the basement. No one would have to know, and he was sure he could scare up a good betting crowd.

"You look like you want to kill somebody," Oswald said, appearing beside him. "Go on and find a girl to chase, would you?"

There's always another girl. Wasn't that what Marie had said? And Marie was smart, the smartest girl he knew, so he would take her advice.

He would dance with all of them, and avoid the girl in the silver dress who looked like a ray of moonlight.

As he walked toward the ballroom, he spotted Leo's familiar golden head bowed low, kissing a girl in the shadows. Isabelle, of course. The two of them were pawing at each other. A last hurrah before the engagement was announced and the dancing began.

Wolf shook his head. His brother was truly brazen and unapologetic. He should know better—what if someone from court saw him? War could be declared again if he embarrassed the queen in this way. On the other hand, he had to hand it to Leo. He didn't let duty get in the way of his fun.

Maybe it was time Wolf did the same.

· 24 ·

Bloom
IS OFF THE ROSE

ure enough, just as she had expected, the minute Isabelle stepped foot inside the Crystal Palace, Leopold pounced. Here he was, all over her at the royal ball, on the night his engagement would be announced. Isabelle pushed him off, balling her hands into fists, and pushed against his chest with all of her might so that Leo finally had to let go of her. She had been struggling against his hold, closing her mouth against his kisses, fighting the urge to scream while he pawed at her chest. "I told you, I don't want this, I never want to see you again," she said, spitting out her words. "Please, leave me alone."

Leo only smirked. "You'll change your mind, *chérie*, you always do. You will be begging for my attention before the night is over. You will be so jealous of Marie-Victoria you won't be able to stand it."

She slapped him as hard as she could, and gasped. She hadn't meant to hit him that hard, but his cheek was red. Her ring had opened his old wound, and the cut on his face was bleeding. "Leave me alone—I am not your toy!" She smoothed her hair and gathered her skirts, but Leo's arm shot out and grabbed her by the wrist.

"I will scream!" she said. "And everyone will know!"

"Everyone will know what?" he asked, his voice soft and amused, even as his hold on her was growing more painful by the moment. She felt as if he could break her bones in half, one by one. She felt like a caged bird, struggling and flapping her wings as the cat pounced. A bird, a mouse; always she felt like an animal around him, and now she wondered, was it her or him who made her feel this way?

"Everyone will know the truth about you—that you take advantage of women! That you are not the hero everyone claims you are!"

"Go ahead," he whispered in her ear, his voice smooth and silky and dangerous. "Tell them. See who they believe— their beloved future king, or you, a descendant of a failed house."

"I hate you," she said. "I hate you so much. I curse you with any power left in our bloodline. I curse the rest of your days. May your light turn to ashes, and everything you hold dear disappear from this earth." She had no idea where the words came from, but it was something her mother used to say when she spoke of the British royal family.

"Hard words, my lady," he said. "But your threats are emptier than a beggar's cup. I will see you on my wedding night."

"I will see you in Hell," she vowed as she twisted away from him. She pushed the curtains aside and stepped back into the party. She hadn't taken one step when someone accosted her.

"Isabelle, what is the matter? I have been looking for you—are you all right?"

For a moment she was scared that Leo had returned to rough her up again, and she cringed away, but it was only her cousin Louis. He was wearing the Valois medals on his gold-trimmed jacket, and he looked so handsome and French that even though they had arrived at the ball together, she fell upon him as if she had not seen him in days. "Louis!" she said, falling into his arms and hugging him tightly. "Thank God! Do I look okay? I tripped, my heel caught on something," she said to explain her disordered appearance. She held on to his arm and leaned on him heavily. She hadn't realized how off-balance she was until now.

"How are you? Are you sure you can go through with this? We can go home, you know—just say the word." Louis had been offering his sympathy since she had signed the papers. He thought she was still in love with Leo.

She smiled thinly. A lock of hair fell onto her cheek, and she tucked it back behind her ear. "No, actually I pity the princess." Now that she knew exactly what kind of a man Leopold was, she was sorry for Marie-Victoria. Isabelle herself still felt confused about the love she had felt for him—was any of it real? Just a few months ago she would have done anything for him, and she had let *him* do anything he wanted to her . . . how had everything changed so quickly?

Her cousin stared at her. "You are different today."

"It is like I was sleepwalking, and finally I am awake," she said slowly. It was as if a veil had been lifted, and she could see Leo for what he was. He was not even as handsome as she had first thought. Upon closer inspection, his hair was dishwater yellow, his eyes set too close together in his face. It was his younger brother Wolf who was the looker in that family. It was odd how no one ever noticed or commented on it. Everyone was always talking about how wonderful Leopold was; no one ever mentioned Wolf, except to chastise or criticize him.

"You look very beautiful today, Izzy," Louis-Philippe said as they approached the dessert sideboard, which was groaning from the weight of many fantastic desserts. "Here." He handed her a cherry ice and a slice of lemon cake. "Eat, you look hungry."

"Thank you," she said. "So do you. I mean, you look very handsome."

He smiled, and she felt better for the first time that day. Her maid had talked her into wearing the daring new style of dress, and while she was worried about going without a corset, she was relieved to be comfortable for the first time at a party. Why did women wear them, anyway? They were awful. In the meantime, the orchestra was playing a Prussian melody in honor of the Crown Prince's home kingdom, and in preparation for the entrance of the prince and princess. They melted into the crowd and scanned it for familiar faces. Isabelle nodded to a few girls she knew, taking note of dresses, gloves, and fans to see if there was anything she wanted her seamstresses at home to replicate. So this was the mythical Bal du Drap d'Or. So far she was not impressed, although she had been a little nervous when she had been presented to the queen earlier. She had been so frightened that the Merlin would cast a spell on her, but he did not. He let her live, let her dance. He had merely nodded, dismissing her like all the rest. She wondered if they even knew who she was, or if they even cared at this point. It had been almost five hundred years ago now, and House Orleans posed no threat to the Crown. As Hugh said, they were merely grateful for scraps. She hoped that at least Louis was having a nice time.

"Have your eye on anyone?" Isabelle asked. "Spill it—who's caught your fancy?"

"Nobody. I don't have 'an eye' on anyone," he said as he finished his ice and set it down on a passing tray.

"Oh. But surely you like somebody?"

Louis-Philippe bowed his head, and when he looked up at her, he was blushing. "I do. I do. I do 'like' someone."

"Who? Tell me!" Isabelle asked, fanning herself with vigor. "Tell me!"

"I can't . . . she doesn't know . . . and I think she might get angry."

"Angry? Why would she be angry? At you?"

"Well, she is a little . . . opinionated," he said.

"Opinionated? You mean she's a bit dramatic? A loud-mouth?" Isabelle laughed. "Sounds like someone I know."

Louis-Philippe looked at her with such a hopeful expression that she felt a flutter in her heart. He couldn't possibly? *Louis-Philippe?* In love with her? Jug Ears, as Hugh always called him? Although his ears were the right size now, and he was not so little anymore—he had grown up *so* tall—but he was just a boy, really. Even if he believed he was in love with her, it was nothing but boyish infatuation, surely. She shook it from her mind. It was too much, too soon, after Leopold. She could still feel his cold hands groping her. The last thing she wanted to think about right now was anything to do with boys. She wanted to be as far away from them as possible— even from Louis, who really didn't count as a boy at all.

"Oh, well, forget about her then. Did you see the American girl? The one who is shining like a diamond? They say she is very, very rich. Find her dance card. See if you can win her heart and her money—we need it!" She pushed him away, almost the same way she had pushed Leo earlier.

Isabelle just wanted to sit down. She had had quite enough of boys for the day.

the PRINCESS DAUPHINE

It was time. The princess's grand entrance. The guests had been presented at court; the party was in full swing. Dinner had been served long ago, and it was time for the ball to officially begin. People needed to dance; they were itching to dance. Gentlemen milled by the sidelines, waiting. Girls new to society couldn't wait to show off the steps they had practiced. The queen on the podium looked like she wanted to go to bed already, she was yawning so much. But still the ball had not yet opened, as the princess had not yet appeared. A few, however, had caught glimpses of the prince—clasping hands here and bowing to guests there, his fine blond head shining like a beacon in the middle of the dark room.

It happened slowly and all at once. First the lights dimmed, then the orchestra stopped playing. In the middle of the Crystal Palace, a small blue fire began to grow. It started as a tiny spark and grew into a ball of flame, as tall as a hedge, now tall as a tree, beautiful and sharp as a phoenix. It grew until it filled the entire room, this strange and beautiful blue light—grew so large, it dispersed among the crowd, covering each and every guest, from royal to aristocrat to servant alike in its strange blue light. Until all at once, it snapped back to the center, intense and blinding, and burst with a huge thunderclap—the sound of the sky breaking open, of the world splitting apart—and then just as suddenly disappeared, sending the room into total darkness, having swallowed every light in the Crystal Palace. When the lights flickered back on, in the middle of the room stood a girl. . . .

Her Royal Highness, Princess Marie-Victoria Grace Eleanor Aquitaine, Dauphine of Viennois, Princess of Wales.

Her dress was the same color as the blue fire. It was made of a thousand tiny blue feathers, a wave that moved with a graceful ripple across her bodice and skirt. And then the dress exploded, and a hundred blue birds flapped away from her dress up toward the ceiling, through the hole in the roof to the sky. There she stood, their princess, her bare shoulders creamy against a blue dress made of midnight satin. Her only jewelry was a small circlet of diamonds on the coronet, entwined with stones representing England and France in her hair.

She was absolutely breathtaking. No one had ever seen her look so beautiful; she was so much taller, her hair darker, her eyes brighter—she was made of light and magic. She was the most dazzling creature in the history of the monarchy. Her entrance would be recounted in history books for years to come, marveled over, picked apart, every detail of her dress obsessed over by millions of young girls all over the empire.

The silence was broken by a hoarse cheer from the back of the room, soon taken up by every guest, hooting and hollering and yelling their lungs out: a jaded court brought back to life by the sight of their beautiful, healthy princess. She was no longer an invalid, no longer ailing; she was an evening star sent down from the heavens. Her beauty and magnetic presence eclipsed every girl in the room. No one remembered Isabelle of Burgundy, or remarked upon Ronan Astor of New York; all eyes in the room were on Marie-Victoria of England and France.

The crowd continued to roar—for a moment it appeared they might mob the princess, so great was their intense passion and patriotism—but when the Merlin held his hand up for silence, the crowd instantly quieted. The show was not yet over. It was time for the prince to make his appearance.

Leopold walked out of the shadows. No fancy magic for him: no blue light, no soaring birds. He did not need any. He simply walked in, tall and handsome as ever; he was dressed in his Prussian gray and reds, his smile as bright as his hair. The crowd stirred in breathless anticipation as he bowed to Marie-Victoria. She curtsied to him. He took her hand, and the orchestra played the first strains of the Lovers' Waltz. There was no announcement from the herald. None was needed to present the future King and Queen of the Holy Franco-British-Prussian Empire.

The Merlin smiled. With that came clapping, cheering, and whistling as the room exploded in joy. They had never seen a couple so enchanting, or so enchanted; their love was pure magic.

Only if one looked very, very closely would one notice the prince had a red mark on his cheek. *As if someone had kissed or slapped him just a few moments before*, the real Marie-Victoria thought as she watched the performance intently through Aelwyn's crystal glass.

"Are you sure you don't wish you were out there with him?" Gill asked, his voice in her ear, his strong arms around her waist.

She shook her head and leaned back, so that her head rested underneath his chin. "No. I'm exactly where I want to be."

They continued to watch the ball unfold through the magic glass. Viviane's crystal allowed them to hear and see everything. One by one—courtiers, lords and ladies, the great and the good, the beautiful and the damned—all joined the royal couple on the dance floor. The princess down below was perfectly executing the steps to the Lovers' Waltz. She was as graceful as a prima ballerina; she was beauty incarnate. Her prince looked absolutely besotted with her.

"See, she has fooled everyone. We will be safe," Marie said. "Aelwyn's magic is formidable. No one will see through the illusion."

"She wouldn't have fooled me," Gill said. "That girl is nothing compared to you."

She smiled and nuzzled his chin in reply.

"I wish we could go now," he said. "Tonight. I wish I could take you away from all of this forever."

"I do too," she sighed. "If only we could go now." They had agreed they needed to escape as soon as possible. Gill wanted them to go abroad, to the American provinces. There they could blend in as new immigrants, and make a new life for themselves away from the empire. But passage would be expensive, and Gill's salary from the Queen's Guard was but a pittance. He was going to try to borrow money from a friend or two. Marie could not help with this. She might be the princess of the realm, but she had no access to any of their wealth. She never carried coin or gold—never needed it—and she was loath to take the jewels and heirlooms of the house to sell or barter. She was adamant that they remain with House Aquitaine; they were not hers to take. When it came down to it, she owned very little.

Marie tried not to worry about taking such a long journey, with the state of her health being what it was. Besides, she had been feeling better since deciding to leave with Gill. She was worried about Aelwyn, however, who would bear the burden of their deception by remaining.

There was also the problem of getting past the wards on the back gates, which were heavily fortified and spell-cast to keep the royal family safe. They would need a spell-key to unlock it, and the spell-keys were kept by the Merlin's order.

Tonight was the first test—to see if Aelwyn's magic could fool a crowd, fool a prince. If she was successful, Aelwyn would tell the sisterhood that she had chosen to return to Avalon. In truth, she would take on Marie-Victoria's visage for good. Slowly, the spell would merge her own features with Marie's until, little by little, it would reveal her own. The people would not remember that their princess had once been pale and plain; they would have always known her to be beautiful and vibrant. Aelwyn would marry Leo, taking ring and crown in one fell swoop, and leaving Marie-Victoria with her wished-for cottage by the sea.

There were pitfalls, of course—the eagle-eyed Merlin, for one, and Eleanor for another. If they caught a whiff of the deception—Marie shuddered to think what they'd do to the two girls. It was treason, what they were planning—a betrayal of the highest order—a dark and terrible magic that would corrupt the very foundation of the empire. No matter how light and pure their intentions were, it was a perversion of the natural order of things. It would mean the Aquitaine bloodline would not continue—the victory Henry had won on the bloody fields of Orleans would be for naught. The treaty the Merlin had crafted to ensure no mage would ever rule—a treaty that protected magic and non-magic alike—would be nullified.

Hell, as they say, would break loose.

To give up an empire for personal happiness was madness, but Marie had never wanted to rule—had never wanted to be queen—had never truly believed she would inherit the crown. She had always felt lesser, unworthy, too small and insignificant for so large a role. All she wanted was to be happy. Although, perhaps if she was being completely honest, Marie would admit that she did feel a little twinge of sadness and jealousy when she saw Aelwyn in all her finery down there, reveling in the love and appreciation of her people. Marie herself would not have chosen a blue column of fire to mark her appearance. No, that was pure Aelwyn: drama, magic, the unknowable mystery of Avalon. Marie would have chosen something simpler to announce herself: perhaps a crown of flowers on her head would have been her only jewel for a public appearance.

Either way, the point was now moot. Once the plan was in effect—a plan she herself had set in motion—she would no longer be the princess. She would never face the court again, never have to wake up to the blank faces of her ladies, never have to sit in session on any issue, never see her mother again. If only they could leave as soon as possible, so she would no longer linger on the doubts that had started to cloud her decision.

Gill kept his strong arms around her, and his heart beat steadily in his chest. Marie decided she would spend her future with him, place her happiness with his. "Let us go, as soon as we can," she whispered. "Please."

"I'm doing everything I can," he whispered. "I promise. It won't be long now."

She nodded and sighed.

"Now I need you to do something for me," he said. "Dance with me, Princess. After all, we know the steps."

She turned to him with a smile. To the strains of the Lovers' Waltz, they danced the night away.

· 26 ·

the
KRONPRINZ

*S*he was the princess. She had the fire, the dress, the magic, and—thanks to the power of the illusion spell—Marie's face on her visage. The joy of the crowd. The hand of the prince on her waist. They finished the waltz and Leo escorted her to the podium, where the queen and the Merlin were waiting.

"My darling daughter!" Eleanor exclaimed, enveloping her in her arms and kissing her profusely on her cheeks. "Well done!"

"Princess," Emrys said, bowing. The Merlin looked at her keenly, but Aelywn would not meet his eye and kept her chin lowered. The white stone that amplified the spell was tucked underneath her neckline, and the glamour it cast made certain that not even those with the power of sight could penetrate its haze. But still she trembled before the Merlin, her treacherous black heart cowering in front of the most powerful mage in the world.

Now Leo was leading her back to the crowd, back to the dance. He was looking at her with a wonder-filled light in his eyes, as if he had never seen her before. As he led her through the dance, holding her in his arms tightly, he was just as strong and confident and handsome as the day when they had first met in that hallway. She felt her body responding all too eagerly to his touch.

She had not felt this way since Lanselin. . . .

She could not think of Lanselin right now. . . .

His hand was on her waist, the other on her shoulder as she swayed to the tune of the music, their steps exquisite and perfect. It felt as if they were the only two people in the room, even while they were surrounded by the entire court. Leo had not said a word to her since her appearance. Instead he had a glazed, dazed look on his face, as if he could not quite believe his luck.

"My prince, you are so quiet," she said coquettishly. "Do you not like the dress?"

"Who are you?" he asked abruptly. Before she could answer, he added, "You are different tonight. Where have you been all this time?"

"I have been right here, my lord. Right in front of you." She smiled.

"Then I am a fool for never noticing before," he said,

and held her even more tightly. It was tradition at the royal ball for the princess to dance with lords and courtiers out of courtesy—to entertain the Viceroy of India and the Minister of Zanzibar, to laugh at the jokes of the Duke of Buckingham—but Leo did not let her go, would not let her leave his side, would not give her up to anyone in the room.

Instead, they danced for hours. With every waltz, every step, Aelwyn understood there was no turning back now. She had fooled the queen and the Merlin, the entire court of England and France: the great empire. She would be the princess. She would have love and power and position, higher than she could have dreamed.

It was everything she'd ever wanted.

· 27 ·

a
DECENT PROPOSAL

er feet were tired. Her dress was made of magic, and fit like it was made for her and her alone, but the shoes were another matter. The heels were very high, and the narrow shape pinched her toes. Ronan wanted nothing more than to sit down, but there were so many lords and gentlemen who had written their names on her dance card, and it felt rude to turn them away.

When she'd found out who "Heath" really was, she had wanted to hit him, or run after him—explain, or apologize— but she understood that it was too late. He had been looking for something, had been testing her, and she had failed. If she ran after him now, his disgust with her would be complete. And Wolf *had* looked a bit disgusted with her, she could tell;

she'd seen his lip curl a little at the sight of her face when she received the news.

So she danced, and looked gay, and pretended that she was having a wonderful time, that she was just glad to be there, to be part of it all. When the princess appeared in a ball of flame that turned into a hundred blue songbirds, Ronan had gasped in delight and marveled at the depth and breadth of the Merlin's magic. Her own moonstones paled in comparison next to the blue fire that was Marie-Victoria's gown. Prince Leopold was as handsome as advertised, but he was too far away to analyze or worship thoroughly; since he was already spoken for, her interest in him had receded. No, she was only thinking of Wolf, dashing Wolf, who had walked away from her without looking back.

Ronan leaned against a wall, hoping that her next partner wouldn't show up or had found someone else to dance with. But no such luck. She spotted Marcus Deveraux winging his way to her with a smug smile.

"Ah, there you are—I was looking for you. I believe you are mine." He looked better than he had the other night, with his hair brushed back from his forehead. Away from the eclipsing glamour of Perry and Archie, one could go as far as to call him handsome—or as handsome as he would ever look in a white tie and tails.

"Lord Deveraux," she said brightly. "What a pleasure to find you here."

"No need to be so formal," he said with a dismissive wave that was meant to be nonchalant. "Just call me Marcus, like everyone does."

"Marcus," she smiled. She was tempted to tell him she would rather sit this one out, if he did not mind, but somehow the words never came out of her mouth. She fell into his arms, and they fell into the small precise steps of a minuet.

"Having a jolly time, are you?" he asked, straining to make his voice heard over the strings.

She smiled and nodded politely.

"Had a chance to see any of the countryside?" When she shook her head, he said, "Oh, no matter. We won't have to live there for a while yet. In fact, we could even live in America, in your 'neck of the woods,' as they say. I'm an adventurous chap."

"Excuse me?" Ronan asked. She wasn't sure she understood what he was saying. What was all this talk about "we"? "Forgive me, my lord, but I'm not quite following you."

"Now, now, you don't want me to get down on one knee, do you? Knee's a bit shot. But I suppose the ladies like it. Ferdie said you would, said I shouldn't muck it up."

"Lord Deveraux," Ronan said firmly, forgetting that they were supposed to be on a first-name basis, "please explain what you are trying to say."

Marcus sighed loudly and blew a raspberry in exasperation, as if she were a particularly slow or dim-witted child.

"Here's the thing, see? I'm supposed to pick a bride this season, or Mummy'll cut off the dosh. And, well . . . you're awful pretty, aren't you? So, um, how about it?"

The pretty ones always go first.

Ronan stopped dancing and stood still in the middle of the ballroom. Several couples had to dance around them to keep from bumping into them. "Are you proposing to me, Lord Deveraux? Proposing marriage, I mean?"

"Yes, of course I am," he said with a big smile, relieved to be understood. "So, what do you say? Want to give it a go? You're a pretty American—I'm a single, titled Brit—it's what you came to the season for, isn't it? Why don't we seal the deal, as you folks like to say? Get this done, right?"

Since it was so businesslike, Ronan was tempted to ask about the amount of his stipend, and for that matter, how much he would inherit—what the estate was worth, and exactly how much of his fortune was liquid. But she did not have to, as what had been presented was enough for her to make a few quick calculations. She factored in their great house on the square (which had been suitably updated with the latest modern conveniences), the fact that his sister would be a bridesmaid to the princess, and what she could remember from the issue of Debrett's—that the Warwick country home was one of the finest castles in all of Franco-England, and they also kept a house in Paris. On paper, he was proposing a very good match indeed—one, he was right to note, that she had come to London for.

"I . . ."

"Yes?"

"Yes—I mean—no. No. I can't," she said. Ronan started to dance again, and he was forced to follow. She gave a small laugh. "I mean, we don't even know each other! We've hardly said two words to each other! And this doesn't count."

Marcus's shoulders slumped. "Ferdie said you'd say that. I suppose I'll have to court you properly, then?" he asked gloomily. "Send flowers, pitch woo, moon about your eyes and such?"

She did not dignify that with a response. Instead, as the orchestra played the last strains of the piece, she curtsied politely. "I am very flattered, Marcus, but . . ."

"But?" he asked hopefully.

Ronan wanted to laugh. She couldn't seem to walk in any direction without someone proposing marriage to her. But she said the same thing she had told Wolf on the boat. "I'm sorry, but the answer is no."

Wolf couldn't help but overhear the conversation, since old Deveraux had had to yell above the orchestra. He had to hand it to Marcus—full points for attempting to make his mark early. Claiming the prettiest girl in the room before the night was even over. Ronan Astor, that was her name. He savored it like a fine wine on his tongue. Unconsciously, he had spent the entire night shadowing her movements, watching her as she danced with his friends and acquaintances, making sure she didn't see him.

Like everyone else at the party, Wolf had been impressed by Marie-Victoria's entrance, amazed to have seen his friend transformed into some kind of magical bird. He wasn't quite sure how he felt about that—it didn't seem very Marie-like to enter the dance in such a showy way—but he supposed it had to do with the Merlin, and the empire wanting to make an impression. During the mandatory dance, his brother seemed happy enough to see the princess transformed like that. After watching them for a few moments, Wolf went back to his regular pastime—tracking the movements of a certain American girl.

Right now she was dancing with the so-called Red Duke, although nothing about him was red, except his face after a few drinks. Hugh Borel. Wolf didn't know him that well—French royals had been practically banned from court since their defeat—but he appeared a nice enough chap, polite to a fault maybe. One of those nervous types.

Wolf downed his glass of champagne and made a decision. It was almost four in the morning, long past supper. All the court insiders had abandoned the ball for the after-parties, and he himself had promised a few friends he would leave soon. He felt a pang to see that Ronan was still at the dance, not realizing that only the losers who had not been invited anywhere else (like Hugh Borel) remained.

Well, it was up to him then, wasn't it? To rescue the fair

maiden and all that. He finger-combed his hair and checked his teeth in the silver. Then he approached, silent as a leopard, as smooth as knife through butter. "Mind if I cut in?" he asked.

Hugh glanced at him. For a moment his eyes were icy, but they turned back to the warm, cloying obsequiousness he was known for. "By all means, she's yours. Excuse me, my lady," he said as he bowed to Ronan.

"You," Ronan said. He took her hand in his, put the other around her waist, and pulled her toward him.

"Me." He smiled.

"I don't think what you did was funny."

"Really? I thought it was a laugh. That Red Duke needs to learn his place around here."

"Not that. You know what I mean. Back on the *Saturnia*. Pretending to be someone else. Getting me to play those games with you," she said, her cheeks turning red.

"All right, so I never told you my real name. But *Wuthering Heights is* one of my favorite books. If you recall, Heathcliff is quite the anti-hero—so in that way, I never pretended to be anyone else. I told you the truth. I fight in the ring, my family herds sheep. Okay, so they herd a lot of sheep. My brother's getting married. All truths. And it was just a game, love—we did nothing wrong, did we? As I recall, you enjoyed it too."

Ronan's face remained frosty. "If you say so, Your Highness."

"Highness! You don't need to mind your P's and Q's with

me, girl." He quite liked the way she fit around him. His hand almost spanned her small waist, and her hand was curled in his like a child's.

She lowered her lashes. "I don't think we've even been properly introduced."

He leaned in to whisper in her ear. "I'm Wolf."

"Ronan Astor," she said, her voice still chilly.

"Don't be that way, Ronan. Come on. I heard you turning down my friend Marcus back there. Now, why would you do a thing like that? I thought you meant to marry well—the Warwick spread not big enough for you? Have your plans changed, my lady?" he asked, his blue eyes twinkling with merriment.

"If they had, why should I alert you?" she asked tartly.

"Point taken," he said. "I do apologize." They danced for a few more songs, taking a whirl across the floor. He leaned over to her ear again. Her skin was so soft, and her hair was fine as silk. He remembered those lazy days of champagne and billiards. "You have to believe, I wasn't . . . I wasn't taking advantage of you, back on the boat. And I wasn't making fun of you . . . the proposal might have been an impulsive gesture, but it was a sincere one. I apologize if I offended you."

She relaxed in his arms and looked him right in the eye. For a moment, she looked like she did the first time they had met: determined, resolute, brave. "If you want to know why I turned down his proposal, it's because I thought it was too early."

"Too early?"

"Too early to exit the game. After all, the season's just begun, hasn't it? It would be a shame to miss all the fun," she said with a raised eyebrow. "And it's all a game, isn't it? Even to you, who proposed to a stranger on the boat. What did you call the London Season? The wedding races? Well, I aim to get my filly past the line."

He'd been about to invite her to the after-party at the Grosvernors', but it was clear she thought their time together was over for the evening.

She curtsied. "Good night, my lord," she said, reaching out her hand. Wolf flinched, thinking she meant to slap him. But she only tweaked his bow tie, which was crooked.

Wolf bowed, watching her leave. He touched his tie where she had fixed it, a small, secret smile on his face.

· 28 ·

Gift
HORSES

The next day, wedding gifts began to pour into St. James Palace in earnest. From the far-flung reaches of the empire and across the globe, friends and allies sent gifts to the newly affianced couple in honor of their upcoming wedding. A date had been set by the Merlin and announced all over the empire: Marie-Victoria and Leopold would be married on the summer solstice, a worthy night for merrymaking. It would be the end of a glorious season, capping the year and signaling the start of something the empire had not seen in decades: peace.

The gifts were remarkable in breadth and variety: dazzling jewels from the mines of Burma and Africa, pineapples and coconut creams from the island provinces, rare animals and exotic fruits from the Australian hinterlands. There were

gifts of ornate furniture and important paintings, gold dou-
bloons and bottles of the finest liquors throughout the land.

Isabelle stood in the center of the royal court, covering her
yawn as Hugh presented their gift to the royal couple. Her
cousin was a bit agitated, as Louis-Philippe was supposed to
have joined them for this reception, but had failed to meet
them at the ordained time. Good for him, Isabelle thought.
She would have preferred to sleep in as well.

Was this truly necessary? Neither the queen nor the prince
or princess were at court to receive the gifts. Instead, only a
minister of the Merlin's and the first lady-in-waiting stood a
few feet away from the throne to officially accept the procession of bounty. Even they looked tired. But this was the royal
protocol—no matter that the entire court had been up until
five in the morning from the festivities.

"With great joy, we bequeath our gift to the royal couple.
Five hundred barrels of our best Burgundy," Hugh said, his
hands shaking a little. He held out a bottle of the same vin-
tage, presenting it to the minister and the lady with a bow.

Isabelle wrinkled her nose. Five hundred barrels! That
was almost their entire harvest. Now this palace would smell
just like home—like a stinky, vinegary, earthy cave. "Awful
generous of you, Hugh," she said as they left the stateroom,
once they were safely out of earshot. "Wasn't it enough that
they chucked me as a bride? Must we provide for the wedding
feast, as well?"

"It is but a small price to pay for our return to court. I can assure you, our generosity will be well rewarded," he replied with a satisfied smile.

She supposed that that meant he'd lined up another match for her. Who cared? She had drunk too much champagne the night before, and her head was pounding. It was the worst kind of hangover, since it wasn't from merry-making—she had refused to dance the entire night, and had instead sat in a corner, downing glass after glass until she could barely stand. She wasn't too sure how she'd gotten home, either. She had woken up in her bed with all of her clothes on, lying on top of the covers, her hair still in a bun, her makeup smeared on her face.

The maid had awoken her to tell her that Hugh had arrived to take her to the gift reception. She had kicked and whined, but Hugh had insisted. So she had scrubbed her face and changed her clothes, while her maid had quickly put up her hair. Now she was walking in the palace courtyard, desperate for a cup of coffee.

She didn't want to bump into anyone, didn't want to gossip about the stupid ball. She had heard enough the night before of Princess Marie-Victoria in her beautiful, magical, astounding blue dress. More annoyingly, it appeared from their passionate kiss in the middle of the waltz that Leo was actually falling in love with the princess, and was happy. She didn't know what else could possibly worsen the very worst day of her life, when she saw Louis-Philippe walking out of one of the apartments of the castle's east side, still in his ball clothes. He was rumpled and sheepish, his bow tie askew, carrying his frock coat folded over his arm. There were lipstick traces on his collar.

She called his name and he jumped a little, startled. "Looks like you had a good night," she said, a little stunned to see him so early in the morning, and obviously just coming home.

He smiled, abashed, but he didn't deny it. In fact, he stood up a little straighter, carrying himself with a newfound confidence. Isabelle understood instinctively that whatever the night had brought, it had made him a man. "Hey, Izz," he said, ruffling her hair with a grin. He had never called her that before, nor had he ever been so casual around her.

Isabelle remembered the shy boy who had looked at her with so much longing last night, and how she had fobbed him off—urging him to meet the rich American, or any other girl. But it looked as though the lucky girl lived in the palace. It was probably one of those daughters of the duke. . . . She felt a pang. How could he have grown up so quickly overnight? One night with one of those floozies had crushed his crush so completely? It wasn't much of a torch he carried for her, then, if it had burned out in less than twenty-four hours. So much for his protestations of love. He was the same as all the rest—just some stupid boy who thought with his little brain.

"Did I miss the gift presentation? Is Hugh mad?" Louis asked.

"I don't think he noticed. He was too busy preening—he was so proud of his overly generous gift," snapped Isabelle. Coffee . . . was there no coffee to be had in this godforsaken palace?

Louis cocked his head and squinted at her. "And how are you feeling this morning?" He fell in step with her as they made their way to the back gates. There were few courtiers out that morning, only the odd page boy, a few yawning footmen, and ladies' maids running with irons to attend to their mistresses.

"Fine," she said through gritted teeth. "Just fine."

"I'm glad you got home safely."

She stopped and stared at him. "That was you, then? You were the one who took me home?"

He nodded, and had the good sense to blush. "I tried to wake your maid, but she wouldn't budge—apparently she had quite a good time at the servants' ball. . . ."

Isabelle was turning a bit red herself, as a few memories from the night before came back to her. She had sobbed in his arms, she remembered now. It all seemed so terribly melodramatic. "So, you dropped me off and went back to the ball?"

He kicked at pebbles in their path. "Well . . . not exactly."

Ah. So he had come back here, then, after dropping her off like a sack of potatoes. She wondered if the girl he was with had witnessed her complete, humiliating breakdown. Isabelle vowed never to drink any champagne again. It was a vow she knew would be forgotten by the evening. "Is she rich, at least?" she asked.

"I have no idea," he laughed.

Just then, footsteps on the pathway alerted them to the fact that they were no longer alone. A girl was coming out of the same apartment that Louis had just vacated. She was radiant and pretty, her hair golden as the sun, her cheeks pink and fresh: a proper English rose. She ran up to Louis-Philippe and gave him a kiss on the cheek. Isabelle had guessed correctly: she was one of those ducal daughters. Lady Celestine was her name. "Oh, hi," she said when she saw Isabelle. "Um, Louis, you forgot your belt," she said, handing him a black satin one.

"Thanks," he said, grinning widely.

She wrapped her robe tightly around her person and looked up at him eagerly. There were red love marks all over her neck, and Isabelle hoped the girl would be wise enough to cover them up. Her father was notorious for his temper. The Duke of Montrose had five daughters, each one wilder and more reckless than the next. Celestine was the youngest, and the prettiest by far. "We're all booked up this week with tiresome dinners, but we'll be at the vernissage next week. See you there?" she asked.

"You can count on it," Louis promised. He glanced around and, finding the courtyard clear, kissed her right on the lips.

"You're so naughty! I've got to get back, I'm late for break-fast." She laughed, pushing him away. "Don't forget me!" she called gaily.

The young couple looked so incredibly happy that Isabelle wanted to vomit. As she followed the whistling Louis to the waiting carriage, she thought she'd been wrong earlier: it *was* possible to feel even worse today.

· 29 ·

Runaway
BRIDE

The wedding-dress fitting was finishing up. Marie was smiling at the mirror, humming to herself as the ladies who surrounded her clucked and chatted. There was a lightness in the air these days since the royal ball. All talk in the palace was of Marie and Leopold, and the kiss that had sealed it on the dance floor. The prince had taken hold of the princess and, in a smooth gesture worthy of a true Romeo, dipped her back till she was bent at the waist and kissed her soundly in front of the whole court. The clapping and cheering were even more deafening than when the princess had first appeared.

The wedding dress was flamboyant: gold in color, resplendent with magic. It was woven with the stars of the sky and the light of the moon; it was the most amazing, ethereal creation that anyone had ever seen. Marie thought that it made even her look beautiful. She couldn't help but feel a twinge of jealousy at the thought of Aelwyn alighting from her carriage, glowing in the gown, mounting the steps of St. Paul's, and walking down its long, long aisle between hundreds of beaming guests . . .

My real wedding will be a simpler affair, she told herself, and chuckled. *But it will be a thousand times better, because I will be marrying a man I chose. The man I love.*

Of course, her ladies thought she was in a good mood because of the kiss, because of Leo, and because she was finally happy to be marrying him. None of it was true, but Marie let them think that. It was so much easier. After the ball, the prince had sent a myriad of invitations her way—requests to see her alone, for a stroll in the gardens or dinner à deux. But she had demurred, saying she was ill after the ball—that it had taken too much energy out of her—or that she was busy. This had led to even more desperate and lovesick entreaties, until Marie began to grow nervous. Her plans with Gill were so close to fruition; her new future, her new life, hung tantalizingly before her, like a ripe apple just out of reach. But if she didn't give in to Leo's demands to see her soon, then it might start to look suspicious.

Except there was no way Marie could be alone with him after he had been with Aelwyn. It was strange to hear about her own "first kiss" from everyone else. People had gushed on and on about the look of surprise on her face when he had planted his mouth on hers, the dazed smile on her lips when he stood her up again and whirled her onto the dance floor for "The Lovers' Waltz," followed by a tango so intimate that Countess von Fickenstein, his aunt, had covered her face with her fan.

If she went to see Leo now, he would surely kiss her. And that could not happen. After breakfast that morning she'd begged Aelwyn to don the glamour and visit him one more time. Aelwyn pretended to be reluctant, but Marie could tell her childhood friend had loved being the belle of the ball. Loved being the princess and future queen. And, most of all, that she'd loved kissing Leo, and was eager to do it again.

But so far they had not found the right opportunity to make the switch. They had to be careful; they couldn't take the chance that anyone would notice Princess Marie had been in two different places at the same time. Soon, though, Aelwyn would never have to take off the glamour. She would *be* Marie, and Marie would be . . . free. To be with Gill. To be his wife. The thought made her blush with happiness.

"'The Lovers' Waltz.'" Julia, one of her ladies, smiled.

"Huh?" Marie asked.

"You're humming it," her lady said. "Oh, Marie, your wedding will be wonderful!"

Yes it will be, now, Marie thought. It will be everything I've dreamed of.

When her ladies left, along with the tailor and his seamstresses, Marie put her day dress back on with the help of her nurse, Jenny Wallace. Wallace was the apple-cheeked care-giver who had raised Marie—who had wiped away her tears, fixed her helmet, understood each of her physical regimens.

Marie called her "Wallace" because when she was little it was easier to pronounce than "Jenny." Wallace wasn't a young girl anymore—she was now a sensible matron with several young children of her own. But she still came to the palace once in a while to check in on "her princess" and to make sure the healers were prescribing the right medicines for the wasting plague. Wallace wiped her hands on her apron and frowned at Marie.

"What?" Marie asked, trying to wipe the smile from her face.

"You don't fool me," Wallace said.

"What are you talking about?"

"You cannot go away with that boy, my chick," she said.

Marie put down her book and regarded her nurse with alarm. "You know?"

"Of course I know. I've known you since you were a babe. I've seen how you look at each other—the way he smiles at you. The way you light up when he's around, and *only* when he's around. I wanted this for you, but I wanted it to be with someone you were allowed to love as well. Perhaps it was wrong of me to hope that might happen," Wallace said, putting her hands on her waist and regarding Marie with forthright disapproval.

Marie paled. "What will you do, Wallace?"

"It's not for me to *do* anything," Wallace sighed. "I've already done as much as I can," she said, giving Marie a hard, knowing look.

So it was not the Prussians who had insisted they replace her Queen's Guard, after all. "It was you—you were the one—you told them to send Gill away."

"I suggested to your new family that it might make a nice gesture. Yes I did, my sweet, I did. I thought it would be easier for you if he went away."

Marie fell to her knees and put her head in her nurse's lap. She had always found comfort in that lap. "Wallace, I can't marry Leo. I can't."

"But you looked so happy at the ball dancing with him," Wallace said, as she stroked her hair gently.

"That wasn't me," Marie whispered.

"I knew it was too good to be true. I knew it. What a great actress you are."

Marie thought about disillusioning Wallace but decided it was too risky to drag Aelwyn into this.

"How did you know we were planning to leave?"

The nurse showed her what she had found in Marie's dresser. A pouch full of gold coins; letters; keys that would unlock each door in the secret dungeon passageways. The first few items in their escape plan. All they lacked was the spell-key for the wards.

"What will you do?" Marie asked again, lifting her tear-streaked face.

"It is your life, my dear. I cannot do anything except ask, what are you thinking? You cannot mean to do this. You cannot leave with him—you must know that."

"I have to," Marie whispered. "I love him."

Wallace gave her one of her deep and sympathetic and terribly sad smiles. "But what about your mother? Think of what this will do to her. To lose her only child and heir—to lose the throne . . ."

Marie shook her head. She hardly knew her mother. Her mother had loved her, but she would enjoy having a different daughter. Let Aelwyn be the strong, beautiful, healthy girl that Eleanor had always wanted—the girl Marie had never been. Eleanor was not losing a daughter; she was gaining a finer one than she'd ever known. But Marie could not tell her nurse that. She would have to tell Aelwyn to be kind to Wallace. "Mother will be fine," Marie said.

"You are wrong there—so wrong, my chick. Your mother will be devastated."

"But you won't tell?"

"I won't—I promise, Princess."

There was no deception in Wallace's voice, yet something nagged at Marie's mind.

"But you told her when I ate the shrimp," she said quietly.

"Beg pardon, my lady?"

"When I was eight and Mother had that dinner for the buffoon of a prince from Denmark. The one whose father actually named him Hamlet. Everyone was eating shrimp cocktail and it looked so delicious, but I wasn't allowed to have any because the doctors thought I might be allergic to shellfish and given my 'delicate condition,' an attack could kill me. So I got one of the kitchen maids to bring some to my bedroom, and the silly girl ended up bringing a whole huge pot of it and I ate so much—"

"That you got sick," Wallace finished for her. "Yes, I well remember."

"But I wasn't allergic, just like I thought. Yet you told Mother anyway."

Her nurse shook her head, understanding the point of Marie's story. "This isn't a dish of fish, my lady, and you are not a mischievous girl of eight. It is your life now."

"Does that mean you really won't tell?"

"I said I won't, and I mean I won't!" Wallace said sharply, a trace of some long-vanquished provincial accent sneaking out in her affronted voice. "But I beg you to reconsider," she continued in a softer tone. "Think of the queen, of your country. Think of me. If you leave, I will never see you again. And think of yourself. If the Merlin finds out—your actions will be considered treason. You might lose your life in this venture. Is he worth that much to you?"

Marie opened her mouth to answer, but the words didn't come. It had to be worth it. It was love, right?

Wallace smiled sadly at her charge. She reached for the envelope and shook the keys into her hand.

"I must admit, you certainly planned well. Every key

between here and the outer gate. I recognize them all from my own time at the palace, as a headstrong girl. All but this one," she said, holding up a sliver so thin it seemed less of a key than a lock pick. "What door does this open?"

Marie stifled a gasp. She'd forgotten about that key, which wasn't a key at all, but merely looked like one to allay suspicion. Aelwyn had given it to her as a precaution, in case Marie and Gill were caught as they made their way out of the palace.

"I'm not sure; let me see it," she said in the lightest voice she could muster. She held out a hand, willing it not to tremble. Wallace trustingly placed the key in it.

Marie brought the key close to her face as if she were inspecting it. With a deft gesture, she snapped it in half, and a twinkle of dust fell into her palm.

"My lady, what—"

With a single puff of air, Marie blew the dust in Wallace's face. The nurse's eyes went wide for a moment, then her lids slipped down until they were nearly closed.

"You're very tired, aren't you, Wallace?"

"Yes, my lady," Wallace answered in a distant voice. "I am very tired."

"You're so tired that you fell asleep in your chair right after the seamstress left, didn't you?"

"Indeed, my lady." Wallace sank deeper into the chair. "I feel as if I could sleep all day."

"The last thing you remember is telling me how beautiful I looked in my wedding dress, isn't it?"

A smile flickered over Wallace's mouth. Her eyes were all but closed now. "You did look so lovely in your dress. You'll be a beautiful bride to that fine Prussian prince."

Wallace's chin dropped on her soft bosom. Slow, heavy breaths began to wheeze through her nose. Marie took the small, sad envelope and stuffed it back into the depths of her drawer. Aelwyn had said that the powder would put a person to sleep for four or five hours, and afterward they would remember only what they had been told to remember. It would have come in handy when she and Gill made their escape, but she couldn't risk Wallace ruining everything. She loved her nurse, but when all was said and done, Wallace *had* told the queen about the shrimp.

·30·

VERNISSAGE

*T*he private opening of the Royal Academy of Art was typically the second biggest event of the season. Located in Burlington House, Piccadilly, its annual exhibition showcased the work of the best living artists of the empire. Wolf was looking forward to the event, as he had been a tad disappointed to miss Ronan at the flurry of dances and dinners that had immediately followed the ball. He'd eagerly awaited her appearance at a party at Duchess Wellington's, a dinner at Earl Pembroke's, and at the opera on Thursday. But she was nowhere to be found. He was beginning to worry that she had taken Marcus Deveraux's marriage proposal after all, and was in Avon planning her wedding.

He followed the crowd into the main gallery, where

paintings of every size, shape, and color lined the wall up to the rafters in a jumbled fashion—portraits of the queen and of the Merlin, bucolic landscapes, fruity still-life studies. Wolf remembered a conversation he'd had with Marie about the formulaic stagnation built into the current artistic movements. She had argued that it was the kingdom's very culture that was repressing true and enlivened artistic expression—everyone was too afraid to create something that would offend the Merlin, and so the only art that was produced was boring, pedestrian, inoffensive. Wolf sighed and thought she might have a point. Even the most important pictures—deemed the best by the Academy, and therefore set right at eye level—showcased the same cloying, patriotic tone as the lesser works.

Wolf was bored. It had been weeks now since he'd fought that giant from Brooklyn. He was out of shape, and felt stuffed and lazy. Thankfully he had spoken to a few of the good fellows of the Queen's Guard, and had set up a fight in a few weeks' time. They'd agreed to meet in the dungeons below. He was looking forward to it, but for now his mind felt like it was full of cotton balls, fuzzy and useless—only consumed with gossip from the vain, venal strivers of the Lenoran court. Wolf had no interest in the usual aristocratic pastimes of shoot and hunt. So far the only thing he was interested in tracking was a certain golden-haired American bird.

He spotted Archie and Perry with the aforementioned Marcus, who soon stalked off, and Wolf sidled up to the pair.

He had seen them with Ronan the night of the ball, and guessed correctly that they were good friends of hers. "Hello, lads." Wolf smiled. "Enjoying the exhibition?"

"Wolfgang." Archie nodded, raising his glass.

"Evening, Prince." Perry smiled.

"What's got him all hot and bothered?" Wolf asked, motioning to Marcus, who was haranguing a waiter for bringing him wine instead of champagne.

Perry took a lazy sip from his flute. "Oh, we were just riling him up a bit about being rejected so early."

"Rejected?" Wolf asked, ears cocked.

"He proposed to Ronan Astor—the American girl. Remember her? The looker in the silver dress? I do believe you danced with her at the royal ball."

"He actually proposed?" Wolf asked, raising an eyebrow, even though he had been there when it happened, and had overheard the whole thing.

"To get it over with. His mummy is threatening to cut him off if he doesn't settle down. Lady Julia's worried they'll lose the pile if he doesn't marry soon. Worried he'll fall down, bonk his head, and die—then what'll she and her five daughters do?"

"Good for Ronan for turning him down, then."

"Yes, she's quite available," Archie smiled. "Why? Interested, are you?"

Wolf drained the rest of his glass and winked at the boys. "Maybe."

Perry gave him a fatherly nod. "She's supposed to meet us here—she should be along shortly. I'll tell her to find you. Come on, Arch, let's see what atrocities they've put in the condemned cell." He nodded toward the back of the gallery, where it was so dark and narrow it was hard to get a good look at the paintings.

"Hey, that's where they put my pieces!" Archie said, affronted.

"I know, darling," Perry said. "Maybe now you won't waste so much of your time in your studio?"

Wolf left them bickering fondly with each other, and walked the length of the exhibition by himself. Royal portraiture was always well represented, and soon enough Wolf found himself in front of one that depicted the Prussian court with his family in the middle. The resemblances were passable enough. King Frederick was seated on his throne, with one son to each side of him. Sir Duncan Oswald, master-at-arms, stood next to Wolf, and Lord Edmund Hartwig next to Leo. The queen was next to Altmann von Vilswert, the Bavarian knight who was supposed to have been a favorite of his mother's.

The family hadn't actually sat for the portrait, at least not as a group. They'd posed individually, and the painter had added them to his canvas one at a time, as though assembling a very fancy jigsaw puzzle. Lord Hartwig had been his father's most trusted advisor until his death at Lamac—one of the very few Prussian casualties—but Wolf's mother had loathed him to the day she died, and she refused to be in the same room as him for the portrait. For his part, King Frederick felt the same way about von Vilswert, whose friendship with the queen was a source of malicious gossip. It wasn't the relationship that bothered King Frederick—their marriage had been a purely political affair—but there were some who suggested that von Vilswert was Wolf's father, and that was not to be tolerated.

Wolf squinted at von Vilswert's nose, wondering. It looked more than a little like his, but then, so did Leo's, and Hartwig's for that matter. Well, that was the von Hohenzollems for you. Marrying their cousins since 1061.

"Monstrosity, isn't it?" his brother's voice asked.

Wolf turned to see Leo exchanging a word with the seller, who was writing down a receipt. "I was just thinking how cruel it was of fate to give us all the same honker. You and Hartwig even have the same *adorable* chin dimple," he said teasingly.

To Wolf's surprise, Leo's face darkened. "Come now, little brother," he said, his voice deepening like it did whenever he felt like reminding Wolf that he was the heir and Wolf was just the spare. "We're in a foreign country. It doesn't do to be seen talking disparagingly about a high-ranking member of our court—nor to speak ill of the dead."

The seller stepped obsequiously forward just then, holding out a clipboard and a fountain pen. Leo jotted his name down angrily, the pen slashing so heavily across the page that the clerk had to struggle to hold the clipboard still.

"Wait, are you *buying* this?" Wolf asked. "There must be fifty versions of this painting back home."

Leo's scowl passed as quickly as it had come, and he laughed sheepishly. "It's appalling, I know. That dimple's so deep it looks like you could fit a slice of Cook's sauerbraten in there. I'm taking it off the market so I can put it out of its misery. There are so many here, and I aim to buy every one." Leo sniffed. "I'm uncertain why a portrait of the royal family should include these courtiers anyway. It looks like a bad Nativity scene."

"Ah, well." Wolf smiled. "When did you get here? Is Marie with you?"

"She's coming with the queen," Leo said. "I thought I'd check it out beforehand. Having a good season so far?"

"Fine," Wolf replied. "You and Marie seem to be finally hitting it off," he said to his brother as they moved down the hall, turning heads and drawing appreciative glances along the way.

Leo's forehead crinkled. "Blasted wedding preparations are taking up all her time. But she'll be here with me tonight."

"Well, Marie does love art."

"Yes. I thought I'd get her a painting as a wedding gift. I think our German Expressionists might be a tad much for her, but perhaps a Turner or a Sargent. Not any of these ugly family portraits, of course. The only place they're going is the fire."

"Good choice." Wolf smirked. Leo was entirely too vain;

his brother often argued that only the royal court painter should be allowed to depict their family.

"Speaking of wedding gifts, have you seen the loot? Real drakon eggs, and all sorts of magical exotica. Burgundy sent all of their Burgundy, apparently. There can't be a barrel left in France," said Leo.

"Hopefully his wine is as good as they say. Else your wedding will be a sour one." Wolf shrugged.

"Maybe we should pop one open tonight and find out," Leo said, a sly smile creeping over his face. "As I've insisted father take a few as gifts to his hosts on his tour of the countryside."

"Maybe we should," Wolf agreed. "For diplomacy's sake, of course."

"You know all the secret passages, right? You and Marie were always ducking into one or another when you were kids. Surely you remember which one leads to the cellars."

"But what about the vaults? They'll be locked with the Merlin's magic," said Wolf.

"Come now, brother, you and I both know that's never been a problem," Leo answered, a twinkle in his eye.

Wolf rocked back and forth on his heels and looked around nervously. "Fine."

"Think we can polish off a whole barrel of wine between us?"

"We can give it the old Prussian try," Wolf said.

"Tonight, then," said Leo firmly.

"Sure," Wolf said. It wasn't as if he had anything better

to do. "So," he continued, "you and Marie, eh? Things are good?"

Leo stopped and grinned at Wolf. "I have to say, I am besotted. It's a whole new world. She is a dazzling creature. I only wish she had more time to see me."

Wolf smiled indulgently. "I told you she was a remarkable girl."

"Remarkable is only the tip of the iceberg. I've never met anyone quite like her."

"There aren't many like her in this world, brother," Wolf said, happy that the two were getting along so well after their rocky beginning. "But all this talk of wine has made me thirsty. Let's go find ourselves a couple of glasses."

· 31 ·

Regrets
ONLY

ollowing the Bal du Drap d'Or, the name on everyone's lips was Princess Marie-Victoria, not Ronan Astor. Of course no one could expect to compete with a real princess, so Ronan still felt quite confident in her showing. She was ready to sit back, relax, and enjoy the mountain of missives and invitations for the season. So it came as an awful shock to realize that there were none.

"I'm so sorry, my dear, it appears the claws have come out. The hostesses are afraid you will upstage their own daughters," Lady Constance said that afternoon during their usual tea at Claridge's. "They've closed ranks and decided to keep you out of the party."

"Can they do that?" Ronan asked, horrified. She also couldn't help but notice that Lady Constance never picked up the check, and it was beginning to smart. Although, for some reason, the hotel seemed happy to place it all on the Van Owenses' bill. Ronan had not corrected their error.

"They can do whatever they want, I'm afraid; they are free to invite—or not to invite—anyone they choose," Lady Constance said. "But it is a shame. I will do my best to try to change a few minds. Perhaps some of those who do not have marriageable daughters might be persuaded. Also . . . and I think this is a delicate question, so please forgive me for asking . . . but I have heard a few rumors concerning the evening of the ball."

"Rumors? About me?"

Lady Constance hesitated. "Yes, my dear. It's come to my knowledge that supposedly dear Lord Deveraux asked you to marry him."

"And? So?"

"Well, my child, it can't possibly be true, but the wags say you turned him down."

"That's because I did."

"Oh!" Lady Constance looked scandalized. "I was certain it was a joke. I told everyone not to believe such vicious lies. Can I ask why you rejected dear Marcus?"

"I did not accept him, as I hardly knew him from the footman," she said.

Lady Constance's handkerchief quivered. "Ah. I see. Well, dear, then there is very little I can do for you. Lady Julia was quite insulted when the news got out, and now the rest of the town's hostesses are worried that because you are so beautiful to merit a proposal on the first night of the season, they would rather keep you out than risk losing a chance for one of their girls."

"Are you saying I should have accepted him?"

Lady Constance put down her cup of tea. She looked as if she meant business. "That is what you are here for, is it not? To make a match? I was told by your mother that you could not return from London without an engagement. I am only trying to help."

Ronan flushed. "But I don't love him."

"What is love?" Lady Constance asked serenely, adding a few more spoonfuls of sugar to her tea.

Later that morning, Ronan received a letter from her mother. The situation at home was direr than they had earlier believed. The bank was threatening to foreclose on the house in a month, or take their debts public.

We hope you are enjoying London and making many good friends. But if Mr. Morgan's bank does in fact reveal the extent of your father's debts, the very governorship is in jeopardy. Astor Manor, the townhouse in Albany, and the country place on the Gold

Coast—all of it could be taken from us, along with our name and place in society. Let us know if there is any news. Any news at all. With love, Mother

Ronan put the letter away. She was to meet Archie and Perry at the vernissage at the Royal Academy that evening. The boys weren't any help with any of the London hostesses, but Archie was an artist, and was entitled to invite whoever he liked to his exhibit. She was too proud to tell them her troubles anyway, and worried that they would not understand. They were both fabulously wealthy, and in Ronan's experience, those who did not have to think about money preferred to keep it that way. They would surely think Ronan's impending poverty something of a lark, and wouldn't take it seriously.

Lady Constance's visit had upset her, but it was not Marcus's proposal she was regretting right then. It was the other one: Wolf's. Was she cursed? To have come so close to winning, only to lose in the final round. She had been so confident at the ball, flippant and glib with Wolf—but what if her confidence was misplaced? What if she had played her hand wrong? She would not return to New York without a proposal. She could not.

Ronan decided to take Lady Constance's advice and try to make peace with Lady Julia. She paid a call to their house on the square. Lady Julia was out—supposedly on her way back soon—so Ronan waited for the better part of an hour in the hope that she would return. Finally, the butler allowed that perhaps the madam was not returning any time soon. Ronan left her card with him and hurried over to the Royal Academy, annoyed that she was running late. She hoped she wouldn't miss the boys. The Academy was thinning out as guests left the exhibit, and Ronan was one of the few entering. "Oh, excuse me," she said, bumping into a gentleman staring at a portrait of the royal cat.

"Miss Astor," the gent nodded.

"Lord Audley," she said. She recognized him from the ball and remembered him as an eager dance partner, and one who often stepped on her foot. Robert Tuchet, the Baron Audley, was a portly gentleman of some years.

"So pleased to see you. May I show you around? Have you only just arrived?" He smiled broadly.

"Yes, and yes please," she said. She allowed herself to be led around the exhibit, and properly oohed and ahhed at his every observation. She craned her neck to see if she could catch a glimpse of Archie and Perry anywhere, but they were nowhere to be found. Neither was there a familiar dark head in the crowd, for that matter.

As Ronan strolled through the exhibit, she mused on her current state of social decline—had she truly made such a big blunder in turning down two proposals? If she had accepted Wolf on the boat, she would be married already; and if she had accepted Marcus, she would be picking out china patterns with the Warwick crest. She would not be walking through this dull exhibition of atrocious paintings with a boring baron almost as old as her father.

If only she had the courage of her convictions. It would be so easy to make the baron propose, she could tell—she'd only have to crook a finger in his direction, and he would fall to his knees. No matter. Marcus had promised to keep courting her, and somehow she sensed she had not seen the last of Wolf.

· 32 ·

the
QUEEN'S ROAD

er mother was already waiting for her in the open-air carriage. Marie took the footman's hand and climbed aboard, sitting across from her so they could converse easily. The driver clicked his reins and they rolled toward the Row for their morning ride, a practice they took up every so often for the benefit of their subjects. Eleanor never wore a large hat, or one that obscured her face, when she went on these morning drives. There were people who had waited hours to see their monarch, and she did not want to disappoint them. Now that Marie knew that only she could see her mother as she really was, she was fascinated by her mother's glamour. She could catch a glimpse of it if she looked at Eleanor sideways. What a beauty the young Eleanor had been, with her peaches-and-cream complexion and sumptuous mane of softly curled vermilion locks. Marie had inherited her mother's alabaster skin but not her vivacity. The only color that tinted the princess's cheeks was the flush of the wasting plague.

The streets were lined ten deep with pedestrians who clapped and cheered as the royal procession made the rounds, but their clamor was somewhat dimmed by the protective wards surrounding the carriage.

"You were not at the vernissage last night," Eleanor said.

"I was not feeling well, Mother." Marie waved at a child holding flowers in the air. She had planned to go, but decided to stay in at the last minute. Aelwyn had changed her mind about visiting Leo while using the glamour, at least until Marie was safely gone from the palace. It was just too dangerous. Marie couldn't quite bring herself to moon over Leo like Aelwyn had, so she was still avoiding him.

"You looked very well at the ball," Eleanor said. "The living dress was a thrilling idea."

Marie nodded. "It was Aelwyn's idea."

"She did a fantastic job on you—it was quite a performance," the queen said as the carriage entered Hyde Park. The crowds were not as heavy inside as on the boulevards. Eleanor sniffed and rearranged her blankets, which came only as high as her waist, so her subjects would not think their queen wasn't sturdy enough to deal with the British climate. Even though spring had come to London, the cold and damp never quite went away.

Such a pretty city, Marie thought. She looked out over the park grounds, with their strangely melancholy weeping beech trees. She would miss this when she went to the Americas.

Gill had told her that the *Saturnia* was scheduled to make its return passage to New York, and they would be on that ship when it did. It wouldn't be long. Marie sighed and the queen gave her a sharp glance.

"Sometimes I wonder, my child, if you truly enjoyed the ball that evening," Eleanor said.

"I did—of course I did," Marie said. She attempted a smile, but it was difficult to lie, even then. She had to remember she was doing it for Gill. "All my dreams came true that night. It was such a magical evening. I will remember it forever."

Eleanor settled deeper into her blankets. She looked like a wizened elf. "Funny, I don't recall you ever mentioning 'dancing at the ball' as one of your dreams when you were a child. You always seemed a little bored by the whole spectacle."

Marie shrugged. She couldn't recall sharing *any* of her childhood dreams and fantasies with her mother.

"I, for one, was sad at the end of the evening," Eleanor said, her voice gravelly. "I was so disappointed, truly. I wondered whether I should mention it, and decided it was best if I did."

Her mother's stare was piercing and cold, like that of the gargoyles on top of the palace. For a brief moment Marie felt the hair on her arms stand up in terror. Eleanor was about to tell her that she *knew* about the glamour spell—she was sure of it—and now her mother would send her to the gallows for her deception. This was her mother's way of sentencing her; Marie would not have been surprised if the captain of the Queen's Guard, who was riding in front of them, turned back and apprehended her immediately. "What do you mean, Mother?" Marie said, and coughed loudly and messily into her handkerchief.

"I was sad and disappointed for my girl did not come to my room after the party. Remember when you used to do that?" she asked. "After every royal ball?"

Marie turned to her mother and smiled in relief as she dabbed her mouth. It was one of her favorite childhood memories—sitting in her mother's dressing room, watching her take off her gown and jewels and turn back into her mother once more. How had she forgotten that?

"I was expecting you, I was. I missed you, Marie," Eleanor said. "You are growing up so fast . . . and I think I had hoped to hold on to you for a little longer."

Marie opened her mouth to speak but was stopped by a lump in her throat. Her emotions surprised her. In the past few years she had grown so used to thinking of Eleanor as "the queen" that she had all but forgotten that the wrinkled yet delicate woman sitting opposite her was still her mother. She felt the blood rush to her cheeks and turned away quickly, lest the sight of Eleanor's sad eyes bring tears to her own.

A little girl in a somewhat dingy violet dress with a loose hem caught her gaze and waved wildly with one hand while her other clung to her mother. Marie obliged her by waving back. The little girl began to jump up and down in excitement. She was yelling something, but Marie couldn't hear her through the wards that protected the carriage. Her small body jerked and pulled at her mother's hand until the woman swept her daughter up into her arms and gave her a kiss on one smudged cheek. Marie knew they would remember the moment forever. The day the princess—the future queen—waved to them. Except she would not be queen.

She took a breath, then turned back to Eleanor. "Oh Mother, I'm sorry, I was so selfish—the ball took so much out of me—I just needed to rest—I'm sorry," she said, reaching across the carriage to take her mother's hands in hers.

They remained that way for the second loop of the park, and Eleanor released her grasp first. "You know, my child, you do not have to pretend with me, like you did for everyone at the ball. That kiss—a little over the top, don't you think? I know you do not love him, and that perhaps you are angry that you have to marry him. But you may learn to love him, like I loved your father. That is all you can ask of our life—to do your duty to your country, to protect our interests and serve our people, and hope that happiness comes as well. If you are lucky and try very hard, it will."

And there was the other half of the equation. On the one hand there was Eleanor her mother, who felt spurned when Marie didn't come up to talk about her day. But on the other there was Eleanor the queen, who regarded "family" as synonymous with "duty." The latter would always trump the former, Marie knew. The queen would always put her country's happiness ahead of her daughter's.

"Yes, Mother," Marie said after a long pause, turning away. They were silent for the rest of the trip.

A few days later, Marie visited Aelwyn at the charter house of the Invisible Orders. She found her friend sitting alone, staring out the window pensively. Aelwyn looked as drawn and tired as Marie did, and Marie wondered who, exactly, was benefiting from this. Perhaps it was a sign that she was on the wrong path, that they both were—but she could not admit it to herself. She had to do this; it was their only chance—*her* only chance—for freedom and happiness. She had to shove her feelings aside, especially her loyalty to her mother. *Gill—think of Gill and his love for you, and the life you will share together,* she reminded herself. *That is all that matters.*

"Marie," Aelwyn said. "You startled me."

"I'm sorry—I had to see you—"

"Because you are leaving."

"Yes. Tomorrow evening, at the garden party. You must take my place at the dance. I will tell the court I don't feel well enough for dinner, but will join them for dancing and supper afterward. At midnight, Gill and I will leave the castle through the basement tunnels by the back gates, and you will appear at the dance as the lovely Princess Marie."

"He has the spell-key to let down the wards?"

"No."

"But how will you get past them?"

"I don't know, but he says that the wards will be down when I cross. Can you do anything to help us? Doesn't the sisterhood work on those shield spells?"

"I can't bring them down myself—only the spell-key can do that—but I can give you something that will keep them open once they are down to give you ample time to cross."

"He will be waiting for me outside with a hansom cab. The ship sails tomorrow morn." Marie grabbed Aelwyn's hand. "It's crucial that no one suspects what's happened before we sail. If the Merlin finds us, Gill will be executed, and even I—"

"No." Aelwyn cut her off firmly. "Even if my father wanted to do such a thing, the queen would never allow it. She loves you too much."

"She loves her country more."

"Oh, Marie, you don't really think that, do you? That would be too horrible!"

"Aelwyn, listen," Marie said desperately. "If the Merlin had to choose between saving me and saving the Empire, which do you think it would be?"

Her friend's cheeks went bright red and she looked away. Marie knew she had struck a nerve. After a moment Aelwyn pulled her hand away and tucked it into the long, loose sleeve of her robe of the Order. The gesture seemed habitual, despite Aelwyn's brief time as an acolyte. She would have to abandon the habit, Marie thought, when she started wearing the tightly fitted gowns of her new life.

"Are you truly certain this is what you want?" Aelwyn said now.

Marie nodded, and said the same thing she had said when she first came to ask her friend for aid. "Please. Help us. I am begging. Winnie, I know I am asking so much of you. But, don't you see—this is all for the good—Mother will have a healthy heir, and Leo will have a wife who loves him—won't he? Won't he?"

Finally, Aelwyn nodded. "As you wish. I will play both parts for a while," she said slowly. "It won't be too hard, as the Order is going into its silent recess where the sisters are in seclusion for a month, and I am to remain in my cell for a good part of the day. At the end of it, they will discover that I have 'escaped' as well, leaving a note that makes it clear I have returned to Avalon and that I have bequeathed the powers of the Morgaine to you—who is really me, of course."

Marie was shocked at the detail of Aelwyn's plan. It was as if her friend had been thinking about this for a while.

"But will people really believe that you can transfer the Morgaine's power to me?"

"They will when 'you' demonstrate your power for them. My father won't be fooled, of course, nor your mother. But by then it will be too late. They will have to accept me as Princess and Morgaine both, or risk a revolution that could bring down the Empire."

"It will be done, then," Marie said, putting her hand on Aelwyn's cheek. "You will be me. And I will be with Gill."

"Good luck, Marie," Aelwyn said. "I hope very much that you know what you are doing."

Marie laughed. "I don't . . . but maybe that is for the best. This will be the greatest adventure of my life."

She hugged her friend tightly, said good-bye, and did not look back once.

On the way to her apartments, Marie ran into Hugh Borel, the so-called Red Duke, who had been in and out of St. James Palace throughout the season with the French contingent. She hoped he was happy with the reinstatement of Orleans into the court. Perhaps Aelwyn would do Isabelle a service and take her as one of her attending ladies.

"Princess," he said, bowing.

"Lord Burgundy," she said with a smile, hoping he would not desire anything beyond the usual formalities. She knew she should be flattered by all the attention, but run-ins with obsequious courtiers usually resulted in another round of coughing.

"Congratulations again. I wish you every happiness with Prince Leopold," he said with a shy smile.

"Thank you," she said. "And thank you for your most generous gift. I hear our sommelier is beside himself."

"It is our pleasure." He smiled. "It is an honor to be part of your wedding."

Marie smiled and did not respond, hoping he would get the idea and gracefully end the conversation.

"No one will have seen anything like it, I'm sure," he said. "It will be spectacular, a real thrill." It appeared he had more to say, but Marie had had enough.

"Yes, yes, thank you. Please excuse me," she said, trying not to be too rude and feeling a coughing spell coming on.

"By all means, Your Highness." He bowed, but Marie could tell he was annoyed to have been dismissed so quickly.

She shook it off. She was tired of trying to please everyone. She was looking forward to tomorrow, when she would only have to worry about herself.

Monarch
AND MERLIN

he next morning, before the sisterhood went into seclusion, Aelwyn was called into her father's office. Emrys's back was turned to her. He was facing the window to the garden, where the staff were putting the finishing touches on that night's party. When he turned around to face her at last, he looked grim. Agitated, even, which was not a quality she associated with him. Even when he exiled her to Avalon four years ago, he had not cracked a smile or raised his voice but had merely said that neither she nor London were safe until she learned to control her powers, and then directed the Lord Chamberlain to pack her belongings.

"Father." She bowed.

He motioned for her to sit, and she did, wondering why he had called her in. Did he know exactly what she and Marie were planning? In a moment he could clap chains on them both and put them to the fire. It was a terrible thing to say about your father, but hadn't he banished her to Avalon without a second thought? Without knowing or caring whether she would return? Though he was strict, she was certain he could never inflict the ultimate punishment on his daughter. Could he? Marie certainly believed the queen would, and why would the Merlin be any different?

She touched the white illusion stone around her neck for luck. The Merlin observed this gesture with a frown, and again she wondered if he knew what was afoot. But then he closed his eyes and sighed deeply.

"My time grows ever shorter, my daughter," he said, eyes still closed. "You must be ready when you are called to serve."

"I will be, Father."

His eyes opened, but they were no more readable than when they had been concealed behind his wrinkled lids.

"How do you find the studies of the sisterhood?"

Aelwyn was prepared to trot out another reflexive answer. *The sisterhood's spellbooks are full of wisdom*, or some such platitude. But the sharpness of her father's gaze made her hold her tongue. This was not another of his formal interactions. He wanted the truth.

She shrugged. "Dull," she said. "Rote."

Aelwyn couldn't be sure, but she thought she saw a smile flicker at the edge of her father's mouth.

"You prefer Viviane's approach to magic. Emotional. Elemental. You find the spellbooks too limited."

Aelwyn found her fingers caressing the illusion stone around her neck. "The spellwork of the Invisible Orders is indeed powerful, but devoid of"—she struggled to find the right word—"imagination. Beauty. *Passion*. Whereas Viviane's magic is like a wave of emotion that flows through the body. Solid at its core, but ragged around the edges. Hard to predict what its final effect will be."

"Hard to control, you mean," the Merlin said brusquely. "I too have known the lure of Avalon's magic, daughter. I know how powerful it can be. But it is like a team of horses pulling a carriage. You hold the reins and think that you're in control, but then a dog barks or a firearm discharges and the horses seize the bit and race off and nothing will stop them until they choose to stop themselves. With magic like that you are nothing more than a passenger."

"But if you keep your seat you *can* ride it out," Aelwyn insisted. "And how much more thrilling is that?"

"We do not use magic for the thrill of it!" Emrys said sharply. "It is not a toy. It is a duty." Then his face softened and he settled back into his seat. "I am feeling my age, my child," he said. "And, like it or not, you are my only heir. You must promise me that you will remain bound by the strictures of the Order. The sisters' magic may be literal, as you say, but it is powerful, and it has kept the world safe for five hundred years. You cannot imagine the chaos before I established it.

It made Lamac look like a playground spat. Once you take the oath of service," he continued, "you will be bound to the crown for a thousand years, and I will leave this body that I have inhabited for just as long. You will be Morgaine to Marie-Victoria, Leopold and generations of their descendants, and . . ." His voice trailed off and his expression became almost wistful. "I will return to Avalon."

The tone of her father's voice when he said the name of his homeland caught her off guard. "So you feel the pull of Avalon's magic too, Father."

A kind of bark emerged from her father's thin lips, a sound so strange it took her a moment to recognize it as a laugh.

"Of course I feel it! I have felt it every day for the past five hundred years! And you will feel it too. But you must resist it. For the Empire. And for your subjects. Though you will hold no title other than Morgaine, though you will own no palace or land and will never take a husband or bear children, you will still be the invisible hand that runs the Empire. You must keep that hand steady."

Aelwyn found it hard to digest what she was hearing. "I can't understand why you sent me there in the first place if you knew the life I was to lead here. It's almost as if you hoped I wouldn't come back."

Her father sat back in his chair as if he had been caught.

"But that can't be true," Aelwyn continued. "I am, as you say, your only heir, and the Empire cannot exist without its Merlin or Morgaine. Which raises the question again: why send me to Avalon, when you knew that Viviane would not only instruct me in the wyrdding ways, but teach me to esteem them over the gray magic of the Invisible Orders?"

"I sent instructions to Viviane expressly forbidding—"

It was Aelwyn's turn to laugh.

"When has your sister ever listened to you? When have you ever listened to her, for that matter? Nearly a thousand years ago you divided the world between you like Zeus and Hades, one to Heaven, one to Hell, and ne'er the twain shall meet."

"But they *have* met," the Merlin said, his voice filled with strange urgency, "in *you*."

"I—" Aelwyn's mouth closed. She knew her father wouldn't answer her next question. But why did it seem like he was saying that he had *wanted* her to disobey him? That he wanted her to embrace the lessons she had learned in Avalon, at his sister's side? How strange it must be to be a parent! On the one hand, you wanted your children to obey your every command, to be like you in every way. But you also wanted them to be independent, their own persons. To defy you. To come into their own.

But she would never know, would she, for as the Morgaine, she would never bear children. Not that she cared about offspring at this stage in her life. But the thought that she could never have them in the future was daunting. Except, of course, the Merlin *had* fathered a child. She was living proof. Maybe there were even others like her. . . . But if she ever bore a child, she would have to give the baby up to the Order as her father had done, sentence her own progeny to a life of servitude. *An honor*, Emrys had always said. *A shackle*, Viviane had argued. Perhaps it was both.

Her father peered at her intensely, and Aelwyn couldn't help but wonder, as she had a thousand times before, if he was able to read her mind. But all he said was: "Do you know what the sisterhood and the brotherhood truly do, Aelwyn? Do you know what my job is? What your job will be?"

Aelwyn waited patiently, as she surmised her father was speaking rhetorically.

"We keep the kingdom safe, my daughter. From the rot inside as well as from the dangers outside. Viviane believes that we have surrendered our power, but in truth, we are the power behind the throne. The wizard chooses the monarch. *We* place the crown on their heads. It has always been thus.

"But in order to do our job well, we work in the shadows, we serve. Power must not be concentrated in one person alone. The temptation that comes with the crown is too great for any wizard, and magic unbridled would only bring chaos. A wizard or sorceress must never sit on the Lily Throne. Never. It would be a corruption of the delicate balance that has kept this empire robust for almost a thousand years."

Nervously, she fingered the illusion stone again, thinking that if Marie and Gill went through with their wild plan, her part in it would be the ultimate betrayal. She would become Queen *and* Morgaine, she would bear Leo's children and raise them as well, uniting magical and political power.

Is that what she wanted?

To break her oath?

To betray her father?

To put the empire at risk?

A phrase from her father's speech popped into her mind. *The rot inside.* A hidden enemy.

Did her father know their plan?

She'd thought this deception was a simple thing, for love, for Marie, for freedom, but as she listened to her father's words, she knew what it really was.

Treason.

The rot inside.

A hidden enemy.

Was it her?

She noticed her father's left hand then. It sat on his thigh, all but concealed inside the long sleeve of his dark robe. But she could just glimpse the fingers, curled into a loose fist, the thumb slightly protruding between middle and ring fingers. It was an ancient gesture, as old as magic itself: the ward against dark magic. But the gesture belonged not to the world of gray magic—the contained magic of "spells and books" as Viviane dismissively referred to it—but to the wyrdding ways her aunt had taught her in Avalon. The ancient green magic wielded by Jeanne of Arkk that her father had outlawed and spent more than a century rooting out and destroying after he helped establish the Franco-British Empire in 1429. Why on earth would he resort to such a gesture, and in his sanctum sanctorum no less? The safest place in the palace, in London, in the entire Empire. Why would her father resort to an almost superstitious gesture, like a frightened child?

Was it meant for her?

Just then her father saw where she was looking and ducked his hand deeper in his sleeve.

"Father—"

A knock on the door cut her off. The Merlin sounded almost relieved as he called: "Enter!"

The door opened, revealing the Lord Chamberlain himself, which could only mean a message from the queen.

"Father," she began again.

The Merlin's left hand emerged from his sleeve. The ward had been released, and he waved her silent.

"You may leave us now."

There was nothing else to say. Aelwyn stood, bowed slightly, then turned to the door.

"My Lord Chamberlain," she said coldly. The queen's chief of staff had a knack for showing up at just the wrong time. Only then did she notice that the Lord Chamberlain was not alone. Trailing behind him like a shark after an ocean liner hoping for a bit of chum was Duncan Oswald, master-of-arms in the Prussian court. Oswald's eyes were as bright and calculating as the Merlin's. He stared at her coolly.

"The princess asked after you," the Lord Chamberlain said, his voice professionally inscrutable. "She said she was sorry not to see you at the Bal du Drap d'Or."

Aelwyn's heart beat faster. "What an odd thing to say," she said in the lightest voice she could muster. "The princess knows that as an acolyte of the Invisible Orders I cannot attend such a gathering."

"Indeed," the Lord Chamberlain replied. "It was almost as if she had forgotten that you were the future Morgaine. She said you would have loved to see her dance with Prince Leopold."

Aelwyn peered at the Lord Chamberlain, but if he was hinting that he knew something was going on between her and Marie, his face didn't reveal it.

"Yes," she said finally. "I would have loved to see that." And she slipped past him and Oswald and headed out of the office.

As she hurried down the hall, Aelwyn's thoughts flitted back to the night of the royal ball, when she had danced with Leopold. At first she'd wondered why it was that the prince had accepted Marie's transformation so wholeheartedly. But she'd realized that Leo had just taken her change of heart in stride. To his way of thinking, Marie had simply succumbed to his charm, and the look in his eyes was triumph, not suspicion. To him, it was simply natural that the princess would finally come around to the way everyone else thought about him. But could there be something more to his misperception?

Not trust or even smugness, but somehow, maybe he did know that the Marie who danced with him and returned his kisses was in no way like the shy girl who demurely removed her hand when he placed his over it?

She remembered a conversation they'd had the night of the ball. They had stopped dancing, as Leo wanted to take a stroll through the Crystal Palace.

"Such a beautiful country," he said to her. "When we are married, we will travel the empire. In Paris they have erected the Tour Eiffel."

"Yes, my lord." Aelwyn nodded, thinking it would be wonderful to see the world, to see every part of it. This was what she had left Avalon for—to see and feel and experience everything.

"We must make certain to keep the empire safe and whole. The Iron Knights have reunited after their failed coup d'état. They are only biding their time. One hears that they have found a way to counter Avalon's magic and the protection that keeps us all sleeping soundly in our beds."

"You will keep us safe, my prince?" she asked, her eyes bright.

"Yes, we will start here, in this city. Already there is too much theft, corruption, and danger. One cannot even travel the queen's road without being set upon by bandits. It is a shame. They must learn to fear our strength again. I shall restore order and bring peace."

"A nation needs a strong arm," she said.

"And I will give it to them." He smiled.

"Yes," she said. "You will."

·34·

Lady CALLER

onan, it is simply not done. You cannot think you can go to the palace and call on the prince without an invitation," Vera said, scandalized, as Ronan adjusted her hat in the mirror. She had suggested a few tweaks to the milliner, who complimented her on her good eye for design.

"Why not? It's the twentieth century, Vera, and I am tired of waiting," she said. It had been more than a week since the royal ball. Ronan had been very good and patient, going through the motions of the season: calling on great ladies, attending a few minor suppers and dances with Archie and Perry. But it appeared their circles did not overlap with Wolf's; while Marcus had become a diligent suitor, and had taken to calling on her every other day, the one she was waiting for never showed.

Ronan was a modern American girl, and not one to wait around. She knew Wolf was staying in apartments in St. James Palace with his brother, and what could it hurt? Why couldn't she go to him? Perhaps he was busy, or he did not know where she was staying (doubtful). It appealed to her spirit of adventure—that same bravery, she thought, that he had so admired on the *Saturnia*.

He had admired and loved her once; he could do so again, she was certain. She was going to make him love her once more, or die trying.

And hadn't she already been presented to the queen? That meant she was part of society—didn't it?

"You may call on him *after* he calls on you, but only then! A lady does not call on the gentleman first!" Vera admonished, wringing her hands.

"Relax, Vera. It will be fine. I bet he'll like it."

When she arrived at the black gates of St. James, her confidence wavered a little. Was she doing the right thing? Or was this foolishness? Wolf was reckless and impulsive, and so was she; she wanted to show him that. Also, she wanted to see him again. The days of the season were ticking by; soon it would be over, and she would be back on a ship headed to New York, and not in a grand stateroom courtesy of the Prussian royal family, but in some tiny second- or even third-class cabin where she and Vera would have to bunk one on top of the other. There was so little time. Every day she did not accept Marcus Deveraux's proposal was a day that her parents' investment in her was unmet.

The lord steward of the house greeted her and showed her to a front reception hall. "Is Prince Wolfgang expecting you?" he asked.

Though both his face and his voice remained utterly impassive, he somehow still managed to ooze condescension. But Ronan had been raised by Bits Astor, and if she knew how to do anything, it was how to bend a reluctant servant to her will.

"No, I think not," she said, her voice both casual and imperious at the same time. "I thought I would call on him, as I missed him at the vernissage the other day." She handed him her card, which he stared at for several seconds, as though it were written in Greek or Chinese. At length he bowed, spun on his heel, and slipped out of the reception room.

So far, so good, she thought, studying the portraits in the palace. Each ruler had a portrait next to the Merlin. It was amazing to see the Merlin so unchanged over the centuries. Uncanny. The kings and queens were seated on the Lily Throne, draped in sumptuous robes, festooned with medals, and wearing the crown jewels. But it was the Merlin, standing to one side in the same plain black robe in picture after picture, who managed to convey real authority. The power behind the throne, Ronan thought.

There were footsteps in the hallway. She turned to greet

Wolf, but it was not him who appeared. It was the tall, thin, crusty old man who was always at his side.

"Miss Astor?"

She nodded.

"I am Duncan Oswald, master-at-arms. I am sorry to say that the prince cannot see you this afternoon. He has a very full schedule."

"Oh, it would only take a minute—I just wanted to say hello," she said, disappointed.

"I am afraid he cannot see you."

"Or he doesn't want to," she said, unwilling to apologize for her impudence.

"I am sorry, Miss Astor."

She nodded, her pride burning. She began to walk out of the reception room when she saw who else but Wolf rounding the corner with his brother. "Wolf!" she cried. "Wolf! It's me—Ronan!"

But it was Leo who turned first. Up close he was even more handsome than when she'd seen him at a distance at the ball. If anything, he was possibly more good-looking than Wolf, all golden skin and high cheekbones, his bright hair burnished to a sheen. His eyes narrowed when they landed on her, and something sparked in their depths. As he stared at her, she could have sworn she glimpsed the tip of his tongue poking lasciviously from his lips. A shiver ran down her spine. She didn't know if she was turned on or repulsed. Or she knew, but didn't want to admit it to herself.

Leo turned back to Wolf. "The young lady has called your name, little brother. How odd, as she has not been announced by the steward," he said with a mocking salute before turning and marching down the hall.

"I'm sorry to just burst in on you like this—" she started to say, but Wolf started toward Ronan so violently that she fell silent. He looked . . . scandalized. Ashamed, even. His cheeks were red and his eyes flitted between her and the courtiers, as if he was trying to convince himself they hadn't seen her.

His obvious distress at the sight of her was almost too much, but Bits's training took over.

"I was most sorry not to see you at the vernissage the other night, Your Highness. I hope you were not taken ill," she said. The formality of her tone pleased her. She sounded more royal than the princess herself.

Wolf glanced anxiously at the courtiers again, before stepping closer to her. "Ronan! What do you think you're doing? You can't be here!" he whispered fiercely.

Wolf sounded nothing like a prince when he spoke—he sounded just like a nervous boy from some backwater like Chicago or Prague. A boy whose fling had come back to haunt him. Yet this very lack of pretension revealed that it was he who was to the manor born, and she was just an American girl, uncouth, striving, and, apparently, unwanted. Her composure crumbled.

"I—I'm calling on you. What does it look like I'm doing?" She reached for his hands but he stepped out of reach.

"But—you can't—this is *not done*," he said angrily. "You should have waited for me to call on you first."

"But you didn't call."

"I know—I—" He broke off, his eyes darting to the lord steward, who, though he stared off into the middle distance, gave off the air of a man tapping his watch, indicating that it was time to get a move on.

Wolf took a deep breath. "You should go, Ronan," he said firmly. "For both our sakes."

Ronan felt her eyes widen, her jaw drop. She couldn't believe what she was hearing. "You're telling me to leave?"

Wolf's only answer was to turn to the lord steward. "If you would please arrange for a hansom to take Miss Astor wherever she would like to go."

"Of course, sir." The servant bowed.

Fury seized Ronan.

"That won't be necessary," she said, grabbing her parasol and pushing past him so roughly that one of the courtiers started. He was actually ashamed of her!

"Good-bye, *Your Highness*," she said, her voice dripping with sarcasm. She would be damned if she saw him again.

· 35 ·

Midnight
IN THE GARDEN

$\mathcal{I}$sabelle studied herself in the mirror as she assumed the position, hands braced against the marble top of the dresser, feet splayed on the parquet floor. Her hair was simply yet elegantly braided atop her head, with a few spiraling ringlets framing her face. Her décolletage looked fabulous if she said so herself, her breasts powdered and pushed up by her corset into two pale, plump mounds. *Leo is a fool,* she said to herself. *That skinny Marie may wear the crown, but she'll never boast a chest as* magnifique *as this.*

"Tighter!" she urged.

A cool breeze raised goose bumps on her bare legs as an unseen figure approached her from behind and began to push and pull, tug and twist, until Isabelle felt that her insides were being pushed up and out of her mouth like frosting squeezed through a pastry bag.

"Do please hurry," she moaned. "I don't know how much more of this I can stand."

"I'm sorry, milady, but I can't quite make it fit."

Isabelle sighed as a black-capped face appeared from behind hers in the mirror over the dresser. Her pinched lips and wrinkled brow suggested that it had not been an easy week attending the Lady of Orleans.

"Perhaps you have another corset? A . . . bigger one?" the maid asked, as she lost her grip on the stays and Isabelle's body bounced out of the corset.

"Ugh," Isabelle said in exasperation. "Fine, let's just go with the pink dress I wore to the Bal."

She took one last look at the white dress laid on the bed as the maid snatched it up and hurried into the dressing room. It would have looked exquisite on her, with its hourglass waist and deep square neckline barely concealed beneath the thinnest layer of gossamer tulle. Perhaps the most daring part of the dress was its hemline, though. It stopped mid calf, and would have shown off several inches of ankle, not to mention the most darling pair of shoes—white lambskin as soft as silk, with a button closure intricately embroidered in roses and violets. But there was no way she could squeeze into it without a proper corset.

Normally she would have been aghast at the idea of wearing

the same dress in public more than once—and at court, no less! But now that she had decided to spend her future alone, there was nothing she wanted more than to leave London immediately and start her new life, far away from everything. Hugh, however, insisted she attend the opening party at the palace gardens. She could not refuse lest she arouse suspicion, for he would never let her go if he knew what she was planning. And despite her resolution, she had looked forward to another opportunity to show these English girls how a real Frenchwoman dressed. But fine, she would wear the pink number again. Let them whisper that Lady Orleans was some kind of pauper, that she was lucky to be alive in light of her family's efforts to conquer England five hundred years ago, let alone invited to court. Soon she would be back among her beloved vineyards, while Marie and Leo and all the rest of them grew drunk on her wine. . . .

The pink dress slipped on easily, and in a few moments she was ready to go. The lady's maid stepped back and gave Isabelle one final look to make sure everything was in place.

"'At's a lovely dress, 'at is," she said approvingly. "What my mum calls 'forgiving.'"

"I beg your pardon!" Isabelle thundered. "What are you saying?"

"Oh, oh!" the maid stuttered. "It's just that—" She pointed to Isabelle's waist, her words trailing off.

"What are you trying to say, exactly?!" she said, sucking

in her stomach and pulling herself up to her full five feet two inches. In her fury she slipped into French. *"Dites-moi!"*

The maid's eyes went wide with horror and fear. "Nothing, milady," she mumbled, dropping into a low curtsy. "If that's all . . . ?"

"Go!" Isabelle roared. "And tell the palace I won't be needing your services any longer. I would rather dress myself than suffer such insolence!"

The maid all but ran from the room as Isabelle snatched up a small string purse and stormed out as well, heading for the line of carriages that waited by the palace's side entrance. To dare suggest that she, Isabelle of Orleans, did not have an ideal shape! She had simply outgrown her corset, that was all. Never mind that she'd had them made just last month. The way these seamstresses worked these days, their clothes were practically too small even as they sewed the last stitch. And heaven knew that looser gowns were infinitely more comfortable anyway—she should have ordered three, rather than just the one she wore to the Bal du Drap d'Or, but Hugh monitored her clothing allowance with a miser's obsessive attention to detail. He said the vineyard was losing a fortune in profits off the five hundred barrels of wine they'd gifted Marie and Leo, so there wasn't money to waste on a new dress for every social occasion.

Typically the garden party was an afternoon affair, but since it was a special season—the Wedding Season, as everyone was calling it now—the palace decided to throw the party at night, complete with billowing striped tents, a full orchestra, and dancing. The most magical decoration of all, however—literally as well as figuratively—was the lighting, which was composed of a half dozen transparent globes suspended above the garden, each filled with ten thousand fireflies whose combined luminescence bathed the entire party in a softly pulsing golden glow. The gardens were transformed into a wonderland worthy of Titania and Oberon's court. A true midsummer night's dream—a carnival and a party, all in one.

Yet to Isabelle the scene looked like something out of a Bosch painting, a tableau vivant on the subject of vanity designed expressly to mock her thwarted ambitions. She alit from her carriage and looked around for a darker corner. Maybe no one would notice that she was wearing the same dress she'd had on at the ball. But before she could slink off, the greasy face of her guardian appeared in front of her, a conniving grin on his lumpy lips.

"Ah, Isabelle, there you are! I was wondering if you were ever going to arrive." Hugh's hand wrapped around her upper arm in a gesture whose chivalric appearance was belied by the viselike grip of his fingers as he spun her like a music box ballerina. "May I introduce you to Lord Stanley," he said, gesturing to a handsome young man puffing on a cigar.

Lord Stanley had a swoop of dark hair rolled off his forehead in a pompadour style, and his jacket sleeves were pushed up to his elbows. He looked her over slyly. "So this is the famous Isabelle of Orleans," he said.

Pulling her arm from Hugh's grip, Isabelle waved the smoke away from her face and forced a smile. "Pleasure . . ."

". . . is all mine," William Stanley said, smiling at her with a leer and forgetting to kiss her hand.

Isabelle nodded politely and glanced at Hugh. But her cousin, having displayed his wares like a farmer herding his cows to market, had already tottered to the bar for another drink. Without a look back at Lord Stanley, Isabelle walked away. If Hugh thought he could fob her off on just anyone, he was mistaken. She would never marry any of these arrogant fools.

With relief she spotted the familiar dark head of her cousin Louis, and began to hurry in his direction. Her heart leaped—only to fall again when she saw that he was with the girl from the other morning. She was wrapped around his arm like a koala, a cuddly-looking but apparently quite stupid creature from the Australasian territories—the royal couple had received one as a wedding present.

Louis extricated himself from koala-girl's grip and came up to Isabelle, kissing her on both cheeks with affection. "You look tired," he said, concerned.

Mon Dieu, what was it with people tonight? First her rent-a-maid suggests she is not quite as sylphlike as she had been, and now Louis tells her she looks tired?

"Thanks, that's just what a girl wants to hear," she said dryly. When she saw the hurt look on his face, she apologized. "I'm sorry, I don't feel like myself lately. It's all this bland British food. I can't wait to get back to Orleans for some good old *cornichons et crème glacée.*"

Louis laughed. "It can't be as bad all that. It's all right, Izzy," he continued with a sigh. "I'm used to your moods."

"It's not a 'mood,'" Isabelle said, annoyed. "If you had been treated—" She broke off. There was no point in taking her anger out on dear, sweet Louis. It wasn't his fault that Leo had thrown her over for Marie's stolen crown, or that Hugh was trying to sell her off to some nouveau riche industrialist with a purchased title. "I suppose you've had fun this season," she said in a softer tone. "You seem to have become quite a favorite of Celestine. Be careful—her father might have your head if he finds out you have been taking liberties with his youngest daughter."

"There is nothing to fear from the duke. I aim to propose to Celestine tonight," Louis said as they made their way through the garden maze toward the main tent, where jugglers, acrobats, and fire-eaters were performing for the entertainment of the assembled guests.

Isabelle had been distracted by a mime that came too close, so when Louis's words sank in she was not prepared to hear them. "What do you mean, propose?"

"It's only right," Louis said, clenching his jaw.

"But you are only—"

"I turn eighteen next month, and will come into my inheritance. Hugh is ready to settle the estate for me. I will leave before the summer ends."

Isabelle turned to her cousin with a new light in her eyes. *Of course.* While Louis was a Valois through his mother, he had an inheritance through his father as well. He was the Count Beziers of Languedoc. There was a small castle in Cévennes that came with a yearly income and some land. The vineyards were tiny but the harvest was impeccable. It was nowhere near as large an estate as Orleans, but it would be enough to satisfy the Duke of Montrose. One less daughter to worry about.

Louis held her hand. "I hope you can be happy for me, Isabelle. I hope you will come visit me and Celestine sometime."

"Oh, Louis," she sighed. "I *am* happy for you." Sweet Louis, who had always been such a good person, a good friend, and a good man. Where did she go so wrong? How was it that some silly British girl could capture his heart, his hand, and all the riches of his inheritance in one fell swoop? How did it happen so quickly? What had Isabelle been doing while Louis was growing up and falling in love?

She had been alone with Hugh for too long, and had grasped on to Leopold as an escape, only to find that the raft was sinking. It was a pity one never loved the person who loved you until it was too late. And it was too late; she could see that. Louis was only standing by her to be polite, but his eyes were already scanning the crowd, looking for his love.

"I want to do the right thing—we got a bit carried away before, and I want to make sure that she is taken care of. I want to take care of her," he said. It was as if he was talking to himself more than her. His Adam's apple bobbed painfully.

"Of course you do." She nodded. "Well then, what are you waiting for? Get down on one knee. Isn't that what the season is for?"

· 36 ·

Midnight IN THE GARDEN PART TWO

onan did not think she had merited an invitation to the garden party, but Perry insisted that he had called on Lady Marlborough, who held the lists, and she'd assured him Ronan's name was on it. "Perhaps you made an impression at the royal ball," he told her. "Don't look so shocked. This is what the parties are for, you know, to see beautiful young people out and about. You are very decorative, and just between you and me, the court is looking a wee bit dismal these days. They need fresh blood."

She was pleased to have been selected and excited, too, to see the real palace where the royal family lived. St. James was the center of the world. In the past few days she had been visited by the Boring Baron more times than she could count. He had sent many lovely bouquets and had been very close to proposing, she could tell. He just needed a little nudge from her, a little indication that his proposal would be accepted. It was the same with Marcus, who was soldiering on with his courtship like a lad getting through his finals, checking all the boxes with a dogged determination. Yet Ronan could not do it; could not bring herself to accept either of them. She had simply smiled and thanked them both for their company and sent them away.

Her visit to St. James the other day still made her burn to think about. The way Wolf had dismissed her—as if she were a mere scullery maid! Well, she would show him. She had been *invited* to the palace this time. And if she saw him, she would ignore him until he felt as hurt as she did.

Ronan arrived at the party in a beautiful turquoise gown. Her maid had draped her hair with a string of lustrous pearls. Archie and Perry were dressed in "penguin suits"—practically casual wear. They each had on black jackets and bow ties, though Archie had taken advantage of some minor Scottish title attached to the family through his mother's line to liven up his suit with a cummerbund done in an awfully loud and gaudy plaid. "It's really truly hideous," he said when he unbuttoned his jacket to show it to Ronan, "but the looks on these stuffy old faces is totally worth it."

Perry had sewn a magical pocket into his suit from which he produced a perfectly chilled bottle of champagne. He had just refilled their flutes when Ronan saw one of her suitors approaching from the left, and winced. "Quick, hide me, it's the Boring Baron," she said. "He aims to propose and I can't let him—otherwise I'll face *his* mother's wrath, I'm sure."

She had finally made peace with Lady Julia over tea, who pretended not to know what Ronan was talking about, and insisted that Marcus had most likely been joking.

"Never fear, my lady." Perry smiled, pushing her behind a tent flap while the baron, Lord Audley, looked confused.

"Did I just see Miss Astor?" he said to Archie.

Archie whipped his head side to side theatrically, as if he was just as shocked as Lord Audley to find Ronan gone.

"She was just here a moment ago!" he exclaimed, hamming it up. "I've heard those Americans have worked up some new magical tricks all their own. Maybe she vanished into thin air!"

Lord Audley frowned. "I've heard that such a thing is possible, but the talismans required are *appallingly* expensive. She must be *quite* wealthy indeed."

Ronan bit back a laugh behind the tent flap. The way the Lord Audley said "quite wealthy indeed" made her wonder if he was chasing her for her money. *Wouldn't that be rich?* she thought, all puns intended.

"And if I were a beautiful single American debutante," Archie was saying, "I know just where I'd vanish to: the bar!" He pointed to the opposite end of the party. "It's where all the men are, after all."

"Oh dear," the Boring Baron said, sounding very put out. "Then I had perhaps best make my way toward the libations, hadn't I?"

"Most definitely," Archie said, shooing him off with a little pat on the bottom.

"I saw that!" Perry hissed as he and Ronan tumbled out from behind the tent, laughing hysterically.

"Firmer than it looks," Archie said mischievously. "Sure you're not dismissing him too hastily?" he said to Ronan.

"Some of us are looking for more than a firm bottom in a future husband," Ronan answered in a faux demure tone of voice.

"Hey! I resent that remark!" Perry said, his outrage as fake as Ronan's hauteur.

Archie clapped his boyfriend on the butt. "Don't you worry, darling, Lord Audley's behind doesn't hold a candle to this one."

Ronan laughed so hard she was afraid she was going to split the seam of her latest Whitney Van Owen gown.

This is fun! she thought to herself. If only every evening could be like this. Sipping champagne from crystal flutes that magically refilled themselves and laughing at slightly off-color jokes. But despite the prodigious size of Whitney Van Owen's continental trousseau, this evening's beautiful dress was the third-to-last. Soon she would have to start—shudder—repeating outfits like that sad French girl, Isabelle, whom Ronan had glimpsed when she came in, wearing the same (admittedly lovely) gown she'd worn to the Bal du Drap d'Or a few days ago. A faux pas like that would empty out a girl's marriage prospects like the shelves of Lord & Taylor the day after a sale. Not that any of these duchesses, countesses, and ladies knew what the inside of a department store looked like. All their clothes were bespoke, of course, made by tailors and seamstresses who descended on their palaces and châteaux with reams of silk and velvet and lace. Only the poor provincial Astors had to "go shopping," just like every other untitled colonial subject.

This gloomy train of thought was interrupted when, out of the corner of her eye, she saw him. *Him.* It was as if she had a sixth sense when it came to Wolf—as if she could close her eyes and divine his presence when he was near. But outwardly she gave no indication that she was vibrating with anticipation, and continued to chat gaily with her friends.

"Oh, there's the Lupine One," Perry said, motioning to Wolf, who was talking to three very pretty girls. "With those Montrose lasses. I wonder who he'll choose? Or perhaps he'll take all of them," he said, looking pleased at the naughty idea.

"Rumor has it that Celestine has been going about with that dreamy Louis-Philippe—Count Beziers of Languedoc."

"He *is* dreamy," Perry agreed. "But he doesn't a candle to *Woof*," making the last word more bark than name.

"He asked about you at the vernissage, you know," Archie said, elbowing Ronan.

"Did he, now?" she said, keeping her face serene.

"Mmm-hmm," Perry said.

Ronan shrugged. "He can ask about me all he wants. Questions are free, aren't they?" And turning quickly, she led her two friends deeper into the party—and out of Wolf's line of sight. She knew exactly how to play his game.

After dinner, which was truly lovely—outdoors under the tents, with the fireflies flickering and the moon so pale and white—the evening started with a few dances. Ronan made sure that every time she saw Wolf approaching, she was able to cajole a nearby gentleman to dance with her. In a few minutes, her dance card was full.

She could feel his eyes on her the entire evening, but she paid him no attention. Even when they were practically next to each other and he said, "Excuse me, Miss Astor."

She just shrugged and danced away with Marcus, who was determined to win her over, it seemed, with a variety of whining, mooning, and annoyance. "What is wrong with you? Aren't you here to find a husband?" he said testily. She had just told him she was unsure of her schedule for the next few weeks.

"Can't one simply enjoy the season?" she said lightly. "Oh, come now, Lord Deveraux, let's be friends."

"Friends," he said mournfully. "I have enough friends."

Finally it was the end of the evening, and Ronan had danced with almost every eligible young (and not-so-young) man in the place. She stood to the side, fanning herself. She was glistening, the night was beautiful, and she had quite enjoyed herself. The band played the most marvelous music, and there were many fun and handsome boys to choose from. But even though she refused to acknowledge Wolf's existence, she found it just as hard to concentrate on the other boys on offer.

She saw Wolf nursing a drink on the other side of the room. He caught her eye and walked purposefully toward her. She ignored him, remembering again how insulted she had felt the other day when she had come to call. Truly, these fat-headed Europeans should join the twentieth century. In New York, no one would think twice.

"Ronan," he said.

She turned away. "Did you hear something, Archie?" she said. "I don't see anyone, do you?"

Archie raised his eyebrows. "We don't?"

"Ronan, please," Wolf said. "Please hear me out."

She rolled her eyes. "I guess he can't get enough of me." She nodded to the boys to indicate they could leave her with him. She turned to Wolf coldly. "Enjoying the evening, *mein herr?*" she asked.

Wolf winced at her German. "Your pronunciation is almost as bad as my mother's was."

Ronan was confused. "Your mother wasn't Prussian?"

"At some point in the distant past, maybe."

"I'm afraid I don't follow."

"If I remember correctly, my father's grandfather?—great-grandfather?—married off his youngest daughter to the king of Sweden sometime in the middle of the last century, in order to cement a truce that had just ended the Prussian-Swedish War. That woman's son or grandson became the most recent king of Sweden, and he returned the favor by marrying his daughter—my father's grandfather's sister's granddaughter, or something like that—to my father, who just happens to be her third or fourth cousin."

Ronan couldn't help but laugh. "My goodness, how on earth do you keep track of all that?"

"Clearly I don't," he said, laughing too. It felt good to laugh with Wolf as they had laughed aboard the *Saturnia*, and for a moment Ronan forgot she was angry at him. But then she remembered, and she bit off her laughter and turned to look quite obviously at a handsome boy who waltzed past with some young debutante on his arm.

"Lord Barrymore," she called, "don't forget you're next on my dance card."

Lord Barrymore grinned over his date's shoulder. "Oh, believe me, I won't."

Wolf cleared his throat in annoyance. "I was hoping I would get a chance to speak to you and explain about the other day, yet I find I can barely get a word in before you are whisked off by another ridiculous boy. I mean, what's the point in even being a prince if you can't get a pretty girl to pay attention to you?"

Ronan continued to stare after Lord Barrymore, who

couldn't tear his eyes from hers. "It seems that with girls as well as thrones you're always coming in second. Perhaps next time you won't ignore a girl when she calls on you," she said bitingly.

Wolf winced. "Ronan—I am sorry for the way I acted. I should not have turned you away. You surprised me, and court etiquette is very strict about these things. You don't understand."

"I understand that *you* did not follow the protocol to call on me, either, and so I thought I would give you a chance to make up for that. Instead, I was humiliated."

"My father was there that day, and it looked as if you were one of those girls who are always accusing me of 'siring a child upon them'—and that you'd come after me. And don't forget, I'm a guest in this country, just like you. And Leo's so eager to make a good impression on the court—he's going to be their king, after all."

Ronan rolled her eyes. As if she cared who was going to be king of England and France, or Transylvania, for that matter. "You have girls accusing you of getting them pregnant?"

"Yes—very many."

"And have you?"

"No!" he said. "I've never—it's all lies and entrapment. It's a tactic. They hope to blackmail me into marriage somehow."

"But I assume you did play strip billiards with them, didn't you?"

He did not protest, which she took as a yes. *He'll break your heart, that one—be careful of him.* Wasn't that what Perry had told her?

"It was nice to see you, Prince. But I'm afraid I am full up all evening," she said.

"Oh, you mean this?" he asked, holding up her dance card.

"Where did you get that?" she asked, searching her pockets. "Give it back!"

Wolf smiled as he tore it in half, then into tiny little pieces that fluttered to the ground.

"Excuse me!" Ronan said indignantly.

"Relax—now you are mine all evening." Wolf smiled and took her in his arms. He whispered in her ear, "Come, now—you have made your point, and I have made mine. We are meant for each other, can't you see?"

Ronan knew she should pull free from Wolf's embrace. Should storm out of the party or, better yet, cut into the arms of the first boy she came across and let him whisk her across the dance floor. But Wolf's hands felt so familiar—so natural, as if the curve of her waist had been made to fit the curl of his palm. Over his shoulder, she saw Archie and Perry raising their glasses in celebration.

Wolf's head bowed close to hers and his lips grazed her ear.

"I'm truly sorry about the other day—I was wrong to say the things I did. I was wrong to send you away. And I was wrong not to call on you properly." He spoke with the air of a boy who had so much to tell her, and now that she was in his arms, he wanted to tell her everything. "It's just that I wasn't sure before."

"You weren't sure about me?" she asked softly, doing her best not to sound too eager. She couldn't take another disappointment. Not when Wolf's arms were around her and his breath was soft on her neck.

"I wasn't sure if it was the right thing to do," he said. "To court you. If I am not free."

"Not free, my lord?"

"But it's all right now," he said in a rush. "My father is so happy that Leopold is marrying the princess, he doesn't care who I marry. He told me so this morning."

She bristled at the suggestion that she was less than worthy, and he strove to soothe her doubts. "I'm sorry to speak so bluntly. But there are duties and responsibilities that come with my position, and I didn't want to begin something that I wouldn't be able to finish. . . . I would never want to hurt you."

His cheek was pressed against hers, and her lips were almost brushing his face. She could dance like this forever. "But you are free now?" she whispered. "Free to love me?"

Wolf drew up short on the dance floor, heedless of the whirling couples around them. He looked directly into her eyes.

"Yes. My father has even promised to give his blessing."

For the first time in her life, Ronan found herself speechless. It was all she could do not to gasp, or squeal, or jump up and down for joy. But all she did was pull him back into her arms and they slid back into the waltz as if the musicians were playing for them and them only.

"Oh, Wolf," she whispered. "I'm so happy!"

There was nothing to fear, he told her. He couldn't wait to begin this new adventure with her by his side, how his heart leaped with joy to be able to hold her so closely. If he could, he would marry her now—but they had to follow proper procedure. His brother would marry first, but they could be married a few months later, in the fall. A smaller ceremony, of course, and it would not be in London. Perhaps they could even get married in New York. Who knows, maybe they would even live there. Wolf noted that as *kronprinz*, Leo's ego already filled all of Prussia, and after his wedding it was sure to spread through all of Europe. It made sense for Wolf to reinvent himself outside his brother's shadow, as an American. "Practically a commoner," he finished up, dryly.

Ronan snorted. "You may become many things, but common will never be one of them."

"Be honest. You're disappointed. You want to be a princess," Wolf teased. "Admit it."

"Being a princess is much more about the attitude than the title," Ronan countered.

"If that's true," Wolf laughed, "then you've skipped past princess and gone straight to queen!"

A strong, spirited, and smart girl . . . Ronan Astor . . . Wolf had been looking for a girl like her for so long. And now she was real, in his arms. To make things even better, he had a fight scheduled for later tonight, in the dungeons. . . . He was looking forward to the adrenaline and the exercise. Perhaps he would take her to see one of his fights some time—he wanted to share everything with her, and Ronan seemed like the kind of girl who might even enjoy it. She was different, and never cared what anyone thought. He couldn't believe she had simply walked into the palace and called on him like she had done the other day. The lord steward had been so put out that he had to take a calming potion and retire for the rest of the afternoon.

A girl and a fight. The public was right—this was the best London Season yet.

"Will you wait for me tonight?" he asked, checking his watch. He'd almost forgotten his plans. "I have an . . . appointment. But it should be done by the time the party's over."

"I will wait for you for as long as you need," said Ronan.

It was time. Fifteen to midnight. Marie checked the clock again. She would meet the sun the next morning as an ordinary subject of the realm; she would no longer be the princess dauphine. It was a perfect night, clear and balmy for London. The whole court was in the gardens, far from the basement passageways that would lead to her freedom. Marie-Victoria put on her most practical outfit: a black cotton poplin dress, a traveling cloak, and her gloves and hat. She tucked the envelope with the keys and coins into her pocket, and picked up the small bag she'd stuffed with clothes, books, and tonics for her illness. Starting tomorrow, it was all she would have in the world. Princess Marie-Victoria Grace Eleanor Aquitaine would be plain old Mary Grace.

No, she remembered then. Mary Cameron.

Marie looked around at her beautiful pink room, at the pink wallpaper with the gold filigree, and hoped that Aelwyn would enjoy her life. In the morning, she and Gill would board the ship bound for New York and begin their new existence together. They would find the captain of the ship and have him marry them at sea, so they would arrive in the new land as husband and wife.

Marie had never been so frightened. She was really doing this. She stole out of her room and found the hidden panel in the hallway that allowed her inside the secret passageways. She followed the brass rail down to the basement, unlocking each door until she was in the bowels of the castle. Near her were the dungeons where her ancestors had kept their enemies, until the Merlin forbade the practice several hundred years ago.

The last gate was up ahead—the final door. Marie took a deep breath and pushed forward. Just as promised, even without the spell-key on her, the wards that kept the castle and its residents safe were down, she could tell. There was no feeling, no heaviness in the air. Gill had told her they would only be down for a few minutes after the hour, but Aelwyn had given her the words to keep the threshold open until she crossed. Once she was past the last gate, Gill would be waiting for her right outside.

She walked toward it, and noticed the damp basement had the usual loamy, earthy smell. But there was something else—a vinegary, sour smell—and right underneath, a smoky acridity, so sharp it almost made her sneeze. She stopped to wonder about it, when she heard a noise in the tunnels.

There was someone else down there.

She heard the footsteps come closer and then fade away.

Who was it? Who else knew about these passageways and would be using them on a night like tonight, when almost all the palace was attending the garden party?

But there was no time to wonder about that now. It was a question for another girl, another life. She had to go—the ward would be down for only a little while longer, and Gill was waiting. So was her new life, her new name, her new reality. Good-bye to the princess, good-bye to the palace. . . .

Good-bye . . .

Good-bye . . .

Marie ran as fast as she could through the rest of the tunnels that would lead to the iron bars of the last gate.

·37·

Gauntlet
AND DUEL

hy was she seeing double? Everywhere Isabelle looked was so fuzzy, and her head hurt. She thought she might be laughing too loudly, but what Lord Stanley was saying really was so funny. Hysterical. A little handsy, perhaps, but after the way a certain *kronprinz* who shall remain nameless had treated her it was nice to have a man look at her that way.

Then she felt another, firmer hand on her arm, separating her from Lord Stanley and steering her toward the exit.

"I think you've had enough, Isabelle," Louis said firmly, taking away the glass of champagne in her hand. "Let's get you home."

"Give that back!" she screeched, reaching for the flute

helplessly and dissolving into more giggles. "Don't be a killjoy."

"Aw, come on, let her have it," William Stanley said with a sneer.

"Yeah, I heard she's more fun with a few in her," said Edward Finch-Hatton, with a bit of a knowing air.

"You'd know, wouldn't you, Beziers?" William Stanley said.

"Excuse me?" Louis said, holding her up by her shoulder. "What did you say?"

"Saw you leave with her last night, when she was plastered. Don't tell me you didn't get lucky."

"Lucky? With Leo's sloppy seconds?" Finch-Hatton scoffed. "That's like shooting fish in a barrel. She's a done deal. A sure thing."

"Ignore them, Louis—come on, let's leave, just let it go," Isabelle said, coming to her senses when she understood what they were saying about her. She did feel very floppy and out of water just then. She just needed to get away from this awful party, this awful city. Away from these horrid boys. But she could also feel her face color with shame. To be spoken of that way, and at court, no less! But what could she do? As a Valois, she had no power here, was barely even welcome. Such was her lot in life.

But Louis-Philippe would not let it go. He turned to the rowdy lads. "I don't think I quite understand you. What are you saying about my cousin?"

"C'mon, everyone knows she's been giving it up all winter to Leopold—and that he had her brought here so that he could . . . well, you know. Get his kicks in before he's married off to that poor sickly thing in the palace. She's sloppy seconds and soiled goods, right? But you're a good man, you don't care. All we're saying is, maybe you could share."

Isabelle couldn't look at Louis; she knew the look of horror on his face too well. It was the same face he'd made when the healers told them their parents had succumbed to their illness, leaving them both orphans. He pulled her to one side. "Isabelle, is this true? Did Leopold . . . did he take liberties with you?" Louis asked, his voice hoarse and angry.

She nodded, ashamed. "Yes," she whispered. "Because I was to be his wife anyway. Because we were engaged."

"When did it start? In February? When he came to Orleans with Lord Hartwig?" Louis asked, his face slowly draining of color. "Was it then?"

She hung her head and nodded.

"And after the engagement was dissolved?" Louis whispered. "Did you continue to—did you—did he—"

She looked at him beseechingly, and he knew the answer. "You don't understand, Louis. It's me he loves, not the princess! I thought that if I could remind him of that he'd come to his senses—"

But Louis-Philippe was already putting down his drink and removing his jacket and turning to face the crowded garden. She had never seen him look so angry in her life.

"Leopold!" Louis called, his voice ringing through the party. "Leopold, come here!"

The prince, who had disappeared from the party earlier, was now marveling at a dancing bear in a tutu that was pirouetting for its trainer. He looked up with a bemused expression. "Excuse me?"

"Leopold. A word, please." Louis kept calm, though his fists were clenched in rage.

"Yes?"

"These men have accused my good cousin of harlotry. Surely, as a gentleman and a prince, you will defend Isabelle's honor."

"But your cousin has no honor." Leo smiled. "At least when I knew her. And I knew her very well and very often, didn't I, Isabelle?"

"Let's go, Louis—come on, let's go, please—you're just making it worse," Isabelle pleaded, hanging on his arm. "Please, let's just leave here. Please."

"NO!" Louis threw down his glove at Leo's feet in a rage. The crowd went silent. Even the orchestra stopped playing. There was a dangerous malice, a strange feeling in the air; as if the world were hinged on a precipice, and could fall at any moment.

Leo raised an eyebrow. "Are you mad, sir?"

Louis put up his fists and insisted Leo do the same. It was as Leo said: Louis looked crazed. The vein on his forehead was throbbing, and he looked as if he were about to burst.

Isabelle came between them. "Louis—let's go—what are you doing? Let it go. Stop this!" But he pushed her off. He lunged after the prince.

"I challenge you to a duel! To defend Isabelle's honor," Louis called.

Leo regarded the younger boy for a long moment while the crowd watched with bated breath. Weeks of the same old dresses and same old cocktails and same old waltzes had grown stale. They wanted blood. Leo's nostrils flared as if he could smell it. He was nothing if not a showman.

He knelt and picked up the glove and tucked it in his lapel as though it were a pocket square. "I accept."

A ripple passed through the onlookers. The future king of Franco-England! Accepting a duel just weeks before his wedding! They pretended to be shocked, but it was clear they were thrilled.

"Now." Louis removed the pistol he always carried as part of his gentleman's uniform. He motioned to a nearby gate out of the garden, away from the party. An empty courtyard would accommodate the ritual.

"As you wish," Leopold said lazily.

"Louis!" Isabelle screamed. "No! No! Take it back. Don't do this! He'll kill you!"

"Leave me alone, Isabelle," Louis said. "Hugh, you will be my second?" he asked, finding his white-faced cousin among the crowd.

"What are you doing?" Hugh whispered fiercely. "You cannot challenge the prince to a duel at St. James! This is madness! Apologize and pledge your loyalty, then let's get out of here. This has gone too far. Isabelle will survive this slur. No one will remember unless you go through with this."

But Louis's jaw was clenched and his face was set. Isabelle recognized that same stubbornness in her father. There was no talking him out of it. He would see this through to the very end.

"I look forward to the challenge. I will enjoy winning," Leo called. He looked around. "Find my brother," he said, irritated when he was unable to see Wolf in the crowd. "Tell him to get my guns."

It took a little while to locate Wolf, and by the time a pair of somewhat rough-looking Prussian footman all but dragged him into the courtyard, the combatants had repaired to opposite sides of the space. Wolf came with the asked-for armament and Leo selected a pistol from the bunch.

Across the way, the Valois contingent was in the throes of great agitation. "You must walk away while we still can—they will have our heads!" Hugh screeched. "Louis-Philippe, I forbid you to carry this out!"

"You are no longer my guardian, Hugh. I have come into my father's title. Now, do be quiet, as I have to concentrate,"

Louis-Philippe said as he checked his gun and cocked it back to make sure its single bullet was set. He cleaned the handle and practiced removing it from its holster.

"Louis! Wait!" Isabelle rushed out to the courtyard, pushing away the ladies who attempted to keep her back.

He turned to her, his face open and hopeful. "Yes?"

"Louis . . ." she said, wonderingly. "Louis, I wanted to tell you something, before . . ."

"I'm not going to die, Isabelle," he said.

She gulped and nodded, tears forming in her eyes. She couldn't believe it. Was he truly doing this for her? She did not believe she was worthy of honor, and here was her cousin, wagering his very life on her virtue. The rules of the duel were clear: whoever won was the moral victor. If Louis-Philippe won the duel, Isabelle of Orleans would be as pure as the driven snow. And if Leopold won, then she would be cast out from society as a wicked woman, a loose woman, a harlot. Which Louis had to know is what she was. She had given herself to Leo on nothing more than a false promise, and yet Louis was still willing to put his life on the line to reclaim her standing in society. It was the most amazing thing anyone had ever done for her. It made her feel like the queen she had always wanted to be.

"Louis—I love you," she blurted out quickly, before she lost her nerve. Did she love him? Why had she said that? Because he was about to die for her, and she wanted him to die with that knowledge? To die happy? No. She was not lying. She did love him—she had always loved him, with all of her heart. He was her true love—her childhood friend and protector. But he was a man now.

She had been consumed with sadness to see him with Celestine—to know that he meant to propose to the girl. She had thought she would lose him forever. But the sadness was not just jealousy, like when she had believed herself in love with Leo and wished ill on the princess. She was sad because she wanted Louis to be happy, and she realized that he could be happy without her—perhaps happier, even.

"Isabelle," Louis said, his face conflicted. "Don't."

"I love you. It's okay if you don't love me. But I want you to know that I love you. I . . . I owe you that much."

He closed his eyes and holstered his gun. When he opened them they were filled with feeling. "I think you know how I've always felt about you."

Isabelle couldn't bring herself to speak. She nodded quietly.

"I know this is insane, and I will most likely die tonight, but to do so defending your honor would be enough for me," he told her.

Isabelle felt the tears flow. Here was a good man, standing by her side all along. She turned to look at Leo. The impending duel had brought a spot of color to his cheeks and a little smile to his lips, and he looked more handsome than ever. Yet neither his good looks nor impeccable wardrobe nor even his title could conceal what Isabelle had always known, even when she was desperate to be his wife: he was a cad. A bounder. A good old-fashioned creep.

She turned back to Louis. Though he wasn't as debonair as Leo, as rakish, he was handsome in a more modest way, and the watery depths of his eyes held no secrets or ulterior motives. He loved her, not for her title or her body, but for who she was. He could not die for her. She wouldn't allow it.

She shrugged helplessly. "Don't do this. It doesn't matter," she said finally. "If not by Leo, my honor would have been taken from me anyway."

Confusion clouded Louis' face. "What do you mean, Isabelle?"

"You know what I mean." She turned then, and looked across the courtyard.

Louis turned and followed her gaze. There stood their cousin and his second, Hugh Borel. The Red Duke stared at the garden gate as though contemplating making a break for it.

"Are you saying . . . *Hugh*?"

Isabelle's eyes narrowed. Her hatred was so palpable that Hugh seemed to sense it. His head whipped in her direction, but when he saw the cousins eyeing him contemptuously he jerked away. But not before Louis had seen the guilty expression on his face, and knew that Isabelle was telling the truth.

"If Leo had not claimed me, he would have," Isabelle said. She had chosen the lesser of two evils, or so she had believed.

Louis grabbed Isabelle's hand. "I would never have allowed it!"

She cut him off. "Then he would have had you sent away or killed—orchestrated a convenient accident of some sort. And that would have been infinitely worse than anything he could do to me. It was better that I shared Leo's bed, and his protection."

He started to speak, but she waved him silent. "Louis-Philippe Beziers, as the rightful queen of your country, I command you not to die. Do I have your word?"

Despite the gravity of the situation, Louis couldn't help but smile at her. "You have my word, my queen. My word, and my life."

"Take this," she said, removing a chain from her neck. It had once held a stone, but it was gone now; she had given it away. "It was my mother's. For luck."

Louis nodded. "Hugh," he called in a voice that dripped with acid, "are you ready?"

Hugh nodded glumly, his weak chin disappearing into his neck fat. He held his own weapon distastefully, as though it were a dead snake.

Isabelle watched them walk to the courtyard. Though the sky was pitch-black overhead, she prayed that somehow, her long nightmare was about to be over and not that that another one was just beginning.

On the far side of the courtyard, Wolf was trying to talk his brother out of the duel. He had been wearing only a pair of loose cotton trousers when Leo's men had found him, his hands wrapped in heavy layers of gauze bandages. One of Leo's guards had given him a jacket, but it was obvious that Wolf was shirtless underneath it, and Leo laughed as Wolf marched up to him.

"Forgive me for spoiling your fun, old boy. If I didn't know you any better I would assume you were on your way to see some Spanish *contessa* or Slovakian princess, but judging from those wraps around your hands I'm guessing you had entertainment of a different sort in mind."

"You can't seriously mean to go through with this?" Wolf asked. "The scandal will taint your wedding season. It might even cause Marie to break her engagement."

Leo laughed curtly. He was polishing his gun with the edge of his sleeve—not as if he wanted to prepare it for use, but as if he wanted it to look good while he used it.

"Marie, or her mother for that matter, has no more power to break this engagement than a fly can wriggle itself out of a pot of honey. Fear of renewed war will trump any scandal." Leo held his gun up and inspected it. From the look in his eyes, Wolf suspected his brother was actually checking himself out in the pistol's glossy silver plating. His nonchalance in the face of impending mortality—whether his or Beziers's—was incomprehensible. It was as if he were preparing for a ball, not a duel.

"Down in the dungeons, were you?" said Leo. "How's the wine?" The other evening they had gotten into a barrel as planned. "Oh right, you weren't down there for a drink. No, you were about to have one of your gladiator bouts, weren't you? Tell me, how different is this from what you were about to do?"

"No one dies in my fights," Wolf growled.

"Pity. Although I do have to hand it to you, brother, the fact that you managed to get a fight going under the nose of the Queen's Guard is quite impressive. But then, you and Marie always did run around together when you were young. It's a shame that you're not the one marrying her, really. With you she might actually have a chance at happiness."

His brother's tone was light, which made his words all the more chilling. Leo was talking about the heir to the Franco-British throne—and his future wife—as though he was pointing to the chicken he wanted the cook to prepare for dinner.

"You be nice to Marie, Leo. Her health isn't great, but she's the kindest, most honorable person I know," Wolf said in a warning tone. "She's very dear to me."

"Don't you worry, Wolfgang, I'll be as gentle as a lamb with my bride. She has to bear me an heir, after all, and unite the Hohenzollern and Aquitaine lines. Beyond that, well . . ." Leo's voice trailed off, as if he couldn't be bothered to contemplate his future wife's fate. He picked up a second pistol and holster, and handed it to Wolf. "Ready? We have a duel to fight."

"Leo, come on. Walk away from this. Leave the boy alone." Wolf shook his head in disapproval. "This is madness."

"This'll be fun, watch. He won't be able to touch me."

"If you won't back down, then let me do it. I'm the better shot. Let me take your place," Wolf insisted.

Leo smiled, touched. "I don't hide behind anyone. Now come."

Wolf shrugged his shoulders and holstered his gun. If Leo wanted to duel, then he couldn't stop him. Whether it was girls, guns, or an empire, Leo always got what he wanted.

Wolf followed as Leo walked toward the center of the garden, where Louis-Philippe was already waiting. "Believe me," Leo said, "I plan to be alive for a long, *long* time."

· 38 ·

Mirror
MIRROR

It was midnight at last. Aelwyn checked herself in the mirror. (Real mirrors, being vainglorious devices, weren't allowed in an acolyte's cell, but she had conjured one for the occasion.) She still couldn't get used to the sight of Marie's face staring back at her. The illusion stone created a mask that was uncanny, unreal, not just to everyone else's eyes, but to hers too. She touched the bridge of her nose, her cheekbones; it all felt strange, unfamiliar. She changed from her acolyte robes to the dress that Marie was meant to wear to the garden party, tucking the stone under her collar. Aelwyn stopped to consider what she was doing. After tonight, she would no longer be an acolyte; she would be the princess of the empire.

Marie had made it clear she had no interest in the throne, or in wedding the future king. The ring and the crown were there for the taking—all Aelwyn had to do was claim them. But her heart was heavy as she stole away from the charter house toward the palace proper. She remembered how she and Marie had looked, the night that Marie had told her she and Gill were really leaving, that Aelwyn was to take her place as princess. Their faces had been so ashen, so unhappy . . . was this the right choice? But there was no stopping now. Marie would be gone when the sun rose in the morning, and the throne would be Aelwyn's. And so would Leo.

But even as his handsome face filled up her mind's eye, she remembered again her father's words. *The rot inside.*

Aelwyn had been afraid that perhaps her father had been talking about her, but what if the Merlin had been warning her about someone else . . . ?

As she made her way to the gardens, she thought it seemed oddly quiet—there were no sounds of murmured conversation, no clink of glasses or forks against plates. There was no music playing.

Leo was supposed to meet her in the bower by the courtyard. But when she arrived there was no Leopold. She must be early; it was not midnight yet.

How odd. There were no sounds of merrymaking, no party . . . and when she looked at the courtyard again, she saw why.

Silhouetted against the moonlight were four figures. Two

of them stepped forward. The taller held his hand out, but the shorter one smacked it away. A voice with a light French accent carried clearly across the grass.

"I'd sooner shake hands with a snake."

A venomous chuckle replied. "Since snakes don't have hands," Leo's voice answered, "that would be quite impossible."

Leo? In a duel? During his wedding season? It made no sense.

As the slighter figure stepped forward, a beam of light caught his face. Aelwyn recognized the young Frenchman, Louis-Philippe Beziers, who had come with the Valois party. He leaned in as if to say something, and Aelwyn, thinking quickly, whispered "Listen" into her palm and cupped it behind her ear. Louis's voice came as if he stood right next to her.

"You are no prince but a scoundrel, and you shall forfeit your life for Isabelle's honor. I pray your death is slow and agonizing."

Isabelle's honor? Aelwyn wouldn't have believed her ears if she hadn't used magic to augment them. The entire court knew that Leo had broken his engagement to Isabelle of Orleans in order to marry Princess Marie, and now the young Frenchman was accusing the *kronprinz* of taking advantage of her. Perhaps Isabelle was spreading a malicious rumor merely to get back at him. But Leo's next words dispelled any doubts she had.

"Isabelle was more than happy to give up her honor, as she has none." Leo smirked. "Take your best shot, Beziers."

Isabelle wasn't lying, then; this duel was serious business.

Leo was proud, even preening, and it took a moment for Aelwyn to process what she had just overheard. Only Marie had seen him for what he was, but now Aelwyn's eyes were open and she could see him clearly for the first time.

The boys stopped walking, their backs still turned to each other.

"Ready?" Louis-Philippe called.

"When you are," Leo drawled. So confident and calm.

Aelwyn immediately understood that Louis was a sitting duck, and had walked into a trap. It struck her that Leo was not merely arrogant; he had the serene demeanor and smugness of a man who knew there was no way he would lose this duel.

But how? A protection spell of some kind maybe? It was dishonorable to wear one in a duel, and rules required that both opponents be tapped down by a house mage before starting, which she had just witnessed. So if Leo was wearing one, it was undetectable by the Order.

The boys nodded to each other. They began to walk in opposite directions, counting each step aloud until they got to the end. "TEN!"

The boys whirled around.

It all happened in a flash.

They reached for their pistols.

Without thinking, acting on pure instinct, Aelwyn's hand flew to the second stone she wore upon her neck.

The black one from Avalon.

She squeezed it tightly, drawing all its power into her body. She remembered the awesome, terrible feeling of holding the street urchin's soul within her mind. Summoning every ounce of her concentration, she directed the energy of the stone at Leo, to remove the ward that protected him and give Louis a fair chance in the duel.

That was all she meant to do, truly.

For the briefest of seconds, Leo's soul flickered in her mind's eye. She reached for it, calling it into the stone. The energy took the form of an astral hand, curling around Leo's soul like a crow snatching an egg from a nest. This was not going to be pleasant for him.

Not at—

But just as suddenly, Aelwyn felt her magic shredding like a sail ripped apart by a hurricane, battered against something dark and vicious and infinite. A banshee wind that howled in rage.

This was no mere protection spell—what was it? What kind of magic was this? Aelwyn tried to gather herself together as Leo's head whipped about in the darkness, trying to find his second assailant. Then his eyes met hers in the shadows and widened. *Marie? No. You are not Marie. You are only wearing her face.*

Then, another voice: *I know this face.*

With a snap, the illusion that covered her melted into the mist, until she stood before him as the sorceress she was.

Ah. Now we see each other for what we really are, said a stranger's voice directly into her mind.

The next thing Aelwyn knew she was tumbling backward, a wall of force smashing into her body like an ocean wave and tossing her against the garden wall with such violence that she fell to a heap on the floor, her magic dissolving in tatters.

With a sick smile, Leo raised his gun. *I'm bored of this conversation.* But before he could fire, a shot rang out.

Aelwyn had been so focused on Leo that she had forgotten about Louis.

About the duel.

And apparently, so had Leo.

He staggered backward, his gun falling from his right hand as his left clutched at his chest. Like a branch cracking off a dead tree, the once and future emperor of England, France, and Prussia fell to the ground and lay still, his blood and life seeping out of him.

That was all Aelwyn remembered until she, too, sank into darkness.

It happened in a split second. Leopold had drawn his weapon, but before he could bring it to bear, Louis-Philippe had already fired his pistol, shooting the prince right in the chest.

Wolf screamed and ran to his brother. "LEO! LEO! SOMEONE GET ME A HEALER! LEO!"

Louis-Philippe stood motionless, his pistol still smoking,

until the Red Duke corralled him and dragged him away with a stunned Isabelle by his side. They brushed past Aelwyn without seeing her lying like a corpse in the shadow of the trees.

Wolf heard and saw nothing but his brother on the ground. Leo lay on the gray cobblestones, his shirt ripped open, his chest concealed beneath a layer of blood. His left hand still clutched at the wound. Wolf ripped off his jacket and fell to his knees, hoping to stanch the bleeding. But when he pulled his brother's hand aside, he saw that it wasn't his wound the fingers were clutching. It was a stone.

Though the rest of Leo's chest was smeared with blood, the stone was completely clean, untouched, pristine. It was a lumpy thing, not a gem but some kind of rock.

Wolf knelt to examine the stone but before he could touch it, a dozen men rushed to Leo's side and bundled him on a makeshift stretcher fashioned from an overturned table. The men were dressed as footmen, but Wolf knew they were some of his father's most battle-hardened troops, and with the rough efficiency of soldiers they hustled him and Leo into the palace to find their healers.

He forgot all about the stone around Leo's neck. Probably nothing more than a talisman of some sort.

For now Wolf could only look into Leo's open, unseeing eyes, and pray that a healer got to him before the last of his life leaked away.

Wedding
BELLES

Let me be your ruler,
You can call me Queen Bee.

—LORDE,

"ROYALS"

· 39 ·

People's
PRINCESS

hat was that?" Marie said, hearing the sound of gunshots from the courtyard. She turned, looking back at the palace walls. She remembered the footsteps she had heard in the dungeons as she made her way to the gates. Maybe that person had seen her, and had alerted the palace guards. She couldn't take it if she and Gill were caught before they could escape.

Gill stared in the direction of the garden, his hand reaching instinctively for the hilt of his sword before he realized that he wasn't in uniform.

"Nothing that concerns us anymore," he said, taking her bag and putting it in the carriage. "Come, Marie—please."

She nodded, still shaking, shivering. She was so frightened. She was leaving the only life she'd ever known. Leaving not just St. James Palace, but England, the empire, the Continent. New York was only the first stop; it was Gill's plan to make their way first to Mexico, then as far south as they could go, Brazil maybe, or even across the Pacific to Asia. They could not stay anywhere within the empire's reach; they would have to find an independent country where they could hide and create new lives.

Gill looked tense. His eyes were bloodshot, worried. "What's wrong?" she asked.

"I didn't think you would meet me," he confessed.

If the truth were told, for a brief moment she hadn't thought she would either, that her courage would fail her.

"I am here," she said.

He folded her into his arms and kissed her hair. "This is a dream."

"My dream," she said, putting her arms around him and tenderly kissing him on the lips. "Let us go and make it a reality."

"Here," he said, putting a cloak around her shoulders and helping her into the warm carriage.

"How did you know the wards would be down? And where did you get the money?" Marie asked, when they were safely on their way. "Who helped us?"

"A friend," Gill said. "My captain handed me an envelope, said it came from someone very important. Inside were two thousand emperos, and a note that said the wards would be down at midnight. It said for me to do my best by you. That's all I know, as it was unsigned. I didn't ask any questions, and the captain had no answers. But a friend helped us tonight, Marie—a real friend."

A real friend . . . Marie thought. As the carriage rolled away from the palace, she thought she would feel complete, happy; but she was nervous, agitated. Those gunshots in the courtyard—and that strange smell in the basement . . . She tried to shake them from her mind, tried to focus on the warm body next to her, Gill's reassuring solidity. But something nagged at her. . . .

The hansom turned off Piccadilly onto a narrow street. The close-set brick walls of the buildings echoed the sound of the horses' hooves back at the carriage. Marie listened to the staccato clip-clop for several seconds, unsure why it sounded so strange to her. Then she realized with a start that she'd never been off London's main thoroughfares. Though she'd been fated to rule this city one day, she'd never seen anything but its public face, its elegant stone buildings, immaculate parks, and luxurious haberdasheries—though even these had only been glimpsed from the outside.

As a princess, there was always someone to do her shopping for her, someone to bring messages from Parliament to her, even someone to have a good time for her. All she was expected to do was appear on a balcony or in an open carriage and wave her hand. She wasn't even allowed to toss pennies to her subjects the way they did in smaller kingdoms. It would be "common," her mother said, although Marie sensed the answer was more complex than that. Giving money to the poor would be tantamount to admitting that not everyone in the empire had a warm meal awaiting them at night, or a dry roof to sleep under. And of course it would also require lowering the protective wards around their carriage, which was something they never did.

But she was done with all that now. She was just another citizen in just another street, and she pulled open the shade on the window and eagerly peered out at the darkened sidewalk.

"Marie, please," Gill cautioned.

"It's fine. No one will recognize me, and even if they did they wouldn't believe it. The heiress to the Lily Throne in a hansom? Unthinkable!"

Gill laughed with her, but nervously. Still, he made no move to close the curtain. Marie wondered if it was because he knew she was right, or if because in his head she was still the princess, her orders to be obeyed unquestioningly.

She squinted out the window. It was so dark that she could barely see anything.

"We really should install gaslights on these side streets, like they have on the Mall. It would make things so much easier for pedestrians, not to mention safer."

Gill shifted uneasily, and she could feel him weighing whether to answer. "There are streetlights. They're just not lit."

"What?" Marie said. "But why ever not?"

"London is a vast city. One of the largest and most populous in the world. Piping gas to its thousands of miles of streets would be a great expense."

"No doubt. But the empire is the wealthiest the world has ever known. Surely it behooves us to illuminate our capital city, so that everyone can see just how prosperous we are? And so that our own citizens can find their way around at night?"

Another uneasy pause from Gill. "Wealth is a relative thing, Marie. There are indeed people in the empire who have access to greater comfort and luxury than any other people have ever known in history. But for every one of those there a hundred or a thousand who have . . . not as much."

"What do you mean, not as much?"

Even as she asked her question a shadow took shape in the darkness outside the carriage. Marie thought it was a pile of trash at first, but as her eyes grew more accustomed to the darkness she realized that it wasn't trash it all. It was a group of people—at least five, maybe more—huddled together under a makeshift tent of dirty blankets and other rags. Hungry eyes stared out of sooty faces. A hand separated itself from one body and reached toward the carriage, palm up. Marie couldn't tell if it was covered by a glove or just a thick coating of dirt. She reached for her purse of coins.

"Marie, you can't," Gill said, putting his hand on top of hers. "All you have are gold pieces. One of them is worth more than what these people see in a year. When they see them, they might swarm the carriage. They could be hurt, or . . ."

Gill's voice trailed off, but Marie knew what he meant. *Or we could.*

She stared at the grubby hand and glittering eyes for one more moment, then sat back against the cushioned seat. "I had no idea things were so bad."

"It was kept from you, no doubt."

"Are there many more like them?" she asked, close to tears.

"The indigent population of the capital is estimated to run to many thousands."

"Thousands!" Marie cried.

Gill squeezed her hand. "It is not your fault, my lady. Nor is it your responsibility. Not anymore."

His words fell heavily on her heart.

The people were no longer under her power, nor her protection. She was no longer the princess. These problems were not hers to fix. She was free now. So why was her soul so burdened?

· 40 ·

Aftermath
AND ESCAPE

*Y*ou stupid boy!" Hugh Borel hissed as he pushed and prodded Louis and Isabelle toward a dingy covered carriage parked in the shadow outside the palace walls. "Do you have any idea what you've done?"

"Never mind that!" Isabelle answered. "We have to get out of here before the Queen's Guard is after us! Out of London, out of England!"

Hugh glanced at her sharply, but for once found no reason to argue with her, and they hurried forward. Despite the urgency, however, she hesitated when she reached the carriage, unsure of its provenance. Then the driver turned toward her, and she recognized the familiar face of their loyal servant Pierre-Auguste. He had come as part of the Valois retinue to London, and his ancestors had been in her family's employ for more than three generations, and serfs for a dozen more before that. At least this was safe. She bundled a dazed Louis into the cab, and without waiting for him to extend a hand to help her up, hauled herself in after.

Hugh paused outside the door. "To the docks," he ordered, clambering into the cab even as a whip cracked and the carriage lurched into motion, causing Hugh to tumble unceremoniously into the rear seat.

Fortunately Isabelle and Louis had sat directly behind the driver. Isabelle was tempted to laugh, but as her odious guardian struggled to regain his dignity she caught a glimpse of the pistol he had worn as Louis's second, still holstered at his side. Her right hand sought Louis's left, and curled into it.

Isabelle's touch seemed to rouse Louis. He turned to her with a dazed expression.

"I did it for you," he whispered, looking deep into her eyes. "I did it for you. I won . . . and I saved your honor."

Isabelle was shocked. In the middle of her panic, she had forgotten this part—this essential reason for his valiant action. She stared at him, and realized what she'd told him before the duel was still true. She loved him. She loved him, and he had saved her honor. And when she looked into his eyes, she knew he was not thinking of Celestine anymore.

What was that poor girl compared to a lifetime of loving Isabelle d'Orleans?

"Thank you," she said simply, and squeezed his hand.

"A fat lot of good that will do us if you've actually killed him," Hugh snarled from the opposite seat. "Isabelle's honor won't mean a thing when she's hanging from the gallows, and we're all swinging beside her."

"Duels are protected by law," Isabelle said, turning to Hugh in disgust. "There were a dozen witnesses to Louis's challenge and Leo's acceptance. His own brother served as his second. No court can touch us."

But she couldn't help but wonder if for once her hated guardian was right. For five hundred years House Aquitaine had confined House Valois to the tiniest corner of their rightful dominions, stripping away their titles and lands year by year until she, the true Dauphine of France, who should have ruled a vast empire from Versailles, barely had the credentials to serve as lady-in-waiting to the imposter, Marie-Victoria. Maybe Eleanor would use this excuse to finally eradicate House Valois once and for all—or Marie-Victoria could do it, when she ascended to the throne. Her cousin had shot Marie's fiancé, after all. If Louis hadn't actually killed Leo, he had at the very least humiliated and disgraced him. To the thin-skinned Franco-Brits (and even more thin-skinned Prussians), one's standing in society was in many ways more important than life itself.

But apparently Hugh wasn't thinking about the Aquitaines at all.

"Courts!" he scoffed. "Do you think King Frederick cares a whit about courts where his son is concerned? The man has the Pandora's Box! He defeated the Merlin's armies with it—thousands of soldiers killed in a single afternoon! How do you think our tiny force of a few hundred irregulars—peasant farmers who have had their scythes taken away and replaced with rifles—will fare against that?"

Isabelle had a near-total obsession with the crown that had been taken from her family, and as such had hardly given the Hohenzollerns a second thought. Prussia, on Germany's eastern border, was almost as close to Muscovy as it was to France: not exactly neighbors. But of course King Frederick would be enraged at this attack on his son, especially if it proved fatal, and marching halfway across Europe to avenge it would seem small labor indeed. But to use the Pandora's Box against Orleans?

"He wouldn't dare!" Isabelle said. "He—he *couldn't!*"

"Lady Isabelle is right," Louis said, stirring himself. "If Leo is dead, Frederick's last remaining hope for peace with the empire is to transfer Leo's proposal to Wolfgang. But Eleanor will never consent to the marriage if she thinks Frederick is going to abuse his power so flagrantly, and against one of her sovereign territories, no less. Her French subjects would clamor for revenge, and so would her own people. She would be forced to resume the war, no matter the cost in lives, or risk losing her throne to revolution."

"Listen to you, a mere boy talking as though you have experience with statecraft," Hugh sneered, although it seemed to Isabelle that his voice had softened a bit. Maybe Louis was right. Law and custom would protect them, and the fear of an even more destructive war than the last one would keep the peace.

But Hugh was still speaking. "You have no idea how close I was to exacting vengeance on the empire while safeguarding House Valois from the Prussians! Until you had to ruin it, of course," he said bitterly to Louis.

"What do you mean?" Isabelle demanded. "Have you entered into some kind of treaty? You have no right—no authority. You are a trustee only. All such decisions have to wait until I come of age."

"What did you do, Hugh?" Louis demanded.

But Hugh refused to explain, setting his mouth in a thin line. It was obvious he enjoyed every bit of power he exercised over them. "If only Isabelle learned how to keep her legs closed, this would never have happened."

"You dare insult her honor?" Louis snarled. "May I remind you that I've shot one man tonight already? I'm more than willing to shoot another."

"With a gun that holds only a single bullet." Hugh pushed his jacket open, revealing, first, his pale stomach, then the butt of his holstered pistol. "May I remind *you* that I am the only person in this carriage bearing a fully loaded weapon?"

"Louis, stop!" Isabelle commanded. "Hugh is just trying to get a rise out of you."

Louis continued to shoot daggers at Hugh for another moment. Then he turned to Isabelle, putting his right hand on her waist as if to shield her from her guardian.

"It's okay, Izzy. Once we're back in France you'll never have to see this disgusting creature again. I'll take you to Cévennes with me. You will be safe there."

As Louis spoke, Isabelle grew increasingly tense. It wasn't his fantasy of deliverance that unnerved her. It was his hand resting on her waist. It squeezed gently—unconsciously, even—kneading the unfamiliar flesh beneath the loose folds of her unfitted gown, until finally it was clear that Louis understood what he was feeling, and his voice trailed away in shock.

"Izzy," he said when he could speak again. "Are you—"

"Don't!" Isabelle said out loud, conscious of the weight of Hugh's gaze on her, as heavy as a sodden, moldy fur. "Don't make it real. Not yet." She felt ill.

"Pregnant? She carries a bastard in her belly!" Hugh crowed. "Oh, this is getting richer by the minute!"

In his fury, Louis leaped across the carriage even as Hugh went for his gun. Louis was on the older man before the gun was fully out of the holster, his body crushing Hugh's arm against the back of the seat and preventing him from drawing his weapon. Their fists flew at each other, but in the enclosed space of the carriage it was hard for either of them to throw a solid punch. Within seconds, however, a cut had opened over Hugh's eye and begun to run with blood, while Louis was bleeding from his mouth.

Isabelle didn't know what to do—beg them to stop before Hugh managed to shoot Louis, or cheer Louis on and pray for an end to all her troubles right here, right now? She saw Hugh's right hand fumbling toward his pistol again, and managed to kick it away with her shoe. The one-inch heel penetrated deeply into his flesh, and he screamed like a slapped baby when he jerked away.

Still, if Louis was faster and more nimble than his cousin, Hugh was bigger and stronger, and in this kind of wrestling match that was what mattered. With a yelp like a cornered jackal, he managed to throw Louis back into the seat beside Isabelle, using his foot to hold Louis down while he drew his pistol and pointed it at his attacker.

Click.

Another arm appeared through the carriage window, holding a pistol pointed directly at Hugh's head—not one of the ceremonial antiques from the duel, but a proper American Colt, which even Isabelle knew could hold six bullets, rather than just one. Through the flapping curtain, Isabelle could see the grim face of their driver, Pierre-Auguste. Based on his position, Isabelle figured he was standing on the running boards.

"Drop your weapon, please, Duke Borel," he said in a determined tone.

"You cretin," Hugh snarled. "I'll have you hanged for treason! I'll have you drawn and quartered!"

"My family's oath is to Lady Isabelle, sir, as head of House Valois. You are just another lackey like me."

Suddenly Isabelle heard words bursting from her mouth. "Shoot him, Pierre-Auguste!"

Pierre-Auguste's arm wavered. Then he shook his head. "I am sorry, my lady, but my oath does not extend to murder. Though the Red Duke is as hated among the servants as he is by you and Count Beziers, there are still laws that bind us, and keep us from descending to his level of savagery. But I am only too willing to testify at his trial." He turned back to Hugh. "Your weapon, Duke Borel," he repeated. "Or will you force me to kill you in order to save Count Beziers's life?"

Hugh's lip quivered, and Isabelle thought he might cry. Then, carefully, with no sudden movements, he handed his gun to Pierre-Auguste, who tossed it to the road. Isabelle heard it clatter over the cobblestones, the sound quickly fading as the carriage raced on.

"Pierre!" she said incredulously. "The carriage is still moving!"

Pierre-Auguste smiled wryly. "Magic reins," the older man said, somewhat abashedly. "I use them so I can catch some sleep during overnight journeys." The curtain fell closed and the carriage creaked as he clambered from the running board back to the driver's seat. "I trust that you three will behave yourselves until we reach the docks," he called faintly.

In the carriage, Isabelle found Louis's hand as she had when they first got in. It was warm now, and slick with Hugh's blood, which she could feel soaking into her glove. Normally she would have been repulsed, but now she almost savored it. She stared in triumph at Hugh's bloody, frightened face.

"You mentioned hanging before, but that is not the French

way. I know there's an old guillotine in the château somewhere. The blade is probably a little rusty, but I'm sure it will
still get the job done," she said.

Hugh's eyes narrowed into malevolent slits. But for the
first time there was something there besides hatred: fear.

And as Isabelle held tightly to Louis's bloody hand, she
realized that maybe she didn't need a kingdom after all. Just
one person whose loyalty wasn't based on mere duty or
law. Perhaps at long last, Isabelle had found what she had
been looking for all her life: safety, security, love. Maybe now,
all her dreams would come true.

Life and
DEATH

olf paced maniacally back and forth in the long hallway in their guest apartments. The healers had barred him from the ground-floor reception room where they were frantically working to save his brother's life. To make matters worse, his father, King Frederick, was at a foxhunt all the way up in Lincolnshire and he wouldn't be able to get back to London before morning. Not only was Wolf on his own, but he was in charge.

He wanted something to hit. Or, better yet, something to hit him. Physical pain would make more sense than this emotional ache, which made his limbs twitch helplessly like an old man's. Wolf had always let his fists do the talking. Now he was realizing that the mind needed training just as much as the muscles, and his was woefully out of shape.

His brother had been shot in the heart and was surely dead. It was all Wolf's fault. He should never have let him duel. But Leopold had been so confident in his success, and Wolf had never been able to stop him from doing anything. Still, when the shot rang out, Wolf had been sure it would be the young French boy who fell to the ground, but it was not. It had been his brother. Leo. *I don't need magic to win my fights,* Wolf thought fiercely. *I should have been the one to hold the gun. I could have cut that boy down before he drew a breath.* But Leo had insisted, had assured him nothing would happen, that nothing *could* happen to him.

And so Wolf had let him, because his older brother was always right, and now Leo was dead. There were dozens of people milling about, rushing through the hallways—healers, mages, ministers, functionaries. He was alone among strangers, alone in the hallway with blood on his hands.

"He's not dead," Oswald said, appearing by his side. "Get up, Wolf. Get up."

It was only then that he realized he'd been kneeling. Wolf looked up with bleary eyes at his mentor. "Leo's not dead?"

"He's still breathing," Oswald said. "The healers are looking at him now. The Merlin has just arrived to help. Leo is unconscious and gravely wounded, but he is still breathing."

Wolf said a prayer of thanks. "What now?"

"We will find out tomorrow. He will live through the night, the healers assure me, and the Merlin should be able to set him to rights. But there is a more pressing issue."

"More pressing than my brother almost dying?"

"The princess. She is missing."

Wolf looked at Duncan blankly.

"I just heard from our guards. They discovered Princess Marie is not in her room. She told the court she would appear at the garden party at midnight, but she did not. No one can find her anywhere. They are waking Queen Eleanor now. I cannot tell you how bad this would look for us, how suspicion would fall upon our shoulders if she has truly disappeared. There are those who would surmise that it is retaliation for Leo's injury." Duncan frowned.

"How is that the empire's fault? He walked into a duel on his own will," said Wolf.

"Already our foreign minister is arguing that someone from the Invisible Order should have stopped the duel, or that the treaty has been breached as harm has come to the *kronprinz* while in the empire's domain."

"That is utter foolishness; no one could have stopped Leo from doing this. Hell, even I tried to!" argued Wolf.

"Nevertheless I've sent our men to comb the city before the queen can raise the alarm."

"Marie's really gone?" Wolf repeated, as if he couldn't quite believe the words he was hearing.

"There's more," said Oswald. "Your father. When we sent word to him about Leo, we discovered his train from Lincolnshire had derailed. Foul play is suspected. We are told the king survived, and have sent mages and messengers to locate him, but it looks as if the train was attacked by some kind of firebomb."

Firebomb? But they were at peace with the empire now. Who would want his father dead?

Wolf's thoughts were in a whirl as he walked with Duncan back to his apartments and saw Ronan Astor standing there, pristine and lovely in her turquoise dress. He had asked her to wait for him after the garden party, when he got back from the fight. It felt as if that had been another lifetime ago. But the sight of her jolted something in him.

Marie-Victoria was missing and his father's train had been attacked. London was in chaos, the empire and the Prussian kingdom at odds once more. Marie was in great danger, and he wasn't just going to stand around doing nothing about it.

Ronan ran to him, a ministering angel, a dove. "Wolf, I'm so sorry! We all saw him fall—heavens, your brother . . ." she said, holding him in her arms.

"Is still alive," he said.

"Thank Merlin! But where are you going?" she asked as he pulled away from her, a faraway look in his eyes. "Wolf!"

He faced her, but he was still looking past her. "Ronan, I'm sorry—I can't stay with you right now. The princess is missing, and I think I'm the only one who knows where she is. I will come back to you, I promise. When this is over, I will come back to you."

·42·

Rot
AND ROTGUT

ill had rented them rooms at an inn near the port called the Knight's Arms. Marie knew she should not have been shocked at the shabbiness of her new accommodations, but she was. Just as she had never ventured off London's most elegant thoroughfares before that night, she had never stayed anywhere that was not exquisite and beautiful and perfectly appointed until then. The bed was so plain, the mattress so hard, and the food from the kitchen—Gill brought her up a plate, lest anyone see her—well, the food wasn't exactly what she was used to. The meat was salty and tough, the bread hard, the cheese moldy. An earthenware cup held a dark liquid that Gill assured her was wine, though it smelled more like vinegar, sour and acrid.

"I know it's not what you're used to. I'm sorry."

"Don't be," she said. "It's perfect."

A nervous smile crept on Gill's face. "Really?"

"Really."

His happiness cheered her up and she dutifully cleaned her plate, carving the green spots from the cheese and chewing each bite of bread for what seemed like hours before it was soft enough to swallow. She even risked a sip of wine, but it tasted so much like a musty basement that it was all she could do not to spit it out. Afterward Gill had taken the plates back down to the kitchen, telling Marie he was going to have a pint of ale in the dining room and listen for any news from the palace, leaving his bride-to-be alone in her room.

Do you know what you are giving up for him? Aelwyn had asked her at their last meeting. She had not known then; she was beginning to understand now. But it was all right; Gill was worth it. She would do anything for him, would live anywhere, do whatever she was called upon to do. And hadn't she longed for a cottage, anyway? A simple cottage, not a palace. She was done with castles and palaces; she'd had enough of those to last her a lifetime. She did not need her jewel-box room and her beautiful bed. Really, this clean, small room would more than suffice. Compared to the conditions endured by the homeless people she'd seen earlier, it was its own kind of palace, the meal she had just eaten a feast. She should be thankful she had access to them, rather than pining over privileges that were only hers because of an accident of birth.

I would have helped them, she told herself. *If I had become queen I would have made it my priority to help all of those in need.* But that, too, was something else she had given up. Perhaps Aelwyn would help them, although as a sorceress looking forward to a thousand-year life span, she probably wouldn't feel the urgency of someone like Marie, who had stared her own mortality in the face ever since being diagnosed with the wasting plague as a little girl.

Do you know what you are giving up?

A knock sounded at the door.

Another knock. "Marie? It's me."

Marie opened the door (yet another thing she would have to get used to). Gill hovered nervously on the threshold until she invited him in. She sat on the bed. There was one chair in the room, tucked under a battered writing table, but Gill eyed the bed beside Marie until she realized what was going on and patted the coverlet beside her. Smiling sheepishly, he sat down and took her hand in his.

"Any news?" she asked.

Gill looked grim, and Marie's already upset stomach tightened.

"About you? No. But there has been a rather shocking development."

Marie's head filled with an image of Queen Eleanor stretched out on her bed, her wrinkled skin gone waxy and pale, her open eyes staring blankly at the embroidered canopy that had sheltered her sleep for a century and a half. But what Gill said next was in some ways even more shocking.

"Prince Leopold's been shot," he said.

"What? How?"

Quickly Gill sketched the details of the duel with Louis-Philippe, including the rumors of Leo's violation of Isabelle's honor.

"Even if he survives his wound, he still lost the duel, so this will be an enormous stain on his reputation. And now other accusers are coming forward, saying Isabelle was far from Leo's only conquest. The daughter of the Marquis de Sevilla claims he proposed to her, then abandoned her when he got what he wanted. The Contessa di Castigliori from Naples tells much the same tale, as does the daughter of Freiherr Ziggindorfer from Hungary—and she has a six-month-old son to boot. A girl in every port, as the saying goes."

Marie shook her head incredulously. "And yet all the stories had it that Wolf was the ladies' man. How strange. Is there any news of Leo himself? Will he survive?"

"The bullet nicked his heart, but Prussian healers are among the best in the world. The Merlin is with him too."

Marie absorbed the news quietly, wondering what would happen now, if Leo did not survive. Would Aelwyn go through with the plan to take her place? Or would the palace discover they were missing their princess? And what of Wolf? If Leo died, would he be offered up as heir and suitor? The thought of Aelwyn marrying Wolf did not sit well with her for some reason.

Gill stood up then. "We should retire. We have to be up

early. We'll have to be extra careful. Reports are that Lady Isabelle, Count Beziers, and Duke Borel were making for the docks directly after the duel. Technically Count Beziers committed no crime and they are within their rights to leave, but the Prussian contingent is understandably eager to have a few words with him."

Marie shuddered. "Poor Isabelle. She is the real victim here. I hope she is okay." The thought came to her to write a card, or even to pay her a visit and see if there was something she could do. Then she laughed at herself. As princess and heir to the throne there were many things she could do for Isabelle, whose lot in life as the Valois heir was hard enough already. But as a commoner she could do none of those things now, or ever again.

Gill said good night. His room was next to hers. "I know it's not great," he said, motioning to their surroundings. "But I'm going to work really hard, and one day—one day I will give you riches, more than you desire. I will work so hard for you, Marie."

She put her hands on each side of his face and kissed his lips. "I don't want riches, I want you. The food was delicious. We are off to a great adventure, you and I."

"I cannot wait for tomorrow," he said.

Marie's smile was resolute, though she couldn't quite get Isabelle out of her thoughts, or Leo, or Aelwyn, or Wolf. But all she said was: "Neither can I."

The next morning, Marie dressed for her wedding and the journey. She put on a gray dress, fitted at the waist with the simplest embroidery across the bodice. It was plain, more like the robe of the Invisible Orders that Aelwyn had given up than something a princess might wear, but made of a good, sturdy cloth, and tailored to be comfortable for a tiring day. Still, she wished she had a flower for her hair, or something prettier to wear; she was a bride this morning, and she wanted to look like one—wanted to wear something that would bring a smile to Gill's face.

The innkeeper left her a breakfast tray with salt beef, bread, and wine. Marie's tin fork clattered against her plate when she picked it up, and she noticed that her hand was trembling. There's no reason to be nervous, she told herself. Well, no, there were any number of reasons to be nervous. But now was not the time to give in to them. Now was the time to act like a princess, as her mother always said. It's not the title that makes the princess. It's the princess that makes the title.

She reached for the wine for some liquid courage, downed the biggest draught she could manage. But as the sour taste filled her mouth and nostrils she shook with a jolt of recognition. The wine didn't just smell like a basement. It smelled like *her* basement—the basement in St. James through which she'd sneaked out last night. The basement filled with five hundred barrels of Hugh Borel's famous Burgundy, said to be the finest in the world. Yet the odor it gave off wasn't of fine wine but of rank vinegar, of sulfur and smoke. And she had smelled that odor once before—just over four years ago, right before Aelwyn was banished to Avalon. The smell in the dungeon—in the basement—that earthy, vinegary, smoky smell—it smelled like magefire. Like dark magic.

"Gill," she said, rapping on his door. "Gill!"

He opened his door, looking sleepy but happy. He, too, was dressed in traveling clothes. "Yes, my dear?"

"I need to go back to St. James," she said urgently. "Now."

His face crumpled. "You changed your mind."

"No—it's not that—I have to warn them!"

"About what?"

"They're in terrible danger." She told him about the smell in the basement. "It smelled just like it did four years ago, before Aelwyn set my room on fire. Like vinegar and acid and sulfur. Magefire." The barrels of wine from Orleans were full of it, she was sure. "Someone is planning to burn down the palace, to set off an explosion. I need to hurry—I need to get those wine barrels out of there."

He grabbed his pistol from the desk and put on his coat. "You are certain?"

"I'm not—" she said, losing the conviction in her voice a little. "I just have a feeling—the smell was so strong—and I will never forget that night—"

Gill hesitated. "Listen to me, Marie. If we go back now,

the *Saturnia* will sail without us. We will have to wait at least another day before we leave—another day before we're married and inseparable by law. By then the queen and the Merlin will be using every force in their power to find us, and we may not be able to get away at all. If there's truly something you need to warn them about, we can send a messenger. That will be enough."

Marie didn't know what to do. He was right, of course. A day's delay would almost assuredly foil their plan, and there would be no second chances. Even if she wasn't executed, or thrown in stocks, or disinherited, there would be no chance that Queen Eleanor would ever allow her to see Gill again—doubtful, in fact, that she would let him live. She would be right back where she started, trapped in the protocols of court, slated to be married to Leo or, if he died, then some other prince from some other kingdom whose character was equally dubious.

"You're right, of course. I will send a note. We should head to the *Saturnia*." It would be warning enough. Wouldn't it?

Gill nodded. "I'll settle our bill and roust up a messenger while you write it." He grabbed his coat and hurried from the room.

Marie rummaged through her bag until she found her stationery. The beautiful sheaf of cream-colored paper was softer than the sheets she'd slept on last night, and there at the top was the royal crest, embossed in gilt. BY APPOINTMENT TO HER MAJESTY THE QUEEN. Marie shook her head in wonder.

She had packed the stationery without thinking yesterday, just as she would for any other trip. It seemed that her old life could not be left behind so easily.

She picked up the pen, and began to write a note, then thought better of it and tore it up. She wrote another one instead.

The words seemed to come of their own accord.

> Dear Gill,
>
> You will always have a place in my heart. Please forgive me.
>
> — Marie

Her fingers were trembling too much to fold the letter and put it in an envelope, so she simply left it for him on the small desk. She grabbed her bag and slipped out the door, heading toward the rear of the building. Less than a minute later she was in the unfamiliar, fishy-smelling streets near the docks, racing in what she hoped was the direction of St. James. It didn't matter if there was a princess with her face in the palace. She was the real dauphine—whether she wanted to be or not. It was up to her to make everything right. It wasn't just her duty or her responsibility. It was her destiny. It wasn't about personal happiness or even about herself at all. As her mother had always told her: their lives were not their own.

They belonged to their country. Everyone's security was tied to hers, from the wealthiest dukes and duchesses to the poorest beggars on the street. This was what it really meant to be a princess, to wear the crown, to rule an empire. It wasn't about the stationery, the gowns, the palaces. It was about keeping her people safe, and creating a stable, solid foundation for their peace and prosperity.

Because what was a cottage in the sky, when her castle was about to burn?

· 43 ·

Mean STREETS

"Oi! What's this then? Looks like a little bird has flown its cage!"

The figure rose up in front of Marie, nearly invisible because its face was so covered in soot that it blended in with the shadows cast by the narrow alley, while its clothes were indistinguishable from the pile of trash from which it had risen.

Growing up in St. James, Marie had spent hours studying maps of London, dreaming of the thousands of vital, rough-and-tumble, *real* lives that were closed off to her, locked behind the bars and stones and wards of the palace. She knew the name of every one of her city's neighborhoods, their major thoroughfares, their postal codes, their representatives in Parliament. So when she set out from the inn's back door, she thought getting back to the palace would be a snap. The river, after all, was due east of St. James, and ran a north-south course, so if she walked directly away from the river she would soon enough reach Whitehall and see the green acres of St. James Park up ahead. A snap.

What she didn't realize, however, was that she and Gill had crossed over the river on Westminster Bridge, so when she started walking toward what she thought was west, she was really walking south. She realized something was wrong relatively quickly, and veered right to correct her course. Or tried to veer right: the road she took slithered around a long curve and seemed to double back on itself, though she didn't recognize any landmarks. She could have asked someone for directions, of course, but, well, she was Marie-Victoria, the Princess Dauphine, whose image appeared in the newspapers every day. Someone was going to recognize her, no matter how humble her dress. So she pushed on, looking up at the sun to try to get her bearings. But the sun was invisible behind the usual London clouds, and the shadows seemed to come from three different directions at the same time.

Once again, she was horrified to see how people lived—the poor children in the streets with their hands out, begging. The dirty sidewalks full of horse dung, the sky clogged with gray smoke. The abject poverty in front of her moved her to tears and mortification. How could she sleep on a comfortable bed, dine on rare and fanciful treats, when children were going hungry just a few blocks away from the palace gates?

To make everything worse, it started drizzling, and she didn't have an umbrella. An umbrella wasn't something she'd ever had to think about. When it started raining, an umbrella would open over her head as if by magic. Sometimes it *was* magic, of course, but usually it was just one of the dozens of maids and footmen who trailed after her like ducklings after their mother. Who was she kidding to think that she knew how to make it on her own? She didn't even know how to take shelter from the rain.

She was lost within this train of thought when the snarling voice shook her from her reverie. She looked up to see a sneering, dirty face surrounded by the sooty walls of a small, dark alley. She turned quickly, only to see two more youths materialize from piles of trash, barring her exit.

She turned back to the first one, who seemed to be their leader.

"Please, let me pass," she said.

"Of course I'll let a lady pass!" he said contemptuously. He was about her age, maybe a year or so older. "I's a gentleman, ain't I? Don't I look like a gentleman?"

"You . . . you look the very model of gentility," Marie stuttered.

"Hear that, boys? The very model of genti—genti— What'd you call it, missy?"

"Gentility," Marie whispered.

"Gent'bility," the odious creature said. "'At's me!"

"If you please," Marie tried again. "I have urgent business to which I must attend."

"Well, and what do I look like, some kind of loafer?"

"No, I—"

The ruffian puffed up his skinny chest.

"Do I look like someone who's life is so pampered and full o' luxury that I couldn't possibly have urgent 'busy-ness' to which I must attend to? My job is to collect the tolls for this here alley. Passage ain't free, you know. There's a charge."

"Yes, of course," Marie said, reaching for her string bag—thank God she'd remembered to grab it before she left the inn. "I can pay you whatever you want."

Before she could open the bag, however, the hoodlum had snatched it from her hands.

"Allow me to help you with that," he said sarcastically.

Marie grabbed for the bag but he pulled it out of reach. Any closer and she'd have had to step within range of his breath, which, judging by the color of his teeth, was an experience she didn't want to subject herself to.

"See here!" she said indignantly. "That's *quite* rude of you."

"Quite rude, you say?" He laughed. "You've hurt my feelings." He jingled the bag ruminatively. "There's an extra charge for insulting the toll taker, there is."

He pulled the top of the bag open and let the coins spill carelessly into his grubby palm, some of them bouncing off his hand and falling to the cobblestone surface of the alley. When he saw the solid gold coins, however, his eyes went wide, first with disbelief, then with greed.

"My, my, my. I thought that was a nice frock you was wearing. But I didn't realize it was *this* nice." He shook the coins in his palm before dumping them into a pocket. "Girl who travels with this kind of ready cash likely has a few other goodies on her, jewels or jewelry or some such."

Marie couldn't help herself. "Jewels and jewelry are the same thing. And it's pronounced 'jool-ry,' not 'joo-lu-ry.' The only thing worse than being mugged is being mugged by a group of hoodlums who can't even speak my mother's English properly."

The boy frowned in confusion. "Your mother . . . ?"

"Perhaps you've heard the expression 'the queen's English'?"

One of the fellows behind her sniggered.

"What, yer sayin' yer mum's bloody Queen Nell?" His accent made his friend sound like the Duke of Cornwall.

Marie summoned all the authority that a life at court had taught her, and put it in her voice. "Her Majesty's name is Eleanor, and I'll thank you to speak it with the respect it deserves."

The chatty one in front of her snorted a dumbfounded laugh. "What, and that makes you Princess Mary?"

Marie drew herself to her full height. "I am the Princess Marie-Victoria Grace Eleanor Aquitaine." The words had never been more meaningful to her than they were in that moment. More true. "Now stand aside, sir, and let me be on my way," she said, speaking to him with her mother's voice—the voice that inspired total obedience. The voice of the queen.

He snorted again, but he was clearly thrown. Marie knew it was her only chance. She spun and dashed for the alley's exit. One of the bandits blocked her way, but her hand was curled in a fist and seemed to make contact with his mouth of its own accord. The bandit went down like a bowling pin. She leaped over his body and kept running. *I just hit him!* she exulted. *I'm going to get away—*

But a tug on the back of her dress brought her up short before she'd taken two more steps. She heard buttons snap and fabric tear, but the quality of her dress was her undoing: it held tight and she was jerked to a halt. Rough hands spun her around and pushed her against the wall. She was acutely conscious of her open bodice, her exposed blouse, her heaving chest.

"You're a saucy lass, ain't-cha," the first hoodlum sneered. "That's going to make this more fun."

There were four of them. She wouldn't get away. But she could scream, and so she did—she screamed at the top of her lungs—and then they surrounded her, and she screamed even more—and she thought she would die, or worse—and they pushed her to the ground—and she closed her eyes then, because now she was too frightened to scream, and she only wanted to live. But then, just as suddenly, someone was pulling the men off of her, and she was safe and unharmed.

"Sorry to spoil your plans, boys," a voice said from somewhere to Marie's right. "But this party's over."

Gill! she thought. *He found me.* Then she saw it was not Gill, but someone else—a boy with dark hair and blue eyes.

"Wolf!"

"Stay back, Marie—let me take care of them." Wolf had no weapon. Already he had a cut lip and his fists were red with blood, but his assailants looked even worse. They surrounded him menacingly, and one pulled a broken pipe out of his pocket.

"Hey now, that's not so nice—picking on a girl alone in the city," Wolf said.

"Go on, boy, nothing for you here. There's four of us and only one of ya." Their leader spat at the ground.

"Then it's an even fight." Wolf smiled as he dispatched them in quick succession. A flurry of fists and feet: roundhouse to the jaw, karate chops, well-aimed punches to the gut and face. In a few moments they were all in a heap on the street.

"Are you hurt?" he asked, as he helped her to stand.

"No, just shaky," she said, taking his hand.

He pulled her close and held her in his arms until she stopped trembling. "You're all right now—you're safe, you're with me."

"How did you know where to find me?" she asked.

"I went to the Knight's Arms; it's the cleanest inn near the ports. They told me a young woman of your description had just left. I thought you might be lost, and I know you—you always think if you keep turning right, you'll find your way somehow. Remember how we learned the passageways that way? So I kept turning right, and here you are," he said.

"I ran away. I made a mistake. I don't know what I was thinking." Her heart ached, because she knew what she had to do. She had always thought of herself as gentle and soft-hearted, but in the end she had been as abrupt and brusque as the Merlin. She had left Gill at the inn without even saying good-bye.

Wolf nodded. "I left as soon as I heard you were missing. Leo's been shot. My father's train was attacked. The palace needs you—you belong back in St. James, and I came to bring you home."

"Yes! We must return immediately," she said, remembering what had caused her to leave Gill in the first place. "There are five hundred barrels of Burgundy—the duke's wedding gift—in the castle basement. Yet I suspect they're not filled with wine but with magefire. Hurry, we need to get rid of them before whoever put them there sets them off!"

· 44 ·

Lion and
BEAR

Wolf and Marie raced toward St. James in the hansom that Wolf had commandeered earlier, when he first went out to search for her. He galloped at a breakneck pace through the streets and it was all they could do to stay in the seat.

"What do you mean, someone's trying to blow up the palace?" Wolf shouted above the clattering of steel-shod hooves on the paving stones.

"I sneaked out last night through the old dungeons. They're mostly used for storage these days. Like I said, they contain five hundred barrels of Burgundy from the Red Duke, Hugh Borel. But as I made my way through them I kept getting whiffs of sulfur, vinegar, and smoke. I figured that one of the barrels had split and the wine had gone off, and I didn't give it another thought. But the smell was so familiar and it stayed with me. I was sure I'd smelled it before. And then I remembered—"

Wolf's spine went cold as he listened to Marie's description.

"It was magefire," she told him. "I've only ever smelled it one time before."

He knew when Marie had smelled the magefire. It was when Aelwyn had set fire to her bedroom and almost killed her.

"Is this Aelwyn's plot, then?" he asked, giving the horses another pull on the reins to make them run faster.

Marie hung tightly to his arm. "I don't know." She told Wolf about Aelwyn's part of the plan, how she had taken on Marie's form during the royal ball.

"So that wasn't you dancing with Leo after all," he said.

"It wasn't me," she admitted.

For some reason, Wolf found some joy in this information and did not care to hide his relief upon hearing it. He had been jealous to think that his old friend had finally fallen for his brother. A little part of him had always been proud that Marie was the only person in the world who preferred him over Leo.

"I don't want to suspect her, but she hardly protested at all when I told her my plan; it was hard to think that she didn't just want me out of the way." Marie shook her head. "Except . . ."

"You don't think it's Aelwyn," he said.

"I don't. She might have been tempted to be princess and

to marry Leo but she would never harm anyone in the palace. Never. This isn't her," said Marie.

"You have someone in mind?"

She nodded. "When Gill told me Count Beziers had shot Leo it all came together. The Red Duke is his cousin, after all, and Isabelle of Valois's guardian as well."

"You think the French are making a play for the throne?"

"Maybe," said Marie.

Wolf thought it over. It did make sense. Though their armies and most of their land had been stripped from them after the defeat at Orleans, House Valois had never renounced their claim to the throne of France.

"You look skeptical," Marie said.

"I am. They have no sorcerer to create the magefire," he said, frowning. "And how could they have smuggled in five hundred barrels under the Merlin's nose?"

"It must have been wine when it arrived," said Marie. "Someone turned it into magefire after it was in the palace basements. As for a sorcerer, they could be allied with one."

What Marie was saying made sense to Wolf. It all led back to Burgundy. Or did it? He remembered something suddenly. "Leo."

"Leo?"

"He sent my father north with a few barrels of the burgundy the Red Duke gave you two as a wedding gift," Wolf said slowly. "The king was traveling with it when his train derailed."

"But that would mean . . ."

"I don't know what to think," he said, despairing. It was all so chaotic and confusing. His brother. Shot. The virtual bomb underneath the palace. His brother sending his father off with the booby-trapped wine . . .

His brother insisting on King Frederick taking the barrels as gifts *for his* hosts.

Leo wouldn't take no for an answer.

It couldn't be right. Leo would never. Would he? But why?

Wolf turned ashen. "My God. Do you think he was in on it? With Borel?" Leo knew a little about magic, after all; it was a hobby of his. And magefire could be conjured from ordinary materials. Even Aelwyn, an eleven-year-old apprentice, had been able to create it.

"Oh, Wolf, I don't know. If the French were involved, why would Beziers challenge him to a duel?" she said.

Wolf stewed on it, hoping against hope that the logic didn't point to his older brother, his own flesh and blood. His mentor and friend. Not Leo. It couldn't be Leo. But he turned the facts around in his mind, over and over again, and finally said, "Perhaps Beziers's challenge was unrelated to the plot to take down the empire. I am sorry to admit that Leo did treat Isabelle quite shabbily."

Wolf heard the anguish in his own voice. Apparently Marie did, too, because she rubbed his arm soothingly. Then he realized something else.

"The wine," said Wolf in a hoarse voice. "It had to be

him. The other night, after the vernissage, I showed him how to get into the dungeons, and we tapped a barrel and drank a few cups. But I heard a noise and left him alone for a time. He must have done it then. Changed them. It had to be him. There's no one else who would have had the opportunity. No one outside of Queen Eleanor's retinue, anyway, and they're all so loyal to her that it's impossible to imagine. It—it had to be Leo."

"But why would he do such a thing? He had the empire in his grasp, he was going to be king. Why set it all to ash?" she said.

"I don't know," said Wolf, clicking his tongue against his teeth as the hansom raced down the Mall toward the front entrance to St. James.

But instead of the usual palace guard before the open gates, the way was barred by a contingent of knights from the Order of Articus, one of the oldest and most prestigious military contingents, resplendent in their blue and red. The gates were locked.

"Halt!" one of the knights yelled, stepping in front of the charging horse with his pike leveled. "Halt, I say!"

Wolf grabbed the reins and jerked them tight. The horse pulled up so quickly that his hooves slid on the street and almost danced out from under him before he managed to stop. Wolf moved to jump out of the cab to confront the knights, but Marie had already leaped to the pavement.

"What is going on, lieutenant? Why are the gates closed?"

The knight whirled on the girl speaking to him, his mouth already open to issue a rebuke. When he saw who it was, though, he stammered for several seconds in a fit of confusion, then dropped to one knee and bowed his face nearly to the ground.

"I beg your pardon, Your Highness!"

"Stand up, sir," Marie said in a forceful voice, "and speak plainly. What has happened here?"

Wolf stared in amazement. He had never seen Marie act quite so imperial before, he was impressed by the force of her command. Maybe running away from her titles and duties had made her realize just how much of a monarch she really was.

The knight stood up abashedly. "It's the damned Prussians, your highness. A number of soldiers who were masquerading as butlers and footmen have stormed your mother's apartments." Then he saw who was with Marie and held up his weapon again, pointing it straight at Wolf.

"At ease, sir!" Marie commanded, standing even straighter, and her voice took on even more steel. "The prince is with me."

"Marie—I will get to the bottom of this. This is a terrible misunderstanding," said Wolf, gnashing his teeth at the news.

She nodded and turned to the guard. "Does the queen yet live? Does she remain at liberty?"

"The Queen's Guard was caught unawares and many were killed. But her majesty remains alive, ma'am, and barricaded inside a few rooms. Their magical defenses seem to be holding." The knight whirled on Wolf. "By all accounts it was *Kronprinz* Leopold who gave the order to assassinate the queen."

Wolf wanted to shut his ears from hearing these words. His brother. A traitor. One who had planned the decimation of the empire and the deaths of thousands. It had been one thing merely to suspect him, another thing entirely to know it was true.

"The *kronprinz* healed from his wounds last night, and this morning it is believed he disarmed the Merlin. He was last seen headed for the dungeons."

Marie and Wolf turned to each other. Marie's cheeks were flushing with anger and determination while Wolf had curled his hands into fists.

"Take us there," they said in unison.

· 45 ·

Daughter
OF MERLIN

When Aelwyn awoke the next day in the middle of the courtyard garden, her skirt was damp with dew and her head pounded as if she had been dancing and carousing all night. How long had she been out? What had happened since?

But as soon as she recalled the events of the party, she leaped to her feet and raced through the corridors of St. James toward the ministry offices to find her father and warn him about Leo. That he was . . . not what he seemed, nor something she'd ever seen before. Not mortal, but not magical in the way that she and her father and the few remaining mages were. Whatever he was, he was very powerful, and very, very scary.

That infinite darkness inside him.

That raw pulsing power that had snapped her magic as easily as a child's arm.

He had been shot right in the chest, she recalled. Did it pierce his heart? Was it enough? Did he live?

Aelwyn was so wrapped up in her thoughts that she didn't see the dark-robed figure in the passage in front of her until it was too late. He seemed to materialize from thin air. No, not thin air: from the wall, which he walked through as though it were no more solid than a reflection in a mirror. Which could only mean—

"Father!" Aelwyn bleated as she collided with the Merlin. Despite his advanced age and rail-thin figure, she bounced off him as though his skeleton were made of iron.

Emrys caught his daughter and steadied her. "Where have you been? I have been looking for you!" he said, spinning her around and setting off the way she'd come. "The *kronprinz* was shot last night and we don't have much time."

"Father," she said urgently. "I have to tell you something. Leo is—"

"Missing," said her father, cutting her off. "Impudent demon got away from me."

The Merlin caught her up to speed. After the Prussian healers had healed the prince's wounds, Emrys had entered the room and cast a binding spell on the location as a precaution so that no one inside could leave. But somehow Leo had disarmed him and used the binding spell on the Merlin instead. He had just been able to get away.

"A binding spell—but that would mean—you knew—you knew about Leo," she asked. "About what he is."

"I'd long suspected that the Hohenzollern court has been harboring a powerful sorcerer, and Lamac only confirmed that. I'd guessed it was Hartwig at first, but the man has so little power he couldn't transform a dove into a cat. I just didn't know *who* it was—until the *kronprinz* set foot on Albion."

Albion. The ancient name for England. The name by which it was still referred to in Avalon. A wyrdding word.

"I've known ever since he arrived. But there was little I could do about it since the treaty had already been signed." He sighed. "Which placed him under the queen's protection."

Aelwyn struggled to put her next question into words.

"Who . . . what is he?" she finally asked, shuddering. She had never encountered such wild and vicious magic.

"I don't know. There is wyrdding magic deep in his veins, but not one that I have seen before." The Merlin sounded old, weary, even as they ran through the palace.

"But Viviane told me that wyrdding magic comes from Avalon. How can Leo's be unknown to you?"

"My sister loves her homeland a little too much. Yes, Avalon is the source of *our* magic. But there are many other kinds of magic in the world, some that we know of, and many that we do not. In the far lands of the north and east—Muscovy or Hindustan or Cathay, or the ancient civilizations of the New World, whose magic went into hiding after the Europeans arrived, or perhaps even Africa, whose vast interior remains all but unknown to us."

Aelwyn nodded. "But Leo is the Prussian *kronprinz*. He's not from anywhere else."

"Indeed he isn't," the Merlin agreed. "But that's just it. I don't think Leopold *is* Leopold."

Aelwyn would have stopped dead in her tracks, but her father's hand on her arm dragged her forward.

"Wh-what do you mean?"

"I believe the being who just bested me isn't Leopold von Hohenzollern. At least not entirely. It is something else as well. An incubus in mortal flesh that is concealed from my scrying bowls and magical scans."

"But if that's the case, why were you able to sense it now?"

"I'm not sure," the Merlin admitted. "Maybe it's grown careless, but I doubt it. Clearly it needs Leopold's body, or it wouldn't have expended so much energy saving it from what should have been a mortal wound. But I suspect that the wound made it realize how vulnerable it is. It would have known that once Marie took office, my time as Merlin would come to an end and I would have been forced to depart Albion, leaving you as Morgaine. While you possess even more innate power than I do, you are young and inexperienced, and vulnerable to attack. It probably thought it had a better chance to defeat you than me."

Aelwyn wasn't sure if her father was praising her or criticizing her, but now didn't seem like the time to protest. "But we'll be able to defeat him together, no?"

"Except I am bound by my oath to the throne. Whatever else it is, it is still Leo, and Leo is still the presumptive heir to the empire. The powers of the Merlin are vested in the crown and in the law. It would take an act of the Council of Magic, ratified by Parliament and signed by Queen Eleanor, to cancel the agreement and free me to use my power against him. Needless to say, we don't have time for that. I tried to cast the spell on the room instead of on his body to work around the law, but it backfired on me."

"Where are we going?" she asked, finding it hard to keep up with her father's quick steps.

"To the dungeons. He's gone there, you see. To wreak vengeance on us all and bring down St. James as well as a good section of London. A soldier from the Queen's Guard arrived a few minutes ago to tell us there are five hundred barrels of magefire down there, just waiting for a spark."

Aelwyn gasped. "What are we going to do? How do we stop him?"

The Merlin pulled up short. "Not we, daughter. You. You are not Morgaine yet. As such you are bound by no restrictions to your power."

Aelwyn stared up at her father, shocked. "But I don't possess the powers of the Morgaine either—just the spells I learned from the sisterhood, which any acolyte knows. How can I possibly challenge a being of such strength?"

"Now is not the time for modesty, daughter. You spent four years with Viviane. I may not have seen my sister in half a millennium, but I still know her. She will have taught you to access your wyrdding power—to use it to amplify the sisterhood's spells a hundredfold, and to do things the sisterhood can only dream of."

Aelwyn was shocked.

"But just yesterday you made me promise that I wouldn't use my wyrdding power outside of Avalon!"

A flicker of a smile touched her father's mouth. "A promise I couldn't help but notice you didn't make." The smile was gone as quickly as it came. "Listen to me. I've been hoping he would make a mistake like this and sure enough, his pride got the better of him. During his duel with Beziers, Leo foolishly placed his physical shell in mortal danger. Your attack with the soulstone took him off guard, and Beziers's bullet nicked his heart. The incubus's magic clearly requires a live host. While the Prussian healers are talented, Leopold's body is still weak and the incubus is vulnerable. You must finish him off."

Aelwyn gulped. "You mean?"

The Merlin nodded.

"You need to kill him and whatever is inside him, once and for all."

"And while I'm at it, try to keep him from setting the entire palace—not to mention the entire city—on fire?"

"Exactly."

Aelwyn was still trying to wrap her head around this when her father grabbed her hand and pushed her through a wall.

·46·

Dark
WIZARD

The Merlin disappeared and Aelwyn was alone in the dungeons. She knew where she was headed. She knew these tunnels like the back of her hand. She had Marie to thank for that, Marie with her love of secret passageways and games of hide-and-seek.

She found him standing in the middle of the barrels, green smoke rising from their cracks and seams. It was indeed magefire. The smell was overpowering.

"Surprised?" she asked, startling him.

Leo turned around. His hair was disheveled and his shirt was slightly agape, so she could see the patch that covered his heart. His once-handsome face contorted in a malicious sneer. "You dare challenge me, witch? Haven't you learned by now? Begone with you."

He waved his hand at her, but Aelwyn dodged the spell with swift reflexes and walked firmly into the middle of the room.

"Think your stone magic will hold against mine? Shall we try again? I'd like to hear you scream this time. Yours is a pebble compared to the power at my command," he sneered.

This time Aelwyn saw the stone he wore around his neck. It matched her father's description. For it was the Merlin, of course, who had trapped all the horrors of the world inside it. Pandora's Box. While the worst of its contents had been dissipated at Lamac, she could feel its evil influence, like a heady mixture of misery and temptation.

"That stone you wear has turned you into something you are not," she said. "You were not like this as a child." She remembered him. A little bit of a flirt, a little headstrong maybe, but not vicious. Not cruel. What had he done to himself?

"Don't blame the stone. I was always what I am. I was just . . . biding my time."

"You mean you were too weak to challenge my father," Aelwyn taunted him. "Too afraid. You needed to get your hands on your little toy," she added, nodding at the stone around his neck as though it were a tacky trinket and hoping he couldn't feel the fear in her heart.

Leo smirked. "Why are you fighting me, witch-girl? I know you have no more respect for the sisterhood and their boring idea of what magic is than I do. We are the same.

Don't we have the same plan? Aren't I doing what you wanted to accomplish all those years ago, when you almost burned down the palace?"

Her cheeks flamed as red as her hair. "That was an accident!"

"So you claim." He shrugged.

"You are a monster."

"It takes one to know one, Avalon whore." Without warning, he flung a force that sent her flying across the room, slamming her down onto the nearest barrels, just as the door to the room opened and Wolf and Marie appeared.

"Aelwyn! Are you all right?" Marie cried, running to her friend, who lay dazed on the ground.

Wolf removed a pistol from his holster and pointed it at his brother. "Leo! Stop what you're doing."

"And you're going to stop me? With that?"

With a nod of his head, he sent Wolf's gun careening away. Wolf reached for his blade. He would protect his friends as long as he could. "Marie—go. Take Aelwyn and go!"

"No! We're not leaving you," Marie said.

"How sweet. Friends to the last. But never my friend, right, Princess? You despised me from the beginning," said Leo, stalking the room and keeping to the shadows of the cavern.

Wolf had to divert attention away from Marie, had to keep Leo focused on him. He had no idea how they were going to stop him from lighting those barrels and sending them all to the heavens, but he had to try.

"Leo! Why are you doing this? You're my brother. You were going to be king. You had the empire at your feet. We were at peace. Why destroy it all?"

"Brother," said Leo with a sneer. "We are not brothers. Oh, the wench queen was my mother all right, but my father is not the fat fool who sits on the throne."

"Not your father? Then who—Hartwig!" said Wolf. "So the rumors were true, then? That's why you kept buying all those royal portraits—too scared that anyone would notice the resemblance! But how could it be—mother detested him!"

"Has that ever stopped anyone from taking what they want?" Leo laughed with maniacal glee.

Next to him, Marie shuddered, and Wolf felt a cold anger fill his veins as he understood now why his mother cried all the time, why she went to the grave early.

Leo crowed. "Yes. I am Hartwig's son. We hail from a long and proud order that keeps the dark magic aflame. For five hundred years we have waited for this day when our true mother would have her revenge on the wizard who burned her at the stake and trapped her soul in a box. When our enemies would burn as she burned."

"Jeanne of Arkk," said Aelwyn. "I heard her in you. When I held your soul in my stone." The banshee screams of virulent rage, the seething furor of a twisted spirit.

The Dark Witch of Orleans.

Trapped in the Pandora's Box.

Suddenly Aelwyn realized her father had been wrong. Leo hadn't been possessed by some weak demon that slowly gained power inside his body. He had been bred by the malevolent Lord Hartwig to be a host for an evil creature waiting five hundred years to wreak her revenge.

"She was in the Pandora's stone! Jeanne of Arkk! And when you broke the magical seals that kept it closed, you took the demon into your body," Aelwyn said.

"We are king and queen, bound together in body for eternity, and together we shall destroy anyone who gets in our way."

"Together! Can't you see that she is chasing you from your own body? But of course you can't—there is almost nothing of you left inside, Leo. She will use you as she used countless other men, and when your body is burned out she will trade it in for another."

Leo's face smirked, but now Aelwyn knew it wasn't Leo at all.

"Drive him from his own body? Perish the thought! He's right here with me, like a canary in a cage. There will be nothing left of you, any of you, very soon." There was no doubt that it was the witch speaking now through Leo. He raised his arm and released a flash of light toward the barrels of magefire.

But Aelwyn had raised her arm, too, and had released her

own flame. "I call on the power of Avalon, the strength of our Merlin, the blood of Viviane, the light of the world and every star in the heavens, I call on the spirit of Excalibur and Articus that has kept Albion safe for a millennium, to vanquish and destroy the Dark Witch of Orleans once and for all!" Her arms flew from her side, and a sudden gusting wind blew all over the dark of the dungeon.

There was a great clap of thunder and a flash of white light, as bright as every star in the heavens, as clean and pure as a fairy's wish, a child's laughter, a pure beam of goodness that came from the earth and the heavens. It enveloped them all in its glorious power, overcoming the dark green flame that began to shoot from the barrels, then everything went dark.

When their eyes adjusted to the dim, they saw Leo, lying on the floor with a hole in his chest where his heart should be, a smoking black crater so large that she could see the flagstones through its gaping opening. Smoke leaked from his slack mouth as well, and from his nostrils, and even from his eye sockets.

It was done.

He—and whatever was inside him—was dead.

Aelwyn had killed them both.

· 47 ·

Unmasked
AND UNMADE

*I*t was almost sunset, and Ronan had been taking a late tea when she was paid a visit by the hotel manager. She batted her eyelashes at the liveried steward who stood at the threshold of the Claridge's suite she'd called home for the past month. Something told her feminine wiles weren't going to help her here, however. The steward's perfectly coiffed hair, the slightly floral cologne he sported, and the tiny pink peony pinned to his lapel all suggested he wasn't batting for her team.

"I'm sorry, Mr., ah—"

"Cormorant."

Ronan struggled to keep her voice level. "I'm sorry, Mr. Cormorant, what is the problem?" She licked her lips as she finished speaking, and leaned forward to provide a better view of her cleavage. Just in case.

Cormorant rolled his eyes at this obvious tactic.

"You can save all this"—the steward waved his hand at her general chest area—"for someone else. I prefer a little more hair on the chest, if you know what I mean. Not that the dress isn't fabulous."

Ronan shrugged. "Thank you," she said sheepishly, stepping back.

"No doubt it belongs to Whitney Van Owen, like everything else in this room."

"Yes, and what of it? Miss Van Owen and I are old friends from New York City. My father is the governor of the colony."

"And my father is a dairy farmer on the Isle of Man, but I don't let it hold me back either. Listen, Miss—"

"Astor. Ronan Astor," said Ronan, her head held high.

"Miss Astor, I am here to inform you that Mrs. Van Owen sent a cable from Rome this morning asking that we prepare the room for her sister and nieces, who are arriving on the *Queen Mab*. Imagine her surprise when we told her that the room was already occupied by someone who's been signing her bills as Whitney Van Owen."

"But Whitney told me—"

"Whitney isn't paying the bill for the royal suite and its many amenities. Mrs. Van Owen is. Mimosas for breakfast, consommé for lunch, scones for high tea, and a truly remarkable amount of filet mignon and Bordeaux Supérieur for dinner."

"That was Vera, actually."

"The, how shall I put this, rather broad-shouldered lady who favors the brown serge dresses? My father would put her to good use on the farm, believe me. Nevertheless, there remains a bill that needs settling, not to mention a room that needs vacating so the maids can prepare it for Mrs. Mackenzie and her daughters."

"But Whitney said I could stay here!"

"Apparently Whitney didn't tell her mother that. And while I'm sure three thousand pounds is less than Mrs. Van Owens's shopping allowance, I cannot in good conscience bill a woman for goods and services that she did not, in fact, receive."

"Three thousand pounds! I don't have that kind of money!"

Cormorant circled a white-gloved hand in front of his face. "This is my not-my-problem face. But while you decide how you're going to avoid debtor's prison, I'll have my porters pack up all those fabulous dresses you've been wearing and put them in storage for you. And we've a lovely room in the basement that you and your governess can wait in while you plan."

A room in the basement? It sounded like a cell to Ronan. She was racking her brain to think of some way out of this hairy predicament when the bell for the lift sounded, and the accordion doors rattled open. A stern-faced figure in a Prussian military uniform emerged from the lift, his chest jangling with medals, his boots leaving deep divots in the plush carpet as he marched down the hall. A gilded scabbard hung from the belt of his tunic, but it was somehow less noticeable than the black armband that wreathed his sleeve.

"Ronan Astor?" he said, looking right through Cormorant as if he wasn't there.

"Who is inquiring?" the steward asked in an icy tone.

"I am Sir Duncan Oswald, King Frederick of Prussia's chief of arms, and head of security while His Majesty is here in London. His Royal Highness *Kronprinz* Wolfgang requests the presence of Miss Ronan Elizabeth Astor in the Royal Embassy at St. James Palace at her earliest possible convenience."

Ronan was so excited to hear Wolf's name that she almost missed the word that preceded it. Then it came back to her ears: *Kronprinz.*

"The *kronprinz*? Do you mean Leo?" she asked, confused. "Why would he want to see me?"

A pained expression crossed Oswald's face. "I am sorry to report that Prince Leopold succumbed to injuries sustained in a duel last night. Prince Wolfgang is now the heir to the throne of Prussia. And he would like to see you."

Wolf! Of course. He said he would return to her after everything. But how could Leo be dead, with the Merlin himself attending to him? And—and what did that mean for Wolf? For Wolf and her? *Kronprinz?* Did this mean she was going to be—

"I'm very sorry, Sir Duncan," Cormorant's voice cut into her thoughts, "but Miss Astor cannot leave Claridge's until she settles her rather substantial bill."

Oswald didn't bother to look at the steward. "Send the bill to the palace. Miss Astor needs to come with me. *Now.*"

Oswald said that the new *kronprinz* would answer her questions when they reached the palace, and refused to say another word during the fifteen-minute journey. Ronan was thankful she'd already dressed for the day, because the master-at-arms had refused to let her leave his sight. Although the way he kept his hand on his saber handle made her feel like she was a prisoner rather than a guest. She put it down to Prussian stiffness. Thank God Wolf didn't suffer from any of that.

She fidgeted nervously in her seat, trying to imagine why he'd summoned her to the palace. No, that wasn't quite honest. She tried to imagine any reason to summon her to the palace other than to tell her that the way was finally clear for them to be together, and sadly, she could think of a few.

But as *kronprinz* no one could tell him what to do or whom to marry. He would rule all of Prussia one day—the largest empire in Europe after the Franco-British. And she would be queen by his side.

Wolf had asked for her.

He had returned to her as he'd promised.

Her heart leaped in hope and anticipation for the splendid and happy future that would soon unfold before her. Could it be that the fairy-tale ending she had been working for since arriving in London was finally coming true? It had to be. It just had to.

· 48 ·

Long Live
THE KING

Meanwhile, at the other end of London, Wolf took a few of his most loyal men to the palace's basement. Alongside a second crew provided by the Merlin, they placed the barrels of wine on a decommissioned ferry that had been impressed into duty for the task. It took almost half the day to move and load all five hundred of them, and he and Marie watched tensely throughout the operation. The Merlin had wanted them to retreat to a safe distance, but they both insisted that it was their duty to oversee the operation. Normally the barrels would be rolled up a gangplank, but they didn't want to risk accidentally igniting them by jarring them too much. Although the magefire should remain inert without the spell to activate it, no one knew what kind of booby traps Leo might have concealed. As a consequence the Merlin had to inspect each barrel individually, which was then loaded onto a tumbrel and wheeled laboriously onto the old ferry.

Wolf and Marie stood at the head of the dock, watching the operation. It was the first time the two of them were alone together after what happened in the dungeons earlier that day.

Finally Marie cleared her throat. "When we were down there, I remembered all the time we'd spent in the palace's secret passages when were kids, and all the crazy things we found there—knives crusted with blood from who knew what assassination—"

"Probably a steak dinner stolen by a servant," Wolf said.

"Rubies and sapphires and diamonds that had been pried from the crowns of the aforementioned kings and queens—"

"If I had an empero for every time a jewel fell out of my father's crown, I'd be"—he barked a little laugh—"a lot poorer than if I sold the jewels for what they were really worth."

Marie couldn't help but laugh with him. "Don't try to change the subject. We found all kinds of treasure in those passages. And I just remembered that the best thing of all was that old master spell-key. It opened everything short of the main gates and the door to my mother's private apartments. And somehow you let me talk you into keeping it."

"I believe I found it," Wolf said. "Finders keepers, losers weepers."

"I believe you threatened to kiss me on the lips unless I gave it to you. Which at seven years old I thought was the grossest possible thing in the world."

"And is it still?" Wolf asked lightly.

Marie looked at the horizon, at the ferry that held the wine barrels full of dark magic. After a few moments, she turned back to look at Wolf's profile.

"No," she said softly. "It's not."

His voice was as low as hers. "Good," he said.

She inhaled sharply. She had been meaning to say this for a while now. "I know it was you—you gave Gill the money and lowered the wards so that Gill and I could sneak out that night. I thought it was Aelwyn until she told me she could keep them down once they were lowered, but someone else had to open them first. I should have wondered more about that, but there were so many other preparations that it escaped my attention. But it was you. You were the friend who helped us get away."

"Yes. I'm sorry, Marie, I thought I was helping you," he said. "I thought I was doing the right thing for you. It was wrong of me—it put you in so much danger. But I only wanted your happiness. I thought it was what you wanted."

"It was, but it isn't now," she said. "But why help me escape?"

Wolf shrugged. "I'm not really sure. At the time I told myself that I didn't want to see you separated from the person you really loved, but now I wonder if there wasn't a part of me that knew who Leo really was. What he really was. And I wanted to save you from that. Everyone deserves the chance to be happy. Even princesses."

Marie nodded, her mind a thousand miles away, on a ship where she and Gill Cameron stood side by side while a captain read out the marriage oath. She shook her head, dismissing the image.

"Sometimes I think I loved the idea of escape more than anything really. But when I figured out that the palace was in danger, and the empire itself, I realized that I love that even more. I know it sounds silly, but the empire is part of me."

Wolf nodded vigorously. "I know just how you feel. When we were facing Leo, I wanted to protect my father's empire—my empire." He laughed. "I thought I was the independent-minded son, the rebel, but I guess all that 'duty before self' stuff got to me."

Marie laughed with him. "Well, thanks anyway. For wanting that for me. Happiness, I mean."

He touched her lightly on the shoulder, smiling wryly. "It was my pleasure, Princess."

The last of the barrels was carted out and loaded onto the ferry. The small ship had sunk nearly to its deck beneath the weight of all of them. The Merlin didn't want to light its steam engine for fear of triggering an explosion, so a tugboat had nudged behind the ferry and begun easing it out into the broadest part of the Thames.

"What about you?" Marie said now.

"What do you mean, what about me?" Wolf answered evasively.

"The American girl. I saw you dancing with her the night of the royal ball."

Wolf didn't say anything for a long time. Then: "Well, that doesn't matter now, does it?"

She knew what he was thinking, for it was the same thing that was on her mind. The Merlin had spoken to the two of them earlier.

To Wolf, he had said, "Your parents' marriage was a political alliance, and it is well-known that Frederick and Theresa never enjoyed great affection for each other. Hartwig probably blackmailed your mother into keeping his vile secret by telling her that he would convince your father that she willingly conceived a child with him. I suspect that she kept her silence so that you, too, would not fall under suspicion."

"Wait, are you saying that I'm also—?" Wolf clearly couldn't bring himself to say it out loud.

"No, *Kronprinz*. You are your father's one true son, and the rightful heir to the throne of Prussia. However, for the sake of peace, your father and Queen Eleanor have agreed to keep Leo's true identity, and intentions, a secret."

Emrys Myrddyn had turned to Princess Marie then. "It is your duty, Princess, to wield peace from the ashes of war."

The Merlin's words hung between them now.

Wolf was the rightful heir to the King of Prussia and there was still a treaty between their two countries.

A treaty that required a marriage between kingdoms.

Princess and prince, joined forever.

The tugboat churned water as it pushed the old ferry farther away from shore. Meanwhile, the Merlin's assistants activated a set of protective wards that ran up and down the river's edge. When the last was lit, the Merlin produced a pair of stones from a pocket. He struck them together, making the tiniest of sparks, and in the middle of the river the ferry disappeared in a massive ball of magefire, black at the edges, malevolently green at its core.

The glove of fire spread across the water for nearly half a mile in every direction, until it struck the wards on shore, at which point it began shooting up toward the heavens. Up and up it burned, green, blue, red, and finally back to black, a column of smoke that burned through the clouds and disappeared into the heavens beyond.

Marie shuddered, and Wolf put his hand on her shoulder. "If that had gone off under the palace!"

"It doesn't bear thinking about," Wolf said.

Marie waited until the smoke had gone, though the river water continued to boil for several minutes, so hot until the last. Finally she turned to Wolf. "You need to say good-bye to her. She deserves that much."

"I have already taken care of it," he assured her. Wolf bit back the lump in his throat. He didn't trust himself to speak, so he just nodded, then turned and strode down the dock.

· 49 ·

Paradise LOST

sabelle felt renewed, revitalized. She felt better than she had in days, in weeks, in her whole life. She had a purpose, and something to live for—someone to live for—and he had been there all along. She and Louis-Philippe would leave for Cévennes that day, get the sisterhood's blessing on their marriage, and be happy. They would be happy forever. It was so close now.

She urged her maid to pack faster. Louis would be coming back soon to pick her up, and she wanted to leave before daybreak. Before Eleanor and the Merlin decided to do something about the Frenchman who had killed the princess's intended—let alone what kind of revenge the Prussian contingent would plan. The news was all over the wire: the *kronprinz* had succumbed to the wounds he'd sustained from the duel. Wild rumors were already circulating around the kingdom—that he'd jumped up moments after Louis shot him, that he'd led an assassination attempt on Queen Eleanor and the Merlin, that he'd transformed into a flaming phoenix and had flown away—but these were just the ravings of a superstitious populace. Leo, her tormentor, was dead.

"Where do you think you are going, Isabelle?" Hugh said, entering the room without knocking. "Do you really mean to leave with him? He is nothing but a boy. Cévennes is a small estate—barely worth a mention. Stay with me and you will remain in your ancestral castle, and live as your father would have wanted you to live."

Isabelle stared at him. "No. We are going. I would have left anyway. I would do anything to get away from you. We won't have much, but we will have each other. We have always had each other, and now we will always be together."

"Do you think Jug Ears frightens me, Isabelle?" Hugh asked, his voice dark and threatening. "Do you really believe I'll let that little orphan take you away from me?"

He crossed the room, and she shrank from him. He took her in his arms and licked her cheek. "You are mine, Isabelle—you will always be mine—you can never get away from me," he whispered.

She was nine years old when her parents, aunt, and uncle died of the wasting plague. Hugh Borel had been a boy, ten years older than her and from a poorer branch of the family, but with a better claim through the paternal bloodline. He'd come to Burgundy and, armed with cash from who knows where, bought the title and estate. She was only Isabelle of Orleans, Isabelle of Valois; she was the heir to France—hollow decrees as long as House Aquitaine sat on the throne—but that was the extent of her inheritance according to Salic law.

At first Hugh had been gentle and kind, and she and Louis had considered themselves lucky to have such a fine guardian. But as she grew older, he began to leer at her openly, and it was only a matter of time until he acted on his desires.

The only thing that kept Hugh at bay was the fact that her father had arranged her marriage to Leopold before his death. Even though she had never met Leopold before—her father was the one who had traveled to the Prussian kingdom to make the arrangements—she had fallen in love with Leopold because she thought he would save her from Hugh. But a monster can only control himself for so long, and eventually Hugh took what he wanted, even if it meant his own destruction. Yet somehow it was Leo who'd destroyed her utterly, and Hugh was still here.

Back then, Hugh was particularly frightened of Lord Hartwig, the old minister who insisted on performing a thorough search of their dungeons. He was looking for something he insisted was in their possession.

Somehow Isabelle knew he meant the strange token stolen from the Merlin's camp during the Battle of 1429 that her mother had given her for safekeeping. She knew where it was, and she showed them. She had given it to Leopold freely, thinking that with it, she had bought her freedom as well.

But all that was ancient history. She couldn't care less about Leopold. She didn't even care about the crown that had been stolen from her. She was going to be with Louis, her love, her wonderful boy.

"We are leaving you," she said. "You can have Burgundy and all of Orleans. Take all of France, for that matter. Louis and I will have each other, and after today you will never see us again."

She turned and stalked from the room, half expecting to feel Hugh's clammy grip on her arm, or even a blade sliding between her ribs. But all she felt was his malevolent, shocked stare. She had outmaneuvered him by renouncing everything that should have been rightfully hers.

But it did not matter. She would have her freedom at last. It would be enough.

Louis greeted her at the carriage while Pierre-Auguste loaded her few belongings onto it.

"Are you ready for your new life to finally begin?" Louis said, putting his hands gently on her arms and gazing lovingly into her eyes.

Isabelle nodded. "I'm only sorry I made you wait so long. We could have been together from the beginning."

"I'm the one who should be sorry that you had to spend one more night in his company. I plan to teach him a lesson he will never forget," said Louis, rolling up his sleeves.

"No!" Isabelle said sharply. "It's not worth the risk. I couldn't bear it if I lost you, too, after everything else. Promise me you'll keep your distance! I beg of you. Promise me," Isabelle repeated, "or I won't get in the carriage. There's no point."

Louis shook his head in wonder. "You never cease to amaze me. Fine. I promise not to go after Hugh. But if he comes near you—"

"I'll gut him myself."

The speaker was Pierre-Auguste, who had finished loading the carriage.

"I suggest we get on our way, my lord and lady, before Duke Borel throws what remains of his honor to the ditch and sends his men after us." He nodded at the massive château behind them, and its unseen retinue of footmen and guards and mercenaries.

Louis helped Isabelle into the carriage and Pierre-Auguste cracked the reins. For the first ten minutes Isabelle sat with bated breath, half expecting to hear the sound of hooves as Hugh sent his men to get them. But when the road remained silent and they put first one mile between them and the château, then two, she began to relax. They had done it. They'd escaped.

The roads grew rougher as they drew farther from the château. The bumps played havoc with Isabelle's stomach. She had not been ill for the first few months of her pregnancy, but now she was starting to feel it. A few times she thought she would vomit on the side of the road, she felt so sick from the journey. But Louis held her hand and had such a strong, resolute look on his face that she knew she mustn't fear.

Around noon they stopped at a small inn for lunch. Isabelle was too nauseous to eat anything more than a pair of poached eggs and sip at some water.

"I don't remember Cévennes very much," she said. "But I know we vacationed there sometimes when Papa was still alive, to visit you."

"It is just a small estate, nothing to get too excited about," Louis said with a smile. "But it will be home."

"Home." She nodded. She liked the sound of that very much. She had been looking for home all her life. Now she knew she'd always had one with him.

They finished their meal and walked out of the inn to look for the hansom.

"Where is everybody?" she asked, when Pierre-Auguste did not appear.

"Let me see," Louis said. He walked toward the horses, which were idling by the road, lazily eating grass.

Isabelle saw a large bundle on the ground near the horses. It was red and white like the Burgundy colors, and she thought it was one of her bags at first. She was wondering why it had been unloaded from the carriage when Louis knelt down beside it and lifted a loose flap of fabric as if to retie it.

But then Isabelle realized: it wasn't a strip of fabric. It was an arm.

The bundle wasn't a piece of luggage at all. It was Pierre-Auguste's body.

Louis looked up at her. The fear was visible on his face even from this distance.

"Isabelle! Run!"

But Isabelle was frozen in place—frozen by the sight of six black-clad figures emerging from a copse of trees. They descended on Louis from all directions, and he disappeared beneath them as behind a cloud. The only thing that could be seen in their darkness was the glint of one knife after another, first flashing silver, then red.

"Louis!" Isabelle screamed. She lifted herself heavily and started to run toward him, only to find a cloth coming down over her head and heavy hands pinning her arms to her side. Everything went black. She tried to kick and scream, but there was nothing she could do—there were too many of them. As she was bundled up and taken away, all she could hear were men speaking in French. *"Kill the boy, but keep her alive."*

the
MARRIAGE PLOT

When Marie left the crown room after the meeting with the Prussian and Franco-British advisors to return to her apartments, she was surprised to see Gill stationed at her door as usual, back in his place. They had not seen each other since yesterday morning, when she had promised to write the warning message to the palace and had left him instead.

In the confusion following the duel, the small matter of the princess's short disappearance had been forgotten. No one knew she had almost eloped with Gill—or, if they did, they had decided to diplomatically overlook it. All's well that ends well, as they say, although she was surprised that he had actually been allowed to resume his old post.

She motioned for him to follow her inside. When they

were alone, they sat together on the settee, where they had spent so many wonderful moments reading, talking, and laughing. He slumped down in his seat. There was no happiness on his face. He looked betrayed, lost, and so miserable. She wanted to tell him nothing would change between them.

But that was not why she had asked him inside.

"Don't say it," he said, his brown eyes dark and angry. "Don't apologize, Marie, I don't think I can stand it."

She sat next to him and looked down at her hands. Was it only last night that she had left the palace with no intent of ever returning? Was it only last night that she'd run out through the passageways, never to turn back? Was it only this morning that she'd put on her gray dress, thinking she would be a bride? She looked up at his sad, drawn face. If she had not left him, they would be married now; she would be his wife.

"You're leaving me, aren't you? You're not coming with me to the Americas. You're not leaving St. James," he said.

"I'm so sorry."

"You said you loved me."

"I did, and I do." She wanted to touch his face, wanted to hold his hands, wanted to reassure him nothing was different between them—but everything was different. Everything was wrong. There was no such thing as personal happiness. One hoped that it would come with duty, like a flower you stumbled upon in the wilderness. One could only hope—but one could not desire it, could not live for it. She lived for others.

Her life was not her own, because it was everybody's. She understood that now. As much as her heart was breaking, she had never felt as alive and as vital as she did that day.

She had fallen into her mother's arms in the crown room, and she had told Eleanor she understood now. She understood so many things about her life. She had been a silly little girl before, but now she understood what it meant to be a princess. Royalty meant sacrifice and not privilege, and it would entail the hardest sacrifice of all. She felt a wrenching in her stomach, and she wanted to cry, but she had to be stronger than that. She had to do the right thing for everybody, including him.

Gill would never feel like he deserved her, she realized. He would work so hard, but it would never be enough for him to forget who she was and where she came from. He would have worked himself to death, trying to make it up to her, trying to make up for what she had sacrificed for him. The cottage she'd dreamed of was indeed a cottage in the sky. She had been playing a child's game, for fantasy and escape. She would have been happy with him, but she wondered if in her happiness she would have been depriving him of his. He would never have believed his love was enough for her. He had grown up in the palace as well—he had seen its splendor and grandeur—and for the rest of his life he would have blamed himself for taking it away from her.

"I do love you, Gill," she said, because she did love this sweet boy who would have risked everything for her. He had loved her enough to try to make a new life for the two of them.

"But you are leaving, regardless."

"It's because no matter what happens, I can't—I can't change who I am. No matter how hard I want to be someone else, no matter how much magic is at my disposal, however many spells Aelwyn can cast, I can't change the fact that I am Marie-Victoria of House Aquitaine."

"And I cannot change who I am," said Gill. "Do you know that Prussian friend of yours questioned me when I returned? Because my damned brother is an Iron Knight, because of what happened during the coup earlier this year. As if I could ever betray House Aquitaine, let alone you!"

She had nothing to say to that, so she stroked his back, remembering how he had consoled her when she had discovered she would have to marry Leopold.

Gill hung his head and gripped her hands tightly in his. When he looked up again, she could see that tears were falling silently down his face. "It doesn't matter because you're going to marry him now, aren't you? That Prince Wolf. You have to. Now that his brother's dead. Because that's the way it works, isn't it?"

·51·

Of Kings
AND CONSORTS

Not too far, in the guest wings of the palace, Wolf entered his apartment to find Ronan Astor waiting for him in the reception room as he had requested. Night had fallen across the kingdom, and once again he was struck by her beauty, her lissome silhouette against the dark.

"You came back to me like you promised," she said, rushing to his arms, but he held himself back and gave her only a stiff hug.

He declined to sit. Instead he stood across from her, with Duncan Oswald a few feet to his left. Wolf knew Ronan deserved a private meeting, but he didn't trust himself not to make her some promise he wouldn't be able to keep.

"No, Ronan. I have asked you here to say good-bye."

"Good-bye?"

He explained that the negotiated treaty still stood—and there was no better way to meet its obligation than to have the prince who was still alive marry the princess. That was his job, after all—his purpose in life—to fulfill promises and responsibilities in case his brother failed to deliver. The spare had become heir.

"I am sorry," Wolf said. "I have no choice in the matter."

"Do you love her?" she asked, tears in her eyes.

"I am fond of Marie. She is an old friend of mine." Wolf did not elaborate. He did not tell her about the admiration he felt for her: how smart and strong and brave she was, how her sharp mind and quick reasoning had saved the empire from destruction and war. He said none of these things to Ronan.

"Because there are other ways . . . kings and consorts . . ." Ronan said, her voice low. "I do not care. I only want to be with you. I want to be at your side, at every occasion. I will be in the shadows, but I will love you. I just want to be with you. I will be your mistress if you want, but let me love you. Let me stay with you. Please."

Wolf shook his head, appalled. "No. I will not do to you what my brother did to Isabelle. I will not have you ruined and debauched. I will let you go. I have to let you go."

"No—please—don't say these things, you can't mean them—we only just found each other. . . ."

"It must be done," Wolf said firmly. "You must forget about me, Ronan, and build a life for yourself. Find a man who is free to love you. Find someone who is worthy of you. You think too little of yourself, and of your worth. You're more than just a beautiful girl from New York. You are worth more than any titled aristocrat. You can make your own fortune. I can help you, if you want. I can be a good friend to you."

"But you will not be my husband," Ronan cried. "Or my lover."

"No, Ronan, I cannot," he said. "That part of our relationship has ended."

"Then I will leave court and go back to New York," Ronan said. "I will marry Marcus!" she threatened. "Or the baron!"

"If you must," Wolf said, and his face was tired and drawn, distant.

"You're really going to marry her?" Ronan said. "Though it's me you love?"

All Wolf could do was nod.

"You promised you would come back to me," she said again. "You *promised*."

"As it turns out I was not free to make such a promise. Think about what I am offering, and do what you need to do—but this is good-bye, Ronan."

Ronan could hear the resolve in his voice, and she understood at last that nothing could change his mind. This was not the boy who'd held her in the garden. That boy had also died that night. This was the prince and heir to the throne.

He cleared his throat. "I have taken care of your bill at Claridge's."

She held her head high. She knew he did not mean to be cruel, to insinuate that he had paid for her company, but even so, it still stung. "Then I thank you for your hospitality. Good day, sir." Her lip trembled and her cheeks were flushed, but her eyes were clear and bright, and as determined as his.

"Good-bye, Ronan," he said.

"Good-bye then, Your Highness." She curtsied as she was taught and swept from the rooms, never once looking back.

A knock sounded on Marie's door. Gill sprang up from the bed and answered, doing his best to compose his face. The door opened to reveal the Lord Chamberlain, flanked by a pair of Queen's Guards.

Gill snapped to attention.

"My Lord Chamberlain!" he barked.

"Princess," the Lord Chamberlain said, ignoring Gill. "Her Majesty Queen Eleanor thought it best that even with the Prussian guards dismissed, a more secure guard be provided for you in the wake of recent events. To that end, we are replacing your former guard with a pair of senior officers for the foreseeable future."

Perhaps not everyone had forgotten about the princess's disappearance after all.

Only now did he turn to Gill. "Private Cameron, you are relieved of duty until further notice."

Gill turned to Marie, a look of shock on his face. But Marie kept her eyes firmly fixed on the Lord Chamberlain's.

"Her Majesty's caution seems a bit overzealous, but I understand that it is better to err on the side of safety."

She turned to Gill, her spine straight, chin out, her tone as regal as she could make it. "I thank you for your service, Private Cameron. I—I never once felt unsafe when I was with you."

She didn't say anything else, and a moment later Gill left the room.

the
DUKE'S WARD

hen Isabelle woke up, she was covered in gauze, and everything hurt. She looked outside the window at the rolling hills, the rows of vines. She recognized the familiar smell of vinegar. Home? She was home? Why was she back in Orleans? She sat up with a start, suddenly remembering the attack on the road outside the city.

Louis? Where was Louis?

"Louis?" she called. But it was not Louis who was sitting across from her. It was Hugh. She recoiled. "Why am I here? Where is Louis?"

"You're awake," he said. "Good."

"Why am I here? Where's Louis?" she asked, even though she already knew the answer in her heart. "Louis!"

"Louis is dead," Hugh said flatly. "You can call for him all you want, but he's gone."

"No!" Isabelle said and fell back, sobbing. "No, he can't be dead. Not Louis. What did you do, you bastard?" She remembered the last words she'd heard before she blacked out.

Kill the boy, but keep the girl.

"You killed him," she screamed. "You killed Louis. Oh my God, you killed him!"

"Au contraire, Isabelle!" Hugh said with feigned contrition. "My men liberated you from a band of brigands who killed our poor cousin. You may take some comfort in knowing that Louis's murderers have been brought to justice." Hugh smiled smugly.

"You mean you eliminated anyone who could trace your murder back to you, you monster! Leave me! Leave this room! Leave me alone! Oh my God, Louis . . . my beautiful Louis . . ."

"You truly want to be alone, Isabelle? You cannot think only of yourself now—think of the child."

The fact of her pregnancy hit her with fresh horror. She was carrying Leopold's child.

"My men tell me that Louis-Philippe died before he could make you his wife. If you have this baby out of wedlock, you will be shunned from court and every great house across the Continent. No one will marry you. So I have taken you home to Orleans, where you belong. I am offering you my hand in marriage, and a chance for you to remain with your lands and estate. Come, my dear—haven't I been kind to you? I will accept your child as my own."

"No, no, no," Isabelle sobbed. She was going to escape, she was going to get away from him, from this . . . How had this happened? She was going to live in Cévennes with beautiful Louis, and have a beautiful life together. . . .

"Come here—I have missed you," Hugh said, and he put his slimy hands around her, and he kissed her lips. It felt disgusting and repulsive, but also familiar, like a hurt that she was used to. She had become numb to the pain.

But one day, she would have her revenge, she swore, thinking of the knife she kept in her drawer.

Once the child was born and she was free, she would stick that knife through Hugh's belly and cut him clear down the middle.

In her mind, she could already hear him screaming.

· 53 ·

Good Night, (Not So) SWEET PRINCE

The Prussians would bury their dead in their home country. But before they took Prince Leopold away, his body would lie in state in a chapel at St. James, so that the court and the many members of the public who loved him could pay their last respects. The ceremony was galling to everyone in on the secret, but it was necessary. If the people suspected that even their royal families were vulnerable to magical attack, faith in the Merlin—in the empire itself—would be undermined.

When the crowds had left and the chapel was empty, Aelwyn arrived to say good-bye. She looked down at his face, so serene in eternal rest. It was hard to believe that it had harbored something as evil as what she'd found there.

But then it wasn't him, was it? she said to herself. Leo—the real Leo—had been perverted by Hartwig's evil training. And then the coup de grace had come when Hartwig got him to activate the Pandora's Box, unleashing the spirit of Jeanne of Arkk, which had taken over his body and imprisoned poor Leo's soul in his own flesh. He was just as much a victim of the demon witch's possession as everyone else, a willing victim maybe, but a victim nonetheless.

Marie was sitting in the first pew, and bade her friend join her. They sat and looked at the body of Leo together.

That morning, Aelwyn had destroyed the illusion stone—and with it, the temptation to be something she was not. Her father was right to be wary of the glamour spell, and Sister Mallory was correct; a false victory was a hollow one.

"We made a mistake," Aelwyn said. "I am sorry."

"I am sorry, too, for I made you do it. I'm sorry, Winnie, for pushing you, just like on the night of the fire."

"It is not your fault," Aelwyn sighed. "Not all of it." Her father had been right to send her away four years ago, and the queen had been right to fear her. Because on the night of the fire, the night that she had almost killed the princess, a dark, awful place in Aelwyn's soul had wanted it. All her rage and frustration at her position had manifested that night, and when she saw the flames burn and lick the building, and the princess trapped in the smoke . . .

Aelwyn had been glad, had felt triumphant. *See, I can do this. I can make things burn, I can destroy, I can show you all. . . .*

The power is at my command. . . .

Leo's words echoed in her ear. *You are just like me.*

It was true. She had felt the temptation in her own heart. It had been right of her father to send her away to Avalon, to understand that she must learn to control her power and emotions. She must accept her position and find the good inside herself . . . for there was good in her . . . unlike Leopold and the dark witch to whom he had surrendered his soul.

"It's better that he is dead," Aelwyn said. "The demon that was Jeanne of Arkk was poison. But the worst thing was that Leo was still trapped in there somewhere. I felt him, when I—when I killed him. Beneath the demon there was a little boy lost in the darkness. I can only hope he's found some measure of peace now."

Marie stared at Leo's still form. "You are more generous than I can be on this matter. Jeanne of Arkk may have betrayed Leo after she entered his body, but he invited her in willingly. She did not make him evil. Maybe Hartwig corrupted him, or maybe it was in him from birth. At any rate, the only thing I felt from him was the pure desire for power, no matter the cost."

Aelwyn shook her head in wonder. "Everyone loved him, except for you—you were the only one who was immune to his magic. You saw through him, ever since we were children."

She told Marie what the Merlin had told her: "At last the corruption at the heart of the empire has been expunged. Wolf is the true prince, the true king. For years Leo used his magic to make Wolf seem like the wrong one, the bastard, so that no one would pay attention to him. Because if they did, anyone would see that it was Leo who was wrong. They would notice the resemblance between him and Lord Hartwig."

"He planned everything with Hartwig, didn't he?" asked Marie. "He courted Orleans, found the stone, talked the Red Duke into sending all those barrels of wine for the wedding. He even used Wolf to get into the vaults. Everything was set up for our destruction. Down to every last detail."

"Not everything," Aelwyn said. "He didn't see Count Beziers coming."

"Or you," Marie said. "He missed that. It's kind of ironic, but if I hadn't tried to escape—if we hadn't swapped places—you never would have been there at Leo's duel. He wouldn't have been shot and would have gotten away with everything." She turned to Aelwyn. "The funniest thing is, I thought you loved him."

Aelwyn sighed. She *had* been attracted to him—to his bright and fearless ambition. His focus and his anger had appealed to her too, because rage and resentment were her lot as well. "I was drawn to Leo. I was attracted to his hunger, his weakness. He reminded me of Lanselin, whom I loved in Avalon. A vain and foolish boy, who would put his selfish desires over the peace of the kingdom."

"Did he know you were pretending to be me?"

"Yes, in the end," said Aelwyn.

"I am not sorry that witch is finally dead," Marie said. "And I know I shouldn't feel much for Leo either. And yet I do. He was an innocent once, before the people who should have been nurturing him corrupted him instead. He did not deserve that."

"You are truly merciful," Aelwyn said as she knelt before her. "I serve you, my queen. You have my loyalty. I am your friend, you have been mine . . ."

"Winnie, you don't need to apologize," said Marie.

"There is more, my princess," Aelwyn said, bowing her head. "I must beg for your forgiveness. My father admitted to me this morning that he has been poisoning you since you were young. He made you think you suffered from the wasting plague. Your mother, the queen, began to suspect as much."

"I knew there was a reason I was afraid of your father," said Marie. She paused, shaking her head. "Although I did not think he was trying to kill me."

"He never tried to kill you. It was to make sure your will was strong enough to triumph over a weakened body—strong enough to lead an empire. Testing your strength was a precaution to protect the empire, to protect the realm from weakness inside and out. I'm sorry, it is upsetting news, and it was to me."

Marie laughed without bitterness. "Strangely, I am not upset. I am just relieved that I do not suffer from illness after all."

"You have proven you are the strongest ruler this empire

will know," Aelwyn said. "You will be queen. I will bond to the Order and serve as your Morgaine."

Aelwyn swore fealty to the princess. As she did, she remembered her father's words that morning. *We serve the realm by choosing the monarch. I chose Henry over Charles. I saw the future: I saw this empire standing tall and proud. I saw Camelot lasting a thousand years. I prevented wars, famine, death; instead, I gave this land peace, prosperity, and a succession of worthy sovereigns.*

Your mother and I planned it from the beginning.

When her time to exit came upon her, Eleanor understood what the empire needed: we each needed an heir. One to rule, and one to serve.

She had a dream once, that her daughter would betray her— that her daughter was a traitor. And so we devised a test. We knew Aelwyn's power of illusion and Marie's desire to have a different life. We decided we would announce Marie's engagement to Leopold to set it in motion. Nothing happens in this empire without our knowledge, but we left it to you both to save the kingdom from ruin. If both of you failed, then I would step in, but we would be lost; we would have to try again somehow. Our time was running short.

Eleanor had two daughters sixteen years ago.

One from the seed of her long-dead husband. And the other from the seed of her most trusted advisor.

One to rule, and one to serve.

Aelwyn and Marie were sisters—twins—best friends born into separate destinies.

After telling her the truth, the Merlin had withdrawn. Aelwyn had shifted forward in her seat, one last question burning in her mind.

"Father, have you seen the future in the glass? It will not show me mine," she had asked.

He'd sighed. "I have seen many futures. Each one shows that now is the time for my death. Eleanor will not live the year, and neither will I. But I have seen you taking the vows and taking your place by the throne. For you have chosen the monarch, have you not?"

She had. She thought she had chosen to rule herself, but when she'd seen Leopold in the courtyard, she'd known what had to happen. When she heard the news of Marie's return, Aelwyn knew she could no longer take her place. That had never been her true place in the castle, her true position. When she had chosen to use the soulstone on Leo, she had chosen Marie to be queen and sovereign.

Sweet, compassionate Marie, who would rule the land with a gentle hand and an intelligent heart.

Aelwyn had chosen the monarch, and chosen well.

· 54 ·

Expectations
AND ASSUMPTIONS

*L*ady Constance had arrived for tea again that afternoon. It had been a week since Ronan had been at St. James for her last encounter with Wolf. Lady Constance wanted Ronan to tell her everything that had happened at the palace on the night of the duel. So many rumors were flying around the city, that the French were raising troops, that civil war was imminent, but for now, everyone just wanted to know what happened to that handsome Prussian prince. Was he really a cad and a louse as all the papers now claimed?

"Also I have good news," she said. "Lady Julia thinks Marcus will propose to you again. This time you must accept."

"I must?" asked Ronan.

"Your mother and I made an agreement," Lady Constance said. "Shall I speak plainly?"

"Please do."

"I was to help you land a titled lord. You are a rich American girl, and his family goes back generations. I help set up the match, and voilà."

"Wait—my mother promised you a fee?" Ronan goggled.

Lady Constance shrugged. "It's a typical practice during the season. How else did you get an invitation to the royal ball? I gave you one of my slots."

"But you didn't even get me to any of the best parties, or to your own dinner."

"Your parents' first payment only covered so much," Lady Constance said. "I have been waiting for the next installments. But I did find you Marcus and the baron."

"What does Marcus get out of it?"

"Oh, he's a typical broke Englishman," Lady Constance said gaily. "All of their assets are tied up in the land and the estate. They're practically penniless."

Ronan began to laugh. "Well, then he was barking up the wrong tree if he thought I could change his fortune." They thought she was a rich American, a Van Owen—because of the dresses—because of the royal suite at Claridge's, of course. It all made sense now.

"Pardon?"

"We're broke, Lady Connie," Ronan said. "Penniless as

your friends. It's why Mother couldn't pay the rest of your so-called fee. But here, you've had some wonderful teas on my friend's account. Perhaps I will let you take care of this one."

After Lady Constance left, Ronan returned to packing up her things. Like most days since that fateful good-bye, Ronan spent her time thinking long and hard about what Wolf had told her when they parted. How she had to find a man worthy of her. He would be glad to learn that she had.

Two of them, in fact.

"Darling, are you ready? The duchess really doesn't like to be kept waiting," trilled Archie, as he swanned into the room. It was her last day at the hotel; tomorrow she would move to a new place they'd helped her secure in the city—a small apartment, but serviceable. You had to start somewhere.

"Look at that magnificent hat," said Perry, admiring her daring fascinator, which held the plume of one firebird.

"Thanks, I made it myself," she said.

"That's our girl," said Archie.

Her heart would heal, it was good and sturdy. Besides, who needs a prince, when she had two lords who adored her? Sometimes fairy tales don't go the way you think they will, but a girl could still craft herself a happy ending.

· 55 ·

The Ring
AND THE CROWN

The Prussians were gone for almost a month, but they returned at the end of summer for the final wedding preparations. When Marie entered her drawing room that evening, she found Wolf sitting on his favorite chair, his shoulders slumped. He looked just like he did when he was a little boy. Her favorite friend, she thought. "Pup," she called. "You're back!"

He turned and saw her at the door. A ghost of a smile appeared on his face. "Helmet head."

She took a seat next to him and they both looked out at the garden. The tents were gone now, and the courtyard where Leo had been shot was scrubbed clean. Everything, it seemed, would be scrubbed clean. . . . A prince was dead, but a new prince had been offered in his place. And though there would always be a spot in her heart for Gill, she knew that she had loved the fantasy of freedom more than she had loved him. On some level, she knew that a love match would never be her fate. Wolf had said the same thing. Well, at least they would enter into marriage with no illusions. At least they knew each other—Marie knew a dozen ladies, countesses, duchesses, and princesses who had met their husbands on their wedding day. At least she and Wolf were friends.

They stared at the garden for what seemed like a very long time. They'd both had such different dreams for their lives, but their lives had led them back here, to this room, to each other.

"Did you love him? A silly question," Wolf said at long last. From the tone of his voice Marie knew that Wolf had been brooding about it for a long time. "Don't answer that, of course you loved him. You were going to run away with him. You were going to give up everything for him."

She did not answer, because the answer was clear. At length she cleared her throat. "The American girl. Her name is Ronan, isn't it?" she asked.

"Yes," he said quietly. "Ronan Astor."

"You had planned to marry her, didn't you? And now you cannot marry her—you have to marry me." Marie sighed.

When Wolf looked up at her, his face was as gray and tired as she felt. She thought he would deny it—fight it—but instead he took her hands in his and pressed them to his lips. "I have been thinking, ever since my brother died."

"Yes?"

"We must be kind to each other, Marie. We must forgive each other."

"For what?" she asked, though she already knew. They had to forgive each other for not being the first: the first love, the first kiss. For not being a dream come true from a fairy tale. There was no such thing as fairy tales. Princesses didn't turn into peasants, and princes could not run away to have adventures. She had wanted to be someone else so badly, but perhaps the secret to life was accepting who she was. She was Eleanor's daughter, Princess Marie-Victoria of England and France. She had passed the Merlin's test, carried the blood of generations of rulers, and was to rule an empire that spanned five continents—the most powerful empire the world had ever known.

His lips were warm and soft on her hand. When he let her hand go, she felt a pang.

"So you will marry me, then?" She smiled, her eyes bright. Her heart was breaking, but she was not thinking of Gill just then. She was looking at Wolf—at her dear friend, Wolf— and she was thinking that Ronan Astor was so very beautiful indeed.

"Was there ever a doubt, my friend?" Wolf said lightly.

After the mandatory six-month mourning period for the

sudden and unexpected death of Prince Leopold of Prussia, the court of St. James announced that Marie-Victoria of England and France would be married to the *kronprinz* of Prussia, Wolfgang the First.

The choir sang a hymn of joy as Marie walked into the church on her wedding day, and the court gasped in delight at the sight of her. The princess was dressed simply, her only crown a wreath of wildflowers in her hair: pink, purple, and deep red. Her dress was ivory in color and adorned with English lace. The cut was simple, with a trim of delicately embroidered orange and pink blossoms, but the train was a showstopper: eighteen feet in length, held up by her loyal ladies. She had insisted on no political favors—she wanted only the attendants who had known her from childhood. There was the Lady of the Bedchamber, Evangeline; Paulette, the Lady of the Robes; and her nurse, Jenny Wallace.

Marie wore no jewels, except for the gift of Wolf's mother's diamond ring, the blue stone of Brandenburg. There was no magic or glimmer on her dress or glamour on her visage. Her face was clean and shining, and her smile was gentle. Yet it was said by those who were present for her wedding that she had never looked so beautiful; that on her wedding day, she was even more beautiful than she had been on the night of the royal ball.

Marie walked down the aisle on the arm of the Merlin, and as she did she nodded to the glittering assemblage of honored and titled guests who had come to witness her wedding.

Among the courtiers and dignitaries in attendance were the newlyweds Viscount and Lady Lisle, Marcus and Celestine, who had wed a few months earlier. It was said to be a happy marriage, as both came from similar land-rich estates, and were used to living without heat and plumbing.

The Duke of Burgundy sent his regrets, as he had been taken ill, severely wounded in an attack of some sort. It was rumored that Isabelle, Lady of Orleans, had left the castle in the dark of night. It was said she was living humbly in a seaside town by herself, teaching English and raising the son she had named Charles Louis Valois, who had a remarkable mop of golden hair and the ability to charm everyone with his smile. Marie had asked Aelwyn point-blank if they had anything to fear from this child—he was Leo's son, after all. But Aelwyn had said she thought they were safe, because he had been conceived before Jeanne of Arkk took over Leo's body. "But only time will tell," she had added.

Ronan Astor was also present at the wedding. As a friend of Wolf's she had merited an invitation, and Marie had been kind enough to agree. The two young men seated next to her were Lords Stewart and Fairfax. Ronan had elected to stay in London. They said she had taken a position as a secretary to a rich American heiress who had recently married an Italian count and had set up a home in London. The Astors had lost the governorship of New York, and her parents had decided to move out west instead of remaining in the city. Ronan was living with her former governess Vera in a small flat in

Kensington, but she was starting a business on the side—a millinery shop—and already her hats were sought by the great ladies of London.

Marie turned away from the guests, looking ahead to the smiling face of the newly installed Morgaine. Aelwyn Myrddyn of the sisterhood was resplendent in her white robes, her auburn hair flowing to her shoulders, Avalon's medallion in the hollow of her throat. She had a serene smile on her face. Queen Eleanor was standing next to Aelwyn, and her mother looked as happy as she had ever been. She was an old woman—everyone could see that now. Her hair was snow-white, and there were wrinkles and heavy folds on her face. For the first time, the entire court saw the queen as Marie saw her.

Marie reached the altar, and the Merlin released her with a bow. He too looked as if he had aged a thousand years overnight since he had relinquished his position.

She turned to the front. There, standing in his wedding suit, so handsome and heartbreaking, was Wolf. He winked at her as he took her hand in his. "Nice flowers," he whispered.

"I wore them for you," she said.

They faced the archbishop of the brotherhood, as well as the Sister Superior, who gave the blessings of Avalon on their marriage. After the readings and the songs, it was time to say their vows.

In a clear, loud voice Marie turned to the groom and said, "I, Marie-Victoria Grace Eleanor Aquitaine, take thee,

Wolfgang Friedrich Joachim von Hohenzollern, to have and to hold, from this day forward, in sickness and in health, till death do us part."

Wolf followed. "I, Wolfgang Friedrich Joachim von Hohenzollern, take thee, Marie-Victoria Grace Eleanor Aquitaine . . ."

They were pronounced man and wife to the joyful cheers and applause of the court and all its allies.

Marie was trembling as Wolf took her hand. They began their triumphant march down the aisle. He looked so dashing in his white and gold, so much more handsome than Leopold had ever been. Now that the witch's spell was broken, everyone could see the truth. This was the true prince. And this, the true princess.

"I will be good to you, I promise," Wolf said, leaning down to kiss her forehead. "You will have my heart."

Will.

Because it was not love yet, between them; only friendship. But after everything they had gone through together, and all they had learned about life and war and magic, and the privileges and responsibilities of royalty, it could change.

No, not love, not yet. Holding on to Wolf's warm hand, Marie thought, *But one day, it might be.*

ALSO BY MELISSA DE LA CRUZ

DESCENDANTS

The Isle of the Lost

Return to the Isle of the Lost

THE BLUE BLOODS SERIES

Blue Bloods

Masquerade

Revelations

The Van Alen Legacy

Keys to the Repository

Misguided Angel

Bloody Valentine

Lost in Time

Gates of Paradise